*Book 2 of The Take Charge Series*
# Lady Catherine Takes Charge
### A Pride & Prejudice Variation

*By Shana Granderson, A Lady*

# DEDICATION

This book, like all that I write, is dedicated to the love of life, the holder of my heart. You are my one and only and you complete me. You make it all worthwhile and my world revolves around you. Until we reconnected I had stopped believing in miracles, now I do, you are my miracle.

# ACKNOWLEDGEMENT

First and foremost, thank you E.C.S. for standing by me while I dedicate many hours to my craft. You are my shining light and my one and only.

I want to thank my Alpha, Will Jamison and my Betas Caroline Piediscalzi Lippert and Kimbelle Pease. A special thanks to Kimbelle for her forthright and on point editing. To both Gayle Serrette and Carol M. for taking on the roles of proof-readers and additional editing, a huge thank you to both of you. All of you who have assisted me please know that your assistance is most appreciated.

My undying love and appreciation to Jane Austen for her incredible literary masterpieces is more than can be expressed adequately here. I also thank all of the JAFF readers who make writing these stories a pleasure.

Thank you to Rob Bockholdt: wyndagger@gmail.com, who was commissioned to create the artwork used for the cover.

# INTRODUCTION

### The Series:

The Take Charge series are all stand-alone books. There will be at least four books in the series and as they are not sequels or not connected one to the other, you may read them in any order you choose. None of the books in this series are just about the title character, but how their taking charge affects those around them.

The series tells a Pride & Prejudice Variation/Vagary tale in which one of the characters we know and love from canon takes charge and assert themselves. We see how the actions of that particular character affects the others and the trajectory of each individual tale, both known from canon and some non-canon characters.

We know Elizabeth Bennet and Fitzwilliam (William) Darcy well and how they are depicted in the original, they will not have a book in their names, but will, as it should be, feature very heavily in each of the stories where someone else takes charge.

### Book 2: Lady Catherine Takes Charge:

The great lady is very much like she is in canon until there is a horrific accident in 1804 where both her husband Lewis and her daughter Anne die. For a lady who believed she could control all by force of will and desire, the deaths of her family rock her world down to the foundations. She revaluates all of her priorities, changes direction, and becomes a surrogate mother to both surviving Darcys.

In his will Sir Lewis leaves his estate and all of his holdings to Richard Fitzwilliam as he is the only one of his three nephews to have to shift for himself. Sir Lewis and Anne were the last alive in the de Bourgh line.

Jane Bennet, after losing more than one suitor to her mother's vulgar and inappropriate behaviour has had the blinders removed. Elizabeth is no longer in awe of her father as she has had her eyes opened to his indolence and abrogation of his parental responsibility. Rather than laugh with him at his treatment of his wife and younger daughters, she understands the inappropriateness of how her father behaves.

The story is close to canon with regards to the interactions between the Netherfield and Longbourn residents with the dastardly George Wickham pouring poison on our Lizzy's ear up to a point. We see a lot of that interaction through the eyes of William Collins who is very different from his portrayal in canon. Wickham is exposed, but not by Darcy.

Bingley is his spineless self and allows his sister Caroline to rule his life and manipulate him while at the same time he looks to Darcy to make decisions for him. The Netherfield Party escapes to Town and Bingley deserts Jane without a word except for Miss Bingley's fiction she sends in her note and single reply she sends to Jane's three letters.

Up to a point, Lady Catherine has taken a back seat. Unlike the lady we are used to, she does not want to insert herself into her relative's lives unless absolutely needed. When she sees too much happening which needs correcting, she decides to take charge. She leads her family in berating Darcy for his behaviour in Hertfordshire, his hauteur, and in not taking care of the scourge that is George Wickham.

This story looks at how this iteration of Lady Catherine changes the trajectory of a number of character we all love, and some we dislike intensely.

# PROLOGUE

L ady Catherine de Bourgh's world had just come crashing to a halt. She had always prided herself on being able to control everything around her including her daughter, Anne de Bourgh, who was nineteen, and her husband, Sir Lewis.

She had a forceful personality and had been known to demand, harangue, and cajole those who had the temerity to disagree with her or her point of view. Occasionally, her husband resisted her for a short time, then invariably capitulated so he would have some peace and quiet at Rosings Park, the estate the de Bourgs purchased when they emigrated from France two generations ago.

Theirs had been a forced marriage. After four seasons, Lady Catherine Fitzwilliam could not fathom why she had not a single suitor when her younger sister Anne was being courted by Robert Darcy—untitled, but fabulously wealthy. His line went back to William the Conqueror, when the then D'Arcys were awarded a large swath of land in Derbyshire, which they had named Pemberley.

Catherine could not, would not, countenance her younger sister marrying before her, so she compromised Sir Lewis de Bourgh. Although he was only a baronet, he had a title whereas Anne's Robert did not. He too was wealthy but not at the Darcys' level—he would have to do.

After Catherine became *enceinte* with Anne, she locked her door to her husband. She did not care whether she bore a son or daughter, as Rosings Park was not entailed on heirs

1

male. Anne was born in January of 1785.

Catherine had been a disinterested mother at best, but Lewis had doted on his daughter. Unbeknownst to his wife, Lewis drew up a will naming Anne his heir, not her mother. He added a contingency that if his dear Anne were not alive when he passed, or died before she was married, his nephew Richard Fitzwilliam, the second son of Catherine's brother Reggie, the Earl of Matlock, and his wife Elaine would inherit Rosings Park, de Bourgh House in London, and the entirety of the de Bourgh fortune. All his wife would receive was her dowry, her possessions she brought with her and a settlement from the estate.

Richard had always spoken of a career in the military, which Lewis knew worried his parents, so it was the least he could do as he was the last of the de Bourgh line. His nephews Andrew Fitzwilliam and William Darcy were both heirs to vast estates and wealth, making Richard his logical choice.

To make sure his wife could not claim otherwise with a forged will, Sir Lewis gave copies of his will to both of his brothers-in-law. Lord Reginal Fitzwilliam, Robert Darcy, and Sir Lewis all used the legal services of the same firm of barristers and solicitors, Norman and James, where the third copy of his will resided.

When Anne was six, she took ill with scarlet fever, notwithstanding all of her mother's assertions that she was too highborn to fall ill like a commoner. Anne's case was severe; it was the first time Lady Catherine knew true fear.

The truth was she loved her daughter, even if she did not know how to show it. Anne recovered, but the doctors opined both her heart and lungs had been damaged. At first Lady Catherine dismissed their opinions as so much drivel, but when she saw how quickly Anne tired from a minimum of exertion, she knew in her heart the doctors were correct.

Mrs. Jenkinson, the governess her husband employed for Anne, became more of a nurse than a governess to her young charge, who she loved dearly. Lady Catherine realised mayhap locking her door to her husband and begetting only one child had not been her wisest choice, but she was not one to admit she had erred. Seeing Anne continue to be affected after she had recovered as much as she likely would, she decided in order to protect her daughter, her nephew Fitzwilliam—William to the rest of their family—would marry Anne so she would be protected.

Before her sister Lady Anne died, she began to work on her to gain her agreement for her plan. Lady Catherine had always intimidated her younger sister, so when Lady Anne declined to agree to a betrothal between Lady Catherine's Anne and her Fitzwilliam, Catherine had not been happy.

The older sister had browbeaten her younger and far frailer sister until she gained an agreement—of sorts. The problem was that Lady Anne's husband, Robert Darcy, would not be dictated to by anyone. His wife told him how Catherine had harangued her, causing her to appear to agree with her only to gain some peace.

After Lady Anne passed due to complications from giving birth to Georgiana Darcy in April of 1794, Catherine descended on Pemberley, thinking her brother weak as he had loved her sister. In her mind she would be able to exert her will on the weak-minded fool and get him to sign a betrothal agreement.

She was faced with most unwelcome facts_Robert Darcy was not weak-willed, and she could not work on him to do her bidding. He told her he would never sign a betrothal agreement until and unless William was in love and his love was returned. Catherine was appalled at hearing him consider love to be important. Again, this love nonsense!

Love—such a plebian concept and emotion. The first circles, especially the very top which included the Darcys, Fitzwilliams, and de Bourghs, married for dynastic advancement, fortune, and connections. There was no room in Catherine's world for love; it was all about power, control, and money.

When Robert Darcy died, she again hoped she would be able to carry her point; she would demand her nephew bow to her assertion that his parents had agreed to a betrothal between him and Anne. To Pemberley she had hied, only to be thwarted once again.

Catherine's nephew, like his father, was not weak-willed. Far worse, her late brother-in-law had the temerity to put his wishes in writing, refuting her claims of an agreement and exposing her lie. She returned to Rosings Park in high dudgeon, determined to find a way to work on her nephew.

~~~~~~~/~~~~~~~

Due to her inability to exert herself physically, Anne had taken to driving a small phaeton her loving father gifted her when she was twelve. It was pulled by two ponies so it could not attain high speeds, and Mrs. Jenkinson always accompanied her when she drove out in the park.

Often times, when he was not busy with estate affairs, Sir Lewis would ride his horse alongside his daughter's phaeton. One day, Mrs. Jenkinson had been enjoying her day off and Anne had wanted to drive out in her little vehicle. Sir Lewis, unable to deny his daughter, agreed to ride with her.

With great pride, Anne drove her father out that fateful day in July. They were on a circuit of the park, a path which Anne had driven many times before. On the left was a forest; on the other side was a rocky culvert with a river flowing through it.

A fox bolted out of the trees and between the ponies' legs. They panicked, which in turn caused the fox to try and bite at their legs as he perceived danger. The ponies bolted, and before father or daughter could react, the phaeton careened over the steep edge of the culvert.

Sir Lewis, Anne, and the two ponies were killed instantly as the phaeton crashed onto the rocks below. A tenant farmer was ploughing his fields near the crash site when he heard a commotion followed by the sickening sound of a crash. He rushed to the edge of the culvert and was met with a horrendous sight, a smashed vehicle and the bodies of the master, his daughter, and two ponies. He freed his horse from the plough and rode to Rosings as fast as he was able. When he arrived at the stables and told the stablemaster what he had witnessed, grooms were dispatched to the crash site, while the stable-master ran to the main house and informed the butler.

The butler found the mistress on her *throne* in the main drawing room_the room which looked as though it should be in Buckingham House with all its gaudy and ostentatious dec-orations, and supremely uncomfortable furniture.

When she was informed of the news, Lady Catherine re-fused to believe it. This was not something that could happen —that she would allow to happen—to her family. She and her family were supposed to be above such things.

The great lady had shouted "it is a lie!" and kept repeating those words like a mantra, as if the more times she spoke them, the less likely it was to be true. She continued to deny the truth until the broken bodies of her husband and her daughter were brought to the manor house.

What had her control, all the wealth of the de Bourghs, and all the power in the world achieved? Nothing! Lewis and Anne were dead. Lady Catherine wailed inconsolably as the tentative nature of life and just how little control and actual power she had was brought home to her forcefully.

Mrs. Jenkinson, who mourned her charge as much as Lady Catherine mourned her daughter, was a rock for her mis-tress. She coaxed Lady Catherine into her chambers and as-sisted her maid to change the lady into her night attire. Next, she gave Lady Catherine some tea laced with laudanum.

Once the mistress fell into a troubled sleep, Mrs. Jenkin-son went about the task of informing the Fitzwilliams and the Darcys of the tragedy, who were all in London at the time.

~~~~~~~/~~~~~~~

Their mourning period for their father had just ended. William Darcy and his sister Georgiana, called Gigi, were in London for the first time since Robert Darcy had gone to join his beloved Anne in heaven.

Killion, the Darcy House butler, knocked on Darcy's study

5

door, and was bade enter. With a grave look on his countenance, Killion proffered a salver to the master. Darcy saw a black-edged missive and picked it up, with trepidation.

'*Please God, do not let this be about Richard,*' Darcy looked to the heavens beseechingly. Richard Fitzwilliam, his cousin, the brother of his heart, and co-guardian of Gigi, was two years is elder. Richard joined the Royal Dragoons as a Lieutenant right after he completed his studies at Cambridge, more than four years ago. In May of 1803, England declared war against the self-styled emperor of France—dubbed the 'little tyrant' in the kingdom.

Darcy did not know if Richard, now a major, was still in England, but it was with that concern in mind he broke the seal without looking at it and missed the fact it was the de Bourgh seal.

*14 July 1804*
*Rosings Park, Westerham, Kent*
*Sir,*
*It is my sad duty to inform you that both your Uncle Lewis and Cousin Anne were taken in an accident today.*
*Lady Catherine is sedated and sleeping.*
*With my deepest sympathies,*
*Mrs. Thea Jenkinson*

Darcy was shocked and could not move for a few moments. Although he would never have married the sickly Anne, he did love her as a cousin. Like his Uncle Lewis, he had always appreciated her dry wit and ability to observe that which most did not. He had loved his Uncle Lewis as well.

"Killion, I must to Matlock House immediately. Have Carstens pack my trunks and tell Miss Smithson to have Miss Darcy ready to travel; we depart for Kent as soon as may be," Darcy barked as he ran out of the door.

He met Richard in the middle of Grosvenor Square, on his way to Darcy House. "You know?" the Major asked simply, and Darcy nodded. "Father wanted me to tell you we will depart within the hour. Will you join us?"

"Carstens is packing as we speak, and I left instructions for Gigi's governess to do the same for her," Darcy informed his cousin. After a brief handshake, the cousins turned and returned to their houses.

Less than an hour later, their coaches were on their way to Kent.

~~~~~~~/~~~~~~~

The Bennets of Longbourn, near the market town of Meryton in Hertfordshire, were typical of many lower gentry who had small estates and limited wealth. Their estate was entailed upon heirs male, which did not bode well for the family's future as the Bennets had no son and five daughters.

The master of the estate, Thomas Bennet, was intelligent, but indolent. As each year passed, his wife, Francene—Fanny—grew sillier, consumed with fear of being thrown into the hedgerows when her husband invariably passed away. She had borne only daughters. Her husband, rather than assure her, correct her, or increase his daughters' portions, made sport of her in front of his daughters and others, and did nothing to plan for his family's future.

Mrs. Bennet was of mean understanding, interested only in gossip and fashion. Her husband had been attracted by her beauty and vivacity and had married in haste and was now repenting at leisure.

Too late he realised that Fanny was like her older sister, Hattie, the foremost gossip in Meryton. Both sisters were of similar temperament, interested only in frivolities. Hattie was married to Frank Phillips, who had taken over the Gardiner patriarch's law practice in Meryton twelve years previously. Hattie and Frank had not been blessed with children.

The daughter of a solicitor, Fanny had not been raised as a gentlewoman and did not know how to behave as one; rather than teach her, her husband continued to mock her.

Bennet and his wife married in 1787. In May of 1788, Jane Bennet had been born. Fanny had been certain their next would be a boy, but Elizabeth was born in March of 1790. Her mother could not fathom how she was not the boy she had expected. No matter how many times her husband tried to explain the babe had no control over its gender, Fanny always resented her second daughter for being a girl.

In June of 1792, Mary joined the family, followed by Kitty in January of 1794, and Lydia in October of 1795. There had been complications with Lydia's birth which led Mr. Jones, the apothecary—Meryton did not have a large or wealthy enough population to support a physician—to tell Mr. and Mrs. Bennet they would not be able to have more children.

Bennet's daughters would have fifty pounds per annum on his death and an equal share of his wife's fortune of five thousand pounds on his wife's death. Thanks to the entail, they would essentially be forced into genteel poverty unless the girls married well, which made marrying off their daughters his wife's obsession. Because of this, Jane was pushed out at fifteen, as had each of her daughters when they reached that age.

Jane was a classic beauty, tall, willowy, blond, and blue-eyed. She did not like that all her mother went on about was her beauty, but she was not one for confrontations so she held her peace. Jane's way of protecting herself was to see everyone and everything as innately good—like she was—and ignore any negativity—it was this which led to her being naïve when it came to the way she saw others.

Elizabeth was her father's favourite, due in large part to her mother's ill treatment of her because she was not born a son. Elizabeth loved to walk, climb trees, ride, swim and spend time with her father reading and discussing books.

As soon as Jane and Elizabeth were old enough to do so, they had taken on the duties of looking after Longbourn's tenants; their mother was not interested in tenant concerns. The master should have visited them each quarter to see if there were repairs needed or other concerns, but Bennet was too indolent to bestir himself from his study. When the sisters told him what needed to be done, he would authorise it, as long as he himself did not have to expend energy to help.

From her early years, Bennet had discovered his second daughter was intelligent, so she was the only one he routinely welcomed into the sanctuary that was his study. He educated her as he would a son so she could speak, read, and write Greek, Latin, French, Italian, and German.

He brought in masters when needed, but rather than set an agenda for his daughters' education, he let them decide, so other than Elizabeth, and to a certain extent Jane, none of the others availed themselves of the opportunities offered. Mary decided to be self-sufficient, and the youngest two were not interested in anything that was not fun.

Thanks to her education, by 1804 Elizabeth was running the estate more than her father, whose involvement was limited to signing the documents she placed in front of him when needed. The estate brought in just over two thousand pounds per annum, but thanks to Bennet's refusal to rein in his wife's wasteful spending, much to Elizabeth's frustration, there was nothing left unspent to save for the future.

Edward Gardiner was Fanny's younger, and only, brother. He had a highly successful import-export business, Gardiner Trading Company. Gardiner had tried to convince his lazy brother-in-law to allow him to take Fanny's five thousand pounds and grow it, but it had been too much effort for Bennet to put down his port and book to deal with.

A few years ago, Gardiner married the then Madeline Lambert—Maddie, the only daughter of the rector of the church in Lambton, Derbyshire. They had two children thus far, Lillian—Lily—four, and Edward Junior—Eddy—just two.

The Gardiners, although in trade, were as genteel as any in town, and it was thanks to them that the older two Bennet girls were educated in their duties and had learnt to behave as ladies. Unfortunately, once Lily was born, Maddie Gardiner did not have the time needed to teach the younger three Bennet sisters.

Because Lydia was the daughter who most resembled Mrs. Bennet, both in looks and character, she could do no wrong in her mother's eyes. The result was Lydia was spoilt rotten. The Gardiners stopped trying to help the younger girls when their efforts were spurned.

Mrs. Bennet told Mary she was plain; both her mother and father ignored her, so she turned to moralistic texts in an attempt to stand out. Unfortunately, though she read the words, she never quite plumbed the meaning, and so was wont to spout meaningless moralistic platitudes.

Although she spent a great deal of time practicing on the pianoforte, her playing was pedantic at best. She played the notes correctly, but with a decided lack of feeling. Mary wore her hair in severe styles and chose dark-coloured dresses and gowns which did not suit her complexion.

Kitty was led by the younger Lydia. She was weak willed and had decided the only way to garner attention from her mother was to emulate Lydia —her mother's favourite, even over the beautiful Jane. Jane was their mother's second favourite daughter.

~~~~~~~/~~~~~~~

As it was July, it was still daylight when the Darcy and Matlock coaches halted under the portico at Rosings Park. "Where is my sister Jarvis?" Lord Matlock asked the butler.

"She is still sleeping, my Lord," Mrs. Jenkinson informed the Earl.

"Where are the bodies?" Lady Elaine Fitzwilliam asked.

"They are in the ice-house given the temperature, my Lady," Mrs. Jenkinson replied. Tears started to fall as she thought of the broken body of her charge who she considered more a daughter than a duty.

"Thank you for notifying us Mrs. Jenkinson. Surely you need to rest as well. We are here now. I will act as mistress until my sister is able to do so," Lady Matlock stated.

"We need to bury Lewis and Anne soon," Lord Matlock opined.

"What do you need us to do Father?" Lord Andrew Fitzwilliam, Viscount Hilldale, six and twenty, and the heir to the Matlock earldom asked.

"Please Uncle, give us an occupation," Darcy requested.

"In the morning, you three should see the parson. As Catherine picked him, I am sure he will need a great deal of direction, but we need the funeral to take place the day after tomorrow," Lord Matlock instructed.

"It will be done," Lord Hilldale returned, and the other two younger men nodded.

"Reggie, will you proceed even if Catherine is not lucid?" Lady Matlock asked.

"I believe we must Elaine. I will go view Lewis and Anne. Will you sit with our sister?" Lord Matlock requested.

Lady Matlock headed to Lady Catherine's bedchamber while the four men made for the icehouse. It was a grim business, seeing the damage which had been done to the two crash victims.

When they returned to the drawing room, the stablemaster was summoned after Jarvis informed them he had led the party to recover the bodies. When asked if he knew what the cause was, the man explained they found a dead fox trampled by the ponies, and there were bite marks on the forelegs of one pony.

"It was obvious that the fox spooked the normally docile ponies, which led to the horrendous accident. When Lord Metcalf, the local magistrate, arrived the following day, after hearing from those who has seen the crash site and visiting it himself, he ruled it an accident."

By the next afternoon, Lady Catherine was lucid, but unable, or unwilling, to speak a word. She was silent as she contemplated her former actions and beliefs about her ability to control everything and everyone around her. Regardless of the way she had treated them, the family was with her to offer their support.

The following day, with her sister-in-law holding one

hand and Mrs. Jenkinson the other, Lady Catherine sat crying while her late husband and daughter were laid to rest. Many ladies from the neighbourhood, led by Lady Metcalf, sat with her to offer additional support.

~~~~~~~/~~~~~~~

Mrs. Jenkinson was hired as a companion for Lady Catherine, but after serving for a little over two years, the companion's sister's husband passed away, leaving her with four young children. Mrs. Jenkinson had noted the changes in Lady Catherine since her nephew became master so she hoped the lady would not object too vociferously to her resigning her position.

The opposite had happened. Lady Catherine understood and accepted Mrs. Jenkinson's need to go to her sister. After making a request to her nephew, Richard, Mrs. Jenkinson was sent on her way with a lumpsum payment of five thousand pounds to indicate the gratitude for the way she used to take care of the late Anne de Bourgh coupled with her companionship to Lady Catherine during her mourning period.

# CHAPTER 1

## Easter 1808

For the last three years, the two Darcys and three Fitzwilliams had visited Richard's estate for Easter. This year there were four Fitzwilliams in the party which arrived; Lord Andrew Fitzwilliam had married Lady Marie De Melville, the daughter of the Earl and Countess of Jersey, in January of 1808.

Lady Catherine was not the same person she had been before her husband and Anne were taken from her. Her days of trying to control everything and everyone were behind her. She had learnt a hard lesson—that she could only control how she behaved and the way she treated others.

For the one year of her deep mourning, she was rarely seen. After the funerals, at the reading of her late husband's will, she had sat in silence without a single objection to any of its terms.

Richard was the heir. His aunt had been willing to move to the dower house, but Richard told her that she was welcome to live with him as long as she desired, until the day he took a wife. He told her to choose any suite in the house; she chose her late daughter's suite, for it was where she felt closest to Anne. Mrs. Jenkinson remained as her companion until she left to go help her sister.

At first, the family thought she was ill. Not only had she not objected to the will, but she no longer dominated conversations around her, did not offer advice on subjects she knew nothing about, and stopped writing sermons for the parson, and interfering in the lives of the estate's tenants and the citizens of Hunsford.

What the family did not yet realise was Catherine had become deeply introspective during her deep mourning and had finally learnt to value love. Her greatest regret was she had loved her daughter but had never told her so.

Lady Catherine had never loved her late husband, but she admitted to herself he was a good man and an even better father. Yes, they married due to a compromise, but she had grown to esteem him.

Belatedly, she realised her husband was not weak, he had just preferred peace to confrontation. When she was wrong about the estate—which she now knew was quite often—the steward would go to her husband who would issue the correct instructions quietly.

The late Sir Lewis might have left her nothing but the income from her dowry of twenty thousand pounds. Instead, he settled a further thirty thousand pounds on her, so her jointure was fifty thousand pounds. In addition to the two thousand pounds per annum her money generated, Sir Lewis willed her a further one thousand pounds per annum in his last will and testament.

She appreciated Lewis's logic in choosing Richard as the beneficiary if Anne died unmarried and childless, as neither Andrew nor William needed an estate. Yes, that was another change; she called her nephew "William," a name she had previously eschewed as too common.

William and Gigi became almost like surrogate children to her. Once she had changed her outlook on life, Catherine was welcomed with open arms by her brother's family and the two remaining Darcys.

She had watched as William acquired some of her old attitudes, among them feeling superior to those not of his circle, but there was a contradiction on which she pinned her hopes of improving his attitude. William had befriended the son of a tradesman, Charles Bingley, two years younger than himself.

They had met at Cambridge where William helped Bingley when some lordlings bullied him for no reason other than his roots in trade. The two remained close even after William left school two years before his younger friend.

Before the deaths of her husband and daughter she would have condemned, loudly and vociferously, William's friend's connection to trade. Although she found nothing to object to in the man, his sisters were a different story.

There were two. The eldest, Mrs. Louisa Hurst, was married to Harold Hurst, a gentleman whose family had a small estate in Yorkshire named Winsdale. On her own, Mrs. Hurst was innocuous, but when her younger and much more forceful sister, Miss Caroline Bingley, was with her, she allowed the younger one to lead and followed her blindly.

Lady Catherine had been visiting Pemberley the previous summer when William invited his friend, and only his friend, to visit for the warm months. Somehow, Miss Bingley had convinced her brother the invitation included her and her sister. Rather than the expected guest, four guests arrived.

As she was acting as her nephew's hostess, Lady Catherine was with him when the Bingley carriage arrived. There was no mistaking the avaricious look on Miss Bingley's face as she was handed out. She looked like Catherine imagined a lion would when it spied its prey.

The woman fawned over her niece, nephew, and herself, dropping many not-so-subtle hints about how the estate needed a permanent mistress and about how her first-class education had prepared her for such a role.

Lady Catherine had been unable to understand why the brother allowed his sister to behave as she did, especially when it had been made clear to him the invitation to visit Pemberley was extended to him alone. It did not take Lady Catherine long to take the man's measure; he had no spine, and she was ashamed of ever having thought the same of her own late husband. His sister had him twisted around her finger and could manipulate him with little effort. It seemed his aim in life was a conflict-free existence.

It soon became evident to her the relationship between her nephew and his friend was not that of equals, but more akin to a father-son relationship. Bingley, it seemed, was willing to defer to her nephew and allow him to make decisions for him, and for some reason William allowed things to proceed in that fashion. More puppy and master than equal friends.

No matter how much Miss Bingley fawned over him, or how many hints she dropped, it did not take much perspicacity to see that her nephew did not like the woman and would not offer for her if she were the last available option on earth. The woman herself was wilfully blind to his disdain.

Catherine was surprised when the shrewish harpy—there was no more delicate way to describe her—held herself far above her station and denigrated others who were above her in all ways. Neither her brother nor William said or did anything to correct her.

Had she been the Lady Catherine of old, she would have given both brother and sister a set down for the ages and sent them packing with a flea in their ears. She decided to hold her peace unless her nephew asked her opinion. He did not.

Poor Georgiana hid with her aunt as much as she could. The objectionable Miss Bingley fawned over the shy Gigi, thinking it was a means to attract the brother. It was not. Catherine saw him seethe every time the harridan called his sister 'dear Georgiana' but he never corrected her, even though no one had granted her permission to use Gigi's familiar name.

It was a great relief to the residents of Pemberley when the Bingley party departed, especially the servants—from the housekeeper and butler on down. Lady Catherine departed for Rosings Park a month later, still shaking her head as her nephew had not stepped in to rid his house of the woman before she departed voluntarily.

Now she stood with her ex-army officer nephew, Richard, waiting for the coaches bearing their family to arrive. According to a letter from William in February, the Bingley woman had hinted many times that she would like an invitation to

Rosings Park for Easter. When Richard asked her advice, Catherine shared her observations with him and no invitation had been forthcoming.

Both Richard and Catherine perked up as they spied the first of the coaches approaching the portico.

~~~~~~~/~~~~~~~

"How could you allow my—I mean Mr. Darcy to leave for Easter at his cousin's estate and not invite me—I mean us?" Miss Bingley continued to harangue her brother.

"Caroline, Darcy explained to me it is a family event. Not only that, but how do you expect him to extend an invitation to a place where he himself is a guest?" Bingley whined. "I am his friend, but I hardly know his cousin. Mr. Fitzwilliam had already left Cambridge before I started and we never met. I only know what Darcy has told me."

"Then you should have convinced Mr. Darcy to invite us to Snowhaven so we could meet the Earl, Countess, and the Viscount," Miss Bingley demanded.

"Caroline, be reasonable. Mr. Darcy could no more invite us to his uncle's estate than he could to his cousin's," Mrs. Hurst attempted to placate her sister.

"Why should that be Louisa? I—we—deserve to be with those of our standing, but yet we languish in the lower circles to which your drunken husband belongs," Miss Bingley spat out nastily. "Why you could not marry someone higher, I do not know. Do you not remember how Mother used to tell us it was our duty to raise the family from our roots?"

Rather than provoke an argument with her sister, Mrs. Hurst stood up and left the room. "Caro, you should not have said that to our sister," Bingley said, weakly.

"And what about you?" Miss Bingley rounded on her brother. "You continue to fall in love with your *angels,* but none of them are good enough to help raise us in society. Also, you are supposed to promote me to Mr. Darcy, but even in that you are failing. You should be aiming for that insipid Miss Darcy as a bride."

"She is only thirteen, Caroline!" Bingley exclaimed. "Darcy told me on several occasions he will not consider a courtship for his sister until she comes out when she is eighteen, perhaps even the year after." Darcy had told Bingley on multiple occasions he would never offer for Caroline, even if she compromised him in front of witnesses. In order to try to keep the peace, Bingley did not dare tell his sister the truth.

Even had he told her, Miss Bingley only heard that which fit her desires.

~~~~~~~/~~~~~~~

Longbourn was in an uproar, brought about—as it normally was—by the mistress having an attack of nerves. Netherfield Park had been let a year earlier by a wealthy gentleman and his wife from Cornwall.

They were considering purchasing the estate for their second son so he would not have to enter a profession. Mr. Lloyd Gravelle was four and twenty and had been taken by Jane Bennet, who was twenty—from the moment he met her.

His father, Nigel Gravelle, owned Gravelle Springs, an estate which cleared over eight thousand pounds per annum. From the instant Jane and young Gravelle met, Fanny Bennet pushed the two together. Even worse, every time the young man visited Longbourn, she forced her other daughters out of the room so Jane and Lloyd would be alone.

Elizabeth begged her father to check her mother, but he only laughed and told her it was good for a young lady to be crossed in love at least once. As much as Elizabeth loved her father, she was starting to become critical of his faults; the scales had long fallen from her eyes.

Yes, her mother was loud, vulgar, inappropriate, and more, but as much as she would have liked to lay the blame solely at her mother's feet; the fact her father laughed when he should teach, sat back when he should check, and did nothing to discipline his unruly youngest daughter opened her eyes to his faults and made her realise there was more than enough blame to go around.

It became so bad Jane—dear Jane who would make an excuse for anyone regardless how egregious their behaviour—was waking up to the fact their mother was driving suitors away, not helping her to marry and assist her family in a way that would allow her sisters to find happiness in their own time.

When Jane was sixteen, Stuart Jamison, the son of a gentleman from an estate in Bedfordshire, started to court her. He wrote her poetry, but he had been unwilling to tolerate Mrs. Bennet's machinations and vulgarity.

He had apologised to Jane then left the area in all haste. While he was calling on Jane, he had been introduced to Charlotte Lucas, four years Jane's senior, and who Mrs. Bennet called plain. Charlotte and Stuart became well acquainted over six months; Stuart requested and was granted a courtship, followed by a betrothal, and the two married early in 1805. Three years later, Charlotte presented her husband with a son, and she was with child again. Jane bore no resentment towards Elizabeth's best friend. Her ire was directed at her mother, who had managed to run off another suitor.

The Gravelles—without warning—abandoned Netherfield Park, informing the agent, Mr. Frank Phillips—Jane's uncle—they would not remain and allow their son to join a family which had Fanny Bennet as a member. They could not countenance being forced into the company of such a vulgar woman.

Jane's resentment against her mother grew; she had liked Lloyd and was well on her way to falling in love with him. The one good outcome of losing him was that Jane Bennet was no longer as naïve as she had been, and now saw the world more realistically. Elizabeth had always seen it so.

Thomas did not leave his study, not even when his brother Phillips berated him for not checking his wife. He continued to find amusement where there was none and lost more of his second daughter's respect in the process.

~~~~~~~/~~~~~~~

"Richard, Aunt Cat, Brother" Georgiana—very recently fourteen—exclaimed as she approached them for hugs. In the years since Sir Lewis and Anne had been lost, Georgiana had become close to both her aunts—Ladies Elaine and Catherine—so much so as to view them as surrogate mothers.

"Welcome Gigi," Catherine hugged her niece to her. Each time she saw the young girl, the more she resembled her mother, her late sister, Lady Anne Darcy.

There had been so much loss in their family. Catherine shook off maudlin thoughts as she hugged her nephew, William. Richard clapped his cousin on the back. "Good to see you, William; your lessons on estate management have been paying off. After almost four years, I believe I am getting the hang of it."

"Do not forget, I was trained from the time I was out of leading strings," Darcy replied, missing the fact his cousin had been jesting with him. Over the preceding years, Darcy had become a dour man who wore a mask in public to discourage those who would try to connect themselves to him or view him as a target for their matrimonial aspirations. Even worse many wanted him to invest money with them in schemes sure to fail. He hated being hunted by the ladies of the *Ton* for his fortune and connections. Ironically, as much as he hated predatory, social climbing, fortune-hunting behaviour, he seemed to turn a blind eye to Miss Bingley's behaviour, which smacked of all three. He continued to tolerate her.

Darcy had always found it difficult to catch the tone of others' conversation and was useless with small talk. He was shy, but hid that fact behind taciturn, and sometimes downright haughty and rude behaviour.

His Aunt Catherine despaired as she watched her nephew continue to adopt many of her old attitudes toward those below his status. She had come to realise how wrong they were long ago, but William had not. It was difficult for her, but she would not interfere unless William asked her a direct question—or she felt there was no other choice—and they had not reached that point yet.

"Mother, Father, Marie, and Andy, welcome to Rosings Park," Richard stated warmly. Richard was a sociable man, and although he loved his Aunt Catherine, he was happy there would be additional company for the next three or four weeks.

~~~~~~~/~~~~~~~

After all the guests returned from washing the dust off and changing from their travel attire, they met in the main drawing room, the one that *used* to be Lady Catherine's throne room.

All of the gaudy, uncomfortable furniture had been sold. Gone were all of the baubles, dour artwork, and other ostentatious pieces which had littered Rosings Park in an attempt to impress visitors with the wealth of the estate owners.

About a year after Richard had become master, once his aunt was out of deep mourning, they travelled to de Bourgh House in London. Lady Catherine remembered a warehouse she had discovered near Cheapside, the Gardiner Trading Company, which had the finest bolts and the best selection of fabrics she had ever seen. As much as she had then disdained lowering herself to shop in such a place, the old Lady Catherine had done so because she had an eye for quality, and that warehouse had the best.

She remembered the genteel owner, Mr. Gardiner, sold everything—furniture, artwork, decorative pieces, in short anything worth buying. Lady Catherine asked her nephew to join her when she met with Mr. Gardiner. Gardiner came to de Bourgh House with a clerk, who inventoried everything the master wanted sold. Two clerks returned to Rosings Park with them for the same reason.

In the end, even after his commission, Mr. Gardiner had sold it all for a little more than it cost when purchased. Richard used the proceeds to refurnish and redecorate both of their homes. The *throne,* which used to be in the drawing room, was one of the first pieces to be sold, and Lady Catherine inwardly winced for the new owner, hoping they too would soon have an epiphany.

A year later, Richard and his Aunt visited Gardiner Trading Company to purchase fabrics for curtains. On this visit, they noticed a lady and two very pretty young ladies. Richard requested an introduction, and Mr. Gardiner proudly introduced his wife and two nieces, Miss Jane Bennet and Miss Elizabeth Bennet. Both were very pretty, but Richard was especially taken with the older young lady, a blond with blue eyes.

~~~~~~~/~~~~~~~

The drawing room at Rosings Park, along with all public and private rooms, were now decorated much like the Fitzwilliam and Darcy homes, with understated elegance and an eye to comfort.

"Next year, I will find a companion for Gigi. Her governess will be leaving at the end of the year," Darcy informed his family.

"Do you not mean *we* will, as we *share* guardianship?" Richard questioned.

"Well, of course I will consult you Richard, but you must own I am the one who is with Gigi most of the time," Darcy replied dismissively.

Darcy did not see most of his family members shake their heads. Some would call him proud, and the way he thought his own counsel infallible only bolstered that impression. '*What has become of you William?*' Lady Catherine asked herself silently. '*One of these days, this pride will lead to your downfall.*'

# CHAPTER 2

"William, I do not have a good feeling about Mrs. Younge, the woman you employed to be Gigi's companion," Lady Catherine shared with her nephew at Darcy House in London.

"You know I am not happy you excluded me from the process," Richard told his cousin with no little asperity. "When we discussed this at Rosings last Easter, I thought we agreed I would be involved in the decision as Gigi's joint guardian."

"If you recall, I never agreed," Darcy replied haughtily. "I am, after all, the one who is with her most of the time. You know I am a good judge of character, and she had excellent references from some well-placed families."

"Did you talk to any of these families Nephew?" Lady Catherine asked.

Darcy waved away their concerns. "I observed Mrs. Younge, and she was exactly as I expected her to be, and *my* sister is doing very well with her."

"Does that mean if, heaven forbid, there is a problem with the woman, the responsibility would be yours alone?" Richard shot back angrily.

Like his aunt, his parents, his brother, and his sister, Richard had no idea why William had become almost insufferable. He thought his Aunt Catherine had been close to the truth when she had shared her worry with him one evening, that Darcy seemed to have adopted some of her former poor behaviour.

"Gigi has become very accomplished in the pianoforte,"

Lady Catherine observed to change the subject to a less contentious one.

"For the last year whenever she was in Town, she had been studying with *Signore* Alberto da Funti, the acclaimed *maestro* from Italy. She has excelled under his direction," William reported proudly.

His relatives did not contest the fact William loved his sister and would never knowingly do anything to hurt her. What they were worried about was that his pride and belief in his own infallibility might blind him to some dangers, as in the case of Mrs. Younge.

"Has Wickham been by with his hand out recently?" Richard asked.

George Wickham was the son of Pemberley's late steward. As good a master as Robert Darcy was, he had a blind spot when it came to his godson, Wickham. It was not entirely his fault, as William hid many truths about his godson from the late Robert Darcy.

It was another one of William's failings. He believed he knew the best way to protect those he loved, and in this case, it was by keeping his silence, not by telling his father the truth about Wickham's vicious propensities, his debts, and his ruination of young women and girls. When Richard wanted to inform his young cousin and ward about Wickham, Darcy forbade it, certain his way was the best way to protect his sister, and completely ignoring Richard's opinion that knowledge was strength.

"Since I refused him the living, to which he had resigned all claims, he abused me abominably and went on his way swearing revenge as he always does," Darcy told them calmly.

"Be careful Nephew. A wounded animal is often the most vicious," Lady Catherine opined.

"What can that wastrel do to me? He is all bluster, and even more, he is a coward," Darcy stated assuredly. "He likes going after those who are not able to protect themselves, and I am not one of those."

None of the three noticed Mrs. Younge, about to walk into the room with her charge. If they had, they would have seen the almost feral look on her face when they mentioned Wickham so dismissively. In an instant, she schooled her features and plastered a fake smile on her face.

~~~~~~~/~~~~~~~

There had been no improvement at Longbourn. In Elizabeth's opinion, things had grown worse. As she had done with her three older daughters, Fanny Bennet pushed Kitty out at fifteen. This precipitated a tantrum from her favourite—Lydia, who was but fourteen.

She objected vociferously to being the only daughter not out. Lydia threw some epic tantrums from time to time, but those paled in comparison to this one. Finally, Mrs. Bennet agreed to let Lydia come out in August of the following year, two months before her fifteenth birthday.

This seemed to placate Lydia, as she loved to think she would come out at a younger age than any of her sisters. "Will it not be a lark if I am the first of my sisters to marry?" Lydia crowed after her perceived victory.

"You are pretty and lively enough; I do not see why it would not be so," Mrs. Bennet stated supportively. "If only those artful Lucases had not stolen the Jamison boy away from Jane for Charlotte. I always thought with her being so plain, she would be an old maid."

"Mama!" Jane and Elizabeth chorused.

"What? It is nothing but the truth," Mrs. Bennet sniffed.

"How can that be, Mama? If what you said had merit, would she be married and expecting her second child now?" Elizabeth asked, knowing full well her mother hated to hear about Charlotte being married to one of the men she had intended for Jane. "It was not Jane who caused Mr. Jamison and Mr. Gravelle to run for the hills."

Jane gave her sister a warning look to keep quiet; although she agreed with Lizzy wholeheartedly, it was not worth it. "Well, I am sure I do not know to what you refer, impertinent miss. At least Jane has her looks; no man will ever want you with your dark hair and coarse skin. You are a blue-stocking to boot," Mrs. Bennet stated nastily. Elizabeth was used to her mother denigrating her, but it did not lessen the blow when the Bennet matriarch spoke thusly.

Her relationship with her father had become more strained as his teasing of his family had only worsened. Even though her mother did not understand one jest in ten made at her expense, Elizabeth did and she felt it was not the way a father and husband should behave.

Elizabeth was certain had her mother given into Lydia and allowed her out at fourteen, her father would have done nothing but comment that Lydia was one of the silliest girls in the realm.

Jane and Elizabeth had long discussions about their younger sisters. They believed with a little attention and re-direction, Mary could be corrected easily, but that Kitty was too dependent on Lydia, who they were sure would ruin all of them one day.

At fourteen, Lydia's womanly curves were those of a much older lady, but her mind was that of a girl younger than fourteen. Both Kitty and Lydia were obsessed with officers after Mrs. Bennet told them a fanciful story of a Colonel Millar's regiment and the officers she used to flirt with before she met their father.

To Jane and Elizabeth, the scariest thing was that Mrs. Bennet and her two youngest daughters all seemed to have the same low level of maturity.

~~~~~~~/~~~~~~~

At first, when her two older sisters started to take notice of her, Mary thought they were making sport of her, but it soon became evident they were in earnest. Mary had always felt like no one in their family loved her, which led her to strike out and forge her own path.

At first, she would not give up reading Fordyce's sermons, but within weeks Elizabeth began to expand the scope of

Mary's reading to include some Shakespeare. Jane would take time to talk to Mary—really talk to her. Jane also started to help Mary with her manner of dressing.

Before the end of the year, Mary was wearing dresses in colours that became her, and no longer wore her hair in the severe bun as had been her wont. The last thing Jane and Elizabeth coaxed their sister to change was to discard the glasses she wore but did not need. It had been part of the persona she hid behind to protect herself from the feeling of being alone. Now that she was included in activities with Jane and Lizzy, she no longer needed them.

Although her beauty was not as great as Jane's or Elizabeth's, she was pretty in her own right. At the December assembly in Meryton, Mary found herself in demand for dances although she had been a wallflower sitting with a book in the past.

So it was that the three oldest Bennet sisters forged a new group within the household. The changes in Mary confounded both parents, for different reasons. Mrs. Bennet had to admit to herself her middle daughter was not plain—even if she would not admit it publicly. Mr. Bennet admitted he now had only two of the silliest girls in all of England as his daughters.

~~~~~~~~/~~~~~~~~

"What do you mean we are not invited to Pemberley for Christmastide," Miss Bingley demanded stridently. "Are we not Mr. Darcy's particular friends?"

Even her older sister had tried to tell Miss Bingley that it was only Charles who Mr. Darcy called a friend. "Caro, the Darcys are to be at Snowhaven, the Earl and Countess of Matlock's estate. How can I demand he invite us to Pemberley, never mind to his uncle's estate?" Bingley whined.

"If you let him know we would be quite on our own for Christmastide, I am sure he would have requested the Countess invite us, as is my—our—due!" Miss Bingley insisted.

"We have covered this on many occasions before Sister." Mr. Hurst, who was usually silent, had reach the limit of his patience. "There is no polite way for a guest to invite other guests to another's home."

"What do you know? Are you even sober enough to contribute to this conversation?" Miss Bingley shot back at her brother-in-law.

The truth was that Mr. Hurst did not over imbibe. He often gave that impression, or pretended that he was asleep, so he would not have to deal with the harpy that was his wife's sister. "May I remind you, *Sister*, that I am the only one here who was raised on an estate by a landed gentleman. No matter how much you deny it, you are, and always have been, the vulgar daughter of a tradesman."

Bingley and Mrs. Hurst cringed, as they were aware how much their sister hated the truth of her roots being pointed out to her. She thought her dowry of twenty thousand—that she was vulgar enough to mention at every turn—trumped her birth, when it did nothing of the kind.

Miss Bingley picked up a figurine from the mantle and hurled it at Hurst's head. Hurst, for someone supposedly in his cups, deftly evaded the missile, which broke into shards as it hit the floor. "Are you going to allow this damned man to talk to me in this way?" Miss Bingley demanded of her sister. Rather than answer her, Louisa looked away and played with the bracelets on her arm.

As was her wont when she was in a snit, Miss Bingley stormed out of the drawing room and soon the sound of her bedchamber door being slammed reverberated throughout the house. That sound was followed by the sound of porcelain figurines being smashed by the irate woman who was having a tantrum any child of five would have been proud of.

"Bingley, I am sorry, but it needed to be said. Neither you nor my wife do her any good feeding her pretentions," Hurst stated firmly. "Have you ever told her what Darcy asked you to?" A chagrined Bingley shook his head.

"I do not want to deal with her anger," Bingley admitted.

"You will have to deal with it one way or another. How

long do you think it will be before Darcy, or one of his family, give her a richly deserved, *public* set down?" Hurst asked pointedly. "When we were at Pemberley, I watched Darcy's aunt, Lady Catherine. I swear she came close to taking your sister to task but restrained herself at the last moment."

His brother-in-law did not tell Bingley anything he did not know, but was not the preservation of peace more important? Charles Bingley hated confrontation.

~~~~~~~~/~~~~~~~~

"Darce, would you ride with me into Hertfordshire, just over twenty miles from Town," Bingley requested of his friend not long after Twelfth Night in 1810, a few days after the Darcys returned to London from Snowhaven.

"What is in Hertfordshire?" Darcy asked.

"An estate by the name of Netherfield Park. You advised me to lease an estate before purchasing one," Bingley stated, seeking his friend and mentor's approval.

"It is convenient to Town; what do you know about it?" Darcy quizzed the younger man.

"It clears around five thousand per annum. The owner, Mr. Morris, is a man who inherited it but has a much larger estate in Scotland where he prefers to live. The house, I am told, was rebuilt less than ten years ago before he inherited it, and it is the preeminent estate in the area. It is two miles from the market town of Meryton," Bingley informed Darcy.

"Is there a local agent?" Darcy inquired further.

"My man of business brought this to me knowing I was looking for something to lease, and yes, the local agent is a solicitor, Mr. Phillips. He will meet us there once I notify him when I would like to view the property. The current tenant is with family until March. If I take it, would you join me there to help me learn about estate management?" Bingley asked enthusiastically.

"It sounds like a place worth viewing. As for me, I would only be able to join you in late August. I have family obligations, including Easter at Rosings Park. My sister's companion has asked if she may take Georgiana to Ramsgate in the summer, so I will escort them there in June. I will be spending part of the summer with my sister after completing business in London," Darcy averred. "Who will be your hostess?"

"One of my sisters, Caroline more than likely," Bingley admitted.

"Bingley, I have tolerated your sister for our friendship, but if it gets too much living under the same roof, you must know that I will depart. You remember that I told you there are *no* circumstances—including a compromise—under which I will offer for Miss Bingley, do you not?" Darcy reminded his friend pointedly.

"Yes, I do remember that Darce." Bingley chose not to mention the message had never been passed onto his sister.

After Bingley departed Darcy House, the master made his way to Matlock House, where his uncle and two aunts were located. "Welcome William," Lord Matlock said in a jovial manner.

"Next week I will be in Hertfordshire for two days and one night. I would be happy if you could host Gigi and Mrs. Younge for those two days," Darcy requested.

"William! For shame that you think you need to ask. Of course, our niece will be welcome," Lady Elaine exclaimed.

"If you choose to, you may give Mrs. Younge two days off, as I believe my brother, sister, and I will be able to look after our niece without losing her," Lady Catherine teased. None of the three sitting across from Darcy liked Mrs. Younge, but their stubborn nephew would not hear any word against her without concrete proof, so they stayed their tongues on the subject.

"Thank you, Aunt Cat; that is a good suggestion. I am sure Mrs. Younge would enjoy a few extra days for herself," William agreed.

~~~~~~~/~~~~~~~

One of the Darcy travelling coaches pulled up under the portico at Netherfield Park the third week of January. Bingley and Darcy were met by Mr. Phillips. After greetings, they entered the manor house.

Darcy saw a solid structure and had seen nothing nega-tive in the Park. The house had been well built, and he did not notice any problems inside that might indicate the estate had been neglected. After a tour of the house, the two men met with the steward and toured the home and tenant farms.

The two visiting men had been supplied horses from Netherfield's stables. Mr. Phillips explained the landlord owned a half dozen horses stabled at Netherfield. Just as with the park and house, Darcy was impressed by the way the farms were maintained.

All tenant dwellings were in good repair and looked reasonably comfortable. With his experienced eye, Darcy could see someone was taking good care of the tenants and their needs.

"Darcy, do you see any reason I should not lease this es-tate?" Bingley asked as the two friends hung back on the walk back to the manor house.

"No Bingley. It looks like a good place for you to learn," Darcy replied.

"So, I may lease it?" Bingley verified enthusiastically.

"It seems so," Darcy permitted.

Before they departed, the two men met Mr. Phillips in Meryton, and Bingley signed a one-year lease commencing on the first day of October. The current lessee would leave by the middle of September at the latest.

~~~~~~~/~~~~~~~

The friends parted ways when they arrived back in Town after an enjoyable night at the Red Rooster Inn in Meryton. On his return to his town home on Curzon Street, Bingley decided discretion was the better part of valour and did not mention the estate he had leased to his sisters.

He was well aware Caroline's desire was for him to take an estate near Pemberley.

# CHAPTER 3

Hunsford was a small market town adjacent to Rosings Park, and the living attached to the parish of Hunsford was under the patronage of the master of that estate. As he had with many things that he counted inconsequential, the late Sir Lewis de Bourgh deferred to his wife when appointing a new rector some eighteen years previously.

The man, Mr. John Branch, was in his fifties when he was awarded the living. He was not the best clergyman Sir Lewis had ever encountered, but he knew his wife chose him for the deference, bordering on sycophantism, the man had shown her.

Until the tragedy six years ago, Lady Catherine had been intimately involved in the running of all aspects of Hunsford Parish, including the text of sermons. The one thing her husband had drawn the line at, however, was when he found out Mr. Branch shared confidences of parishioners with his patroness.

Lady Catherine had been taken aback by the vehemence with which her husband objected. He made clear to his wife that he would inform the Bishop of Kent a clergyman in his diocese was breaking canon law. The disclosure would lead to Mr. Branch being defrocked, which caused the great lady to relent.

At first, after the change in his patroness subsequent to the death of her husband and daughter, Hunsford's parson had been lost until he again started to discharge his duties without detailed instruction from Lady Catherine.

His wife had been most pleased, as for the first time since they had moved into the parsonage, she was able to manage her own household without any officious interference from her husband's patroness. They had two sons and a daughter, all of whom were married and living in their own homes, so Mr. and Mrs. Branch had the parsonage to themselves—when their children and grandchildren were not visiting.

In February, Mr. Branch had passed away in his sleep. Richard allowed his widow as much time as she needed to move out of the parsonage. By mid-March, a grieving Mrs. Branch had left to live with her daughter, son-in-law, and four grandchildren in Surrey.

Not far from Westerham—where Hunsford was located —was the town of Chilham. The town was on the Pilgrims Way leading to Canterbury. St. Mary's, the old church in the town, had employed a curate for the last six months, a Mr. William Collins.

When Richard applied to the rector at St. Mary's, with Mr. Collins agreement, he released his curate from his duties to serve at Hunsford. He would either be gifted the living him-self or would serve until another took up the living. It was the habit of some to sell the livings within their purview, but no one in Richard's extended family believed in that practice.

Lady Catherine allowed Richard to decide who would fill the living on a permanent basis, and never tried to insert her unasked-for opinion. Richard loved his aunt dearly, and he did solicit her opinion whenever he felt the need; he wanted her comfortable and her preferences to be considered with his own.

He asked for her opinion of the curate from St. Mary's after the first service he led, on the last Sunday of March. Both had been impressed by the curate's attention to the congre-gants. He did not ignore them to bow and scrape to the master of Rosings or his highborn aunt.

As the mistress of the estate, Lady Catherine extended

an invitation to Mr. Collins for their after-church meal. "From where do you hail Mr. Collins?" Richard asked when the three were sitting in the drawing room enjoying some tea after a satisfying meal.

"My late parents had a small cottage in Crickdale, Wiltshire. My mother passed twenty years ago, and my father while I was in the seminary before I took orders," Collins shared.

"Do you have any other family, Mr. Collins?" Lady Catherine enquired.

"Yes, I have a distant cousin in Hertfordshire. The family name is Bennet; his estate, Longbourn is entailed away from the female line. My cousin has five daughters and no son, so I am the heir presumptive," Collins explained.

"It would be a terrible thing to be displaced from the home one grew up in simply because they are of the incorrect gender," Lady Catherine opined.

"Unfortunately, there was a breach in the family due to a disagreement between my grandfather and the Bennets of Longbourn," Collins admitted.

"We will not try to force a confidence Mr. Collins," Richard interjected. "I must tell you we were both impressed by your way of conducting the service, and your sermon spoke to everyone."

"Thank you, Mr. Fitzwilliam. I thank you both for your hospitality. I am invited to dinner at one of the parishioners, so it is with appreciation I take my leave," Collins bowed to both and made his exit.

"What do you think Aunt Cat?" Richard asked after they heard the butler close the front door.

"We have only seen him perform his duties once—with aplomb I must say. In my opinion, however, we need to see how he executes his duties over the next few weeks. The opinion of the Hunsford parishioners will be most important."

"In that case, we will wait and see. There is no need to make a hasty choice," Richard agreed.

~~~~~~~/~~~~~~~

"How pleasant it would be not to be alone for Easter," Miss Bingley said, dropping a none too subtle hint as she and her older sister were visiting their *dear friend*, Miss Georgiana Darcy.

The fact that the girl was but fifteen made no difference to the insincere woman. Darcy knew full well the harridan thought he would take notice of her if she fawned over his sister. It seemed she would never learn. "Bingley told me you were invited to spend the holiday with your family in Scarborough," Darcy averred, not taking the bait Miss Bingley so liberally spread around for him.

"That is so far, and there are no people of fashion there. It would be better if we were invited to visit a place closer to Town," Miss Bingley cooed as she batted her eyelids in what she believed was a coquettish fashion.

Rather than attract him, it made Darcy's stomach turn. He could see his sister wanted nothing more than to be rid of the cloying woman as well. "We have an appointment, Miss Bingley, Mrs. Hurst. Have a good day," Darcy stated in dismissal. Even Miss Bingley could not mistake that they were being asked to leave. With as much good grace as she could muster —which was not much—the woman, who looked like she was dressed for a ball at St. James, and her sister departed reluctantly.

An hour later, Bingley was shown in. Darcy had no doubt he had been sent by his sister to solicit an invitation to Rosings. He held up his hand before he allowed Bingley to speak. "If you are here to plead for an invitation to Rosings Park, save your breath to cool your porridge. Even *if* I desired to invite your sisters and Hurst, it is not my place to do so. How many times must your sister be told the same thing?"

"She was so disappointed I had to..." Bingley started, "I do not want to prevaricate, she demanded I not return without an invitation."

"You have my sympathy, my friend, but unless you are willing to stand up to your sister, you will never achieve the peace you desire." Darcy was sure his friend would not do so, but he needed to say it, nonetheless.

~~~~~~~~/~~~~~~~~

"What do you think Aunt Cat?" Richard asked after Mr. Collins third Sunday in the pulpit at Hunsford.

"Let me ask you nephew, what have you heard from the parishioners?" Lady Catherine answered with her own question.

"You know I liked it more when you took charge and just told everyone what to do Woman," Richard jested.

"No, you did not." She smiled, as he helped her laugh at her former faults and attitudes.

"The reports from the parishioners are all positive," Richard informed his aunt as he became more serious. "That, coupled with his manner of conducting services, leads me to think he is the man for the job."

"Then it seems you know what to do without my input, do you not?" she replied serenely.

"Collins will be joining us for the meal after services. I will offer him the living then," Richard decided.

"Richard, are you concerned—like the rest of us are—about Mrs. Younge not being what she seems?" Lady Catherine asked worriedly.

"My thoughts and feelings have been expressed to William, but he insists his judgement is sound. If I try to bring up the fact we are supposed to be co-guardians, he is dismissive." Richard paused for a thought. "I am worried about him Aunt Cat. The proud, haughty man he is now is not the one I knew before Uncle Robert passed away. He is almost rude to those he thinks below him."

"Except to the Bingleys," Lady Catherine pointed out. "He does not see the contradiction in his treatment of others, while he is seems blind to their status as children of a tradesman. Personally, I think Bingley is a good man, just without any backbone and too easily manipulated by his sister—who he refuses to take in hand—and abrogates his responsibility for decisions by deferring to others, especially William."

The butler announced Mr. Collins, so discussion of their concerns about Darcy ceased. After the meal, Richard asked Collins to meet him in his study where he offered the living to the clergyman.

Collins accepted gratefully and asked for a few days to move his possessions from his little cottage near St. Mary's church, which Richard readily granted. In addition, a cart and trap were placed at the new parson's disposal to assist with his move.

~~~~~~~/~~~~~~~

"Your new rector seems to do a credible job," Darcy announced after Easter services at the Hunsford Church. "He is mayhap a little young to have a living, but from what I can tell he is well liked by the congregants."

"As your approval is hard to earn," Richard jested—only partly, "it is that much more appreciated when granted." Richard gave his younger cousin a bow with a flourish.

"Do not be facetious Richard," Darcy returned. He did not miss that his cousin's jest was a disguised criticism.

After Easter dinner, Georgiana sat with her aunts and cousin Marie while the three men enjoyed their drinks. "Do you think I have done something to upset William?" she asked the three older women.

"Why on earth would you think that Gigi?" Lady Catherine asked concernedly.

"I hardly see him. He created an establishment for me, where it is only Mrs. Younge, other servants, and me. He is always busy, and I see him less than once a week. I must have done something to anger him because he hardly has time for me." The young girl was crying softly by the end of her speech.

"He obviously has a lot of business to attend to Gigi," Lady Matlock tried to think of a reason for her nephew's change in behaviour.

"When I asked if I was allowed to come visit Rosings to be with Richard and Aunt Cat, he told me I have too many les-

SHANA GRANDERSON A LADY

sons," Georgiana shared.

*'Could it be my nephew is punishing us for questioning the companion he selected? Is his pride so great he cannot accept anyone disagreeing with him? I worry William has turned inward far too much. I do not know how much longer I will be able to remain silent. William needs to be woken up. It will take some patience, as I do not want to push him away so he withdraws even further into himself.'* Lady Catherine mused silently.

By the time the men entered the drawing room, Georgiana had dried her eyes and put herself to rights so her brother did not notice anything amiss. Georgiana agreed to play for her relations. It was something new for her as she had always been too shy to exhibit in front of others, even her family members.

In mid-May, the Fitzwilliams departed for Snowhaven and Hilldale, and the Darcys for Town. Darcy had business to see to before he transported his sister and her companion to his house in Ramsgate.

~~~~~~~/~~~~~~~

In mid-June, Mr. Collins was a dinner guest at Rosings. "Mr. Collins, may I ask a question?" Lady Catherine opened after she poured three cups of tea as they relaxed in the drawing room. "If you feel it is not something you wish to answer, please tell me so."

"Please ask, your Ladyship," Collins allowed.

"We only have so much family in this world, and if I understood what you told us when we first met, your only family are these Bennets, from whom you are estranged." Collins allowed it was so. "Do you have any personal issue with them?"

Collins considered the question for a minute. "No Lady Catherine, I do not. In fact, I have never met them," he admitted.

"Do you know what caused the breach?" Lady Catherine prodded gently.

"I do. My late grandfather used to be named Bennet. Some generations before a younger Bennet son had moved to

Wiltshire and over the years the Wiltshire Bennets became estranged from the Hertfordshire family. The reason for the estrangement is not known. My grandfather compromised the current master of Longbourn's aunt thinking it would somehow gain him access to Longbourn's coffers. He never received anything besides a fraction of his wife's dowry as there was a stipulation about compromise and only allowing ten percent of the dowry to be released in that circumstance.

"The Bennets refused to acknowledge him after that, so he changed his name to Collins—his mother was a Collins—and passed his hate of that branch of the Bennet family onto his son—my father," Collins revealed.

"And I assume your father did—or tried to do the same with you? Did he succeed in turning you against your unknown cousins?" Lady Catherine asked.

"He tried, but I have always kept my own counsel on the subject; he merely assumed I felt as he did. One of the tenets of our faith is forgiveness. I feel as a clergyman it is my humble duty to offer an olive branch and heal the breach. I am not sure, however, that if I make an overture it will be welcomed by my Cousin Bennet," Collins said contemplatively.

"It sounds like a laudable aim," Richard opined.

"Unless you reach out to him, you will never know. I have heard it said, nothing ventured, nothing gained," Lady Catherine prompted.

"It is a good suggestion. I am not willing to leave the congregation yet. Mayhap I will write to my cousin later in the year and see if he would agree to my visiting Longbourn. Would you be willing to allow me a sennight if he is receptive Mr. Fitzwilliam?" Collins asked.

"Up to a fortnight will be acceptable, as long as we have a clergyman able to fill your place while you are away," Richard granted.

So it was that Collins resolved to write to his cousin near the end of the summer.

# CHAPTER 4

Rosings Park was hosting Richard's parents, his brother Andrew, and his sister-in-law Marie, who was with child and who had felt the quickening a few days past. The family arrived at the end of June, bearing a letter containing the news that William had decided to visit his sister earlier than planned as his business had concluded unexpectedly.

On the second day of July, the family spied a coach approaching the portico while they were in the gardens, enjoying a cool breeze. Richard stood to get a better look at the carriage. "Why, that is William's; I did not think he was to visit us. Did he not go to Ramsgate to spend time with Gigi?"

"That is what his letter said," Lady Catherine confirmed.

Everyone in the garden walked over to greet their cousin as his vehicle came to a halt. What they saw inside it caused them to stop in their tracks. Darcy was sitting hunched over with his head in his hands, looking like the world was ending. What frightened them was that Gigi was crying and would not look at any of them. Of even greater concern, Mrs. Younge was conspicuously absent.

The ladies, shocked at the level of despair within the carriage, and that no one extended a happy greeting, made their way to where the men stood. "Come Gigi," Lady Catherine said as she reached into the coach and coaxed her niece out.

"You will all...want to...cut me when..." Georgiana attempted to speak while sobbing. She spoke no further as she was quietly shushed and tucked tightly into her aunt's embrace.

"Elaine and Marie, let us help this poor girl into the house," Lady Catherine said. She turned to her brother. "Reggie, find out what happened so we are able to help." She and Elaine led the distraught girl inside; Marie followed closely behind. "Marie, please have Mrs. Toppin have water sent up for a bath for Gigi."

"William. WILLIAM!" Richard demanded his cousin's attention when the ladies were inside. "What in the blazes is going on? Why is Gigi weeping, and why were you not comforting her? Why are you sitting there doing nothing, looking like there has been a disaster?"

"There has been one," Darcy returned weakly.

"Not here," Lord Matlock interrupted abruptly. "Let us go inside to a sitting room. There is no need for anyone else to hear whatever it is that William needs to tell us."

It was when Darcy stepped out of the coach—as if in a stupor—his tear-stained cheeks were visible to his uncle and cousins. "Have my cousins' trunks unloaded and brought up to their suites," Richard instructed Mr. Toppin, the butler.

The men made their way to a sitting room; the Countess and Lady Catherine were but a few minutes behind them. "Gigi is bathing and Marie is with her, after that she will be given a calming draught to help her sleep. Once she has drifted off, Marie will join us," Lady Catherine reported. "What happened?"

"That is what we want to know," Lord Matlock stated, staring down at his nephew sitting in a chair and holding his head in his hands again.

"My arrogance and pride almost caused my sister to be lost forever," Darcy stated in a barely audible voice. None had ever seen William looking this close to being broken before.

The family members present all had a strong suspicion that whatever had happened was connected to the missing companion. There was no point in his family reminding him he had been unwilling to listen to any criticism of Mrs. Younge, because they understood he was berating himself more than any of them could.

"Here William, drink this," Lady Catherine handed him a snifter of brandy—two fingers high. "All of it," she insisted when he was about to put it down with half still in it.

"I was so sure of my own judgment, I ignored you all, especially Aunt Cat, when you told me you saw something which did not add up regarding Mrs. Younge," Darcy stated, his voice now a little louder.

"William, tell us what *happened*," Lord Matlock insisted.

"May I have some more brandy pleas Aunt?" Darcy held out the snifter.

"One finger this time," Lady Catherine said, handing her nephew the brandy.

"Gigi is asleep, although it is a fitful slumber," Marie reported when she joined the rest of the family.

Darcy gulped the brown liquor down. "As you know, I decided to visit Gigi in Ramsgate a few days earlier than expected." There were nods from the six members of his family. "Thank God I did."

"Whatever it is, we will address it as a family; there is strength in numbers," Lady Catherine attempted to assure her nephew.

"If I had listened to you about Mrs. Younge, *none* of this would have happened; it was all my fault," Darcy rasped plaintively.

"Now is not the time for recriminations William," Richard attempted. He knew the family's imaginations were running as rampant as his own.

They were now sure whatever had happened was connected to Mrs. Younge and had caused Georgiana to regress greatly. She had been blooming and shedding her shyness when last they saw her, the girl who arrived at Rosings was unable to speak.

"When I arrived, I did not see a footman on duty at the door, so I opened it myself and entered my house. I saw Mrs.

Younge looking through a slightly open door into the drawing room. She heard me behind her and spun around to chastise one she assumed was a footman—I found out later she had given all of the servants the night off. When she saw me, she blanched and almost fainted. I ordered one of the footmen who had arrived with me to detain her, as my suspicion was aroused.

"It was then I heard Gigi giggle inside the drawing room followed by *his* voice!" William's look went from despondent to fury in an instant. "Wickham was in the drawing room with Gigi, unchaperoned! When I threw the door open, he turned white, and then recovered enough to tell me smugly we were to be brothers as he was betrothed to my sister. Gigi saw my look of absolute fury and all happiness vanished from her countenance as she realised, contrary to whatever her *suitor* told her, I was anything but happy."

"Did that libertine ruin our girl?" Lady Catherine asked the pertinent question, one she dreaded to hear answered, as they all did.

"No, I do not believe so. From what I was able to gather from her, the most they did was kiss. I informed the blackguard that without the *prior* approval of both her guardians, not one penny of her dowry—not even the interest—would be released until she was five and thirty. As you can imagine, that placed a dent in his plans. He wanted money as soon as he crossed the border with her, not twenty years later.

"When he learnt he would receive nothing of her dowry, Wickham became most abusive, telling Gigi the only attractive thing about her was her fortune. Then the libertine told my poor sister he would not wait twenty years with one so unappealing and made to leave. It was not until his disdainful and hurtful words in the drawing room that Gigi realised her supposed protector had assisted a snake to manipulate her and her tender loving heart from the beginning," Darcy related to his family.

"Gigi started to cry and reminded him that he told her

he loved her. The bastard, sorry ladies, laughed! When he did, I planted a facer, and I do believe I broke his nose. In my fury, I told him if he breathed one word about this escapade to anyone, I would call in the over two thousand pounds of his vowels I hold and have him in Marshalsea for the rest of his miserable life." As he continued the story some of his anger dissipated, while it increased for the other men in the room. Unlike them, Darcy had some time to face the facts, and now thought only about his sister, who had believed herself in love and was nursing a broken heart.

"What about Mrs. Younge?" Lady Catherine enquired.

"She is one of Wickham's paramours. Her characters were counterfeits." Darcy hung his head in shame. How many times had his relatives urged him to check her characters in person, not just accept them at face value? "The two of them planned to isolate my sister from me. Wickham met Gigi *by chance* one day as she and Mrs. Younge were walking on the boardwalk near the beach. After that, he seemed to be wherever they were. Gigi thought it providence that they met each day. After a few days, Wickham was calling on her at the house, and Mrs. Younge would contrive to leave them alone.

"When Gigi asked her companion if it was proper for her to be alone with Wickham, Mrs. Younge assured her no one would object to an old family friend calling on her. Thanks to my neglect, she was lonely, and in but a few days believed herself in love with him. She agreed to an elopement, which would have taken place two days after I arrived. She was convinced it would be a pleasant surprise if they could greet me as man and wife when they arrived at Darcy House.

"If she is not ruined, why is Gigi so devastated?" Richard asked.

"She feels shame as she knew better. She knew that the family would never accept a steward's son as her husband and she should never have agreed to an elopement. When I asked why, given her awareness of those two salient points, she told me she was lonely and wanted to feel loved," Darcy stated sorrowfully. "I have made so many errors. It started with my arrogant thinking that I the son, was protecting my father by not telling him about Wickham, and then trying to protect and shelter my sister in the same manner. You were correct Richard, I did her no favours by hiding the truth about Wickham from her."

"William, all you can do is learn from your mistakes. There is no way to change the past. Self-flagellation will not help you, and it certainly will not heal Gigi," Lady Catherine told her nephew gently. "The question is, what do we do going forward?"

"I will cancel my visit with Bingley at his new estate at the end of next month," Darcy stated.

"Before you do that, let us see how Gigi is first. It may be better for her recovery if you are not here to hover over her constantly. You wear that damnable mask of late, even around us. I wager if she sees it, she will think you are angry with her," Lady Catherine proposed. "My suggestion is she remain here so I will be able to help her. And Richard is, after all, her *co*-guardian."

"William, I agree with my sister," Lady Elaine added. "It may be better for both of you to separate while she recovers here with us."

"Will you and Uncle Reggie remain in Kent if I agree, and leave her to recuperate here?" Darcy asked. *'Mayhap time with her aunts and Richard will be good for her. It certainly cannot be worse than my actions,'* Darcy reproved himself silently.

"We must return to Hilldale, so we are not able to remain," Andrew informed the family as he looked lovingly at his Marie.

"In that case, I will remain with all of you here until I meet Bingley in London next month." Seeing his Aunt Cat's raised eyebrows Darcy added. "I promise I will not inhibit Gigi's recovery."

The rest of the family agreed it would achieve nothing to point out all of William's errors, so they moved forward and concentrated on trying to repair the damage to Gigi's psyche.

~~~~~~~/~~~~~~~

"What do you mean by leasing an estate in the wilds of Hertfordshire? Did I not tell you we needed to find one near Pemberley?" Miss Bingley screeched. "How could you take an estate without allowing me to inspect it first? What will Mr. Darcy say about this estate in the middle of nowhere?"

"Actually Caroline, Darcy was with me when I inspected the estate. He heartily approved of it as a good situation for me to learn about estate management, and it is only a one-year lease after all. I have not purchased the place and will not do so unless Darcy advises me to," Bingley explained.

As soon as he mentioned Mr. Darcy's approval, Miss Bingley's mouth shut with a clack. One thing she would never do was gainsay Mr. Darcy. Therefore, if he approved of the estate Charles leased, she was satisfied.

"Why did you not tell me that right away?" Miss Bingley demanded.

"You were too busy berating him," Hurst added. It amused him how easy it was to make his wife's sister change a position merely by mentioning Mr. Darcy.

"Have some more brandy," Miss Bingley sniped.

"If you do not want to be my hostess, then I will ask Louisa to fill the office for me," Bingley gave his sister the choice.

"It may be worth my while to stay in town with Miss Hampton-Jones." Miss Bingley thought about how many times she would be able to call on her *dear friend*, Miss Darcy.

"In that case, Louisa will be my hostess. Lulu, you know Mr. Darcy's preferences, do you not?" Bingley slyly asked his older sister.

"Why would Louisa need to know about my—err—Mr. Darcy's preferences?" Miss Bingley demanded.

"Did I not mention Darcy will join us about a week after we take up residence? He plans to remain until a few weeks prior to Christmastide," Bingley informed his sister nonchalantly.

"I will be willing to forgo my *best* friend's company to be your hostess," Miss Bingley made another about face.

"You will not disappoint Miss Hampton-Jones?" Hurst asked. "I am sure she will be bereft of your scintillating company."

Miss Bingley glared at her lout of a brother-in-law and flounced out of the drawing room; her nose high in the air.

~~~~~~~~/~~~~~~~~

Darcy planned on leaving Rosings Park for Town and continuing to Hertfordshire a day later. He felt more like himself again, and although he admitted in *this* case he had erred, he continued to feel he was generally correct in his judgements.

He had been chastened, and was still worried about his sister, but in essentials he was the same haughty man—quick to judge and believing most others were below him in consequence. His Aunt Cat had hinted at the contradiction between how he thought of most people, and how he related to the Bingleys; like much else, Darcy dismissed what she said as it did not square with what he believed of himself.

He was unable to see how similar his thinking was to that which had led him to reject others' opinions about Mrs. Younge before Ramsgate. At least he had been open to his family's input in finding a new companion.

A good friend of his Aunt Elaine had a daughter who was about to marry. A Mrs. Annesley had been her companion for over five years; she was a lady who had been widowed at two and twenty and left with little in the way of funds. Her current employer, the Countess of Ridley, gave a glowing report, as did three other employers whose daughters she had shepherded for some years each.

This time, he spoke with everyone providing the characters in person. Unlike Gigi's previous companion, Mrs. Annesley was all that was good, so although she was older—in her forties—she was employed as Miss Darcy's new companion.

Since Mrs. Annesley joined his household, his sister had

begun to recover more than she had with only her two aunts for support. Lady Catherine opined that, as Mrs. Annesley was an outsider, her niece saw her as objective. Regardless of the reason, Darcy was pleased his sister was improving, so he decided to keep his appointment with Bingley at his friend's leased estate.

~~~~~~~/~~~~~~~

A few days subsequent to the new tenants of Netherfield taking up residence, Mr. Bennet had called on Mr. Bingley, after telling his wife he would not, he sat in his study with a letter in his hand. It was from Mr. William Collins.

Bennet had no idea if the man was different from his grandfather or father, both of whom had been anathema to his family. He thought if the son was as ignorant as the father, he would be amused by the letter, so he read it; he would never turn down an opportunity to laugh at someone.

*1 August 1810*

*Hunsford Parsonage, Westerham, Kent*

*Cousin Bennet,*

*The disagreement existing between you and my late father always made me wonder why said disagreement survived my grandfather—who was the one who offended your family.*

*Moreover, as a clergyman I feel it my duty to promote and establish peace in all families within the reach of my influence; how am I able to do so credibly if I ignore the breach in our own? You and your family are all the family I have left in the world, and as far as I can tell, the reverse is true as well.*

*I pray you will not reject this offered olive-branch. I am sure the entail hanging over the heads of your family cannot be easy. Neither you nor I were party to its creation, so all we can do is to live with the consequences of our great-grandfather's decision. I beg leave to apologise for the actions of my grandfather, as I am sure no one in my family has ventured the same before.*

*This past Easter, I was gifted the living at the parish of Hunsford by the Honourable Mr. Richard Fitzwilliam, second son of the Earl of Matlock. His aunt, Lady Catherine de Bourgh, resides with him and is the mistress of his estate of Rosings Park. She suggested that unless I attempted to reach out to you, I would never know if you might be open to a reconciliation. Hence, my letter to you is long overdue.*

*If you have no objection to receiving me into your home and are willing to extend an invitation, I propose the satisfaction of waiting on you and your family, Monday, 19 November, in the afternoon.*

*I trust you have enough time to consult with your wife and let me know if you are willing to invite me to Longbourn. Among the many topics I am sure we would find to discuss as strangers are wont to do, I would like to discuss all the ways we may be able to alleviate the stress of the entail on your family.*

*If you are amenable to inviting me, I shall probably trespass on your hospitality for about a sennight. Again, this would depend on your convenience and agreement.*

*I look forward to meeting you and your family and placing the disagreements of the past where they belong—squarely in the past.*

*Sincerely,*
*William Collins*

'How am I able to make sport of a sensible, well written, and thoughtful letter?' Bennet asked himself, astounded that it was the farthest thing from what he expected when he broke the seal.

Bennet agreed with his cousin's sentiment neither of them should be beholden to a disagreement that began over forty years in the past. Still shocked by how different William Collins seemed from his father, Bennet sought out his wife and wordlessly handed her the missive.

"Why would I want to read a letter from that disagreeable man who will steal my home from me when you die," Fanny Bennet sniffed with disdain.

"Mrs. Bennet, read the letter and then make your pronouncements," Bennet suggested.

After complaining about how the man's name would cause her to have an attack of her *nerves*, Mrs. Bennet read the letter. To her own surprise, she too was not unhappy. "Oh yes, Mr. Bennet, please invite your cousin for as long as he chooses to remain. Mr. Bingley will marry Jane, and mayhap he will want a lively wife like my Lydia." Fanny jumped right to making matrimonial plans. After all, getting all her girls married—well married—was her life's work.

"In that case, I will reply to my cousin forthwith and extend an open-ended invitation." Bennet was not sure if his cousin would look for—never mind find—a wife among his daughters, but he would not pass up a chance to laugh at his wife's inept matchmaking attempts.

# CHAPTER 5

"**W**elcome home Mr. Collins. I understand from what Richard told me of your letter that you are courting one of your cousins?" Lady Catherine enquired as she poured tea after dinner.

"Yes, I am. That was not my aim in visiting my cousins, but Miss Mary Bennet, Mary, and I are very compatible. She is a studious young lady. I understand from my cousins Jane and Elizabeth—Jane is the eldest, and Elizabeth next before Mary—that she is always helping Longbourn's parson with good works, not to be seen doing them, but for the correct reasons. While all five of my cousins are very pretty, in my opinion none were more so than Mary." Collins was not normally so verbose, so it was telling that he was so voluble about his cousins in general and Miss Mary Bennet in particular.

"Did you happen to see my nephew while you were at your cousin's estate?" Lady Catherine asked.

"If you did, I would like to know how William acquitted himself with the locals," Richard said. Both wanted to hear the parson's impressions, as on several occasions Gigi had innocently mentioned how her brother had written of a Miss Elizabeth Bennet in his letters. Normally, Darcy would not give attention to any particular lady, so for him to mention any lady once, never mind multiple times, was exceptional.

"If it is all the same to you, I would prefer not to speak ill of your relative," Collins stated diplomatically.

"What has my nephew done?" Lady Catherine asked exasperatedly.

"Are you sure you want to know?" Collins asked. "It was very surprising that a close relative of yours would behave in such a way, regardless of his position in society."

"We must know. If we are to address his behaviour, it will not do to be ignorant of what is attributed to him," Lady Catherine confirmed. '*I think it is time for my nephew to be addressed regarding his manners and mannerisms. I thought what happened to Gigi due to his blockheadedness regarding the companion he chose for her would have made him look at himself critically. Unfortunately, he did not apply what he learnt in that case to the rest of his life.*' Lady Catherine shook her head sadly then returned her attention to Mr. Collins.

"Let me start from when I arrived. My reception was all that was gracious and welcoming, and both my Cousin Bennet and I agreed the past belonged in the past. It must be said my cousin is an indolent man, and it takes much to bestir him from his study. There are five daughters. The oldest is Jane—considered the prettiest girl in the neighbourhood. She is tall and willowy, blond with blue eyes. Next is Elizabeth—or Lizzy as most call her. She is also very pretty—wavy mahogany hair with the greenest of eyes one can imagine—just not in the same way as her older sister. In addition, she is intelligent and possesses a wit as quick as any I have seen.

"After Elizabeth is the sister I am courting, Mary. She has Jane's height and Elizabeth's colouring, but her eyes are hazel with flecks of green and gold, and in my humble opinion is no less pretty than her older sisters. The youngest two are Kitty—Catherine—and Lydia. They are rather undisciplined and wild.

"Catherine, who is almost two years Lydia's senior, follows the girl of fifteen who is brash, flirtatious, and has a head full of officers only. The three older girls are mortified by the behaviour of the younger two. Unfortunately, Lydia is her mother's favourite, so rather than check her, she encourages her outrageous behaviour. I have learnt her youngest is just like she was as a young girl. In my observance, in many ways

Mrs. Bennet still is young in mind, and I wonder at my studious cousin's choice as they are quite mismatched.

"The mother's main, or rather only concern, is to see her daughters married, regardless of their inclination. I have spoken to my three oldest cousins, and they are adamant they will only marry for the deepest love, regardless of their mother's desires.

My cousin does nothing to discipline his youngest two no matter how much Lizzy—his favourite—begs him to do so. He merely laughs at them and calls them the silliest girls in all of England. He mocks and teases his wife in company. That she does not understand she is the butt of his jokes makes it no less objectionable.

One could believe the three older sisters were unrelated to their mother or their younger two sisters. They are poised, observe propriety at all times, intelligent, and act just as gentlewomen should. The older two were taught by their Aunt Gardiner in London, and they took my Mary under their wing. They tried with the two youngest, but neither was interested in changing their ways." Collins completed his picture of his cousins.

"Gardiner? Is this Aunt Gardiner married to an Edward Gardiner who owns Gardiner Trading Company near Cheapside?

"Yes Your Ladyship; he is their uncle," Collins confirmed.

"We briefly met the two eldest Bennet sisters some years ago. Do you remember Aunt?" Richard asked. He had never forgotten the blond who had caught his eye.

"Yes Richard, I do. Please continue, Mr. Collins; I assume we will hear about William—my nephew Darcy—soon."

"There is a bi-monthly assembly in Meryton, one of which was held not long after Mr. Bingley took possession of Netherfield Park. He and his party, including your nephew, attended. I was not in the area yet, but it would be an understatement to say the Netherfield party in general, and your cousin and nephew in particular, left a strong impression, and it was not positive, other than Mr. Bingley.

"I am told there are many more ladies than men at the assemblies, so the local ladies choose to sit out two to three sets each to allow everyone the chance to dance. Your nephew and friends arrived late, I am told, because of Miss Bingley's belief one should always be *fashionably late.*

"Sir William Lucas, a knight and neighbour to my cousins, who acts as host at the assemblies, was introducing the Bingley party to my cousins, when your nephew refused the introduction and stalked off. He ignored the number of women without partners, and only danced a set each with Miss Bingley and her older sister, Mrs. Hurst.

"Bingley became fixated on my Cousin Jane immediately and danced with her. Before his second set with my cousin, he tried to convince Mr. Darcy to dance. Mr. Bingley told his friend there were many pretty girls; then Mr. Darcy told him he was dancing with the only pretty girl in the room. My cousin Elizabeth was sitting out one of her sets for the reason I described earlier, and Mr. Bingley suggested her as a dance partner, asking if his friend wanted to be introduced.

"My cousin Elizabeth told me she will never forget his words: '*She is tolerable, but not handsome enough to tempt me; I am in no humour at present to give consequence to young ladies who are slighted by other men. You had better return to your partner and enjoy her smiles, for you are wasting your time with me.*' She told me he looked directly at her before uttering those ungentlemanly words loudly enough for others to hear.

"I am sorry if this pains you," Collins stated.

"It is not the hearing of it that pains me Mr. Collins, it is that my nephew has not learnt yet. We had hopes after... Let me say only there was almost a disaster after a serious lapse in his judgement and we hoped it would have lessened his pride, but I see it has not," Lady Catherine replied sadly.

"Is there more Mr. Collins?" Richard asked, even though he feared the answer would be in the affirmative.

"Yes, there *is* more. At gatherings in the neighbourhood,

I am told your nephew would stare at Lizzy. Her interpretation is he looks at her to find fault. My opinion is quite the opposite, although I would not chance her sharp tongue to express my opinion to her directly," Collins explained.

"Do you believe my nephew is fixated on Miss Elizabeth?" Lady Catherine asked.

"Yes, Your Ladyship, I do," Collins averred.

"If I know my nephew, due to his wrongheaded pride, and his belief in what honouring the Darcy name means, he is fighting an inclination for Miss Elizabeth, as he feels she is too far below him. In that he is wrong. She is the daughter of a gentleman and he the son of one; in that they are equal," Lady Catherine opined. "He has mentioned Miss Elizabeth at least once in each of his letters to his sister. I would wager he is not doing so consciously."

"Just before I arrived, Miss Bingley invited Jane to Netherfield Park for dinner on an evening when the men had been invited to dine with the newly arrived Derbyshire Militia. Her mother, in a misguided attempt to ensure my cousin would spend more time at Netherfield, sent her on horseback even though it was about to rain. Jane was soaked to the skin, took ill, and had to spend the night. The next day, Lizzy walked three miles—if I have not mentioned it, she loves to walk and can cover great distances on her own two feet—to Netherfield Park and ended up residing there to nurse Jane for four days. I arrived while my cousins were at Mr. Bingley's estate.

"Mr. Bingley decided to hold a ball which was held two days before I was to return to Rosings. He invited the whole neighbourhood, and all of the officers. But I get ahead of myself. Lizzy reported that although Miss Bingley and Mrs. Hurst —who she calls both the superior and the supercilious sisters —styled themselves Jane's friends, they were looking for anything they could to separate her from their brother. By then he had shown a strong inclination to my cousin, and she was falling in love with him. In addition, Lizzy told me when Mr. Darcy was not looking at her with disdain or ignoring her—they sat in the library on one occasion and he never acknowledged her and left without a word after a half hour—he argued with her and seemed to bait her.

"Their mother did not want to send the carriage to collect them until the following week, but after services that Sunday, Jane and Elizabeth took matters into their own hands and borrowed Mr. Bingley's equipage to return home. My cousin's wife was most put out, yet she harangued only Lizzy. I did not mention this, but for a reason I cannot fathom she seems to dislike her second daughter. When I asked my cousin, he thought it was a great joke, explaining that his wife blames Lizzy for being born a girl, but not any of the three subsequent daughters she bore." Collins paused to drink some tea in order to lubricate his throat.

"As a mother who lost her daughter, I will never understand a parent who does not treasure their children," Lady Catherine stated. She sorrowed anew whenever she thought of all the years she would not have with Anne.

"The next day, we walked into Meryton and that is where we had the distinct *pleasure* of meeting a man who was about to purchase a lieutenant's commission in the militia, one George Wickham." Collins reported.

"WICKHAM!" Richard fairly shouted, "what is that wolf in sheep's clothing doing in the militia?"

"I take it you feel no easier about him than your cousin?" Collins asked. "My cousins and I were talking to Mr. Wickham and another officer when Mr. Bingley and Mr. Darcy rode up. Mr. Bingley made a beeline for Cousin Jane. Both Lizzy and I saw the moment Mr. Darcy and Wickham saw one another. The former had a thunderous look of fury while the latter went white and appeared fearful. Mr. Darcy wheeled his stallion around and took off at a gallop from whence he came. Mr. Bingley soon followed after he handed the invitation to the ball to Jane.

"That night there was a card party at Mrs. Phillips's house. She is sister to Mrs. Bennet, and her husband is the local solicitor. Lieutenant Wickham attended with a few other officers. When he found out how much my cousin disliked Mr. Darcy, he spun a yarn which I could tell was full of contradictions, not to mention the impropriety of such a disclosure to a new acquaintance. Lizzy, who is normally an intelligent lady, absorbed the tale without question as it fed her need to dislike Mr. Darcy.

"Both Jane and I tried to point out the impropriety of such a disclosure, never mind the contradictions I identified, but she had closed her mind on the subject. Rather it was that she felt vindicated in her complete disdain and dislike of Mr. Darcy, who she calls *'that insufferable, haughty, hateful man'*. She felt with Mr. Wickham's open and honest—her words—countenance he could not have possibly lied." Collins relayed with a smile as he remembered the moue of distaste his cousin would affect whenever anyone mentioned Mr. Darcy in her presence.

"How did my cousin behave at the ball?" Richard asked. "He did not insult anyone that night, did he?"

"As far as I know, he did not. In fact, much to Miss Bingley's distaste, he danced with none but my Cousin Elizabeth. I was close to them in the line, dancing with Mary, who had agreed to a courtship that morning. I noticed they argued for part of the dance, and if I were to hazard a guess, I would say the subject was Mr. Wickham.

"Lizzy still does not see it. Lieutenant Wickham claimed he would not allow Mr. Darcy to chase him away, yet he made your nephew's presence at the ball his excuse for not attending. The next day, the entire Netherfield Party unexpectedly closed up the house and departed for London. Mr. Bingley let it be known that he had business in Town and would return in— at the most—a sennight. This leads to a delicate question," Collins informed his listeners.

"Do not stop now, Mr. Collins. Knowledge is power, so we need to hear what the question is," Lady Catherine informed the parson.

"As your niece is in residence with you at this estate, I

know part of what Miss Bingley wrote was a lie, but is there some sort of understanding between Miss Darcy and Mr. Bingley?" Collins enquired.

"ABSOLUTELY NOT!" Richard emphasised. "My cousin is not yet out; she just turned sixteen!"

"The reason I ask is Miss Bingley wrote a letter to Jane, implying an understanding between her brother and Miss Darcy and claiming she would soon be her sister." Collins waited as the two opposite him seethed.

"It has always been my opinion that Miss Bingley is vulgar, but this is beyond the pale. The woman is naught but a *liar*. Without going into the whole story, you should know that *Mr.* Wickham is a liar, seducer, libertine, profligate, degenerate wastrel. There are other words I might use, but I will be a lady," Lady Catherine informed the parson.

"Wherever Wickham goes, he leaves debts and trifles with maidens. He left a string of ruined girls across the country; he is the worst kind of blackguard," Richard spat out.

"Mr. Darcy knows about Mr. Wickham, does he not?" Collins asked. Both nodded. "But why did he not warn anyone in Meryton? If Mr. Wickham leaves debts, he will ruin some of the merchants."

"Do you happen to know the name of the colonel commanding the Derbyshire Militia?" Richard asked.

"A Colonel Forster," Collins replied.

"Good, I know him well," Richard returned.

"By the time you left, had Miss Bennet heard from Mr. Bingley?" Lady Catherine changed the subject.

"No Your Ladyship. Jane's plan is to return to London with the Gardiners, who will travel to Longbourn for Christmastide. She hopes to make contact with her *friends* while in London," Collins informed them. "If you are agreeable, Mr. Fitzwilliam, I will be travelling to Longbourn as much as I can to further my courtship with Mary."

"As long as there is someone to conduct services as needed, go to it," Richard permitted." Make sure you secure her, for it seems she is your perfect match."

After Mr. Collins departed, Lady Catherine turned to her nephew. "You know we cannot allow that dastard to wreak havoc on the people of Meryton, do you not Richard?" It was not a question, but a command. "What was William thinking? Is it some warped sense of protecting Gigi that he left the entire town at that wastrel's mercy?"

"We are going to Meryton, are we not?" Richard asked, and Lady Catherine gave an emphatic nod of her head. "I know Colonel Forster as he and I were captains in the Dragoons together. He was injured, and rather than resign, he took a post in the Militia."

"Have a good night's sleep Richard, for we depart for Meryton early in the morning. We will go via London to drop off Gigi with Elaine and Reggie for the day," Lady Catherine decided.

"I heard my name," Georgiana said. She had completed her lessons for the day and joined her aunt and cousin in the drawing room.

Without telling her why—as neither thought she was ready to hear the name Wickham yet—Georgiana was informed of their trip to London the next day. She did not ask about her brother, for she was unaware he left Hertfordshire and could be in Town.

Later that day, a letter from her brother arrived. He told his sister he was for Pemberley to meet with his steward and would see her at Snowhaven for the Christmastide holidays.

# CHAPTER 6

"**F**itzwilliam! Welcome to my humble militia office! Are you no longer with the Dragoons?" Colonel Forster indicated chairs for his guests to sit.

"Richard, will you introduce me please," Lady Catherine requested.

"Aunt Catherine, this reprobate is Colonel Leonardo Forster; Forster, my aunt, the Honourable Lady Catherine de Bourgh." Richard made the introductions. "I inherited an estate, resigned, and sold my commission, so I am no longer in the army."

"Your Ladyship, Fitzwilliam, how may I be of service?" Colonel Forster was wondering what the two were doing in his office. Richard was always welcome but bringing a lady with him meant there could be a serious matter to discuss.

"It is more like what we can do for you Colonel," Lady Catherine informed him.

"Excuse me if I seem deficient, but how is it that you could help me?" A confused Forster asked.

"Colonel, if I am not mistaken, if you want to be allowed back into a neighbourhood where your unit has been, the goodwill of the citizens is crucial, is it not?" Lady Catherine asked.

"That is so, Your Ladyship," the Colonel agreed.

"If, hypothetically, you had a cur in your ranks, one who meddles with maidens and runs up debts he has no intention of paying, would you be welcome again in that location?" Lady Catherine challenged.

"No, we most assuredly would not; such a man would

blacken the name of the whole battalion, not just this unit," the Colonel stated. He became concerned, for never had a woman asked him such questions; he was sure there was a pointed purpose for them.

"You have one such man in your midst Forster," Richard informed his acquaintance.

"Who is he, and how do you know?" Forster asked sharply.

"Lieutenant George Wickham," Richard replied concisely.

"Wickham? How can that be? He is very popular with both his fellow officers and the residents of the neighbourhood," Forster exclaimed.

"He is very good at making friends, but whether he is able to retain them is another thing altogether," Lady Catherine stated plainly. "He has been known to my family since his birth and has intruded on our peace more times than I care to remember."

"Wait, are you related to that proud, unpleasant man, Darcy?" Forster had been warned by his Lieutenant that Darcy might attempt to blacken his name out of jealousy. "Has Mr. Darcy put you up to this so he may injure Wickham's prospects again?"

"You know me better than that Forster; Darcy is back in Derbyshire at his estate and has no idea we are here. Until a day ago, we did not know he had run into Wickham until my pastor returned home and informed us," Richard replied with some asperity.

"Let me guess, the libertine has been spreading his lie my nephew denied him a living at Kympton my late brother-in-law recommended be proffered to him?" Colonel Forster allowed it was so. "As all good liars do, they build their web of deceit on a kernel of truth. My nephew Darcy did deny Wickham the living—a more unsuitable man to be a clergyman I have never known—but that was *after* the wastrel refused to take orders and demanded a pecuniary preferment in lieu of the living." Lady Catherine looked directly into the Colonel's eyes so he could see the truth in hers. "Some four years ago, Wickham signed a release of all claims to the living and received a payment of three thousand pounds from my nephew for doing so. That was in addition to one thousand pounds my brother left him in his will. Did your officer tell you that he lived a life of debauchery and dissipation, and then tried to claim the living to which he resigned all claims? He wasted four thousand pounds in but two years."

"No, he most certainly never told us that." The Colonel began to think he had been played for a fool and started to feel anger.

"He told you my nephew is jealous of him, did he not?" Lady Catherine continued. The Colonel nodded slowly, guessing this too was a lie. "The reverse is the truth. That individual has always been jealous of my nephew. He thinks he should be handed a fortune just because he wants it. If you check, you will see he has debts with almost every local merchant and has trifled with some young girls, for it has long been his habit to leave debts and a string of ruined girls behind wherever he has resided."

"My cousin, Darcy, the one whose name this bastard blackens—sorry Aunt Catherine—holds more than two thousand pounds worth of Wickham's vowels," Richard revealed.

"Sanderson!" The Colonel called for his adjutant; the captain entered and saluted his commander. "Take some officers and go to every merchant in Meryton, but discreetly. I want to know how much Wickham and the rest of my men owe on credit. Also, find out what his debts of honour and outstanding loans from his fellow officers are. Before you leave, have Wickham brought to my office. Do you know where he is?"

"He is trying to charm one of the Bennet sisters on the High Street." Saunderson was gratified it was finally time to address this dastard, as he was one of the officers who had not been taken in by Wickham's slick ways. "I will tell him you have a special task for him."

"I suggest you two wait in my residence." The Colonel indicated a door. "I will call you when I am ready for you to join us once again, but you will be able to hear every word."

~~~~~~~/~~~~~~~

Lieutenant George Wickham was speaking with Miss Bennet and Miss Elizabeth, oozing charm, when Captain Sanderson found him. "The Colonel needs you Lieutenant," the Captain informed the man.

"Miss Bennet, Miss Elizabeth, honour and duty call. I hope I will see you charming and beautiful ladies later," Wickham bowed over both ladies' hands.

"Until later, Mr. Wickham," Elizabeth returned for both sisters.

As the officers walked away, Jane asked, "Lizzy, do you have a tendre for the Lieutenant?"

"No Jane. He is only a friend," Elizabeth owned. "I have no tender feelings for the man. Sometimes he seems to try too hard to be charming."

"Do you still discount the opinion of Cousin Collins concerning Lieutenant Wickham?" Jane probed.

"I do. I saw honesty and openness in his countenance; one who looked so open and pleasant would not prevaricate," Elizabeth insisted.

"You know I try to see the best in everyone, do you not Lizzy?" Jane tried again to open her sister's eyes. Elizabeth nodded. "What does it say to you that I tend to agree with Mary's suitor?"

"It is my belief Mr. Wickham was being truthful," Elizabeth insisted stubbornly.

Jane dropped the subject. She knew as long as her sister was being wilfully blind, there was no point in talking to her about it. "I heard from Caroline today—finally. She tells of all the time they are in Mr. Darcy's company and how Mr. Bingley cannot tear himself away from Miss Darcy's side." A tear ran down Jane's cheek. She believed she had fallen in love with Mr. Bingley and now he was gone. Her journey to London could not come fast enough.

~~~~~~~/~~~~~~~

When Lieutenant Wickham arrived at his Colonel's office, he was shown directly in without waiting. "At ease Lieutenant," the Colonel ordered after Wickham gave his version of a salute. "Lieutenant, I want to verify everything you told me about Mr. Darcy denying you a living is true, as I have a connection in the Archbishop's office and we can have this injustice corrected."

"Err...I mean...ahem..." Wickham spluttered.

"Guests, please enter," the Colonel said with raised voice.

Wickham was confused—until his worst nightmare walked in from the Colonel's residence with a malevolent look on his face, followed by his aunt who looked no less malevolent than her nephew.

"W-what a-are t-they d-doing h-here?" Wickham stammered.

"Are you not happy to see us, Georgie boy? Or is our being here inconvenient to all of the lies you have been telling?" Richard leaned toward the cowering man who shrank back from him until he could go no further as a wall blocked his retreat.

"You are lucky your Colonel is here to protect you, you snivelling coward," Lady Catherine stated menacingly. "If I had my way, you would disappear and never be heard from again, and I doubt there would be anyone who would miss you."

"It seems you omitted many—actually all of the—facts from your tale of woe Wickham. Just so you know, Captain Sanderson and a contingent of your fellow officers are canvassing the merchants of Meryton to discover your debts. Your penchant for leaving them behind you has been explained to me, but I am willing to give you the benefit of the doubt until it is proven otherwise," the Colonel told Wickham, watching the man become decidedly unsteady as if he could hardly hold himself up by his own power.

How could it have gone so bad so fast? Darcy had left some days earlier, and there was no one in this little nowhere town that knew him_was there? "I s-should g-go to m-my quarters..." Wickham tried to say.

"Do you think your Colonel a simpleton boy?" Lady Catherine asked incredulously. "Go to your quarters indeed. You think you can escape this as you have so many times before? Let me tell you, you ingrate, there is no escaping this time. My nephew Darcy is not here to cover your debts out of some warped sense of honouring his father. You will feel the consequences of your actions for once in your miserable life."

"W-what a-are you g-going to d-do w-with me?" Wickham asked in a tremulous voice.

"For now, we will wait," the Colonel told the milksop. "It should not be too long before we know the truth of your debts in Meryton."

Wickham blanched. He had always been able to make his escape before he was held to account. Darcy would pick up after him, as was only right, for he had so much. Even after ingratiating himself with old Mr. Darcy, what he was given had been an insult! One thousand pounds was all he was left, that and a promise of a living. Wickham never had any intention of taking orders, but it was a story he could tell that never failed to gain him sympathy.

He had been beyond happy to weave his tale for Miss Elizabeth after she expressed her disdain for Darcy. The added bonus was that Wickham believed Darcy might have tender feelings for the lady, so he had stoked her hate, thereby injuring his nemesis. Being able to blacken Darcy's name was one of the greatest pleasures in his life. All of that was worthless now. The doors were blocked and Wickham did not fail to notice the soldiers guarding the window even if he were willing to risk his face by diving out of it.

~~~~~~~/~~~~~~~

Jane and Elizabeth were watching the officers. "Why do you think that group of officers seem to be visiting every merchant in Meryton?" Jane asked.

"My dearest sister, I have no more knowledge than you," Elizabeth returned. Having a thirst for knowledge, she hated not being able to solve a mystery. "Here comes Captain Sanderson; mayhap he will be able to enlighten us."

"Good afternoon ladies," Sanderson gave the two Bennet sisters a crisp bow.

"Captain, do you mind if I enquire why you and your fellow officers are visiting all of the merchants?" Elizabeth asked.

"It has come to our notice that a certain officer has been running up debts in the town, far more than he is able to cover," Sanderson informed the sisters.

"Is that officer Mr. Wickham?" Elizabeth asked as she had a suspicion based on the man being ordered to the Colonel before the other officers started their enquiries. "Has Mr. Darcy not blasted Mr. Wickham's prospects enough? Is he now casting aspersions on the man's name? It cannot be very much; I am willing to cover his debts with my pin money."

"Do you have upwards of five hundred pounds in pin money, Miss Elizabeth?" Sanderson asked.

The colour drained out of Elizabeth's face, robbing it of her normal healthy colouring. "How is half such a sum to be repaid?" she gasped in horror.

"Mr. Darcy had nothing to do with this; it was brought to our attention by another man and lady altogether. It seems the man had fooled many of us. The debts I mention pale in comparison to his debts of honour and loans he owes to his fellow officers." Sanderson bowed again and led his men back towards the Colonel's office.

"At some point, Lizzy, you are going to have to start being objective. Not every ill in the world can be laid at Mr. Darcy's door. I fear we may have been misled about Mr. Wickham's character." Jane led her sister back towards Longbourn, as the latter looked to be in shock.

~~~~~~~/~~~~~~~

"Welcome back Sanderson. What did you discover?" the Colonel asked his adjutant.

"The merchants are owed roughly five hundred and

twenty pounds," Sanderson reported.

"How did one man accumulate that much debt in two months? It is more than most men earn in several years," a flabbergasted Colonel asked.

"The three biggest are to the cobbler, the tailor, and the inn. He told the former two he was days away from receiving a large inheritance, which he had won from Mr. Darcy in court after the man tried to cheat him out of it. With the poor impression Mr. Darcy made and Mr. Wickham's charming ways, they accepted his order for a large new wardrobe," the Captain clarified.

"And this libertine would have run as soon as he had received the items. The merchants would have been ruined. He has done this before; the only reason there are not a larger number of bankrupted merchants is thanks to my nephew buying up his debts," Lady Catherine informed the militia officers.

"The amount of his debts of honour combined with funds borrowed from his fellow officers is just under one thousand pounds," Sanderson concluded his report.

"Wicky, why do you bother gambling? You are terrible at it. I suppose when you never intend to pay your debts it makes no difference to you, does it?" Richard barked at the now sullen man.

"I will cover his debts on condition you punish him, and then make sure he cannot harm anyone again. If he steps out of line one more time, to debtor's prison he will go. I will purchase his vowels from my nephew Darcy. The over two thousand pounds worth he holds combined with those I am to acquire today will put him in debtors' prison for the rest of his natural life." Lady Catherine turned to the squanderer, who would not meet her eyes. "If you had used the education my late brother provided you, you could have been a well-off man. When you took the three thousand for the living—which in my opinion once you refused it you should not have received a ha'penny—you told my nephew you were to read the law. You have wasted every chance you were given in order to chase a fortune by dishonest means."

"You will be flogged and receive twenty lashes. Thereafter, you will remain in the brig until we arrive in Brighton. The merchants in Brighton will be warned not to issue you *any* credit. As lady Catherine stated, if you step out of line I will transport you to Marshalsea, or whichever debtor's prison she prefers myself," the Colonel pronounced to the officer who was now shaking with fear.

"Keep an eye on that one Forster, he is as slippery as an eel," Richard warned.

"He will be under watch at all times once we arrive in Brighton," the Colonel assured them as he looked at Wickham disdainfully.

Once a bank draft had been provided for all of the debts, Wickham signed the vowel to Lady Catherine and was led away to the brig.

"Again, I must express my thanks for your timely intervention. We would never have been allowed back in this town —if it had survived Wickham's perfidy—and the honour of the Derbyshire Militia would have been irreparably tarnished." Colonel Forster bowed to Lady Catherine, who inclined her head in acknowledgement, and then he shook Richard's hand. The two left for London to prepare for their journey north to Snowhaven for Christmas.

~~~~~~~/~~~~~~~

A few days later, Mr. Bennet returned home after meeting with Colonel Forster and most of the men in the Meryton area. "It seems my cousin was correct in his conclusions about Mr. Wickham's tale of woe Lizzy," Mr. Bennet told his second daughter after asking her to join him in his study. "The entire story about being denied a living was a lie built on one tiny truth. Mr. Darcy did deny him the living," Bennet paused as his daughter interjected.

"I knew he was not lying," Elizabeth crowed triumphantly.

"Elizabeth Rose Bennet! Allow me to finish," Elizabeth lost her feeling of vindication as quickly as it had come, for her father never called her by her full name unless he was displeased with her. "It was refused *after* Mr. Wickham refused to take orders and gave up all claim to the living—in writing —and received *three thousand pounds* in lieu of it. That was in addition to a one-thousand-pound legacy Mr. Darcy's father willed the man."

Elizabeth felt like casting up her accounts. How had she been so wilfully blind? Unfortunately, it was easy to see the how. As much as she had laughed about Mr. Darcy's slight at the assembly, it had wounded her pride and vanity very deeply, and she had actively sought any information to confirm her growing disdain for the man.

How many, Jane included, had warned her she only knew one side of the story, only for her to ignore them? She wanted the story to be true to justify her estimation of Mr. Darcy being a black-hearted, proud, haughty, insufferable man. Only now, hearing the bald truth, were her convictions shaken; she hung her head in shame.

"Mayhap in future you will not be so quick to judge and be more open to the opinions of others if they contradict your beliefs." With that, Mr. Bennet waved his daughter away and returned to his book and port.

Later, when Mrs. Hattie Phillips arrived to share the gossip about Mr. Wickham with her sister's family, it was with the added information that the blackguard had meddled with at least three merchants' daughters with a promise of marriage.

Mrs. Bennet swooned and had an attack of her *nerves*, calling loudly for her salts. Lydia had loudly and vociferously proclaimed that she did not believe one word spoken against Mr. Wickham. Mr. Bennet had already lost good reading time that day by having to attend the meeting so he did not share the information he could have imparted, other than telling Elizabeth.

~~~~~~~/~~~~~~~

Wickham passed out by the fourth of his twenty lashes. As he lay on his stomach—his back on fire with pain—in the brig, he stewed, imagining ways to revenge himself on those who had wronged him. Whatever he did would need to be subtle as the threat of a lifetime in debtor's prison hung over his head.

The last thing he wanted was an angry Richard Fitzwilliam on his trail. Fitzwilliam's leaving the army had in no way diminished the fear Wickham felt for Darcy's cousin. A man as deadly as Richard was the type of man he always steered well clear of, as they were the type that seemed immune to his charms.

# CHAPTER 7

February 1811

**M**r. Collins had proposed to Mary Bennet before Twelfth Night, and she had happily accepted him. The wedding was to take place on the last Friday in February. Mary would be attended by both of her older sisters.

All three ignored their youngest sister, who was acting out and pouting constantly because she would not be the first of her sisters to marry. For once, Kitty did not enter the fray to support Lydia. It seemed Kitty had the decency to know it was Mary's time, and that Lydia's attention demanding behaviour was not acceptable. Lydia, angered, verbally attacked Kitty loudly.

Lydia's behaviour pushed Kitty out of her younger sister's orbit and into that of her three older sisters. As for the older sisters, they were pleased at the result, inasmuch as they abhorred Lydia's behaviour. They had long hoped to be able to assist as least one—if not both—of their younger sisters to become gentlewomen.

As usual, Mr. Bennet found amusement in his youngest's behaviour and did nothing to restrain her. While her father laughed at her antics, Mrs. Bennet—as pleased as she was to have one of her daughters marry the heir to Longbourn—refused to discipline her youngest daughter.

No one who cared to notice missed the anger bubbling below the surface of Jane's serene countenance. Elizabeth, Mary, and Kitty did what they could to change the subject when either Mr. or Mrs. Bennet brought up Mr. Bingley yet again, which caused Jane to lose her equanimity. The former thought himself amusing and joked about Jane being crossed in love, while the latter berated her daughter for *allowing* dear Mr. Bingley to escape before securing him.

~~~~~~~/~~~~~~~

The night before the wedding, Mrs. Bennet had given Mary the *talk* as she saw it, which frightened her middle daughter so much she was nearly ill. Thankfully, Aunt Maddie had spoken to Mary when the four older Bennet sisters travelled to London to purchase Mary's trousseau. Aunt Maddie had warned her that her sister Bennet would talk to her before the wedding and told her to forget everything her mother might say. As Mary remembered her aunt's words and talk, it undid the damage done by Mrs. Bennet, as Aunt Maddie had given her niece information which actually would be useful to her. By the time Mary remembered all her aunt had told her, she was only slightly nervous and far more in anticipation of her wedding night than she ever imagined she might be.

Once their mother left her chambers, Jane, Elizabeth, and Kitty joined Mary to spend time with her on her last night at Longbourn before she resigned the name Bennet. They knew this was the last time they could claim her exclusively; during all future visits her husband, and hopefully their children, would require most of her attention.

"Jane, how can you still think Miss Bingley is not playing you false given the way she treated you when you called on her?" Elizabeth asked pointedly. "Would you make a *friend* wait three weeks for a return call? And Aunt Maddie told me of her rudeness."

"You may have the right of it, Lizzy, but that does not change the fact that Mr. Bingley is paying court to Miss Darcy. It seems Mama is correct about one thing; Mr. Bingley used me ill," Jane responded.

"Jane, Miss Bingley lied to you," Mary asserted. "We are not talking about a misunderstanding, but absolute prevarication."

"How can you say that with certainty Mary?" Jane enquired sceptically.

"You know my betrothed's patron is Mr. Darcy's cousin Mr. Fitzwilliam, do you not?" Her three sisters nodded. "When he returned to Hunsford in November of last year, he met with his patron and Lady Catherine de Bourgh, Mr. Fitzwilliam and Mr. Darcy's aunt. They asked about Mr. Darcy and how he behaved in Hertfordshire. William was reluctant to speak negatively about Mr. Darcy, but his cousin and aunt encouraged him to tell all, which he did," Mary reported.

"Are you telling me they know of my folly in believing that blackguard Mr. Wickham?" asked a mortified Elizabeth. "Mr. Fitzwilliam and Lady Catherine will be at your wedding; how can I face them? If only I had not been so prejudiced and had not given into my vanity and pride and listened to what all of you were telling me."

"Lizzy, the man is an accomplished liar, libertine, profligate, and seducer. You are not the first young lady who has believed his web of lies. Further, William specifically told me that neither Mr. Fitzwilliam nor Lady Catherine think worse of you for it. My fiancé added that many women have fallen victim to Mr. Wickham's silver tongue, and far worse than just believing his lies." Mary tried to soothe her older sister.

"What do Mr. Darcy's relatives have to do with your knowing Miss Bingley lied?" Kitty asked, redirecting the group back to the main topic of conversation.

"Yes, back to that. He asked them if there was some sort of understanding between Miss Darcy and Mr. Bingley. Mr. Fitzwilliam is one of Miss Darcy's guardians, and both were angry at there being such a suggestion. In addition, Miss Darcy was at Rosings Park with her family since before Mr. Darcy had arrived at Netherfield Park, so she was not in Mr. Bingley's company as Miss Bingley had written.

"Miss Darcy is just sixteen and will not be out for two or three years. William was very forthright when he reiterated that no one in her family will entertain her being called on, never mind a deeper attachment, until a *season after* she comes out." When Mary completed her recitation, a number of emotions crossed Jane Bennet's face, none of them was sorrow. In the end, anger won out.

"You did not listen to me about that scoundrel, and I ignored your warnings about Miss Bingley. It is probable poor Mr. Bingley was never told I was in London," Jane said angrily.

The lying harpy was lucky she was not near Jane at that moment as she would not have left the room unscathed. As serene as Jane could be, once angered, one did not want to be around for the explosion that would surely follow. Her sisters well knew the fastest way to anger her was to lie to her. *'Mayhap there is a chance Mr. Bingley will come back to me,'* Jane told herself hopefully.

"Lizzy, have you changed your opinion of Mr. Darcy now that we know about Wickham's perfidy?" Mary asked.

"Of cruelty to Mr. Wickham I have fully acquitted the man," Elizabeth acknowledged. "However, his bad behaviour, not only toward me while here, shows disdain directed at those he thinks below him. He is still insufferable."

"Had he not slighted you as he did at the first assembly he attended, would you still feel the same way about him?" Jane asked.

"I believe so, yes. There is no reason for him to treat our neighbours in the rude, disdainful, and dismissive way he did while he was here. I have no interest in someone who is so arrogant in their treatment of others," Elizabeth asserted.

"That is a valid objection against the man," Mary agreed. "William told me that Mr. Darcy's cousin and aunt are all that are good and affable, and even though they are the offspring of Earls—the current Earl of Matlock is his father and her brother—they do not treat those below them with disdain."

"Then I look forward to meeting them, and most especially if, as you say, they will not think less of me for being taken by the libertine's lies," Elizabeth declared.

The four then talked about their childhood for another

hour or so, and after many hugs and kisses, her three visitors left Mary's chambers to return to their own. Mary, who had fallen in love with her soon-to-be husband, stayed awake for some time thinking about her William, who was being hosted by their close friends the Lucases at Lucas Lodge for the night. She finally succumbed to sleep as she counted the many blessings in her life, which included her friends, her sisters, and the man who fell in love with her regardless of the attempts of her mother to persuade him to another of her sisters.

~~~~~~~/~~~~~~~

The night before Mr. Collins's wedding, Lady Catherine, Richard, and Georgiana Darcy spent the night at the renamed Fitzwilliam House. Darcy was still hiding at Pemberley, licking his wounds from the discussion he had been subjected to. His family could only hope he would finally wake up to the way others saw his behaviour. As Lady Catherine sat in her sitting room, she thought back to December of last year at Snowhaven.

*When the family had gathered at the main Matlock estate for Christmastide, Darcy had boasted how he had saved his friend Bingley from a woman who was unsuitable. She had no fortune, connections, and no feelings for Bingley. He was proud of how he and Bingley's sisters had separated his friend from the lady before he had made for Pemberley.*

*He went further, crowing about how when Miss Bingley wrote —ostensibly to Gigi—and told him Miss Bennet had called on her and Mrs. Hurst how he had agreed they should not tell her brother.*

*The smug man had not been prepared for the reaction of his family, from the Earl down to his mild-mannered sister. Lady Catherine had led the charge, asking him—a man who did all he could to hide his true feelings from everyone—how he could determine what another felt.*

*His aunt wanted to know when he was to marry Miss Bingley, as allowing her to write to him meant she would be able to claim a compromise, even given the thin excuse of the letter being for Gigi. She could state everyone knew his sister was not at Pemberley.*

Darcy had shrunk back from the harsh reaction of his family. He had been so sure of himself, and yet his family was talking to him as if he were in the wrong. He had only tried to help his friend, had he not?

But that had been nothing to the mortification he felt when Lady Catherine informed him that she and Richard had done what he had failed to do, warn the citizens of Meryton about the wolf in sheep's clothing in their midst. He had started to feel the burn of shame when he was asked why he felt the people unworthy of being warned, especially as he enabled the problem by cleaning up after Wickham and paying his debts, rather than preventing him from harming others. When Lady Catherine told the rest of her family the amount of debts the wastrel had accumulated, the disdainful looks Darcy received from all of his family, including Gigi, had hit him hard.

The family judged his sister had recovered enough to be told of Wickham's perfidy in Meryton. Gigi had been unhappy with her brother for not protecting the locals, in the same way he had not protected her and their father by deciding they did not need to be told the truth about the blackguard. When he used the excuse he did not want to expose her, he was met with a chorus of condemnation. Lady Catherine asked him if he thought when she and Richard stepped in and protected the merchants in Meryton that they mentioned Gigi's name.

Lord Matlock told him he should be ashamed of himself. As Wickham had done in other places, he had ruined at least three girls that the family knew of, so far. The Earl demanded to know if his nephew thought those people too far below him to lift a finger to protect them.

Lastly, Lady Catherine broached the subject of her nephew's hypocrisy with regards to the Bingleys. She wanted to know how one who was so cognisant of his position in society could overlook Miss Bingley's vulgarity. The question was asked whether Bingley was his friend, or merely a puppet for him to direct and control.

Darcy had been dumbstruck. He had never been called to account like this before, and it finally started to sink in; his behaviour *was seen as wanting by all of his family, even though he still be-lieved them wrong on a number of points. He had left Snowhaven right after Christmas Day, telling his family he had a lot to think about.*

Lady Catherine's thoughts returned to the present. On the morrow, they would leave for Hertfordshire to attend Mr. Collins's wedding. After all she had heard of the Bennet sisters, she was keen to meet the two older ones again and make the acquaintance of the others. She wondered if the two eldest sisters would remember meeting her and Richard at their uncle's warehouse a few years ago.

Georgiana's willingness to accompany her and Richard to the wedding was a positive sign. With the aid of her two aunts and Mrs. Annesley, the girl continued to recover. She was still shy, but far less than when she returned from Ramsgate. She did regress at times, but on the whole her progress was positive. To their great relief, the days of her spontaneously bursting into tears were behind her—for the most part.

The three older ladies had not absolved Georgiana of all culpability, but they had helped her see the lion's share of the blame rested with the lying libertine and his paramour who manipulated a young girl's tender heart. They did not white-wash William's part in not listening and properly vetting Mrs. Younge as he should have, nor of not sharing the truth about Wickham and his banishment from any Darcy residences.

The name Wickham no longer sent her young niece into tears and wailings, and that, coupled with the fact that the brigand would be locked in the brig until after his unit moved to their summer quarters near Brighton, made the decision to bring her along an easy one.

~~~~~~~/~~~~~~~

"Charles," Miss Bingley berated, "why have we not seen Mr. Darcy since your escape from that fortune-hunting hussy?"

"As you have been told often, he is at Pemberley, and will make the journey directly from there to Kent without a sojourn in Town as he normally does," Bingley explained—again.

"Then you must press him for an invitation to Pemberley. I need to plan the changes I will make when I am mistress there anyway," Miss Bingley demanded.

"You are delusional Caroline," Mr. Hurst piped up. "Do you not think if Darcy ever intended to offer for you, he would have done so long ago? It is not as though you have been subtle in your desire to be his wife. Mayhap your brother has some relevant information on the subject."

"What do you know you useless, drunken lout?" Miss Bingley hissed.

She did not notice her brother blanch at the suggestion of his having information to share on the subject of Mr. Darcy offering for her. Darcy had wanted him to inform his sister that he would never offer for her—even if she engineered a compromise—but Bingley had chosen the path of least resistance by not saying anything. "Whatever I am, I was *born* a gentleman. You, Sister dearest, were born the daughter of a tradesman, and for all of your pretentions and vulgar utterances about the size of your dowry, that will *never* change," Hurst shot back.

Hurst was concerned his sister-in-law would have an apoplexy given how many colour changes her countenance went through, from white to a shade of red, and lastly to a deep shade of purple, which denoted her fury.

Mrs. Hurst knew her younger sister was about to erupt like a volcano, so she quickly stood and led her infuriated sister out of the drawing room with a look to her husband that seemed to ask why he antagonised Caroline so. Mrs. Hurst led Miss Bingley to her bedchamber, and not long after the door closed the expected tantrum erupted. Her screeching could be heard by the men in the drawing room.

Hurst knew he should not provoke Miss Bingley as he was wont to do, but she made his life, and his wife's, miserable, and it was an outlet for his frustration. He was close to deciding that he and his wife would return to his family's estate in

Yorkshire, a place where Miss Bingley had worn out her welcome some years earlier. However, he was aware his wife felt a responsibility for her younger sister. He had indulged her long enough; it was time to do what his brother-in-law Bingley was not able to do—assert his will.

"Bingley, I know you do not want a confrontation with your sister, but are you really willing to risk your friendship with Darcy by sustaining her delusion? How many times now has Darcy responded to your letters when Caroline demanded an invitation, informing you that you were welcome, but only *without* your sister?" Hurst laid out the truth for Bingley, who seemed to cocoon himself from the truth and live in an almost delusional state, not unlike his younger sister.

"Darcy will not break with me," Bingley replied weakly.

"What do you think will happen if you show up with your sister in tow again when the invitation does not specifically include her? You know Darcy as well as I do. When he makes a decision, he sticks by it." Hurst looked at his weak-willed brother-in-law with something akin to pity.

"Let us hope you are wrong," Bingley returned half-heartedly.

Hearing his brother's non-committal response, Hurst firmed his resolve and stated further, "One more thing Bingley. I have decided that Louisa and I will be returning to Winsdale. As your younger sister is no longer welcome there, she will be with you alone,"

"How am I to manage Caroline without Louisa?" Bingley almost burst into tears.

"Mayhap it is time that you exert yourself in your role as the head of the family." With that, Hurst stood and made his way to his and his wife's chambers. Louisa would complain a little about being separated from Caroline, but they would both reap the benefits soon enough.

# CHAPTER 8

Mary woke up early the morning of her wedding. She felt no apprehension; she was looking forward to becoming Mrs. Collins with true anticipation. She believed—and her sensible sisters agreed—she was meant to be a clergyman's wife.

Although she did not spout moralistic quotes and had not touched Fordyce's sermons since her older sisters included her in their circle of friendship and care, she was a devout woman, one who would see helping her husband's parishioners as a pleasure rather than a duty one needed to be seen doing.

As she watched the sun creep over the eastern horizon, Mary remembered with pleasure the conversation she had with her elder sisters the previous afternoon.

*"Janie and Lizzy, will you both come visit me at Hunsford in March and remain until after Easter?"* she requested.

*"My plans are to return to London to be with Aunt and Uncle Gardiner,"* Jane had replied. *"Papa will send me in the Bennet carriage with Sarah and Mr. Hill to escort me."*

*"As I have no fixed plans, I will be glad to, dependant on Papa permitting me to visit—and he will, as long as it will not require him to exert himself,"* Elizabeth had said.

*"Lizzy, that is not a nice thing to say about our father,"* Jane had admonished. She then added, *"even if it is naught but the truth."* Jane had smiled to reinforce the fact she was teasing.

*"Jane, must you return to London to visit our aunt and uncle?"* Mary had pressed.

*"I think I must. If Mr. Bingley never exerts himself to seek me out, then at least I will know for sure he never loved me as a man*

should love a woman," Jane had rationalised. "I must know or I will be driven to distraction."

"For my part, I am looking forward to seeing your and my soon-to-be brother's home," Elizabeth had stated. "In addition, I suspect I will enjoy walking around the paths of Rosings Park. Mr. Collins has excited my imagination as he has made it sound like a good place to walk, especially in the untamed forest land they have."

Elizabeth had since shared that she requested permission from their father, who had granted it willingly as long as he would not be required to bestir himself from his study and his books and waved her away.

Lizzy would join her in just over a fortnight, giving the newly married couple time to become better acquainted, without having to entertain guests. Just then there was a light knock on Mary's bedchamber door, and she was joined by the same three sisters who had been with her the previous night.

"Is it not sad the Gardiners are unable to attend with Aunt Maddie not feeling well?" Jane lamented.

"They will be missed," Mary stated sincerely. From the time she had become close with Jane and Lizzy, she had joined whichever one went to visit the Gardiners and had been the recipient of the same teaching bestowed on her older sisters. She had become very close to her Aunt and Uncle Gardiner and wished they could be there to witness her marry but understood the reason for their not attending.

Even though Mary did not eat much, the four had trays brought up to Mary's bedchamber to break their fasts. After the small meal, Sarah, the upstairs maid who served the five Miss Bennets, informed Miss Mary her bath was ready for her. Jane and Lizzy would return once Sarah called them after Mary was bathed to assist their sister to don her wedding gown and veil. It was no surprise to any of them Mrs. Bennet had not stirred from her warm bed to be useful to her daughter on the day she would leave Longbourn, nor was the absence of the youngest Bennet unexpected—or missed.

~~~~~~~/~~~~~~~

The Rosings barouche departed London before sunup. The wedding would commence at ten that morning, and Richard did not want to chance a delay on the road that might cause them to be late. Lady Catherine agreed wholeheartedly, and being used to country hours, both she and Georgiana were ready and waiting for Richard in the Fitzwilliam House's dining parlour—Richard had renamed the house with his aunt's blessing. It warmed Richard's heart how often he heard her saying how proud of her nephew she was and how well he had taken to his new role in life.

It was not hard to see Georgiana looked nervous. "Gigi, what bothers you?" Lady Catherine asked an hour into the trip, having given her ample time to bring up whatever was concerning her of her own accord. "The way you are contorting your face will produce premature lines on your forehead," she added; the tease immediately lightened her niece's expression.

"The lady who is marrying Mr. Collins has four sisters," Georgiana verified.

"Yes, what of it?" Lady Catherine enquired.

"What if they can tell of my disgrace when they see me? I am afraid they will rightfully scorn me for my folly," Georgiana expressed her fear. It was one of the times her fears caused her to regress.

"First, how would someone know anything about your past by simply seeing you? From what Mr. Collins has told us, all five Bennet sisters are regular girls, not a coven of witches, for that is what they would have to be to look at you and know what you have done in the past," Lady Catherine stated.

"Gigi, I believe you are worrying needlessly," Richard interjected. "If I remember what Mr. Collins has told us, especially about the three older sisters, they are everything that is good and proper. Even *if* they knew what happened in Ramsgate, they would not hold it against you."

"I can only second Richard's wise words," Lady Catherine stated in support of both her nephew and niece. "Let he among us who has never erred cast the first stone. What you did was to make a mistake. As we have discussed, it was an error in judgement. However, do not forget you were but fifteen and wholly unprepared to deal with a reprobate like that man. At the same time, your companion, who was supposed to protect you, was working against you."

"Even though I feel somewhat better, I still feel a deep and abiding shame over my actions." Georgiana looked down at the floor of the equipage.

"Georgiana Ellen Darcy! Enough self-indulgence. Let me ask you something. No matter how much shame you feel, no matter how much you take yourself to task for your *past* errors, will that change anything that has happened?" Lady Catherine asked stridently.

"No, nothing I do now can change the past," Georgiana admitted.

"Then I suggest you accept a philosophy I have adopted in the years since my husband and my Anne were taken from me. Only remember the past as that remembrance gives you pleasure." Lady Catherine held up her hand as her niece was about to object. "I am *not* saying forget the past, and I am most *certainly* not saying do not learn from past mistakes, but what I *am* saying is to dwell on the past and use it as a crutch to stop yourself moving forward is meaningless. It is the very height of selfish self-indulgence."

"Listen to Aunt Cat, Gigi. Her words are very wise," Richard enthused.

"Would you fall for a silver-tongued devil again?" Lady Catherine pushed further.

"No, I would not," Georgiana replied indignantly.

"That is the spirit I want to see, and you yourself have just proved my point. You *have* learnt from your errors, so please, niece of mine, elucidate this for me. What are you achieving by constantly living in the past?" Lady Catherine asked the salient question.

Georgiana was silent for a little while as she cogitated on

her aunt's sage words. "I see now I was hiding behind the past, in the same way William hides behind his mask. That is not the way I want to be," Georgiana acknowledged.

"As you are the master of how you relate to others, it is up to you," Lady Catherine told her niece.

"William said I was never to talk to anyone else about Ramsgate," Georgiana informed her travelling companions. "However, I do not know if I agree with him. Is not an omission a lie just the same?"

"I disagree with your brother," Lady Catherine stated. "It is not something to tell new acquaintances as soon as you meet them; however, once you become true friends, then if you *choose* to inform others, it would be appropriate as it will save them from a similar mistake. Then your lesson would be valuable to more than yourself and your family. Possibly talking to Miss Elizabeth earlier than others would be appropriate as she was taken in by the same blackguard as you."

Lady Catherine and Richard could not help but see Mrs. Annesley's smile as she *slept*. It seemed the lady knew her charge needed to speak with her relations, and her feigning sleep would make that easier. Their suspicions were borne out when the companion *awoke* but a few minutes after the conversation was completed.

All three adults felt a sense of satisfaction at the change in the way Georgiana Darcy carried herself; she had gained some much-needed confidence.

~~~~~~~/~~~~~~~

William Collins attempted to remain calm as he spoke to Charlotte and Stuart Jamison in the dining parlour at Lucas Lodge. When he had followed Lady Catherine's good advice to reach out to his cousin, the most he had hoped for was a reconciliation in the family and to allow disagreements of the past to reside where they belonged.

He had always wanted to marry, but he did not want the type of marriage he had seen at home. As thankful as he was for being born, he could never understand why a kind, compassionate, and intelligent woman like his mother had married his father. The man was illiterate, and, if Collins were honest, not an intelligent man in any facet of his life.

By the time he was old enough to inquire of his maternal grandparents why they agreed to match their only daughter with his father, said grandparents had left the mortal world.

His mother, who he loved beyond reason, had become ill with influenza, and rather than recover as most do, there had been complications. Knowing she would never leave her sickbed while still living, Collins's mother told her son how his father compromised her when she was but sixteen. She extracted a promise from her son that he would never compromise anyone like his grandfather and father before him had, and, furthermore, he would only marry for love and respect.

Armed with the knowledge his mother shared with him, William Collins started to question everything his father told him, and as he had inherited his mother's intelligence and good sense, it did not take long for him to see how ridiculous his father's pronouncements had been.

His mother left her son a legacy which consisted of her dowry and the funds her parents had received when they sold their farm. Rather than give his father access to these funds, William Collins asked the executor of his grandparents' and mother's wills to release some money for him to attend a seminary.

Mr. Collins senior was an extremely bitter man when he passed away not long after his son began at the seminary. After his reconciliation with the Bennets, William Collins found— as if he needed further proof—additional evidence of his late father's wrongheaded opinions.

Like many men of good sense, he was troubled by the Bennet parents. He was able to put that aside because he had found a gem of the first order in his Mary. They had connected on many levels from the first time they met. They could discuss anything from literature, to politics, the war, as well as theology and religion. Some men might have been intimidated by a wife as intelligent as his Mary, but William Collins considered it a boon. It was one of the many things he loved about his wife-to-be.

"Mr. Collins, Mr. Collins," Charlotte Jamison again attempted to gain the man's attention.

"You have my sincere apologies, Mrs. Jamison, and you too Sir. I was wool-gathering, thinking about how lucky I am to be marrying my Mary in a few short hours," Collins explained.

"As I remember I was also thinking of my Charlotte the morning before we married; I fully understand your preoccupation," Mr. Jamison grinned as he winked at his wife who rolled her eyes at his tease, further proof of their wedded bliss.

"And I was sitting at this table doing the same thing as I considered how fortunate I was to be marrying my Stuart," Charlotte Jamison smiled at her husband.

"Is one of your classmates from the seminary standing up with you Mr. Collins?" Mr. Jamison asked.

"Yes, Mr. Gilcrest will meet us at the church...oh, in less than an hour. I did not notice the time. It is time for me to make myself ready and head for Longbourn's church." Collins stood and bowed to the Jamisons and the Lucases who entered the room as he exited.

~~~~~~~/~~~~~~~

"Collins," Richard caught the attention of his pastor who arrived at Longbourn's church just a little after he, his aunt, and his cousin had alighted from the barouche.

"Good morning, Mr. Fitzwilliam, Lady Catherine, and Miss Darcy." Collins bowed to the group who returned his courtesy. "You are most welcome, and I again thank you for coming to witness this, the most important day in my life—so far."

"We are honoured you thought to invite us Mr. Collins," Lady Catherine inclined her head.

Just then Collins spied Mr. and Mrs. Bennet, with Lydia and Kitty, walking towards the church. "Would you permit me to introduce my cousin and part of his family?" Collins asked his patron quietly. After looking to his aunt, Richard nodded.

Bennet was about to make some inane comment he thought amusing when he noticed three people in very fine clothing standing with Cousin Collins. "Please introduce us to your family," Lady Catherine requested.

"Lady Catherine, Mr. Fitzwilliam, and Miss Darcy," he did not miss the looks the four Bennets gave when they heard the name Darcy, "it is my pleasure to introduce my cousins. Mr. Thomas Bennet, the master of Longbourn, Mrs. Francene Bennet, Miss Catherine Bennet, and Miss Lydia Bennet. Cousins, my patron's Aunt, the honourable Lady Catherine de Bourgh, my patron, the honourable Mr. Richard Fitzwilliam, and my patron's cousin and ward, Miss Georgiana Darcy." Mr. Collins completed the introductions.

Luckily, Mrs. Bennet, awed by the highborn personages she had been introduced to, did no more than curtsy. Her daughters followed her lead and Mr. Bennet bowed. Without further conversation, the Bennets entered the church.

"The mother is not attending her daughter?" Lady Catherine asked quietly with raised eyebrows.

"It was my Mary's choice," Collins informed the Rosings Park party softly. "For the whole of her life, Mary was either ignored by Mrs. Bennet or told she was plain. With the strong bond she had with her older sisters, she asked them to attend her, and, as politely as she could, told her mother she could be seen at the church rather than arrive just before the services."

"It is time for us to sit," Richard stated after looking at his timepiece.

"And for me to take my position. Ah, here is Gilcrest now." Collins made quick introductions and then he and his best man followed Lady Catherine and her party into the church, taking their positions next to the vicar in front of the altar.

~~~~~~~/~~~~~~~

"Mary, you look gorgeous," Elizabeth exclaimed just as her father entered the front door after escorting his wife and younger daughters into the church.

For once, Bennet found no fodder for teasing. His oldest

three daughters were all as pretty as pictures, especially Mary who had so often been called plain by his wife. The young woman in front of him was anything but plain.

"It is time girls. I must say all of you look extremely well today, Mary, you more than any," Bennet stated.

Mary was stunned; she could not remember a previous time her father had complimented her. "Thank you Papa," she managed.

Jane and Elizabeth followed behind Mary and their father, and the four reached the outer vestibule doors in mere minutes. Elizabeth opened one of the inner doors and nodded to Longbourn's rector, Mr. Dudley. After pausing less than a minute, she entered the church and made her way up the aisle. Once she arrived at her position, Jane followed her.

Richard Fitzwilliam felt his breath hitch as he spied the oldest Bennet sister. She was far more beautiful than the first time he had met her at the Gardiner Trading Company; today she was ethereal. Was this the woman William found not good enough for a tradesman's son? What an arrogant arse his cousin could be!

As soon as Jane took her position, the rector gave the signal for the congregation to rise, and this time both inner vestibule doors opened wide and Bennet entered with Mary on his arm. As they walked up the aisle, all those who had heard Mrs. Bennet denigrate her middle daughter as plain over the years had evidence to give lie to those words.

Just below the marble steps that led up to the altar, Bennet halted, kissed his daughter on her cheek, replaced her veil, and placed her hand on her betrothed's arm. Once his duty was discharged, Bennet joined his wife and two youngest daughters in the family pew.

Mr. Dudley opened the Book of Common Prayer and began the liturgy that had married countless couples from the first days of the Church of England. As expected, there was no one who objected, and soon he pronounced them man and wife. All that was left was to sign the register, which they did in the company of their three attendants, and Mary penned 'Bennet' for the final time.

After a brief moment of privacy, the couple joined the Bennets in the church. They were wished well by all of the family, including the Phillipses. The most effusive wishes were from the current mistress of Longbourn to its future mistress.

As much as Fanny had ignored her middle daughter, she was not so deficient of mind to be unaware that her future comfort would be controlled by Mr. and Mrs. Collins. She was vociferous in her explosion of good wishes and compliments for her middle daughter, and Mary smiled inwardly at her mother's transparent display.

For all of Mary's life until the beginning of her courtship with Mr. Collins, Fanny had denigrated her middle daughter as plain. She had not changed her attitude publicly even after Jane and Elizabeth took Mary under their wing and changed the way she dressed and wore her hair.

Many times Fanny Bennet verbalised how Mary would be a spinster firmly on the shelf one day. She had not even noticed the quiet courtship between Mary and Mr. Collins, exclaiming her surprise when it had been announced. Mary had no illusions as to the reason for her mother's sudden approbation.

The newlyweds were congratulated sincerely by everyone except Lydia, who was still miffed that she had not been the first to marry. The six who still bore the name Bennet walked to Longbourn, and the Collinses followed but a few minutes later.

# CHAPTER 9

"Mr. and Mrs. William Collins," Mr. Hill announced which led to cheers and a slew of congratulations interspersed with wishes of happy. Mary and her husband were beaming with happiness as they made the rounds to thank their friends and neighbours for attending their nuptials.

As Jane and Elizabeth walked past the three from Rosings Park, they stopped when the older lady beckoned for them to join her. "Miss Bennet and Miss Elizabeth, I do not know if you remember, but we were introduced at your Uncle Gardiner's business a few years ago."

A memory stirred. "I do remember. You were there with Mr. Fitzwilliam, were you not?" Elizabeth asked.

"Your memory is correct, Miss Elizabeth," Richard bowed to both.

"Kitty," Jane caught the second youngest Bennet's attention. "May I introduce my sister to you?"

"We were introduced prior to the ceremony. Please allow me to introduce my niece." The two sisters who had not been introduced nodded. "Miss Bennet and Miss Elizabeth, my niece Miss Georgiana *Darcy*. Gigi, Miss Jane Bennet, Miss Elizabeth Bennet, and you remember meeting Miss Catherine Bennet— for some reason I do so like your name—before church," Lady Catherine watched the second Bennet daughter's reaction as she emphasised her niece's family name.

Elizabeth, whose eyebrows had shot up at hearing the young lady's name, looked at Miss Darcy. She had deep blue eyes and blond hair and was tall for a young lady of her age. If she had not known what a liar Wickham was already, she would have known it upon meeting Miss Darcy, who mumbled a greeting while not looking directly at the sisters.

From what Elizabeth could tell, since the girl did not talk much, it seemed Miss Darcy had no pride about her, only a deep shyness. Elizabeth then tried to draw the young Darcy out. "We have heard much of you, Miss Darcy, from an *unimpeachable* source." Elizabeth, as did her sisters, did not miss the look of panic that overspread the young girl's face. "From Miss Bingley; she sang your praises to the heavens. If she is to be believed, then you are a virtuoso on the pianoforte, and the most accomplished young lady who ever was," Elizabeth teased. As soon as Georgiana heard who Miss Elizabeth was referring to, she relaxed considerably, for she had been terrified that Wickham had spread stories about her abroad.

Seeing her niece's relief, Lady Catherine made to answer the jest. "My niece is accomplished and loves to play the pianoforte, but, as I am sure you are aware, anything Miss Bingley says must be taken with a grain of salt. You could not have missed how she has her cap set at my nephew and refused to see clear indications of his disinterest. I understand from Mr. Collins you ladies had the *pleasure* of her acquaintance."

"We learnt from Mary that the lady has been less than truthful with our Jane," Elizabeth observed.

"Would the three of you agree to accompany us to that little wilderness I noticed on the side of the house? There is some information I would like to impart, but in this crowd it would not be appropriate." Lady Catherine looked at the Bennet sisters.

"Jane, you and Lizzy go; I will stay to attend Mary if she needs one of us," Kitty volunteered. Her older sisters were very proud of her, for Mary had grown close to Kitty as they both were disregarded by their mother; Kitty would not leave Mary this day of all days.

Leaving Mrs. Annesley to enjoy the feast, the five walked to the natural garden, where they seated themselves on some benches. Jane and Elizabeth sat on one; Lady Catherine and

Miss Darcy sat on another, and Mr. Fitzwilliam sat on a third.

"Miss Elizabeth, on behalf of my family, I wish to apologise for my nephew Darcy's poor behaviour while he was in your neighbourhood, starting with his slight to you at the assembly," Lady Catherine opened.

"It is difficult for me to comprehend William behaved in such an ungentlemanlike manner," Georgiana stated softly, speaking barely above a whisper as she shook her head.

"He had good reason for being disinclined to join in a festive occasion, but once he decided to attend, there was no excuse for his behaviour to you and the rest of the neighbourhood," Lady Catherine stated.

"It is forgotten your Ladyship," Elizabeth stated.

"Lizzy!" Jane admonished. "You still resent the unjust slight Mr. Darcy delivered at the assembly."

"To tell the truth, it still bothers me, but I am *attempting* to forget it," Elizabeth clarified. "I am heartily ashamed that I allowed myself to believe Mr. Wickham's lies. For that I must apologise; I have recognised my wilful blindness and so am trying to move past how I allowed him to manipulate me."

"At least you did not agree to elope with him," came a soft voice.

Jane and Elizabeth looked at one another, unsure if they had heard the same thing from Miss Darcy. "Did you say elope with him?" Jane asked gently.

"Oh Aunt, it slipped out," Georgiana put her head in her hands and allowed the tears to flow, worried her aunt would be angry with her.

"If I am not mistaken Gigi, the Miss Bennets will be the very souls of discretion; do you notice neither have fled from your company?" Lady Catherine soothed her niece.

"May I tell you what occurred?" Georgiana asked as she dried her eyes, relieved her new acquaintances agreed. "I used to have a companion, Mrs. Younge..." She told them the whole of the tale in a voice which became steadier and grew stronger as she told it.

When she was finished with her recitation, she saw abhorrence reflected in the looks of the two Bennets—exactly as she feared—until Miss Elizabeth spoke. "What a waste of a man. Miss Darcy, we are so very sorry you had to suffer the manipulation and lies of those two criminals."

As soon as Georgiana realised none of the anger and disgust was directed at her—just like Aunt Cat had told her it would not be—but only at her erstwhile suitor and his paramour, she started to feel more self-assured.

"If he were not in the militia's brig, I would love to see that man dealt with—permanently!" Jane stated angrily. That so much evil was encapsulated in one man who thought nothing of hurting someone, regardless of their age, infuriated Jane Bennet.

"You are a woman after my own heart Miss Bennet," Richard stated approvingly. The woman was magnificent, and Bingley was a complete fool. *'Let us see if his loss will be my gain,'* Richard watched her reaction to his approbation.

"How could your nephew leave the area and leave us at the mercy of that man?" Elizabeth asked incredulously. "Did he not care that without your intervention half of the merchants in town would have been put out of business by the cad?" All of the righteous indignation she felt towards the insufferable man was rekindled.

"His excuse is if he had warned anyone it would have put Gigi here at risk of exposure," Lady Catherine raised her hand as Elizabeth and Jane were both about to protest vehemently. "He was wrong. We—Richard and I—were able to deal with the man without a hint about Gigi being raised. I purchased the vowels my nephew held in Wickham's name—over two thousand pounds worth—and added them to the thousand-pound vowel I had him sign while I was here. I own over three thousand pounds' worth of his debts. If he pushes his nose over the line, I will call them in and the man will spend the rest of his wasted life in Marshalsea, Coldbath Fields, or the Clink Prison.

"He may have wasted four thousand pounds in two years,

but he will not be able to pay back half of what he owes in a lifetime," Lady Catherine stated malevolently. None of those listening to her said a word in opposition.

"Mary told us how Miss Bingley lied about her brother's supposed understanding with Miss Darcy. There was hardly a word in any of her letters which was the truth," Jane reported.

"Miss Bennet, may I request those letters if you still have them in your possession?" Lady Catherine asked.

"You may your Ladyship," Jane allowed, glad she did not cast them into the fire as she had been inclined initially.

"Please call me Lady Catherine, not Lady Kitty," she smiled, "even if my irreverent nephews and nieces call me Aunt Cat."

"In that case, please call me Jane," Jane granted.

"And I am Elizabeth or Lizzy," Elizabeth added.

"It will please me if you address me as Georgiana, or Gigi," Georgiana requested.

"May I ask what you need the letters for?" Jane probed.

"It is no secret, my dear. The family has all pointed out to William—Mr. Darcy—the contradiction in the way he relates to the Bingleys versus others of his acquaintance. I do not believe he will be so sanguine on the subject when he sees her lies in her own hand," Lady Catherine explained.

"You told me Miss Bingley was praising me to the skies?" Georgiana asked to verify she had heard them correctly, and both Bennets nodded. "The truth is I do not like her at all. When Mrs. Hurst is not with her sister, she is pleasant, but when together she is more like her younger sister. They talk down to me as though I were a child in leading strings, and Miss Bingley fawns all over me as she holds the mistaken belief that doing so will garner William's notice. Like Aunt Cat, I do not understand why he tolerates the woman; he cannot stand her either."

"He stood by while she attacked me and my family verbally. Surely he knows a tradesman's daughter is below a landed gentlewoman—regardless of fortune—but he never once corrected her. He seems most fastidious, so I could not reconcile his behaviour regarding the pretentious, vulgar woman," Elizabeth mused.

"I believe it is for the brother he puts up with her. We will see how her pretentions hold up after I next speak with that woman," Lady Catherine indicated. "You are due an apology as well, Miss Bennet. In addition to the lies Miss Bingley told regarding my niece, my nephew acted to separate you from Mr. Bingley as well. From what I now know, the man was never informed you were in London. You already know he was not spending time with my niece and nephew, which is what you were told. However, the former was at Rosings Park and the latter was at Pemberley."

"So he may still love me?" Jane surmised, hopefully.

"Miss Bennet—Jane, please allow me to ask you some questions, and please let me know if you do not feel it is my place to ask and I will cease. I promise not to take umbrage if you tell me so," Lady Catherine enquired.

"It would be good to talk to someone who is objective," Jane allowed.

"Do you believe that his sisters locked Mr. Bingley away or chained him to a chair so he could not seek you out on his own?" Lady Catherine asked bluntly.

"No, I do not suppose they would have done that," Jane admitted.

"If it were you, and you loved someone, truly loved them, could you be persuaded away from the other person so easily—or at all? Jane, would you allow anyone—no matter who or how many—to talk you out of your inclination so that you would disappear without a word?" Lady Catherine asked gently.

"I would not. Capriciousness is not part of my character, but we do not know..." Jane tapered off what she was about to say as she heard her own words and realised how hollow they rang. At the same time she truly heard what Lady Catherine was driving at. "It does not speak well to his strength of character or the love he professes if he allows others to direct him in that way. If he truly loved me, no one would have been able to dissuade him from returning to me, would they?" Jane concluded. "If he is like that now, would he be resolute enough to make decisions when he is married, or would he defer to others as he seems to now? When I look at Mr. Bingley in this light, his image becomes quite tarnished."

"You are too intelligent not to know the answer to that question Jane. Let me tell you a little more about Mr. Bingley." Lady Catherine requested permission and was relieved when Jane nodded. "He does not like to make his own decisions. He prefers to rely on others so that if things do not go well, he is able to claim it was not his fault, stating that he was but following advice."

"In other words Janie, he is weak and irresolute. That is *not* the kind of man you would be happy with. You, my dearest sister, need a man and not a puppy." Elizabeth paused to cogitate. "When I heard Mr. Darcy assisted in separating Mr. Bingley from you, I was angrier with him than I had ever been for myself. But now—and I know it was not his intent—I believe he has done you a favour. How would it have been if Mr. Bingley had returned, offered for you, and you had accepted him? You would have discovered his lack of character only after you were married; you would have been trapped in a marriage and lost to us. I am sure it will be but the work of a moment for you to get over him, and I believe this knowledge will assist you in that endeavour," Elizabeth opined.

"And I will add Jane, you would not have been mistress of your own home; Miss Bingley would have ruled it as she does now. Mr. Bingley does not have the strength to stand up to his sister from what we have observed, and will not gainsay her," Lady Catherine pointed out.

"Jane, if you see this now, then why not join me in March to visit Mary? She did invite you as well," Elizabeth suggested.

"You will be at Hunsford Lizzy?" Georgiana asked excitedly. "I am so pleased there will be young ladies near my age in the area."

"Are we so easily thrown over?" Richard jested with his ward.

"Do not tease my niece Richard," Lady Catherine swatted toward her nephew playfully even though his bench kept him out of range of her arm. "Jane, it would be a pleasure to have you in the area with Elizabeth. How old is your sister Catherine —Kitty you call her?"

"She turned seventeen in January," Jane replied.

"Mayhap she will make the journey with you. I am recently sixteen so we are very close in age," Georgiana suggested enthusiastically.

"The *whole* of the family will join us for Easter," Lady Catherine looked at Elizabeth as she stated the last.

"Who else besides your nephew Darcy?" Elizabeth asked.

"My brother and his wife, the Earl and Countess of Matlock, and Richard's older brother Andrew and his wife Marie, who are the Viscount and Viscountess Hilldale. Of course, little Reggie, who is not much more than six months old, will be with his parents. The rest of the family are *not* like my nephew Darcy, so I am confident you will like them as much as they will like you," Lady Catherine opined.

"If Papa does not object, I will join the party who will be visiting Mary and our new brother. I am sure Mary would invite Kitty to join us," Jane decided.

"The parsonage should have enough room, but if not, any of you will be more than welcome to stay at Rosings Park," Richard offered. "I have a feeling it would make our Gigi very happy to have one or more of you at the manor house with her."

As they walked back to the house, Jane hung back a little when Elizabeth placed her hand on her sister's arm. "I am so glad I did not jump to conclusions about Mr. Darcy's relatives; they are none of them like him. I believe I like his aunt very well indeed," Elizabeth told her sister.

"I agree completely with you Lizzy. You must allow that people can change, just as you are learning to. I am relieved you were open to seeing what his family was like before jumping to conclusions." Jane looked at her sister with an eyebrow arched in challenge, causing Elizabeth to raise her hands in surrender.

"That snake in the grass called Gigi proud and disagreeable. As if I need any more, it is further proof of his lies," Elizabeth stated. Jane refrained from pointing out which of them had believed that man blindly.

~~~~~~~/~~~~~~~

By the time they returned to the wedding celebration, Mary was ready to change out of her wedding gown and into her travel attire. Jane, Elizabeth, and Kitty accompanied her. Before they arrived at Mary's chamber, Jane delayed Kitty and asked her if she would like to join them when they went to visit Mary, and Kitty excitedly agreed.

"Mary, you remember I turned down your invitation in order to return to London?" Jane asked as they entered the room and Mary nodded. "I have at last decided that Mr. Bingley is not worth my time, so if your invitation still stands, I would like to join Lizzy when she comes to visit you," Jane informed a beaming Mary.

"Of course it does. What about you Kitty? Would you like to join us?" Mary asked hopefully. Kitty nodded vigorously; her days of being Lydia's shadow were over.

"Oh yes, I would love to. Thank you!" Kitty agreed.

They helped Mary change and organise the last few things she needed to take to the carriage that, generously, Mr. Fitzwilliam had placed at the newlyweds' disposal.

They joined their parents and a surly Lydia to see the Collinses off. Just before he was to return indoors, Mr. Bennet was waylaid by Jane and Kitty, who asked if they could join Lizzy and visit Mary in March.

On the one hand, he felt there would be no sensible conversation at Longbourn. However, it would save him money with fewer mouths to feed, More importantly to him, there would be relative peace and quiet. That trumped all else for Bennet, so he consented to Jane and Kitty joining Elizabeth for as long as they desired.

Rather than send his carriage to Town, he would send it to Kent to convey his three daughters. Now if he could only send his wife and youngest daughter away...

~~~~~~~/~~~~~~~

Fitzwilliam Darcy began to examine his character after his family took him to task at Snowhaven. After reaching Pemberley, at first he allowed his indignation full reign and scoffed at their assertions. By the middle of January, alone at his estate, he started to look at his behaviour through the eyes of others.

The thing that hit him hardest was when he realised that his parents would have been disappointed, no more than that, ashamed by his actions. Aunt Cat was correct; he *had* turned into a version of how she used to be.

For the first time in a very long time, the mighty Mr. Darcy, a powerful and wealthy member of the *Ton,* started to look at his character and behaviour critically. The more he looked, the less pleased he was with what he saw.

# CHAPTER 10

"Welcome sisters," Mr. Collins said, greeting his wife's sisters warmly.

"My goodness Mary, you look so very happy," Jane noted.

"That is because I am," Mary responded with a shy smile as she looked at her husband.

"In that case, I will not have to take our brother to task, as I can see he is ensuring your happiness, which is his most important task, after all," Elizabeth said with a wide smile as she hugged her glowing sister. "Marriage looks good on you Mary. Brother, you look just as happy, which portends a felicitous marriage."

"Kitty, welcome to our home." Collins made sure to include the youngest sister present who was standing quietly in the background.

"It is good to see you Kitty," Mary seconded her husband's welcome.

Before they could talk further, Mr. Hill told them their trunks had been off-loaded, placed in the charge of the Collins's man, and asked if he and Sarah could begin their return to Longbourn. After making sure Mr. Hill had enough coin for any needs during the trip home and a basket of food, Jane wished them well for the return journey.

"If you are agreeable, we have been invited to Rosings Park for dinner to welcome you to the neighbourhood. It is but a ten to fifteen minute walk to the great house," Collins informed his sisters.

"I cannot speak for Jane and Kitty, but for my part it would be good to see Lady Catherine, Gigi, and Mr. Fitzwilliam again," Elizabeth stated.

Jane looked at Kitty who nodded. "Kitty and I have no objection. We are not tired, for we all slept for more than half of the journey into Kent."

Mary led her sisters into her home. It was a multi-level grey stone building abutting the church. On the ground level there were a sitting room, the mistress's parlour, the master's study, and a dining parlour. From the dining parlour stairs led down to the kitchen and scullery in the cellar.

Mary explained she had a housekeeper and cook in the person of Mrs. Ethel Cookson, a maid of all work, an upstairs maid, and a man of all work. The housekeeper had a room off the kitchen, while the two maids had rooms in the attic. The man lived with his wife, their children, and his parents in a cottage on the outskirts of Hunsford.

The floor above the ground floor had the mistress and master chambers and one guest chamber; there were three guest chambers on the floor above that. Given that Mary and her husband had been married less than three weeks, the Bennet sisters decided to avail themselves of the three chambers on the floor above those of their sister and brother to give them as much privacy as possible.

After they changed from their travel attire and washed up, they joined Mary in the sitting room, leaving the maid to unpack their trunks. The man employed at the parsonage had placed them in the chambers according to the mistress's instruction.

"Where is our brother?" Jane asked.

Mary asked the maid of all work to tell Mrs. Cookson she was ready for the tea service, then said "He is in his study working on his sermon for this Sunday. Unlike many of his fellow clergymen, William does not like to use sermons written by others; he prefers to write his own. He will let me read it at some point to give him my opinion. If he feels I raise a valid point, he will adjust his sermon. If he disagrees with my interpretation, then we will debate it. More often than not, he convinces me of the rectitude of his point of view—but not always."

"I don't like to trouble you, but there is something occurring at home that worries all three of us considerably," Elizabeth informed Mary.

"What has Lydia done now?" Mary asked, guessing the source of her sisters' vexation.

"Nothing—yet," Jane replied. Mary looked at her sisters questioningly.

"You know the Derbyshire Militia will decamp for Brighton at the end of March, do you not?" Elizabeth verified.

"Yes, I remember how bereft Lydia said she would be without all of her *precious* redcoats," Mary frowned.

"You met Mrs. Forster, did you not?" Jane took up the telling.

"Yes, she was at the wedding, and not much older than Kitty, I believe," Mary stated. "Almost as silly, brash, and flirtatious as Lydia."

"That is the very one. Since your wedding and with plans to visit you without her, Lydia has been spending a great deal of time with Mrs. Forster and now calls herself Mrs. Forster's *particular friend*. Rather than discouraging the connection, Papa is only too happy for Lydia to be out of the house as it gives him more peace and quiet. With Mama spending most of her time gossiping with Aunt Hattie, Papa feels it is *nirvana*," Jane explained.

"If it were not bad enough that Lydia, who is not mature enough to be out of the schoolroom, spends so much of her time with her equally silly and vapid friend, our sister has been invited to travel to Brighton to be hosted by the Forsters. How that girl will be able to chaperon Lydia, I do not know," Elizabeth continued. "I begged Papa not to grant his permission, but he said if he did not allow her to go, there would be no peace at Longbourn. When I pointed out she would ruin us all, he waved away my concerns and told me that Lydia would not be happy until she exposed herself in some public place. He says she will find out her own insignificance, and it could not be done with so little expense and trouble to himself. All he cares about is that he is left alone with his port and books; he would not care if Rome burned around him!"

"Jane and Lizzy had an idea. They suggested I become closer to Lydia again," Kitty joined the recitation. "I made her believe I was jealous of her and I would much rather have been joining her in Brighton instead of going on a *boring* holiday to a parsonage. You know Lydia; she loves nothing more than lording it over others, so she condescended to write and tell me about her wonderful times with officers and balls while I *languish* here."

"That was clever of all of you. Let us pray we will have some warning if she is planning something irrevocable. Brighton is but three or four hours from here," Mary told her sisters.

~~~~~~~/~~~~~~~

"Mr. Collins sent a note," Lady Catherine informed her niece and nephew. "Mrs. Collins's sisters arrived safely. They are not too tired and happily accepted our invitation to dinner."

"Three friends in the neighbourhood," Georgiana gushed. "I am so pleased. When do my aunt, uncle, and other Fitzwilliam cousins arrive, and what about William?"

"My parents, brother, and sister-in-law are in Town, and will arrive here the first Wednesday in April. William is still at Pemberley. He plans to arrive here after spending a single night in Town. That will put him here the Saturday following the arrival of the party from London," Richard explained everyone's plans as he understood them to be.

"I have an idea how to put Miss Bingley in her place once and for all. Would you be willing to issue an invitation for the Tuesday after Easter, the sixteenth of April?" Richard nodded still not seeing the whole plan. "I think the invitation should be issued through William," Lady Catherine decided. "I do not want to take William unawares or embarrass him, so we will make sure he understands everything before issuing the invitation."

"What do you intend for the harpy?" Richard asked, pre-emptively grinning. He loved it when his aunt took others to task for their offensive natures, just as she had done for herself.

"She will be taught just how insignificant she is and her pretentions will be put to rest," Lady Catherine stated with purpose.

"Do you think William will agree?" Georgiana asked.

"If I know your brother, he went to Pemberley after he left Snowhaven believing we were all in the wrong. I believe, however, that soon after he took a good, long, hard look at himself. The whole family's opposition to his arrogance would have given him pause," Lady Catherine supposed. "In addition, I have a feeling once he sees that vulgar woman's letters, that Jane gifted me, he will have no objection to my plan."

"What will you do if he has not learnt his lesson yet?" Richard enquired.

"Then he will not be consulted about the reason for the Bingleys' invitation. However, I pray that course of action will not be needed. Regardless of how William behaves at times, he is a good and honourable man. He looks after all who depend on him. He is considered the best of masters, and if he were beyond redemption he would not be such a liberal estate owner," Lady Catherine expressed. She had not been certain he would accept what was said to him at Snowhaven. What gave her the hope she had was based on his last letter. From its tone she suspected William had been looking at himself in the mirror.

~~~~~~~/~~~~~~~

"The park is so pretty," Elizabeth exclaimed as the parsonage party walked toward the manor house. "I cannot wait to walk the path from the parsonage into the forested area. I will be up with the sun on the morrow."

"As long as you do not expect any of us to join you at such an ungodly hour," Jane teased Elizabeth.

"We know how much sleep you need to maintain your beauty Jane," Elizabeth returned playfully.

Just then, as they transitioned from the trees into the formal gardens, the three Bennet sisters got their first view of the great house at Rosings Park. Even in the twilight it was easy to see the gardens were a riot of colour. They were more ordered and formal than Jane and Elizabeth preferred, but notwithstanding, it was an extremely pleasing vista.

Mr. Toppin showed them to the drawing room. As they walked, the sisters looked around in wonder. The house was light and airy with artwork on the walls; all the pieces selected added to the house's warmth.

As they were shown into the drawing room, Georgiana could no longer restrain herself and approached Jane and Lizzy with evident pleasure. She had met Kitty at Longbourn, but they did not then have much time to talk.

"Jane, Lizzy, and Miss Kitty, you are all most welcome," the young girl gushed.

At that moment, Georgiana realised she usurped her aunt's role as mistress and blushed profusely. She was about to apologise to Lady Catherine but her aunt waved it away, letting her know she took no offence and understood her niece's exuberance at the Bennet sisters' arrival, for she too was glad they were present.

"We thank you for the honour of an invitation to Rosings on the first day of our arrival," Jane spoke for herself and her sisters.

"It is we who are honoured by your presence," Richard stated sincerely. "It is good to see you do not think all of us are *insufferable*." Richard looked at Elizabeth who blushed deeply.

Kitty went to sit with Georgiana while Elizabeth joined the Collinses in talking with Lady Catherine. That left Jane, who took a seat the master of the estate indicated in a bid for her company.

"It is a *pleasure* to see you again Miss Bennet—you and your sisters," Richard told Jane as he looked at her steadily.

Jane had been thinking about Mr. Richard Fitzwilliam quite a lot since Mary's wedding. It was far too soon to consider if she might develop tender feelings for the man—that was the operative word—man. He was all man, no boy or puppy about him. What she was sure about was *no one*, no matter who or how many, could direct him away from one he loved. For that matter, he was not a man who could be directed away from his inclinations once he was set on a course.

He was not as handsome as Mr. Bingley, but that had never been important to her. Character was far more important than some arbitrary physical attribute, and as far as Jane could tell, Richard had character in spades. She trusted Lady Catherine's opinion after their conversation, and she obviously loved and respected her nephew.

Regardless of anything that might or might not develop between her and Richard Fitzwilliam, Jane knew one thing for certain_if Mr. Bingley had in fact been in love with her, it was not a strong love. Jane had considered Lady Catherine's questions after their talk at Mary's wedding, and she had reached a resolve.

Any man who could be redirected by his sisters or a friend, and who substituted their judgements for his own, was not the man for her. It was not a discussion she could have with her mother. She felt she could talk to Lady Catherine about anything, and when the lady had time she hoped to have that conversation.

"From what I can see, your sister is no longer pining for Mr. Bingley," Lady Catherine observed.

"It is my belief you have the right of it, Lady Cat," Elizabeth replied playfully, watching to see if the lady would let her impertinence pass.

There was no remonstration. Lady Catherine leaned her head back and let out a hearty laugh, which caused her eyes to water. "I knew I would like you when I heard about you from your newly-acquired brother," Lady Catherine stated as she dried her eyes. "I wish my Anne was still with us. She had a weak constitution but was in possession of a dry wit, so she would have loved you."

"It would have been an honour to have known the late Miss de Bourgh," Elizabeth inclined her head.

"I am looking forward to your meeting my brother and his wife, as well as Richard's brother and sister-in-law," Lady Catherine told Elizabeth as she patted her hand.

"You mean the Earl and Countess?" Elizabeth verified.

"Indeed. As we mentioned at Longbourn, they do not look down on those below them as some do," Lady Catherine confirmed.

"Like your nephew, Darcy," Elizabeth let the words escape before she had considered her intimation.

"Lizzy!" Mary admonished even as her husband looked away and bit back a smile.

"No Mary dear, I am not offended. Elizabeth only spoke the truth. We hope after his set down at Christmastide my nephew has amended his character," Lady Catherine told them.

"Set down?" Elizabeth stated quizzically.

"Yes…" Lady Catherine gave them a synopsis of the family pointing out certain deficiencies of his character to Mr. Darcy. "It is my fervent hope that he has addressed the reproofs which were laid at his door. We will not know until he arrives next week."

"As much as I hope your confidence is not misplaced, I do not have a high level of expectation the man who behaved as he did in our neighbourhood is able to amend his character and behaviour. He may take your reproofs as insults, for I remember what he told us when I was at Netherfield Park nursing Jane. He told us his good opinion once lost is lost forever. A man who holds implacable resentment may not be able to make the changes needed." Elizabeth wanted to believe he would, but her confidence was low.

She blushed as she remembered her own faults, how her pride and prejudice had led her to believe Wickham. The fact was, she shared an unattractive trait with Mr. Darcy. When she believed she was right, it was very hard to get her to change her position, even in the face of mounting evidence. If she was able to recognise her faults and determine they needed amending, surely it was arrogant, even hypocritical, of her to pre-determine that Mr. Darcy would not be able to do the same?

"It would be wrong of me to pre-judge. I will wait until he arrives and see how he is now rather than see him through the filter of the past," Elizabeth conceded. "For one who says only remember the past…"

"As that remembrance gives you pleasure," Lady Catherine completed. "It seems we share a philosophy. It is one I adopted after Lewis and Anne were taken from me."

The butler announced dinner. No precedence was observed as the group ambled into the small family dining parlour to enjoy the abundant repast and pleasant company.

It became evident that Georgiana and Kitty were well on their way to becoming firm friends. That impression was cemented when Gigi requested that Kitty stay at the manor house, in the second bedchamber of her suite.

And so it was the very next morning one of Rosings Park's coaches collected Kitty and her trunk and moved her to the great house.

# CHAPTER 11

Each morning since arriving at the Hunsford parsonage, Elizabeth walked paths among the trees, invariably finding her way to a glade. The wooded areas had silver and downy birches, ash trees, and Lawson cypress trees; wildflowers and shrubs grew between the trees and alongside the pathways. There was nowhere Elizabeth felt more at home than walking in the midst of untamed nature.

Elizabeth rose before the sun, washed and dressed herself, donned her half boots, and was on her way as the sun started to peek over the horizon. After visiting Mrs. Cookson in the kitchen to be gifted with an apple, a warm roll, or a muffin, she would commence her ramble.

Jane was not one to while the day away in bed, but she did not enjoy walking as much as Elizabeth and did not join her younger sister on her rambles. Jane would wake a little after the sun started its climb into the morning sky. After performing her morning ablutions, she would join Mary and her brother Collins in the sitting room. When Elizabeth returned after her walk, the four of them would break their fasts together.

It was easy for Jane and Elizabeth to see the felicity that Mary enjoyed in her marriage. Mary and Collins took any opportunity for contact between them as if by *chance*; there was no missing the loving looks that passed between them.

Both of her older sisters prayed they would have such felicity in their own marriages as they saw at the parsonage. They hoped they would be fortunate enough to find a man who would love and respect them, and to whom they could returned the same sentiments in equal measure.

After their fasts were broken, Collins would retire to his study to work on any outstanding parish business and then visit his parishioners on a rotation. He met with his patron once a week, unless a pressing need to meet before the next scheduled meeting arose unexpectedly, which was rare.

After Mary dealt with the household needs, she would make her own visits to parishioners. Some visits were to the sick or those needing extra assistance, but the bulk were social calls just to make sure all was well. Having learnt about caring for and visiting Longbourn's tenants from Jane and Elizabeth, Mary was able to apply those lessons in the Hunsford Parish.

While the Collinses were attending to their duties, some days Kitty and Gigi—always escorted by Richard—would visit the parsonage. On other days, Jane and Elizabeth would make the short walk to the manor house. Whenever in company together, Jane and Richard would soon find a reason to talk.

In little more than a week after the sisters' arrival, when in company Richard and Jane seemed to be gravitating one to the other more and more. One particular morning, just before Jane and Elizabeth were to depart for the great house, the post was delivered.

Elizabeth had written to her father, making one more attempt to convince him not to allow Lydia to go to Brighton, so she was apprehensive when she spied a letter addressed to her in her father's hand. She broke the seal and read the short, curt missive.

*23 March 1811*

*Elizabeth:*

*Please do not importune me on this subject again. I made my decision and I am, I believe, still the father and parent.*

*Lydia will soon learn her insignificance at no trouble or expense to myself.*

*Leave my bailiwick to me and worry about yourself,*

*TB*

Elizabeth felt the rebuke jump off the parchment at her.

*'Papa, you are so worried about having peace and quiet you cannot see the danger in letting her go. Lydia will be the ruin of us all. Thank goodness Mary is well married already, but I am afraid you are going to consign the rest of us to lonely spinsterhood by your wilful blindness and refusal to take your youngest in hand. You neither know nor care what an outrageous flirt Lydia is, nor how she makes her family look ridiculous.'* Elizabeth prayed she was wrong but was almost certain she was not.

"Lizzy, why do you look so distressed? Is there bad news from home? Is everyone well?" Jane asked, concerned as she watched the emotions play across her sister's face.

Wordlessly, Elizabeth handed Jane the offending note from their father. "Oh Lizzy, I am so sorry. But you know Father has long been wilfully blind to the danger which Lydia's unrestrained behaviour poses to all of us," Jane commiserated.

"That is the most unforgiving statement I have ever heard you make Janie. In the past you would have made excuses and tried to explain our father's lack of action in some positive light. I am relieved you are seeing things the way they are rather than how you might hope they could be," Elizabeth stated.

"Come Lizzy, it is time to walk to Rosings, for we do not want to cause Kitty and Gigi to wait for us too long." Jane stood to prepare herself for the short walk.

"Is it just the girls you are keen to see, Miss Jane Eloise Bennet?" Elizabeth asked archly. "It seems to me you are just as happy to see a certain ex-soldier who happens to be the master of the estate we are visiting." Elizabeth raised her eyebrow in question and was rewarded with a deep blush from her sister.

"Lizzy!" Jane exclaimed as she playfully swatted her younger sister's arm, never denying her assertion.

~~~~~~~/~~~~~~~

"You will be sorely missed Lydia," Fanny Bennet shrilled as her lace handkerchief waved up and down with the excited movements of its owner. "Oh, how I wish your father would have agreed we all could travel to Brighton. Some sea bathing would have set me up for life!"

Although she was her mother's favourite and professed much love for the woman—but only to the extent that it gained her what she desired—Lydia was pleased her father had refused to bring his wife to Brighton or allow her to travel there without him.

Lydia aimed to flirt and have fun with the officers; she was sure she would catch one, as who could resist her abundant charms? An added incentive for being free of much supervision was that the handsome Mr. Wickham would finally be released from the brig after having been so falsely accused and unjustly punished.

The man was everything she desired in a husband, a handsome officer in a scarlet coat. The other thing that drove Lydia's desire to catch an officer as soon as might be was her desire to wed before any of the rest of her sisters.

That plain Mary had destroyed her plans to be the first of the Bennet sisters to marry, but to marry before her other three sisters would be most satisfying. At least Kitty had realised that she was nothing without her and had started to pay her deference before being dragged off against her will to boring old Hunsford. Lydia would take pleasure in writing many letters to rub Kitty's nose in how much fun she, the youngest and prettiest of the Bennet sisters, was having.

Mr. Bennet had not bestirred himself from his study to see his youngest off. He felt a momentary pang of guilt over the rebuke in his missive to Lizzy, but he consoled himself with the fact that with Lydia out of the house there would be absolute peace and quiet.

He was not worried about his wife interrupting him while there was no one else in the house with them, as she would spend her time with her equally senseless sister, Hattie Phillips, to indulge in gossip and talk of lace and other fripperies all day long.

Bennet knew he should feel guilt at having manipulated his wife to go to her sister's, thereby imposing on his brother

Phillips. She should have invited her to their home, but regret was one of the emotions on which Mr. Bennet did not waste time. Like so many other things he did not do, it was too much trouble to expend thought about his behaviour and inaction towards his family and how it impacted them. He was sure—or at least had convinced himself—that Lizzy's assertions were so outlandish they could not but be wrong.

~~~~~~~/~~~~~~~

George Wickham was seething with anger, for he was still stuck in the bloody Derbyshire Militia. Everything had been set up: he was to have a new wardrobe, shoes, boots, everything he needed to present himself as a gentleman, when that damned Lady Catherine and Richard Fitzwilliam had spoiled his plans.

In the weeks since his flogging, his back had begun to heal at last. There was still pain, but not as great as it had been right after the lashes had been administered. Luckily, the wounds had not become infected—much. There had been some nights with fever, but thankfully, the unit's doctor had applied a salve which protected his open wounds.

Since all his wounds had at last closed, he was finally able to wear a shirt again. There were scabs; those would drop off soon enough but would leave him with scars for the rest of his life—a reminder of what Darcy's relations' interference had cost him.

The only positive for the former lieutenant—now demoted to ensign—was the fact that once they arrived in Brighton, he would be released from the brig. After all, riding in the wagon to Brighton—even with the bars—was preferable to marching for miles each day towards their new encampment, as most of his unit would be required to do.

He had not yet determined how he would get back at his tormenters. He was sure after he was set free he would settle on an infallible plan to exact his revenge. As always, he was confident in his abilities.

If only Darcy had not arrived two days early and spoiled

his and Mrs. Younge's plans with mousy Georgiana! Wickham was now certain that Darcy had lied about the restrictions on his sister's dowry and believed her thirty thousand pounds could have been his.

He still smarted from the facer Darcy had planted on his person. At least his nose had set at an almost normal angle so his greatest asset, his looks, had not been materially affected. Although he needed to exact revenge on Darcy, his priority was the de Bourgh woman, and her nephew Richard Fitzwilliam.

~~~~~~~/~~~~~~~

As much as he hated to admit he was deficient, the more Darcy looked at his behaviour, the more he found it wanting. Was Aunt Catherine correct in her assertions about his contradictory—even hypocritical—behaviour with regards to the Bingleys?

After weeks of thought, Darcy now saw that Bingley, rather than being a friend, was a dependant, one who Darcy could easily control. The enjoyment of being able to direct Bingley led to him turning a blind eye to the abhorrent behaviour of Miss Caroline Bingley, and to a lesser extent, Mrs. Louisa Hurst.

He had sworn to protect his sister, yet there were multiple times he failed her. Yes, Mrs. Younge was his biggest failure, but he was well aware that Gigi disliked Bingley's sisters. In order to maintain his control over their brother, he ignored Gigi's discomfort and did nothing to alleviate her suffering when she was imposed upon by the fawning sisters.

He had heard Miss Elizabeth—the woman who unknowingly owned his heart—call Miss Bingley and Mrs. Hurst the *supercilious sisters*. Looking back on their behaviour with a critical eye, he could not but agree with her.

No wonder Lady Catherine said Miss Elizabeth disliked him. Not only had he insulted her in the most ungentlemanlike fashion at the assembly where they had met, but he had been insufferably rude to all of her family save Miss Bennet, and to all of her neighbours. Then he had hurt her sister while convincing himself he was protecting his *friend*.

He was ashamed; he claimed to abhor deception but had practiced it. He admitted to himself he had no understanding of what Miss Bennet had felt for Bingley but had issued an opinion which fit his needs so he would be removed from the temptation that was Miss Elizabeth.

He hung his head as he remembered Bingley rejected his sisters' arguments and had only agreed to separate himself from Miss Bennet when he, *Mr. High and Mighty Darcy*, had told him the woman was indifferent to him and would only accept an offer to appease her mother.

The arrogant disdain for the feelings of others he had displayed mortified him. As he thought about Miss Elizabeth with his new understanding, he could hear Miss Bingley's pernicious attacks against her, and how Miss Elizabeth had with both wit and class deflected and turned those attacks back on their source without becoming rude. He smiled—a ghost of one—when he remembered how the harridan, harpy, and hoyden all wrapped up into one that was Miss Bingley had always been dismayed when she could not discompose Miss Elizabeth, and he guessed she had often been unsure if she had been insulted by any of Miss Elizabeth's arch replies.

What had he, a gentleman, done while a tradesman's daughter tried to denigrate the daughter of a gentleman? Nothing! He had even agreed with some of Miss Bingley's paltry attacks! Another error he made was on the day after the assembly. Miss Bingley had commented on *Miss Eliza's* reputed beauty, even as she denigrated the woman's looks.

What had he done? Staying silent would have been better than uttering '*She* a beauty!—I should as soon call her mother a wit.' He had known his words at the assembly were untrue as soon as they passed his lips, just as he had known how false this statement was. Miss Bingley had preened, and seeing his mistake, Darcy had hidden from her for the next two days.

Miss Bingley's attacks against Miss Elizabeth had escalated after he confessed his attraction to Miss Elizabeth while replying to Miss Bingley at Lucas Lodge. How selfish he had been. Even though he was the cause of the intensified vitriol, he remained silent and allowed the shrew to keep attacking the woman he loved.

He shook these melancholy thoughts from his brain and realised that he had many amends to make. He was thankful all of his family would be in one place so he would be able to beg their pardon for his offences at one time.

Darcy would have desired the chance to apologise to the Bennets, especially Miss Elizabeth, but only the middle sister was in the area as she had married Richard's parson. In her letters to her brother, Gigi had *forgotten* to mention the presence of the Miss Bennets to him.

~~~~~~~/~~~~~~~

"Elizabeth, you seem out of sorts today," Lady Catherine noted after the two Bennet sisters had been welcomed into the house. "Should I have Mrs. Toppin prepare a chamber for you to rest in?"

"No, Lady Cat, I am well. I am only disappointed by a response I received from my father. I should not be, because he has been this way for as long as I can remember. It was foolish of me to think that he might change now." Elizabeth sighed resignedly.

"In my experience, a problem shared is a problem halved, but I will not force a confidence if you choose not to," Lady Catherine told Elizabeth gently.

"You have met my parents and have seen how they behave. You also met Lydia, my youngest sister, at Mary's wedding," Elizabeth stated.

"Yes, and I remember all of them," Lady Catherine agreed.

Elizabeth told Lady Catherine of her worries about Lydia being allowed to travel to Brighton where she would be chaperoned only by an equally silly girl—Colonel Forster's wife, who was not much older than Lydia. She explained how she had advised against it before she and her sisters departed for

Hunsford, and how she was opposed by both parents for very different reasons.

After explaining about the beseeching letter she posted to her father, begging him to reconsider allowing Lydia's trip, Elizabeth withdrew the curt, chastising response from her father and handed it to Lady Catherine.

"And this is all the answer you can expect to receive from your father? I wonder at his dismissing your concerns with such incivility. Are his peace and quiet worth his daughter's possible ruin?" Lady Catherine asked incredulously.

"As much as it pains me to say so, yes. So long as my father can sit in his study sipping his port while he is reading, the world could come to an end outside the door and he would not bestir himself," Elizabeth replied dejectedly.

"In my opinion, what you and Jane did with Kitty, having her ingratiate herself with her younger sister, will be a saving grace. I believe Mary told you how close we are to Brighton, and having seen and heard about your youngest sister, we can rely on her to boast to Kitty, who will keep us informed of any intemperate actions she might plan to take." Lady Catherine turned to where Kitty was sitting with Jane and Gigi. "Kitty dear, please attend us."

"Yes Aunt Cat?" Kitty said as she obediently joined her sister and Lady Catherine.

Lady Catherine did not miss Elizabeth's questioning look at Kitty's form of address. "It was my desire that Kitty address me as Aunt, and I would be most pleased if you," Lady Catherine looked to where Jane sat, "and Jane would address me thus." Both older Bennet sisters inclined their heads in acceptance.

"Kitty, you must make Lydia believe you are jealous of how much fun she is having, and to highlight what a boring time you are being subjected to here. Ask her to tell you of her fun so you may live vicariously through her. I am sure that if you tickle her ego, she will keep you informed of what she is up to. I believe that if she plans something scandalous, she will not be able to stop herself from boasting about it to you,"

Lady Catherine suggested, then waited while Kitty digested her speech.

"Now that I understand how brittle a lady's reputation is, and how fully her family will be tainted by association, I will do exactly as you suggest Aunt Cat," Kitty promised. Lady Catherine kissed Kitty on the cheek, and the beaming girl returned to her friend and sister, who had waited for her before continuing their conversation.

Elizabeth and Jane could see the attention Kitty was receiving was helping her to gain in confidence and improve her manners. Elizabeth felt guilt for the years when she ignored her sister, writing her off as *one of the silliest girls in all of England,* as her father would say while he made sport of Kitty and Lydia.

Her father was unable to see it, but Elizabeth was aware there was only one silly Bennet, and she was currently on her way to Brighton.

# CHAPTER 12

The Earl and Countess of Matlock, along with the Viscount and Viscountess Hilldale, arrived at Rosings Park on the first Wednesday in April. The occupants of Rosings Park and the Hunsford Parsonage welcomed the adults, but the babe Reginald Andrew Fitzwilliam—little Reggie—was the centre of attention.

He had a mop of sandy blond hair that looked just like his father's hair colour, and after six months he still had the Fitzwilliam blue eyes. Although his mother had blue eyes, they were not the deep blue the Fitzwilliams were known for.

Marie's parents, the Earl and Countess of Jersey, had been invited to join the family for Easter, but declined as they had accepted an invitation from their son's, Wesley De Melville, Viscount Westmore, in-laws and family.

After they changed from their travel attire, washed off the dust of the road, and saw little Reggie settled in the nursery, the Matlock party met Lady Catherine and Gigi in the largest of Rosings Park's drawing rooms.

Lady Elaine, the Countess of Matlock, looked across the room in wonder, happy beyond words at how her niece had recovered. Gigi and Marie sat chatting easily. "Cathy, you have worked wonders with our girl," Lady Elaine told her sister.

"As much as I would like to claim the credit, the truth is that the greatest improvements Gigi made were after she attended the Collins wedding in Hertfordshire with Richard and me," Lady Catherine revealed.

"What happened in Hertfordshire to be such a catalyst?" Lady Elaine enquired.

"Our Gigi met the Bennet sisters. The middle sister is the new Mrs. Collins. Some of her sisters joined her in March," Lady Catherine informed her sister.

"Are you referring to the sister William insulted and the older sister he separated from his friend Bingley?" Lady Elaine asked with raised eyebrows.

"The very same. The eldest, who holds the interest of your second son, is Miss Jane Bennet. She is a classic beauty, a willowy blond with blue eyes. She was hurt by our nephew's officious interference, but now she feels he did her a favour." Lady Elaine inclined her head as Lady Catherine continued. "I hope I helped her see that a man who loved her would not allow anyone to talk him out of his inclination." Lady Catherine waited, her happiness at having been so helpful evident while her sister assimilated the information.

"In other words, you helped her see that the man is capricious and is merely a boy. If she and Richard reach an understanding, they will have our full support, no matter what her connections or dowry may be," Lady Elaine stated resolutely. "What about this Miss Elizabeth?"

"She is a spitfire. Elizabeth is shorter than Jane—Miss Bennet—but no less pretty. Evidently, the mother has told her for years that she is nothing to her older sister because she has mahogany tresses and darker colouring. She is blessed with the greenest eyes you have ever seen and is extremely intelligent with a rapier wit. You will see for yourself soon enough when the Collinses and their three sisters arrive for tea. Anyone who thinks she is less than Jane in looks is blind or stupid, likelier both," Lady Catherine informed her sister.

"And they get along well with Gigi?" Lady Elaine verified.

"All of them do; they are very solicitous of our niece, but unlike that harpy Miss Bingley, they never fawn over her. She is treated like another sister by all four Bennet sisters," Lady Catherine explained.

"I thought from your letters that there would only be three? Do you mean there are three sisters here in addition to the parson's wife?" Lady Elaine asked.

"Correct. Mrs. Collins is Mary, the middle Bennet sister as was. Catherine Bennet—called Kitty—is the next youngest after Mrs. Collins; she turned seventeen this January past. She is residing at the manor house so Gigi is not alone. Gigi is close to all four of the sisters present, but more so with Kitty as they are closest in age. Kitty was a little shy at first and decided she would visit her sisters so as to not intrude on our reunion." Lady Catherine took a sip of her tea before it became cold.

"Is there not a fifth sister?" Lady Elaine asked, remembering what she learned at Christmastide.

"There is. She is but fifteen, a little girl in a woman's body. I also met her at the wedding. She is spoilt and has to be the centre of attention or she acts out badly. Unfortunately, she is nothing like her older sisters." Lady Catherine went on to explain the family dynamic. "The mother spoils her and encourages her pursuit of officers. The father ignores her, and never checks her. As if that were not enough, they allowed such a girl to go to Brighton to be around an encampment of militia officers_one of whom is that libertine Wickham!"

"You did say the father is supposed to be intelligent did you not Cathy?" Lady Elaine was amazed and disgusted at the same time that two such parents could be found in the same household.

"Now you will understand why the sisters who are here are worried that the youngest one will be caught up in scandal and ruin herself, and her family along with her. I will do anything within my power to stop that from happening." Lady Catherine vowed.

~~~~~~~/~~~~~~~

By the time Darcy entered his coach on Wednesday morning, he was feeling better about himself. He had accepted much—most—of what his relations had pointed out to him and now they would be able to judge how he had changed, based on his behaviour.

Would he be able to put away his mask? What about relating to people who were not of his station or those he was not acquainted with? Darcy had no problems interacting with his servants and the tenants at his estates; he treated them all well, so he firmly believed he was capable of both.

The question he had to answer for himself is why he treated other members of the gentry, from lower circles, with such disdain at times. He also had to reconcile his words about the Bennets' connections to trade with his own. Yes, he was uncomfortable in crowds, especially when he did not know the people, but that was no excuse; he was a gentleman after all.

It was not just his friendship with Bingley; he actively invested with some tradesmen. Not only that, but some of the businesses he owned, a grist mill, a brewery, and his shipping interests, were by very definition trades. Part of his introspection had been trying to answer that question for himself, though as of yet, he had not done so fully.

Darcy knew that he often had a problem when talking. He would make nonsensical statements and lose sight of the point he was trying to make. At other times, such as at the Meryton assembly, he might say something rude and inappropriate without meaning it. So, before he departed from Pemberley, he began writing down points that he would use when he made his apologies to the family. As his coach travelled south, Darcy studied his notes, adjusting or adding words that reinforced what he wanted to say to each member of the family.

He knew he needed to beg the Bennets' pardon as well, but he did not know when, or if, he would see them again, Mayhap he could write a letter, which would be a relief, as he was far more eloquent with his pen than his conversation. He would request that the sister who married Richard's parson post it along with hers. He felt it would be presumptuous of him to write to Mr. Bennet on his own; it was not as if they were intimates.

~~~~~~~/~~~~~~~

Both Bingleys were slack-jawed. Their normally mild-mannered brother Hurst had meant what he said. This very day, the Hursts departed for Winsdale, and when Caroline tried to inveigle an invitation, Hurst told her in no uncertain terms that she was not welcome—ever.

"Who will accompany me when I make visits and shop?" Miss Bingley whined.

She would not miss her sister; she would miss all the things that Louisa used to do for her. This was too much! Mr. Darcy remained at Pemberley, and now her sister was gone as well.

"We will have to hire a companion for you," Bingley suggested weakly.

"A companion! I am not a young ignorant girl like Miss Darcy. If I were to suddenly have a companion, all of my friends would think me on the shelf," Miss Bingley stated dismissively. "As I will soon be Mrs. Darcy, what need have I for a companion?"

It would have been the ideal time to inform his sister what Darcy had told him, but Bingley was too cowardly to anger his younger sister, since he did not have his older sister to mitigate the effects of a Caroline Bingley tantrum. He would have been hesitant to do so even were Louisa still present.

"Without a companion, how will you call on your friends, go shopping, or engage in the other activities you enjoy? If only my angel had loved me, we would have had someone to be with you when you needed," Bingley stated wistfully.

For a moment, Miss Bingley considered her brother's words. If he married, it would help alleviate her problems, but nothing was worth *her* family being aligned with those awful country mushrooms, the Bennets. "I dare say you do need to find a wife, an appropriate one for our station, not some fortune hunter from the wilds of Hertfordshire."

As was his wont, Bingley said nothing to refute his sisters' ridiculous statement. Without Louisa to help him, keeping Caroline happy was imperative. "Would you like to go visit Uncle Paul in Scarborough for Easter?" Bingley asked meekly.

"I do not want to spend Easter with our tradesmen relatives. We do not need the stench of trade around us. I am sure we will see Mr. Darcy soon," Miss Bingley stated assuredly. Her brother was unaware that she paid men to watch Darcy House.

Bingley was not so sure they would see his friend in the near term, but he hoped for such a happening as it would distract his younger sister and make his life easier. He wondered how badly his sister would explode in anger if she ever discovered he was still active in trade.

~~~~~~~~/~~~~~~~~

It did not take many minutes after the Hunsford party arrived for tea that the Bennet sisters saw the rectitude of Lady Catherine's words regarding her brother and his family. The Earl was a jovial man who exuded intelligence. The Countess was as pleasant and as welcoming as Lady Catherine, especially towards Jane. Lord Andrew and Lady Marie Fitzwilliam rounded out the party, and they were extremely affable as well.

'Mayhap there is hope for Mr. Darcy, as all of his nearest relations are so pleasant. Gigi says he is the best brother, master, and landlord. Yes, she is his sister, but I have heard the same from Aunt Cat and Mr. Fitzwilliam, and they have no reason to exaggerate. If he has truly taken the reproofs of his family to heart, mayhap I will enjoy Mr. Darcy's company for the first time since the day I met him and he slighted me so rudely," Elizabeth mused as she watched the interactions between her family members and the newly-arrived Fitzwilliams.

"Elizabeth," Lady Catherine called.

"My apologies Aunt Cat, I was wool-gathering," Elizabeth replied contritely. "Did you say something?"

"Do you want some more tea my dear?" Lady Catherine smiled.

"No, thank you, I am no longer thirsty after my first cup," Elizabeth replied.

"Aunt Cat?" Lady Elaine asked in amusement.

"Yes, with the Bennet sisters counted as Gigi's older sisters it made sense, did it not Sister?" Lady Catherine responded, her eyes gleaming with pleasure.

"In that case, you may call me Aunt Elaine, if and when you feel comfortable doing so," Lady Elaine granted.

Upon the arrival of the Bennet sisters, another of Lady Catherine's statements was proven true, for none of his arriving family missed the marked attention Richard was paying to the eldest Bennet sister. They observed that tender feelings seemed to be developing in both directions.

"Miss Bennet," Richard leaned closer to the lady so as to not be overheard.

"Yes Mr. Fitzwilliam," Jane said softly.

"Hypothetically, if one were to request a formal courtship with you, would he have to ride to Hertfordshire to ask permission of your father?" Richard enquired. As it always did when Jane Bennet was near, Richard's heartbeat faster as he breathed in her intoxicating scent.

"No Mr. Fitzwilliam. The hypothetical man would not have to address my father for two reasons. First, I am of age, and second, our brother Collins has permission in writing to act in our father's stead in all matters if needs be," Jane informed him, relieved her answer caused such a beaming smile from Richard.

Richard had both met and heard more than enough about the Bennet parents. He did not relish the thought of having to meet with the indolent man or coping with the effusions of the vulgar Mrs. Bennet. He would as soon ride into battle again.

"In that case, Miss Bennet, will you take a turn in the gardens with me?" Richard requested.

"It would be a great pleasure to take some air with you Sir." They both stood.

"We are taking a turn in the gardens," Richard informed the room. There was no missing the looks of pleasure on Richard's and Jane's faces as they departed, leaving little doubt as to Richard's purpose.

"Kitty, you and Gigi join them," Lady Catherine instructed. Then in a softer voice—still loud enough for all to hear, she said "As long as you can see them, you do not have to be close enough to hear them."

After the three ladies donned their shawls, the four made for the front gardens.

# CHAPTER 13

"Miss Bennet, you can be at no loss why I requested you to walk out in the garden with me," Richard stated.

"I am not sure of the reason for this great honour, although I find myself hopeful," Jane replied shyly. "After my last experience with a man, I would rather not make assumptions even after being given a strong indication of your intentions."

"Surely Jane, you must know I am nothing like the man who hurt you. No one, not even my parents, could turn me away from you—not that my parents would try to do so. I do ask advice when I feel I need it, but I do not rely on others to direct my actions or make decisions for me. I weigh advice with what I know, and if I am convinced that there is a better way, I will make a change, but it will *always* be my decision. You will find—if you have not already—that capriciousness is not an element of my character." Richard paused to assess his walking partner, the lady he hoped to make his partner in every facet of his life.

"If there is one thing I know about you Mr. Fitzwilliam," Jane began to answer.

"Richard, if you please," he interjected.

"Then you must call me Jane," Jane replied. She had missed the fact he had already done so. Her blush was caused by the pleasure from the deepening intimacy between them. "As I was saying, *Richard*, I had not known you very long when I understood that you were *nothing* like Mr. Bingley. As much as he seems to lack character, you have it in spades, so no, I would never think you like him. To make sure I do not allow myself to be misled a second time, I will make no assumptions."

"It warms my heart that you know I am nothing like anyone else. I am not in love with you yet, but I do have a tender regard for you, and I would like to see if—as I suspect it will—love develops between us. Jane Bennet, will you grant me a formal courtship?"

Both Jane's heart rate and her breathing sped up as Richard declared his regard and intentions. How happy it made her to be valued by such a man. "I find my feelings mirror yours. There is no love—yet, but I believe between us there is very fertile ground where love may sprout, blossom, and thrive. I have tender feelings for you, so yes, Richard Fitzwilliam, I most definitely accept your offer of a formal courtship."

Richard lifted both of Jane's hands, gently turned them over, and bestowed a tender kiss on the underside of each wrist. If Jane's heart had been beating fast before, now it felt like a drum was being played at great speed in her chest.

Kitty and Gigi, sitting on a bench on the other side of the garden from Jane and Richard, exchanged knowing looks as they saw Richard kiss Jane's wrists. "So romantic," Kitty sighed. "I used to think that only a man in regimentals would do for me, but now I hope to win the love of a good and honourable man regardless of his occupation."

"We will find such men; we just need to be patient and careful. No one wants to make the mistake I almost made," Georgiana stated introspectively.

"Come, you two," Richard called, "we are for the drawing room." He turned to Jane. "I have a very important question to ask of your brother," Richard told Jane softly.

"My brother will not dare to refuse you anything you ask," Jane smiled beatifically. "Mary would never allow him to impinge on my happiness, and even should he dare, I am of age. Just in case you needed reminding," Jane teased lightheartedly.

~~~~~~~/~~~~~~~

Though Wickham relished his regained freedom, there were a few major inconveniences. He could not run up any debts, nor could he trifle with any maidens. He was aware he was being watched, so he was forced to tamp down his inclinations.

It was one more sin he had to lay at Darcy and his family's door. Who were they to restrict his ability to live as he felt he deserved? From the day he had been flogged, he had attempted to formulate a plan of revenge, but so far nothing in his reach could be used to gain their attention or cause them to beg for that which only he could give.

Then, like a sign from the gods, he had been gifted with the person of Lydia Bennet. She was as stupid a chit as he had ever encountered, and he knew it would not take long to have her eating out of his hand.

Earlier that day, he had encountered her and the equally silly Mrs. Forster near the shops. How he would like to pluck Mrs. Forster before he scarpered to repay Colonel Forster for flogging him.

Lydia Bennet had batted her eyelashes at him and told him she knew what was being said about him in Meryton were lies spread by those who were jealous of him. Even Wickham, who lied with the best of them, could hear how ridiculous the chit's statement was, but of course he played along with her.

What made her even more attractive as a tool for revenge was the fact she had twenty pounds with her, which she boasted that her mother had given her without her father's knowledge. When he needed to make his escape, he would need her funds. Then she had revealed that her sisters were all at Hunsford.

Out of her inane chattering, he gleaned that one sister was married to the parson at Hunsford and the other three were visiting her. Mayhap he should pluck her or take her with him and abandon her in London; it would even the score with that uppity Miss Elizabeth who had snubbed him when he had been sure she was his for the taking.

A plan started to form. If he could convince her they were to elope, he could sell her to a brothel in London. As long as he did not despoil her, he could get an additional fifty pounds for a maiden, mayhap more for a gentleman's daughter. It was disappointing he could not enjoy her himself, but she would fetch so much more as a virgin and he desperately needed the funds.

Wickham knew he would have to be careful to avoid the watchers who seemed to be taking their duty seriously, day or night. It would force him to exercise patience and would require a longer-term plan than he would like, but he knew he would succeed. From the first assembly they both attended in Brighton and all those thereafter, he requested Lydia's first and last sets.

Lydia was flattered that the exceedingly handsome Mr. Wickham singled her out from among all the ladies available to him. She thought the slight crookedness in his nose made him even more handsome and was amused that Mr. Darcy had done him an unintended service in such a way. 'Yes,' she told herself with glee, '*I was not the first to marry, but I will be the next before my older sisters. I must write to Kitty; she will be so jealous that he prefers me,*' Lydia thought spitefully. In her opinion, Kitty deserved to be jealous, as she had not been as obedient as she should have been. Lydia forgave Kitty for her momentary disloyalty, but that did not mean she would not take pleasure in retelling of all her fun as she knew Kitty would likely cry again for being left behind.

One thing she was sure of was that Kitty would keep her secrets, as her next older sister would not want to lose her favour again. If she did, Kitty had been warned that her regard would be lost forever and she would never be allowed to visit so she too could dance with all the officers, save the ones she wanted for herself.

~~~~~~~/~~~~~~~

"Mr. Collins, may I have a word with you in private?" Richard requested as the four returned to the drawing room.

"Of course Mr. Fitzwilliam, please lead the way," Collins replied. Seeing his sister Jane's countenance when she returned from the garden, he had a fairly good idea what his patron wanted to discuss.

"My, my Jane, I have never seen you look this happy before, not even when..." Elizabeth stopped herself before she said the irresolute man's name. "Not even when another was calling on you did you ever look this happy."

"Which only proves that not only was he not in love with me as a man should be, but neither was I in love with him as I thought I was," Jane opined. "Yes, Lizzy, you are perceptive, and I am as happy as could be."

"Are you betrothed Jane?" Elizabeth asked as Mary joined them.

"Is the subject of the discussion our incandescently happy sister?" Mary asked.

"It seems so," Jane responded drolly. "And no Lizzy, I am not betrothed. We have not known one another long enough for that step...yet. Richard requested a courtship, and I accepted with much pleasure. We do not yet love one another, but we both have tender feelings for the other."

"Oh, I knew how it would be," Mary exclaimed louder than she intended, causing the older persons and Lord and Lady Hilldale to look at her quizzically while Kitty and Gigi giggled into their hands.

"Please allow us to inform everyone officially, which will clear up any question anyone might have about the grins you are seeing," Collins announced as he returned to the drawing room with a beaming patron in tow. Collins nodded to Jane, who joined the two men. "Mr. Fitzwilliam has requested a formal courtship from my sister Jane, and she has granted it. As I was given the authority by my cousin Bennet, I have conferred my consent and blessing." As Collins completed the announcement, Lord Andrew leapt from his chair and wrapped his brother in a bear hug.

"Everything of the best, *little* brother," Andrew clapped his brother on the back after he released him from the hug. "I am not sure you are good enough for Miss Bennet, but I wish you well, nevertheless."

"Andrew!" His mother swatted his arm playfully. "Let me hug my younger son."

Meanwhile, Lady Marie reached Jane and took both her hands. "I think I will enjoy having you—and the rest of your sisters—as my sisters," Marie stated.

"Please call me Jane," Jane requested as she accepted good wishes from Richard's sister. "You too My Lord," she addressed the Matlock heir.

"In that case, please call me Marie and my husband is Andrew," Marie averred.

While all the good wishes for future felicity were being conveyed, Lady Catherine rang for the butler and asked him to open some bottles of champagne. "Is she as good as she seems Cathy?" the Earl asked as he assisted his sister up from her chair.

"Better," Lady Catherine replied succinctly.

Lord Matlock knew his sister was not one prone to hyperbole, so he accepted her word without question. "In that case, I can see my younger son is to be very happy," he surmised.

By the time the hugs and wishes for the future were done, all of the younger set had agreed to address one another by first names_or, among the men, by last name or title, including Mr. Collins. The Earl and Countess also insisted that all of the Bennet sisters, including the one who had resigned that name, call them Uncle Reggie and Aunt Elaine. Mr. Collins was given leave to address both ladies with the appellation 'aunt' as well.

~~~~~~~/~~~~~~~

Later that evening, when the four residing at the parsonage returned home, the three sisters sat together in the sitting room while Collins read the day's correspondence. The tea became tea and dinner, and no one repined as a joyous time was had by all.

"Jane, when do you want to write to Mama and Papa?" Elizabeth asked.

"It is prudent to wait, I believe," Jane stated resolutely. "Papa will only make silly jokes, but Mama will invite herself here. You know she will."

"As much as I would like to tell you I disagree, I cannot," Mary agreed.

"I know you are correct," Elizabeth added.

"It is not that I think Richard will be discouraged by Mama's outrageous comments or her vulgar behaviour, but I would rather not put my hopefully soon-to-be family through that exhibition if I can help it," Jane told her sisters.

"We support you fully Janie," Elizabeth spoke for both younger sisters after receiving an emphatic nod from Mary.

Just then, Collins returned to the sitting room. "Will it be strange for you that your patron will become your brother if Jane and Richard wed?" Elizabeth asked.

After cogitating for a few moments Collins shook his head. "No Lizzy, it will not. I will not be the first clergyman who served a parish where a brother or another close relation is the patron, and I am sure I will not be the last. Fitzwilliam and I have an excellent working relationship, so I do not envisage that changing regardless of the familial connection."

"William and Richard have worked well together from day one, according to what my William told me while we were courting," Mary reported. "Nothing I have seen since we have been married has contradicted that. There are patrons and patronesses who try to interfere in the parish under their gift, thinking their wealth and position give them the right to do so. William would not stand for that, and from the beginning of his tenure it was never an issue."

Each of the residents drank a cup of tea and then retired for the night. Once Elizabeth had washed and changed, she knocked on Jane's bedchamber door and joined her when summoned to enter. "You will be a very happy woman, I believe," Elizabeth stated as she sat down on the bed next to her older sister.

"Yes, I dare say I will, if things progress to their natural conclusion," Jane replied.

"Jane, you cannot doubt it. Richard is an honourable and

resolute man," Elizabeth insisted. "He would not take the step he did tonight if he did not mean to propose to you at some point."

"Lizzy, I do not worry about that. I just refuse to anticipate a proposal until Richard addresses me," Jane explained. "Do you remember how Mama was proclaiming my wedding to Mr. Bingley to one and all before he had even requested a courtship? I never want to have expectations raised beyond reality again. Richard is courting me. When—if—he addresses me with his proposals, then, and *only* then, will I plan for the future."

"Mama's proclamations are part of the reason you do not want our parents notified, are they not?" Elizabeth guessed.

"They are. I know we are to respect and obey our parents, and I used to obey and respect blindly. I would never contravene an instruction from our parents if they gave a direct one, but Lizzy, am I a bad daughter to need some distance from them?" Jane wondered.

"If you are, then all four of us sisters here are the same as we all feel as you do," Elizabeth averred with certainty. "I was talking to Aunt Cat, and I agreed with her when she told me that respect should be earned and not merely expected. We can respect the roles of parents that Mama and Papa have, but as people, it saddens me to say that neither have done anything to earn our respect. In fact, the opposite is true."

"It must be hard for you to see Papa thusly, as you were always his favourite," Jane stated.

"At first it was. It has been some time now that I have seen Papa as he truly is," Elizabeth said with a sigh. "The fact that he places his own selfish desires above the welfare of his family was the last straw for me. I still love him as my father, but I cannot look at him any longer with the same admiration and respect I once did."

"If Richard proposes and I accept him, I will inform our parents then. If Mama cannot control her effusions and outbursts, then I will ask Richard if we can marry here or at his parents' estate in Derbyshire. I love Mama too Lizzy, but I will not allow my wedding to become about her and her desire to impress the neighbourhood. Does that make me selfish?" Jane asked sadly.

"No Jane, it does not!" Elizabeth exclaimed. "I would not want that if I were to find a man to marry. The only reason Mary was spared Mama's behaviour was Mama was so used to ignoring her that she did little or nothing to counter Mary's requests. She did not boast about the union far and wide in the neighbourhood, which was indicative of her lack of interest in Mary's marriage. It did not make sense, as the marriage secured Longbourn for our mother.

"Mary and I have discussed this very subject, and she was not sorry to be spared Mama's machinations and effusions. A wedding is supposed to be about the bride and groom. We know that in many ways Mama is an older version of Lydia, who is never happy unless she is the centre of attention," Elizabeth assured Jane.

"Speaking of our youngest sister, I hope Kitty receives a letter soon. I am sure Lydia is not behaving as she should. I will rest easier if I am proven wrong, but it pains me to say that I do not believe I will be," Jane stated.

"With her belief in Kitty's renewed subservience, coupled with Lydia's desire to make Kitty jealous, I am sure it will not be long before Kitty receives a letter," Elizabeth estimated. "Off to bed with me. Good night, and I wish you happy again. You deserve everything good that comes to you, my dearest sister."

"Thank you Lizzy. You deserve happiness too. Sleep well." Jane wished her sister a good night as they hugged, and thereafter Elizabeth made her way to her own bedchamber.

# CHAPTER 14

The following morning the three sisters who still bore the name Bennet, Mary, and Gigi were taking a turn in the gardens. This was, Elizabeth's second walk of the day, for she could not resist her early morning ramble. Far from objecting to walking again, she relished the additional exercise—for what others would call a hike she called a mere ramble.

"Still no letter from Lydia?" Mary asked.

"Nothing yet. I would have thought she would have been crowing about her *fun* from the first day, relishing the thought that I am languishing in Kent," Kitty replied.

"You know how careless Lydia can be. It is possible—if she wrote a letter—that she wrote the direction most ill," Jane guessed.

"What if Kitty wrote a letter to your youngest sister," Gigi suggested.

"That is a fine idea," Elizabeth affirmed. She turned toward Kitty. "You should write to our sister telling her what a terrible time you are having here. You need to make it sound like you are envious of her and beg for some news to relieve the monotony of your boring life without her."

Jane and Mary nodded their agreement. "I will write to her as soon as Gigi and I return to the manor house," Kitty said. "We will be ready to chaperone you and Richard this afternoon Janie."

"If you and Gigi would rather do something else, I am sure Mrs. Annesley would not object to filling the office," Jane offered.

"Kitty and I will be there gladly. Even were we busy, other

than Mrs. Annesley there are more than enough chaperones between the parsonage and Rosings," Georgiana noted.

"If you like, I will volunteer. I want to discuss Richard's opinions on the war," Elizabeth teased.

"No thank you very much! Kitty and Gigi will be fine chaperones," Jane returned with mock afront.

Elizabeth loosed her tinkling laugh. It made her warm inside to see how happy Jane and all of her sisters were. Jane had exorcised the ghost of Mr. Bingley; Mary was as happy as Elizabeth had ever seen her, with a husband that was her match in every way; Kitty was joyful to have escaped from Lydia's influence.

The sad truth was Lizzy realised how much happier they all were away from their parents and youngest sister. This was not how things were supposed to be. In Lady Catherine, they had found a kindly aunt, much like Aunt Maddie. She was sure when Aunt Maddie met Lady Catherine the two would get along well.

"It is time for us to return to the parsonage to take tea with William," Mary stated. "He will be home from visiting parishioners soon."

"Come Gigi, you may assist me with my letter to Lydia." Kitty took their friend by the hand, and after saying their farewells, the two skipped off towards the manor house while the other three turned and started the short walk to the parsonage.

~~~~~~~/~~~~~~~

"Did you complete all your estate business Richard?" Jane asked as the two sat on the terrace in the shade of an enormous ancient oak, sipping fresh lemonade.

Jane and Richard were at one end of the terrace, while Kitty and Gigi were on the other, so they could be seen but not heard. Kitty had reported her letter had been posted, and she had remembered to write her direction as the Hunsford Parsonage.

"Yes, I met with my steward and completed all of my

correspondence. I am able to return letters faster than my fastidious cousin Darcy, who likes to fill his missives with four-syllable words," Richard gave a wry smile.

"After talking to Aunts Cat and Elaine, I am convinced what your cousin did was not malicious. He was trying to save his friend heartache from what he thought was a match of unequal affections. I have been told I am too serene and I do not show my feelings for all to see plainly," Jane stated.

"Then my cousin was blind, for I am able to read your affections plainly." Jane blushed deeply at Richard's statement, for it told her Richard had no doubt her feelings were just as engaged as his. "You will not feel awkward with William—Mr. Darcy—here, will you?" he asked, changing the subject to allow them both to relax.

"No Richard, I will not, but thank you for being so solicitous of my feelings; it is greatly appreciated," Jane replied. "If one of us were to feel uncomfortable, it would be Lizzy." Jane placed her hand on his arm to stop what he was about to say. "She will feel that way for believing Mr. Wickham's falsehoods and repeating them to others. She knows she is not the first to fall victim to his lies and machinations, but she had always prided herself on her ability to read the character of others. Getting it so wrong for both men was quite a shock to her."

"We will keep an eye out when he arrives on Saturday. I am hopeful he has examined his actions critically. It will be clear soon enough after he arrives," Richard stated thoughtfully.

"Will you please tell me about your time in the army before you became master here Richard?" Jane requested.

Unable to deny her anything, Richard told her a sanitised version of his time in the army. He told her about his experiences on the Peninsula, and she thanked God he had not been seriously injured, or worse, before his return to England.

The more time the two spent together, the more they wanted to spend in each other's company. Neither had fallen in love with the other, but they were much closer than the day their courtship began. Without realising it, both were fast coming to the realisation that the other was his or her perfect fit.

For Jane, being with a man who valued her, all of her and not just her physical attributes, was much more fulfilling than her time with the men who had made inept attempts at courting her before Richard. The men who tried to court her complimented only her looks, and none of them had treated her as an intelligent being who was more than her physical attributes.

When she was with Richard, they spoke about anything and everything. He would occasionally allude to her beauty_he was not blind, after all_but it was seldom. Jane was interested in the history of the Kingdom, especially the Wars of the Roses, and discovered it was one of many interests they both shared.

Jane was not a bibliophile like her father or Lizzy, but she did read, and not only Gothic novels. She would read a novel occasionally but gravitated towards books of history and poetry.

~~~~~~~~/~~~~~~~~

"It seems my younger son has met his match," Lady Elaine said to her sister. The two older ladies were with Marie in the nursery, watching little Reggie try to pull himself up as he gripped the side of the cot.

"I had a feeling it would be so," Lady Catherine smiled.

"Catherine, have you been matchmaking?" Lady Elaine asked with raised eyebrows.

"Not really," Lady Catherine allowed.

"Aunt Cat!" Marie exclaimed, not too loudly as she did not want to frighten her son with a raised voice.

"All I did was give them the opportunity to know one another," Lady Catherine acknowledged. "I am not the one who caused that spineless Bingley man to abandon Jane."

"No, you were not Cathy," Lady Elaine agreed. "However, I did hear you encouraged her to come to Rosings Park with Lizzy rather than go to London."

"You make my point for me Elaine. I but gave them a

chance; everything else was and is up to them," Lady Catherine pointed out. "Richard did not confer with me before requesting a courtship and I did nothing to push him at her or her at him."

"The old Catherine would have simply ordered them to do her bidding," Lady Elaine teased.

"Do not remind me how ridiculous I used to be. Thankfully, I learnt discretion," Lady Catherine owned.

"It was noted at Snowhaven that you were taking a more active role in pointing William in the right direction. I was only surprised you waited as long as you did. Reggie wanted to take the boy in hand, but he deferred to your judgement in the matter. I am glad he did; it would not have gone well if William were not ready to hear what we needed to tell him," Lady Elaine opined.

"If he were not such a great, big, tall thing, I would have bent him over my knee," Lady Catherine revealed. It did not take long for all three ladies to laugh at the vision of William over his aunt's knee as she paddled him.

"He has always been polite to me," Marie added.

"Your rank is greater than his, so you would not have seen the disdain he used to—we hope used to—direct at those he considered below him in consequence while out in society. It was always a conundrum, as he treats his servants and tenants well, even warmly. Additionally, his close connection with the Bingleys never squared with his other behaviour," Lady Catherine explained.

"On Saturday, we will see if the boy has learnt anything from the richly deserved set down he received at Snowhaven," Lady Elaine stated.

~~~~~~~/~~~~~~~

"La, Harriet, Kitty is bored and sad in Kent," Lydia told her friend as she read the letter from Kitty. "After the way she treated me, she deserves no less. She says she has not received any letters from me, but I did send one…" Lydia tapered her speech off as a memory stirred. "Oh my, I sent it to Longbourn. I forgot to write her direction at the boring old parsonage. I am sure Mama or Papa will send it on one of these days."

"What does she say for herself?" Harriet Forster asked, glad she had Lydia with her rather than the too-innocent Kitty as she and Lydia were peas in a pod.

"Here, let me read from this point," Lydia found the first paragraph after Kitty's greetings.

*I am so sorry I was not solicitous of your feelings in Hertford-shire. Of course you deserve to be the first of us to marry. You are, as you say, the prettiest and liveliest of us all.*

"You see Harriet, she has realised my superiority," Lydia preened and then returned to reading.

*You were correct Sister! It is so boring here at this dingy old parsonage. No balls, assemblies, or fun of any kind. Worse, there is not a single officer anywhere to be seen. How I wish I were there with you and having fun with all of the officers. I envy you so very much Lyddie.*

*There is one way I can feel like I am there. If you tell me all about your fun and adventures, it will irk me that I am not there with you, but at least I will get some enjoyment in hearing what you are doing.*

*If I hear Mary moralise, or her husband read from Fordyce's Sermons again, I will pull all of my hair out, but Papa will not hear of me returning home early. If Jane or Lizzy asked, he would allow it, but you know how he is with us.*

"How can I not send her all of my news?" Lydia asked. "Will I not be a perfect sister to entertain mine?"

"Yes, you will Lydia," Harriet agreed.

'*I will be able to tell Kitty about my Wicky. He said to tell no one here, but he did not tell me I cannot tell Kitty. How jealous she will be that I will be the next to marry, and such a handsome man in a scarlet coat. I was willing to anticipate our vows, but my hon-ourable Wicky wants to wait until we are married. Only another sennight and we will start our life together. How I love him!*'

~~~~~~~/~~~~~~~

'*How stupid that Bennet girl is. Not only did she not believe what was put abroad about me in Meryton, but the emptyheaded doxy thinks I will marry her. As hard as it was, I resisted her offer to take her virtue. I have at least managed to convince her not to spend her money so I will have her twenty pounds, and then I will get at least another fifty pounds when I sell her.*

*Mrs. Younge will help me. That foolish woman still thinks I love her. At least it is useful to me as she will know the best place to sell the chit. Mayhap she will be able to help me auction her to some lordlings, and who knows how much I will get that way.'* Wickham's brain was actively engaged in planning.

It was a pity that his first liberty would not be until the next Wednesday. He would make his watchers believe he was asleep and then slip out and collect the ridiculous twit. He hoped she would be able to follow directions to Humboldt Square to meet the small, hired carriage that would take them to London. It would burn one or two pounds, but it was an unavoidable expense.

What a pity he would not be able to remain in England to exact his revenge on Darcy and his family as he wanted, but he would not risk spending the rest of his days in a debtor's prison. Knowing Lady Catherine, she would have him consigned to the Clink Prison, the worst of them all, and Wickham was not about to let that happen.

So far it seemed the silly girl had not mentioned a word to the Colonel's bit of fluff. He had relaxed more each day which passed since Lydia Bennet agreed to *elope* with him without Colonel Forster flogging him and throwing him back in the brig. At least she had not been so stupid as to blurt out their plan.

~~~~~~~/~~~~~~~

Darcy arrived at Darcy House on Grosvenor Square Friday afternoon as planned. He would leave for Kent at sunrise on the morrow. He instructed his butler to keep the knocker off the door, and that he was at home to *no one*!

It was well the master issued this instruction, because not an hour after arriving, Mr. and Miss Bingley arrived at the front door. Killion shook his head at the lack of class shown by banging on a door with the knocker down.

Darcy looked out of the side window in his study. *'Damn it, Miss Bingley must have paid someone to watch my house! Will that harpy never learn? My family was completely on point. I have overlooked her atrocious behaviour far too long.'* Darcy shook his head as the woman kept beating on his front door with her parasol's handle.

He opened his study door and beckoned Killion over to him. Darcy closed the door, as he did not want the orange monstrosity to hear his voice. "Killion, my order stands. Open the door—only a crack as she will try and push her way into the house—and have Thomson and Smithers behind the door so it will not open more than you want. Tell her if she does not remove herself, you will send a groom to summon the constable, as I am not home," Darcy instructed.

Killion bowed and left the study to execute the master's orders. He positioned Thompson and Smithers, two of the burliest footmen employed by Mr. Darcy, and then looked to the master. Darcy nodded once before closing his study door all but a crack.

Miss Bingley was about to strike the door again with her now-broken parasol handle when the door cracked open but not very far. She pushed with her shoulder with all of her might—which was not much—while her brother stood in the background not saying or doing anything.

"You hurt me, you oaf! Open the door immediately, Mr. Darcy will sack you as soon as he hears how you have treated his close friends," Miss Bingley shrieked at the top of her voice.

"Madame, if you do not vacate the premises, a groom will be sent to summon the constable and you *will* be arrested for trespassing. My master is not at home," Killion stated succinctly, and then nodded at the two footmen who pushed the door closed.

Miss Bingley had been trying to push the door again, so when it shut with the footmen's forceful push, she fell backward on the stones at the top of the steps leading from the street to Darcy House's front door, right onto her *derriere*.

She was about to have a tantrum sitting in front of Darcy House when her brother finally acted. He pulled her up, down the stairs, and bundled her into the Bingley coach. A group of watchers had gathered to view the spectacle; he realised they were all members of the *Ton*.

"My first action as Mrs. Darcy will be to sack that disrespectful man. Just wait until Mr. Darcy hears how one of his underlings treated me—us!" Miss Bingley raged as the carriage was driven back towards Curzon street.

Bingley had a sneaking suspicion the butler was under orders from his master but did not dare mention that to his sister, who was as angry as he had ever seen her.

Darcy decided to leave earlier than he originally planned. He did not want to take a chance the harridan would return early in the morning to try again.

~~~~~~~/~~~~~~~

Two letters for Kitty were delivered on Saturday morning. The older of the two had been addressed to Longbourn. From the dates on the franking, it seemed it had sat there for some days before someone—their father, perhaps—bothered to look at it.

As the parsonage party was breaking its fast, a large coach turned into the drive leading to Rosings Park. It seemed Mr. Darcy was about to arrive. Jane and Mary both looked at Elizabeth, who merely raised a questioning eyebrow.

"The past is behind us. There have been many misunderstandings between Mr. Darcy and me. I am responsible for several of them, so I will wait to see how he behaves and reserve judgement. I know my fault has been to judge too quickly and then stubbornly hold onto my opinions, to the point of defying logic at times. I will try to not repeat that error. My mind is open," Elizabeth claimed.

Her sisters hoped that was the case. Both were happy she was willing to acknowledge her faults. That in itself was a welcome change.

# CHAPTER 15

Darcy alighted from his travelling coach and a blond streak launched herself into his arms. "I have missed you so much William," Georgiana informed her stunned brother.

"Who is this wild woman who attacked me? What have you done with my shy sister?" Darcy asked in amazement. His sister was not merely back to how she had been pre-Ramsgate; she was far better. She looked him in the eye without flinching, something she had done rarely, even before Ramsgate.

"Come William," Georgiana tugged her brother's hand to lead him inside the house before Richard was able to say anything.

"Good to see you Cousin," Richard managed as Gigi pulled her brother past him.

"You too Richard," Darcy returned as he turned his head towards his cousin.

Darcy allowed his sister to lead him to the drawing room where his aunts, uncle, and other cousins awaited him. "William, it is good to see you. How are you Nephew?" Lady Catherine welcomed him first.

"Much better than I was at Christmastide and thereafter," Darcy stated to all in the room after his sister relinquished his hand. "Allow me to wash and change, and I will return to talk to all of you."

"Go, we will be here when you return," Lady Catherine allowed. "You are in your normal chambers."

Darcy walked forward and kissed his Aunt Catherine on the cheek, then repeated the same for his Aunt Elaine. He shook hands with his uncle, Richard, and Andrew, inclined his head to Marie, and then made his way to his suite, where Carstens was ready for him.

~~~~~~~/~~~~~~~

'I wonder if Kitty has received my letter?' Lydia Bennet asked herself. 'How she will envy me when she finds out that my Wicky is in love with me, and that we will elope on Wednesday next. Mrs. Wickham, how well that will sound! I will be married before Jane and Lizzy. What a joke! I wonder why my Wicky does not want to anticipate our wedding vows, for I know the girl that Captain Carter intends to marry has done so.'

Lydia imagined how much fun her future would be as the wife of her handsome husband. She had turned her twenty pounds over to the man for—as he stated—safe keeping, and she was gratified to have been able to prove that she trusted him as well as loving him.

She did not understand why they had to be so secretive, but she had obeyed his request and not mentioned their attachment to anyone in Brighton. Even Harriet, who was a kindred soul, had not been told a word of her attachment to Ensign Wickham.

It was another thing that angered Lydia on behalf of her soon-to-be husband. He had been demoted from Lieutenant to Ensign because of those slanderous lies told about him in Meryton. Even her mother, who usually supported her unquestioningly, had believed the defamation of her poor Wicky's character.

How was it that no one other than herself believed the stories were planted by that vile Mr. Darcy and his family? Had not everyone heard how ill Mr. Darcy had used his former friend? Mayhap it was one of the reasons her Wicky loved her; she was the only one who seemed to see the truth of the matter.

Not built for melancholy, Lydia returned to her gleeful thoughts of how jealous Kitty would be when she read the letter she had posted. If Kitty had been more loyal, she would have asked Harriet to include her in the invitation. Perhaps it was for the best, as Kitty would have taken away attention that was hers, though it would have been but a small amount as Kitty was so plain.

~~~~~~~/~~~~~~~

"I wonder how long Lydia's first letter sat at Longbourn before our father bestirred himself to redirect it to Kent?" Mary asked as the four sisters gathered in the sitting room to read the inane chatter they were sure would fill the pages of their youngest sister's missives.

"Let me start with the one that was sent to Longbourn," Kitty informed her sisters as she broke the seal. She cleared her throat and began to read.

*26 March 1811*
*Indigo House, Kindle Street, Brighton*
*Kitty,*

*How much fun you are missing while you are stuck with only our older sisters' company and let me not forget Mary's husband. Does he read from Fordyce's Sermons to you every day? If so, you deserve no less for ignoring me for our fun-killing older sisters.*

*Mary may have been first to marry, but it was to our father's heir so there is some solace in that. It was necessary for one of us to marry him so our mother would cease spouting about being thrown into the hedgerows. I never really listened as I knew I would marry before our father passed, and so I will, and before even Jane and Lizzy. La, what a joke it will be when I will go higher in order than my older sisters.*

*Oh Kitty, I have never seen so many handsome officers in one place. There has been one assembly so far, and guess what? Never mind, you will never guess. I danced every single set.*

*It was the first time I danced with Ensign Wickham. He is free from his unjust imprisonment based on the lies of that hateful Mr. Darcy. If I ever see that horrid man again, I will kick him as hard as I am able.*

*But I digress. I allowed three officers to kiss me at the assembly when they escorted me outside for some fresh air. One's hands started to wander most scandalously, but I told him I had to know him better before I would allow such. How glorious it was! Even better, there are dances almost every week! Can you imagine how much I will enjoy flirting freely with the officers in their scarlet coats?*

*Harriet and I visit the soldiers' encampment every day, and we spend time looking in shop windows and imagining all of the things we could buy. The street where we have been staying is the last one before the beach which lines the sea.*

*I have not gone sea bathing yet, but Harriet has convinced her husband to rent a bathing machine for us soon.*

*Do not be too jealous Kitty, for when you are able to visit me, I will find you a husband after I have secured mine.*

*Yours etc,*

*Lydia*

"It is worse than we feared," Jane worried. "What a thoughtless girl, to boast of her inappropriate behaviour and place all of our reputations at risk with her selfishness and stupidity."

"Lydia is far more wanton than I imagined her to be," Elizabeth stated as she shook her head in disgust at their youngest sister.

"Let us pray the next one is not worse than the first," Mary added.

Kitty broke the seal on the second letter and began to read:

*4 April 1811*

*Indigo House, Kindle Street, Brighton*

*Oh Kitty,*

*I am bursting to tell you all, as I am not allowed to share my good news with anyone in Brighton. You are not here so I may tell you.*

*I am in love with the most amiable and handsome man! Let me start at the beginning. If you received my first letter you will know of the first assembly I attended. At the ball the following week, the man of my dreams asked to dance with me twice. Twice, Kitty! He singled me out for such notice.*

*You may be wondering who this paragon is, so I will tell you, it is Mr. Wickham, the one on whom all in Meryton—even his former favourite Lizzy—turned their backs so unjustly.*

"How can that girl be so blind?" Elizabeth asked exasperatedly.

"She is like Mama in that way. She only sees that which she chooses to see," Kitty stated, demonstrating perspicacity her sisters had never before credited to her.

"Read on Kitty," Mary instructed.

*He loves me too, but he has told me I am not allowed to mention our connection to anyone in Brighton, given how unfairly his Colonel and the men he had counted as friends treated him in Meryton. He tells me I am his only true friend.*

*We are to be married! On Wednesday coming, we will elope. Oh how romantic it will be! He has duty until Wednesday morning, and so we will not be able to leave until Wednesday night. How I would love to see Harriet's face when she finds the note I will leave. As much as I want you and my other sisters to attend my wedding and to bask in the glow of your envy for my catching such a man, it will not be possible.*

*Do you know he is such a gentleman he refused to anticipate our wedding vows when I offered? My Wicky looks after me so well; he is protecting me by keeping my twenty pounds safe until we leave.*

*I know well Mama will be in raptures when I return home as Mrs. Wickham. How well that sounds! I am sure you are green with envy by now Kitty.*

"Lydia offered to find me a husband. For my part I have no interest, as I do not like her way of finding a husband," Kitty spat out as she broke from reading the offensive letter.

"Please finish her drivel so we may decide how to proceed," Elizabeth requested. "Her thoughts fly from one subject to the next with no connection—stupid, stupid, thoughtless girl."

*We are to London first. My Wicky tells me that nasty Mr. Darcy has finally agreed to pay him the money he cheated him out of. I will stay with a kindly aunt of my Wicky's while he goes to collect his money from that dreary man, and then we will make for Gretna Green.*

*At least I experienced sea bathing with Harriet. It was wonderful Kitty. The machine is pushed out into the seawater by two horses. There was a servant who helped us dip in the sea. You cannot be seen from the shore thanks to the barrier built onto the machine. What a joke! We were as naked as the day we were born! I am sure you would have loved to bathe in the sea.*

*Wish me happy Kitty, as the next time you see me, I will be Mrs. George Wickham.*

*Yours etc,*

*Lydia*

"What is that girl thinking? That is the problem—she does not think!" Elizabeth answered her own question.

"At least she believes she is in love with him and he with her," Jane stated.

"We need to make for Rosings now. Lady Catherine has the means to deal with him. Her assistance is needed," Mary opined.

"Will she not be disgusted and dismiss us because we are her sisters?" Kitty asked in concern.

"No Kitty, she loves to be useful, and she and her family hate Wickham for the way he has imposed on them and others over the years," Mary averred.

Kitty folded the letters and the four donned their outerwear. Mary left a note for her husband on his desk before they departed in case he returned home from parish business and found his wife missing.

~~~~~~~/~~~~~~~

Darcy had returned to the drawing room and was about to extend his apologies to his family when the butler announced Mrs. Collins, Miss Bennet, Miss Elizabeth, and Miss Catherine.

It astounded him to see the four sisters. He knew one was married to Hunsford's parson, but no one had informed him that her sisters were visiting, especially not the enchanting Miss Elizabeth Bennet. Upon seeing her, all of the feelings for her that he had tried to tamp down returned with full force. While soaking in the sight of her, he noticed the looks of distress on all four women.

"My goodness," said Lady Catherine, who also noticed the looks of consternation on the sisters' faces. "What has happened? Is someone ill?"

"Were that the case, Aunt Cat, it would be far better than the reality," Elizabeth replied as a single tear ran down her cheek.

Darcy's head snapped around, for Elizabeth had just addressed his Aunt in a very familiar way. He was about to open his mouth and insert his hessian into it when he saw his aunt open her arms and enfold all of the Bennet sisters in a hug.

"Do you need privacy to discuss what has happened?" Lady Catherine asked.

"No thank you Aunt Catherine, it concerns one well known to all of you," Jane Bennet replied.

Darcy was thankful he had held his peace, for there was a level of intimacy between his relations and the Bennet sisters of which he had previously been unaware. The irony of his almost action when he wanted to apologise for his officious and prideful behaviour of the past was not lost on him. He acknowledged to himself he had work to do yet on his attitudes and judgmental ways. If only he were the one who was allowed to offer succour to Elizabeth. In his mind—for some time now—she was Elizabeth, not Miss anything.

Lady Catherine urged the sisters to sit, which they did on a sofa next to her. Darcy did not miss his cousin Richard's moving to stand protectively behind Miss Bennet, nor how his action seemed to comfort her.

"I finally received letters from Brighton," Kitty informed the group. "The first one is almost a fortnight old as Lydia posted it to Longbourn, where it was not forwarded for some time. The second is the troubling letter."

"May I read it?" Lady Catherine requested gently. Kitty handed over the letter. Richard moved to stand behind his aunt to read over her shoulder. He was soon joined by his father and Darcy.

Before anyone else could react, Darcy spoke. "This is my fault. If I had not remained silent about Wickham's propensities while I was in Meryton..."

"You take too much on yourself Sir," Elizabeth responded. Darcy's head swung toward Elizabeth, and his eyes locked with hers. "Lydia was informed about Mr. Wickham after Aunt Cat and Richard visited Colonel Forster."

"She refused to believe the facts about the man," Mary continued. "No matter what we, or anyone else in Meryton, pointed out, she clung to the stubborn belief it was all lies. You read her words, so you can see for yourself the depths of our youngest sister's descent."

"Most to blame are our parents, especially my father..." Elizabeth explained all to those in the room who were unfamiliar with their father's lackadaisical way of parenting and their mother's indulgence of her *baby*. "We understand why you were reticent to anger Mr. Wickham, given his actions against Gigi."

Seeing the thunderous look on her brother's mien, Georgiana stepped in. "*I chose* to tell them Brother. They are all my particular friends, sisters of the heart. In fact, Kitty is resident at the manor house so I have someone of my own age with me."

"I am not the vapid girl you met in Meryton Mr. Darcy," Kitty stated challengingly as she saw the hint of distaste forming on his countenance.

Her statement rocked Darcy. He shook his head, wondering if he would ever learn to stop judging others before acquainting himself with the facts. "Please accept my apology

Miss Catherine. It is the first of many I owe. If I may before we proceed?" Darcy looked to his Aunt Catherine and Richard.

"Go ahead William," Lady Catherine granted.

"My plan was to apologise to all of the family," Darcy indicated his family members. "I knew I needed to make my apologies to the Bennets as well, but I just did not think it would be at the same time."

Elizabeth shook her head. Was she dreaming? Was the proud, insufferable Mr. Darcy humbling himself before all of them? She caught herself and remembered she had promised to be less judgemental. She needed to listen first, and then she would decide how to act.

"When I departed Snowhaven, you can well imagine how angry I was. I tried to reject everything out of hand for which you, all of you, had called me to account. Once the anger dissipated and I was able to consider what you actually said, I reviewed my actions as they might be viewed by a third-party observer. The deeper I delved, the more I saw how wanting my behaviour was.

"I have been a selfish being all my life, in practice, and indeed in principle. As a child, I was taught what was right, but I was not taught to correct my temper. I was given good principles but left to follow them in pride and conceit. Unfortunately, as an only son—for many years an only child—I was unintentionally spoilt by my parents, though they themselves were good. My father, in particular, though all that was benevolent and amiable, allowed me to become selfish and overbearing; to care for none beyond my own family circle; to think meanly of all the rest of the world; to devalue their sense of worth compared with my own without correcting me," Darcy admitted.

"When my sister passed away and my late brother withdrew into his grief, he never had the conversations he intended to have with you William," Lady Catherine shared. "When we have time, I will tell you more, but we have pressing issues to address." Lady Catherine inclined her head to the four sisters.

"Then allow me to apologise to all of you for my *insufferable*," he looked directly at Elizabeth, "and wrongheaded behaviour. When we have more time, I will apologise to each of you individually."

"Thank you William," Lord Matlock replied for his family. "We are relieved you have been able to come to these conclusions."

"On behalf of my sisters and myself, we accept your initial apology," Jane spoke for her sisters.

"If you knew all I have done, you would not be so quick..." Darcy started to reply to Miss Bennet in particular.

"We do know *all* Mr. Darcy, but now is not the time nor the place to discuss it," Jane stated firmly, and Darcy inclined his head in acknowledgement.

"Now, back to the issue at hand. On Monday, Richard and I will make for Brighton and put this libertine where he belongs—in the Clink Prison for the rest of his wasted life," Lady Catherine stated, brooking no opposition should one have been so inclined.

"Elizabeth and I will accompany you to take charge of our sister," Jane stated. Her statement was not up for debate, either.

"If you would allow me, I would like to join the party. If I had not enabled him for so long, we would not have to deal with this situation now," Darcy requested.

And so it was decided, on Monday two carriages would make the three-hour journey to Brighton. Mrs. Annesley would accompany the Bennet sisters as a chaperone.

# CHAPTER 16

"**M**rs. Collins, Miss Bennet, Miss Elizabeth, and Miss Catherine, may I beg a moment of your time before you return to the parsonage?" Darcy requested.

The four looked to one another and Jane nodded.

"You may use the parlour opposite William," Lady Catherine said, guessing he was about to ask which room he could use. "To observe propriety, you will keep the door semi-open, and Mrs. Annesley will sit in the hall."

The sisters sat together on a settee while Mr. Darcy paced back and forth for a little while. Elizabeth suspected it was not a manifestation of his pride or disdain as she had thought in the past, but that he was trying to order his thoughts.

Once he had a good idea of what he wanted to say, Darcy took a seat opposite the four sisters. "It takes me a while to find the words I want to use. When I talk without thought, it often comes out nothing like I intend." Darcy paused, and Elizabeth had the decency to feel some shame for her past misjudgements of him and his motives. "A prime example was the first night we met. When Bingley was trying to cajole me into dancing, rather than consider my words, I unleashed a vile and untrue insult against you Miss Elizabeth. All I was trying to do was make Bingley leave me be, but rather than say what I actually meant, I insulted you in the worst of ways. For my intemperate and false words, I beg your pardon Miss Elizabeth."

"Thank you, both for the explanation and the apology Mr. Darcy. I do forgive you fully," Elizabeth granted. "I need to ask your forgiveness for allowing that blackguard with the silver tongue to pour poison in my ear about you and repeating his lies when I should not have," Elizabeth returned.

"There is nothing to excuse Miss Elizabeth. As you now know, he has manipulated and fooled many young ladies, including Gigi, and I had given you no reason to be suspicious of his words against myself," Darcy allowed.

"Although I told my friends and family, your words did not harm me, it was a lie. My vanity was wounded, and it led me to suspend my good judgement. I was looking for anything to confirm my bad opinion of you." Elizabeth looked at Jane, who inclined her head. "There were not a few, one of whom is in this room, who told me how improper it was for Mr. Wickham to share confidences with me on so short an acquaintance. In addition, there were glaring contradictions which, had I not refused to look at them, I should have seen."

"There is nothing for me to forgive, but if you will feel easier, then I forgive you unreservedly," Darcy inclined his head towards Elizabeth. "Speaking of contradictions, it has been brought to my notice how contradictory, hypocritical even, my behaviour was towards the Bingleys versus the rest of society. I derided your connections along with Miss Bingley, all the while not pointing out to her that she is below you in society. All of her pretentions cannot change the fact she is but the daughter of a tradesman.

"That fact is not the crux of the matter. It is her behaviour. That I—a supposed gentleman—stood idly by as she denigrated you and your family was beyond the pale. I am sorry if my silence gave the impression I agreed with her, for I most certainly did not. That leads me to the apology I owe to you Miss Bennet," Darcy bowed his head to Jane.

"Before you go into details Mr. Darcy, I am well aware you did what you thought was best for your friend. *Like you*, I do not wear my heart on my sleeve." Darcy coloured at Jane's statement, remembering how Lady Catherine and others had made that exact point to him. "Do not make yourself uneasy Mr. Darcy; in the end you did me a favour."

"I do not understand your meaning. How was I of service

to you?" Darcy asked in confusion.

"I will ask you the same question Aunt Catherine asked me. If you truly loved someone, would *anyone* be able to talk you out of your inclination?" Jane challenged.

Darcy's gaze immediately shifted to Elizabeth, who blushed deeply. That moment of clarity forced her to understand he was not looking at her to find fault; he *admired* her! "No Miss Bennet, no one would be able to turn me away from one I truly loved," Darcy stated, his gaze never breaking away from Elizabeth's.

"There is your answer Mr. Darcy. As has been pointed out to me if I had discovered Mr. Bingley's capriciousness after we married it would have been too late. Once I realised he does not have the backbone a man should, it did not take long for the love I thought I felt for him to dissolve," Jane stated emphatically.

"It is good you know my intention was not malicious. That leads me to the apology I owe all of you, the rest of your family, and your neighbours in Meryton. I behaved like a prig while visiting your shire. As Aunt Cat pointed out, I live in a similar neighbourhood, and interact perfectly amiably with the denizens of Lambton.

"I am not trying to excuse my actions, but to give you some insight into my character. I believe my actions were a defence mechanism. As soon as I hear people discussing my wealth, my estate, or my connections while ignoring me as a man, I put my mask in place. I freely acknowledge how incongruous my behaviour was for a long time. I treated you all as if you were fortune hunters, though you never gave me reason to believe that—while I said nothing to Miss Bingley who *constantly* demonstrated that she was." Darcy summed up, then went still as he waited for the sisters' verdict.

After receiving nods from her three sisters, Jane addressed Mr. Darcy. "We forgive you for all of your transgressions, real and perceived, and hope as we move forward, we may all start again. We feel very close to your family, so it would be pleasing to have a similar connection with you," Jane granted on her behalf and that of her sisters.

~~~~~~~/~~~~~~~

"Wicky," Lydia cooed. She did not notice how the man winced when she called him that. "How jealous Kitty will be when she receives my letter."

"**WHAT**!" Wickham grabbed Lydia's arm. "I told you to tell no one about us," Wickham roared.

"Wicky, you are hurting me," Lidia cried. "You said to tell no one in Brighton, and I did not. Kitty will tell no one, she has *always* kept my confidences." Wickham released the chit's arm. "She is bored and upset in Hunsford and will be relieved to have something to entertain her. She will be happy for us and will tell not a soul."

"You told her we would leave Brighton on Wednesday night?" Wickham asked.

"Yes, it is what you told me," Lydia confirmed.

Wickham was forced to reconsider his options. It would be far more risky, but he would slip away in the early hours of the morning during his Monday to Tuesday duty. By two in the morning, his fellow officers would all be asleep. He had a few drops of laudanum he had been saving to use when he could suffer this piece of fluff's inane chatter no longer. He would put a drop in each of his fellow officers' tea. Even if it did not put them to sleep, they would be too groggy to stop him.

"I find that I am unable to live without you, Lydia my love. I am moving the elopement to Monday night, or rather early Tuesday morning. Do you remember my instructions for Wednesday night?" Wickham asked.

"Yes Wicky," Lydia confirmed excitedly.

He explained she was to be in the square near the Forster's house a few minutes before two on Tuesday morning. "Do you understand the new instructions my dear?"

"I do, my darling Wicky. I am so excited." Lydia would have liked to have Kitty know ahead of time, but she would write, and Kitty would receive her letter on Tuesday when she and her love were already on their romantic journey.

Wickham had to use all of his self-control to not hit the stupid girl. If he did not need the money he would get for her, he would take her money and leave her behind in Brighton. Wickham had written to his other hanger-on, Mrs. Agnes Younge, asking her to make some discreet enquiries about how much a brothel would pay for a maiden.

To his relief, Agnes had written to say a maiden who was not a gentlewoman would net him about fifty pounds. An unspoiled gentlewoman might gain him a hundred pounds or more.

He would have liked to organise an auction, but time was not on his side. He would negotiate for as much as he could, then start his journey to leave the shores of England forever. He was sure there would be rich pickings for one such as he in the Americas.

~~~~~~~/~~~~~~~

On Sunday morning before church, not long after the sun peeked above the eastern horizon, Andrew, Richard, and Darcy took an early morning ride. "Richard, may I ask you something without giving offence?" Darcy asked.

"Go ahead, out with it," Richard agreed.

"Is there something between you and Miss Bennet?" William enquired.

"And what if there is?" Richard replied with asperity. "Do not mistake me for your puppy Bingley who you are able to direct and have him follow your whims. I would be very careful what the next words out of your mouth are about the lady I am courting and who will be my wife one day!"

"I have no intention of trying to interfere in your relationship with Miss Bennet," Darcy assured his cousin who visibly relaxed. "As much as I understand your thinking thusly based on my past behaviour, I have learnt I am the last one to advise on matters of the heart. The question was but for me to confirm my suspicion based on observing the two of you reacting to each other yesterday."

"Given the vehemence of your reaction to William, am I to infer that my *little* brother is finally ready to admit he is in love with Jane?" Andrew asked as he grinned widely.

"Younger brother, yes, but I am not smaller than you Andy," Richard returned. "And yes, that is what it means. How could one not fall in love with her? She is so much more than her beauty. Do you know I have been thinking about her for some years now?" Andrew and Darcy looked at Richard in question. He explained how he and their aunt had met the two older Bennet sisters at the Gardiner Trading Company a few years back. "As you can see, Bingley never stood a chance with *my* Jane."

"You said you were courting; when did it commence?" Darcy asked.

"Only a few weeks ago, but when you know you know," Richard explained. "I intend to pay my addresses after we rescue her youngest sister. On that subject, before I forget, Aunt Cat wants to depart this evening. She would not travel on the Sabbath unless she felt it was imperative." Darcy nodded, indicating his understanding of the change.

"I wish you all of the best, truly Rich. I think Jane will make a wonderful wife for you," Andrew stated as he slowed his mount so he could ride next to his brother. Darcy took up station on the other side of Richard's horse.

"William, if I did not know better, I would say I am not the only one in love with a Bennet sister," Richard challenged.

"You are not wrong. I used to worry about raising her expectations, but it seems I only raised my own as she dislikes—disliked—me intensely. We have all begun again, so I can only hope she will see I am not the same man she met in Hertfordshire last year. If I had proposed to her, she would have refused me. I was so blind," Darcy acknowledged.

"William, if I may change the subject. Aunt Cat wants to invite Bingley and his sister here for a *chat*," Richard informed his cousin. There was no missing the look of confusion on his cousin's face, and Richard grinned. "When we return to the house—well after church—Aunt Cat will explain everything."

~~~~~~~/~~~~~~~

After an enjoyable Sunday service conducted by Mr. Collins the week before Easter, everyone walked back to the manor house as one large group, as the Hunsford party had accepted an invitation for tea and dinner.

Kitty and Gigi walked ahead. Elizabeth found herself last, not a normal position for her when walking, and it did not take long before she sensed a presence next to her. Based on the smell of sandalwood and spice, Elizabeth guessed it was Mr. Darcy.

"Do you object if I walk with you Miss Elizabeth?" Darcy enquired.

"I have no objection Mr. Darcy," Elizabeth granted. He offered his arm, and she gently laid her delicate gloved hand on his strong forearm. Neither said anything for a little while.

"Are you usually silent when you are walking?" Darcy asked with a grin, twisting her words from their dance at the Netherfield Ball.

"I am at your disposal Sir. I will talk about any subject you desire," Elizabeth returned playfully. She had just made two important discoveries. Mr. Darcy had a sense of humour, and he did not mind jokes at his own expense.

"I could comment on the number of trees, and you could say something about how pleasant nature's décor is," Darcy smiled fully, revealing his dimples to Elizabeth for the first time.

"Please Mr. Darcy, let us talk about something that does not remind us of that unpleasant dance," Elizabeth asked quietly.

"It was not wholly unpleasant for me as I was dancing with you. It only became such when *his* name was mentioned." Darcy realised he had just made an overt declaration of his feelings and hoped he had not pushed her away.

Unbeknownst to him, Elizabeth was not willing to consider his statement at that moment. "It is to my shame I ever defended that scoundrel," she stated.

"We have already canvassed that subject, and you have received my unreserved pardon as you have granted me yours, so let us move beyond the unpleasant past," Darcy suggested. "My aunt tells me you enjoy walking along the paths in the wooded area near the parsonage, most especially the area around the glade."

"Aunt Cat is correct; it is my favourite morning walk," Elizabeth acknowledged.

"Would you object if I were to join you from time to time?" Seeing her surprise, he rushed to clarify his request. "I have no nefarious purpose. I think if we are to become comfortable with one another and move past the misunderstandings that plagued our time in Hertfordshire, we need to come to know one another better."

"In that case, I have no objection," Elizabeth allowed.

A little ahead of them, Jane and Richard were walking together. As soon as Jane placed her hand on Richard's arm, it felt right. She no longer had any doubt that she was in love with Richard Fitzwilliam.

With the depth of feelings Jane felt for Richard she was more certain than ever that she had not been truly in love with any other. She never could commit her life to anyone other than Richard. If Richard asked, she would accept him as long as she knew he loved her in return—which she already suspected. She and Lizzy had sworn they would only marry for the deepest love, and no amount of wealth would sway either from their course. They did not talk; words were superfluous. He did not miss the way she lit up when she placed her hand on his arm, nor did she miss the loving looks directed at her.

Once everyone had seated themselves in the drawing room and Marie returned from checking on little Reggie, Lady Catherine served tea and cakes to her family and friends. After the last crumbs of cake were consumed and the final drops of tea drained, Lady Catherine rang the bell, and two maids cleared the tea service away. She nodded at a footman posted by the door and he closed them behind him as he exited.

"William, Richard mentioned on your ride this morning about my wanting to invite the Bingleys to Rosings Park, but he did not explain my reasoning." Lady Catherine verified and Darcy nodded in confirmation. "I think these will explain much." Lady Catherine handed Darcy the letters Jane had permitted her to share.

As Darcy read, his visage went from calm to thunderous fury in but seconds. "How dare that shrew make claims about Gigi like this! Now I am doubly pleased I did not grant her access to Darcy House," Darcy spat out angrily.

"Explain William," Lord Matlock commanded. Darcy told them about the ill-fated mission Miss Bingley had undertaken to Darcy House the Friday he had stopped over. His telling led to not a little laughter at the picture of the woman sitting in front of the closed door.

"Are you telling me the harpy had people spying on your home?" Lady Catherine exclaimed in disgust. "Are there no depths to which the woman will not sink? It makes putting her in her place all the more imperative."

"You have no idea how angry I was when Jane informed me of that woman's absolute temerity in using my name to further her lies," Georgiana stated pointedly. "Please tell me I will never have to endure her company again."

"You will not Gigi," Lady Catherine assured her surrogate daughter. "When Aunt Elaine is done with her, she will not bother you or anyone else in society again."

"Now, if you are able to work on our youngest sister and parents, we," Elizabeth indicated her sisters who were nodding in agreement, "will all be most pleased."

"Give me time," Lady Catherine returned, only half in jest. "Jane and Lizzy, you will be ready to depart at five?"

"Yes Aunt Catherine, we will be," Jane confirmed.

"Mr. Collins, you understand the reason I feel we need to depart this evening, do you not?" Lady Catherine asked.

"I do and have no issue with it," Collins assured her. "It

has always been acceptable to travel on the Lord's day when there is cause, and the good name of Lydia and her family is an excellent reason."

Darcy asked Richard if he could avail himself of his study to write a note to Bingley, and Richard did not hesitate to grant his cousin's request. Darcy penned an invitation to the Bingleys for the Wednesday after Easter. Darcy pointedly noted to Bingley they were not welcome to arrive before then and requested a note of acceptance or rejection to be sent back with the messenger who would carry the note to Curzon Street.

Just after five that evening, two coaches—neither with coats of arms on the doors—departed Hunsford for Brighton.

# CHAPTER 17

The two carriages arrived at the Blue Parrot Inn in Brighton at about eight that evening. The drivers had slowed once daylight began to wane, but the full moon cast enough light for them to drive safely.

At his Aunt Catherine's suggestion, Richard had sent a rider out that morning to secure lodgings at the Inn. Much to the landlord's pleasure, they rented all of his rooms.

Lady Catherine, Mrs. Annesley, and the two Bennet sisters were on one floor, while Darcy and Richard were on another. Lady Catherine and Mrs. Annesley shared one of the suites, while Jane and Elizabeth shared the other.

The first thing Lady Catherine did was to direct the landlord to send a runner to Indigo House on Kindle Street with a note for Colonel Forster. If Lydia were to observe the boy, he would not arouse her suspicion, as he was not someone she would have seen before. In addition, it was not out of the ordinary for the commander of a unit to be summoned from home late at night.

Little more than an hour later, an unhappy Colonel Forster arrived at the Blue Parrot. He was shown to a private sitting room, where he was welcomed by his friend Richard Fitzwilliam. He looked around, surprised, and greeted Lady Catherine, Mr. Darcy, and the two older Bennet sisters.

"This must be about Wickham," the Colonel assumed correctly. "What has he done now? He has raised no suspicions in the men I have watching him."

"It is not what he has done Colonel, but what he is about to do and with whom," Lady Catherine informed the commander of the Derbyshire Militia. By way of explanation, she simply handed him Lydia's letter.

The more the Colonel read, the redder his face grew. "I will flog him within an inch of his life this time!" Colonel Forster exclaimed.

"As much as he deserves such, I believe if we act prematurely, he will simply claim it was all in Lydia's head and disavow any connection to her," Elizabeth opined.

"Elizabeth has the right of it. He needs to be caught in the act," Lady Catherine stated.

"If Wickham finds out she wrote to her sister, he may very well advance his timetable," Darcy surmised.

"In that case, we need to keep both of them under surveillance, unobtrusively, at all times," Richard stated. "We must take care that Wickham not see any of us, but I understand my old unit is here relaxing after deployment on the continent. The Colonel is a good friend of mine, and while it will make for a late night, I will send a note to him asking for his assistance."

Within minutes, the messenger boy, who had never seen a guinea before, never mind two, was on his way to the encampment of the Royal Dragoons. Just before eleven, Colonel Grant Atherton walked into the sitting room and slapped his former comrade-in-arms on the back.

"Only for you would I leave my wife and a warm bed at this ungodly hour. You know I would do anything for the man who saved my sorry hide in battle, so tell me what you need Fitzwilliam." Colonel Atherton pre-emptively vowed his assistance.

Colonels Forster and Atherton, acquainted from the time they served together with Richard, greeted each other affably. They had been reunited some days after Atherton and his unit had arrived in the area. It did not take long for Richard to explain the problem. "Do you have men who could do what we need Atherton?" Richard asked.

"I do, and they will enjoy sharpening their skills without anyone shooting at them," Colonel Atherton assured his friend. "As soon as I return to the encampment, I will send a group dressed as labourers to watch each of the two. They will be inconspicuously dressed. It will be my pleasure to help rid our army of one so unworthy of the uniform."

The two colonels departed, and the weary travellers finally made ready for bed.

~~~~~~~/~~~~~~~

On Monday morning in London, there was a loud screech from Miss Bingley as she recognised the writing on a missive to her brother. She *accidentally* opened the note and read it.

"I knew how it would be! Look Charles, Mr. Darcy was *not* angry with us, for we are invited to Rosings Park for Easter. I am to be introduced to his family before he offers for me!" Miss Bingley gushed.

"Have I not asked you to refrain from opening letters addressed to me? Please, hand it over." Bingley asked tiredly, and Miss Bingley handed the note to her brother reluctantly, because she now knew she would not be able to manipulate him into going earlier. "This is an invitation for Wednesday, the seventeenth day of April. In fact, Darcy is unambiguous in his statement we are not to arrive early." Bingley would have liked to call his sister to account for lying to him, but he chose peace and quiet over correcting his irascible sister.

"Oh, I am sure Mr. Darcy would not mind…" Miss Bingley was shocked when her brother cut her off. It was not something he did very often.

"Caroline, it is *not* his home. As you see, the invitation is from his cousin who is the master there. We cannot, and will not, arrive before the day we were invited," Bingley affirmed.

"Well, I suppose it must be that way. I need to go shopping, for I cannot allow my, err, Mr. Darcy's family to see me in something old." With that, Miss Bingley collected her outerwear, summoned her maid, and had the butler call for the carriage.

This was her chance, and she would not waste it. Her Mr. Darcy's family would have no doubt of her suitability to become the mistress of Pemberley, Darcy House, and his other properties.

~~~~~~~/~~~~~~~

A messenger arrived with a note for Mr. Fitzwilliam from one of the dragoons trailing Wickham not long after midday. "It seems it is to be tonight. The presage you felt was correct Aunt. The message says Wickham hired a carriage, and it is set to meet both he and Miss Lydia at the northwest corner of Humboldt Square at two in the morning. That is a little over twelve hours from now. I will send a message to Forster. Humboldt Square is close to his house," Richard said.

Richard found the rest of his party in their private sitting room at the Blue Parrot. Elizabeth was pacing nervously; she would be unable to feel easy until Lydia was safe and the blackguard on his way to debtors' prison.

"It is tonight, or rather at two in the morning tomorrow that Wickham will attempt to escape with Miss Lydia," Richard informed his party.

"Thank goodness we came earlier," Lady Catherine exhaled the breath she had been holding since he had entered with a note in his hand.

"You mean, thank goodness *you* insisted we depart Kent last night Aunt Cat," Elizabeth pointed out.

"Why we are here in time is unimportant," Lady Catherine demurred, "only that we are here and are in a position to save Miss Lydia from herself."

"I have an idea. William, Wickham has never seen your new driver, has he?" Richard asked.

"No, I do not believe so." Darcy agreed, though was confused as to what Richard's question heralded.

"We need to offer the hired driver money to *get sick* tonight and send his *trusted friend* in his stead. Then we will have both Wickham and Miss Lydia under surveillance the whole time. Let them enter the carriage, and your man can drive them right to Forster's house where we will be waiting for them," Richard suggested.

"What if Wickham sees they are not going the way he expects?" Jane asked.

"He will have the shades drawn. As he will be leaving his duty post without permission, he will not want to take the chance—no matter how small—of being spied by someone in the militia while he makes his getaway," Richard explained. "Do not forget our men will be close to the conveyance from the second they enter it until it halts on Kindle Street."

"Do you have an occupation for me?" Darcy asked.

"No William. We all should remain indoors until we leave tonight. It is not worth risking tipping off the libertine to our presence in Brighton," Richard informed his cousin.

"Like you, Mr. Darcy, I hate being confined indoors," Elizabeth shared. "I would have liked nothing more than to take a ramble this morning, but I understand today it is impossible."

"Will you not call me William?" Darcy invited. "I am the last member of my family you do not address by a familiar name."

"In that case William, you may call me Elizabeth or Lizzy," Elizabeth allowed.

Darcy was pleased at being allowed to call her by her familiar name—he tried to school his features, but unsuccessfully. Seeing his pleasure, Elizabeth decided she quite enjoyed the company of this new Mr. Darcy—William.

"Please call me Jane Mr. Darcy," Jane requested.

"It will be my pleasure to do so Jane; please use William when addressing me," Darcy granted.

Lady Catherine could not be more pleased by what she was seeing. It had not taken her long observing Elizabeth and William together to see they would best suit one another—though she was aware at least one of them would be unwilling to admit it at this time. She was amused to know it was Lizzy who would be the naysayer if pressed, not her reserved nephew.

When William had proffered his apologies to the family on Saturday night, they were full, complete, and sincere. Lady Catherine had at last seen William begin to transform into the man her sister and brother Darcy had hoped he would become.

She watched as Jane and Richard spoke quietly, their heads closer than propriety allowed. She was pleased and sure it would be but days before Richard paid his addresses to the eldest Bennet sister.

On the other side of the room, Elizabeth and William were debating the latest offering by the scandalous poet, Lord Byron. For the first time, there was no rancour or antagonism in their debate. As far as Lady Catherine could see, the two were enjoying one another's company. She also knew both were very stubborn and might yet need a little nudge.

~~~~~~~/~~~~~~~

At a little after one in the morning, Wickham volunteered to make tea for the three fellow officers on duty with him. The men were surprised that the sullen Wickham would volunteer to do anything for others, and gratefully accepted.

Wickham had just enough laudanum left for one drop in each cup, so he stirred in additional sugar to mask the bitter taste of the drug. He first removed his own cup and settled it next to his seat and held the small tray out for each of them to take one. Wickham watched the three men begin to drink their warm beverage. One of the men remarked it was sweeter than he usually preferred, but he appreciated the warmth of the drink.

It took less than ten minutes before the three were asleep, or close enough to it. Even if they were not asleep soundly, at least they would not be able to raise the alarm for hours. He slipped out of the encampment, and, keeping to the shadows, made his way towards Humboldt Square.

~~~~~~~/~~~~~~~

Lydia Bennet had not allowed herself to go to sleep. It was too important a date to miss due to sleeping. Instead, she sat and composed letters. One was to Harriet, informing her of the elopement.

When that letter was completed, Lydia folded it and placed it on her pillow, where her head would never rest again.

She wrote to Kitty next, telling her of the great romantic adventure she was embarking on and announcing that when next she saw Kitty, she would be Mrs. Lydia Wickham.

Each time she said her soon-to-be new name, she told herself how well it sounded. She expected her sisters—other than Kitty—might scold her for eloping, but she would be married and her unmarried sisters would be expressing their jealousy that their youngest sister had married before them. Kitty's letter was placed on the pillow next to Harriet's, for she was sure Harriet would post it for her.

Wanting to make sure she was in Humboldt Square with time to spare, Lydia crept down the stairs, valise in hand, at twenty minutes before two. She closed the front door quietly; the only sound it made was a dull click.

At the end of the short drive, she turned left on Kindle Street. The walk to the square took less than ten minutes. Lydia was focused only on her goal and did not notice the half dozen men following her.

When she arrived in the square, she crossed to the northwest corner to wait as instructed. The men tracking her movements melted into the shadows, joining the others already posted in the square.

~~~~~~~/~~~~~~~

Wickham arrived a few minutes later, relieved to see the airheaded hussy waiting for him. The thought of the silly girl forced to serve in a brothel gave him pleasure. Only a few more hours of suffering her company, and he would be well paid for his efforts. To keep her from seeing his true thoughts, he plastered a false smile on his face as he approached her.

"My love, you are here." The words stuck in Wickham's craw, but he needed her relaxed and pliable until he sold her to the brothel.

"Wicky! I am so excited. The day for us to become man and wife has finally arrived," Lydia gushed.

"Do not forget you will be with my family until I receive the money Darcy owes me, then we will be off to Gretna Green, so it will be a few days before we become man and wife." As he finished his speech, and before Lydia could reply with whatever whining plea she intended, the hired carriage pulled to a halt near them.

Wickham was about to follow Lydia into the conveyance when he noticed the driver was not the man he hired. "Who the hell are you?"

"Wicky, such language before your lady love," Lydia cooed.

"Quiet Lydia!" Wickham growled.

"Me good mate Thatcher be take'n sick. 'E asked me to make the trip fir ya so ya can still reach London as planned," Darcy's carriage driver told Wickham.

"Just get us there with all haste. The moon is still full; you will be able to see the road," Wickham bit out, hating any change to what he had planned. However, he felt the driver was, in the end, the least consequential part of his plan.

"Aye Sir," the driver retorted. Satisfied, Wickham entered the coach and slammed the door.

"Wicky, I want to open the shades," Lydia whined. How could this be romantic and fun if no one could see her triumph?

"Do not touch the shades," Wickham barked. Seeing Lydia shrink back, he spoke in a seductive voice, "If I want to be romantic with my wife-to-be, how can I when the shades are open?"

When the carriage came to a sudden halt, Wickham leaned over giving Lydia a kiss to placate her, as distasteful as it was to him. "Wicky, what is wrong?" Lydia asked nervously.

"Georgie boy, the game is up! Step out unless you would rather I drag your worthless body out of the carriage." Wickham froze in fear as he heard Richard Fitzwilliam taunt him.

He moved the shade on his side slightly and saw armed soldiers outside. In the vain hope there was an avenue of escape on the other side, he leaned over the girl, and what he saw there was even worse.

Not only were there more soldiers, but he saw Richard Fitzwilliam, Lady Catherine, Darcy, and the two eldest Bennet sisters standing outside of Colonel Forster's house. It was then he noticed the murderous look on his militia commander's visage. How could all of his careful plans have turned to dust?

"Why are we not moving Wicky?" Lydia whined.

"Just shut up," Wickham spat as he opened the door. He did not want to get out, but it was preferable to Richard Fitzwilliam dragging him out.

Once her erstwhile suitor exited, Lydia saw her sisters and the hateful Mr. Darcy standing outside. She left the carriage, intending to berate her sisters. "You are jealous of me! You could not stand it that I was to marry..." Lydia shut her mouth in shock as a hard slap was delivered to her face.

"That will be all for now *Miss* Lydia!" Lady Catherine hissed. Seeing Lydia was about to protest again, Lady Catherine drew back her arm, which was enough to convince the girl that now was not the time to speak. "Jane and Elizabeth, is your sister's valise out of the carriage?"

"Yes Aunt," the two chorused.

Lady Catherine summoned two large footmen to her. "Make sure this," she pointed to Lydia, "enters the carriage with her sisters and remains there *quietly*." Lady Catherine gave the cowering girl a withering look as she spoke the last words.

Lydia did not miss that the lady who hit her was holding the two letters she had written. Silly she might be, but she was not as stupid as people thought; the one thing Lydia knew for sure was now was the time for compliance, not defiance. She allowed herself to be led to the carriage with no sound passing her lips.

Jane and Elizabeth joined their youngest sister in the carriage, but both were too angry to say a word to her, so all sat in silence for disparate reasons.

For his part, Wickham found himself in irons and again facing an irate Colonel Forster. There was a colonel in a Royal Dragoon uniform standing next to his colonel, along with

Lady Catherine, Richard, and Darcy. "Wickham," Colonel Forster barked. "Not only were you deserting during wartime, but you drugged three fellow officers and left your post without permission. You have much for which to answer." Wickham was reeling. He prayed this was a nightmare from which he would awaken, but he had no such luck.

"I am greatly displeased to see you again so soon after Meryton," Lady Catherine addressed him. "We will speak of your punishment at a decent time in the morning, during which we will see if you cooperate enough to earn yourself any sort of commutation."

Wickham turned to his former friend. "Surely to honour the memory of your late father you will…" Whatever he was about to say was cut off when Darcy drove his fist into the man's stomach.

"Do not dare to mention my father or *any* member of my family again if you want to live, you miserable cur," Darcy spat angrily.

"He will be in the brig, in irons. If you need to talk to him before he receives military justice, please let me know," Colonel Foster offered.

After thanking all the men who helped, the three joined the Misses Bennet in the carriage and departed for the Blue Parrot Inn.

# CHAPTER 18

After only a few hours' sleep, Lady Catherine, Richard, Darcy, Jane, and Elizabeth met in the private parlour to break their fasts. "Lizzy and I have spoken to Lydia, but she will not believe anything we say about her favourite. She just repeats we are jealous of her and do not want her to marry before us," Jane reported. "Mrs. Annesley is with Lydia, and there are footmen outside the door as well as a few under the window, just in case the wilful girl tries to run."

"The only way we convinced her to speak calmly was to ask her if we should summon you to come address her Aunt Cat," Elizabeth added.

"Then she will need to hear the truth from Wickham's lips," Lady Catherine decided.

"How will this be achieved?" Darcy asked.

"Richard, you and William can join Colonel Forster to interrogate the man, can you not?" Lady Catherine asked. Richard nodded. "The Bennet sisters, Mrs. Annesley, and I will be in an adjoining room with the door cracked so we can hear what is said."

"How will you keep Lydia quiet?" Jane asked.

"Jane dear, if the threat of me is enough to calm her, what will she do if I am sitting next to her, gag at the ready if needs be?" Lady Catherine stated matter-of-factly. Both Jane and Elizabeth agreed it would be an effective way to keep their brash sister quiet. "As sad as I am to say it, what she will hear will occasion her much pain, but if it aids in teaching her a lesson and helps her to mature, then it will be a good thing," Lady Catherine opined.

Jane and Elizabeth returned to the room where a sullen Lydia was sitting, refusing to look at either of them when they entered. "Lydia, prepare to leave; we are to Colonel Forster's offices," Elizabeth informed her surly sister.

"Are you taking me back to my Wicky?" Lydia perked up. Conveniently she had forgotten how Wickham had spoken to her in a dismissive and downright nasty manner, both before they entered the carriage and while in it for their extremely short journey.

"You will hear him but not see him as we discover his true motives," Jane informed Lydia.

"Good. All of you will have to eat humble pie when you hear my Wicky tell everyone how much he loves me, and how cruel that Mr. Darcy is to have lied so," Lydia crowed.

"Take this as a fair warning Sister. While we are in the room next to the office you may not say a word," Elizabeth held up her hand to stop the protest which was forming on Lydia's lips. "Before you think of making a sound, Aunt Cat—Lady Catherine—will be seated next to you."

Lydia's jaw closed with a clack. She would not risk the lady punishing her again.

~~~~~~~/~~~~~~~

After a return note from Colonel Forster agreeing to help, the group, with a sullen Lydia in tow, departed the inn for Colonel Forster's offices. The Colonel's adjutant met them outside, then led them to a parlour just off his Colonel's office. Richard and Darcy followed Captain Sanderson into the office, and the door was left open a few inches so those in the parlour could hear the words being spoken clearly.

Lydia, who would have normally fawned over Captain Sanderson, punished him by not recognising him. He, like so many others, was a traitor to her dear Wickham. She would not have felt as good about her action had she noticed that the Captain cared not a whit if she paid him attention or not.

Lady Catherine turned to Lydia and admonished her to be quiet silently with a finger over her lips. Lydia flushed with anger but nodded her agreement as they heard Wickham being led into the Colonel's office.

Colonel Forster, Captain Sanderson, Richard Fitzwilliam, and Fitzwilliam Darcy, his foremost nemesis, were seated in the office waiting for him. The Colonel nodded to the soldiers who escorted the prisoner, the signal to leave him standing with the manacles still attached to his ankles.

"Do you know what the penalty for desertion during war is Wickham?" Colonel Forster asked. "Let me tell you," he proceeded before Wickham had a chance to reply. "It is death by hanging."

"S-surely t-that i-is o-only f-for t-the r-r-regular a-army," Wickham stammered, overcome with the need to cast up his accounts.

"No. In time of war it includes the militia," Richard informed the quaking man.

In the adjoining parlour, Lydia suddenly became less sure of herself as she listened to the conversation taking place. She could not have been wrong about Wicky, could she? He had worked hard so he could have the leave needed to marry her, did he not?

"There is one way you can save your miserable neck, and that is to answer our questions absolutely truthfully," Darcy informed the cowardly man, amused Wickham simply nodded, for once out of sarcastic replies.

"Where is Miss Lydia's twenty pounds?" The Colonel asked.

Wickham briefly considered lying, the money was not worth his neck. "In the lining of my pocket. There is fifteen pounds left. I paid for the carriage and a courtesan or two over the last week," Wickham admitted. A soldier who had walked him in removed the money and placed it on the Colonel's desk.

Lydia put her hands over her mouth to stop herself from crying out. She had trusted him with her money, yet he had used it to visit *those* women while professing his love for her. Jane, sitting on her other side, took her free hand and rubbed it gently.

"According to the letter she wrote, Miss Lydia thought you were going to marry her after a stop at family while you collected money from me," Darcy stated. "As I owe you no money and I know you have no family in London—or anywhere else—what was your plan? Were you going to sell her to a brothel?"

"That is what it sounds like to me. When have you ever turned down a maiden's favours when she offered them freely? It cannot be her age; it has never stopped you before," Richard stated with disgust.

"I would never have married that hussy! I was tempted when she all but threw herself at me, but I needed her intact. She has no fortune and is the silliest girl I have ever met. I was using her money to get us to London, and then yes, I was going to sell her to a brothel because I needed funds for passage to the Americas. I knew it was only a matter of time before your aunt would call in my debts and send me to the Clink, as no one can live so cleanly as she demanded." Wickham looked away when he saw the looks of disgust on the four men with him in the office.

He heard a commotion behind him as a door flew open and slammed against the wall. Wickham half turned, just in time to see a feral Lydia Bennet running at him with pure hate in her eyes, her nails extended. The screeching girl flew into him, scratching his face with all of her pent-up fury, and sending Wickham flying back against the desk as she continued to sink her nails into his face, scratching him deeply and wildly.

Wickham collided with the corner of the desk with his right arm; the sickening crack was unmistakable as the bone in his upper arm shattered. Lydia would have jumped onto him as Wickham writhed in pain on the floor had Richard not restrained her with the help of her sisters, who had followed their youngest sister into the office.

"I want to kill him! Let me go!" Lydia screamed madly as Richard held her.

The fallen man was rolling on the floor crying out in pain. Blood poured from his face, around his eye where Lydia's talons had found their mark, and a piece of bone was protruding from his arm.

As Jane and Elizabeth, with Lady Catherine's help, shepherded Lydia, sobbing as her sisters had never seen before, back to their carriage. She often used crocodile tears to get her way, but these tears expressed a real pain, a deeper pain than they could imagine. Lady Catherine offered Lydia a handkerchief to wipe the blood from her hands and pulled the sobbing girl into a hug as the conveyance was driven back to the inn. Once the four ladies exited, the carriage returned to Colonel Forster's office to wait for Richard and Darcy.

Lydia's sobbing had not lessened, so Lady Catherine suggested some wine with a drop of laudanum. Jane and Elizabeth agreed, and the landlord was applied to. He kept a small bottle of the narcotic on the premisses for just such a case.

Soon after drinking her wine, Lydia fell into a deep, restless sleep.

~~~~~~~/~~~~~~~

After the apothecary had seen the prisoner, he made his report to the men in the Colonel's office. "Mr. Wickham has deep lacerations around his eye and on his cheek and has lost an eye. In addition, his right arm is so badly broken, I suggest the military surgeon be summoned, as it may need to be amputated if the bones cannot be set again," the man reported.

After the apothecary left, Colonel Forster ordered his adjutant to request the Royal Dragoons' surgeon attend his man. "It seems Miss Lydia's punishment may be sufficient. It has cost him an eye, his looks, and possibly an arm. When he is able to be moved, he will be sent to the Clink on your aunt's behalf. Considering his inability to work while injured, with the size of the debt, he will never leave the prison alive," Colonel Forster stated.

"He has none to blame but himself, although he will try to do so. He has always been one to concoct schemes he believes infallible, but his confidence is greater than his abilities, and his schemes invariably fail," Darcy told the Colonel.

"When do you return to your estate Fitzwilliam?" the Colonel enquired.

"As soon as Miss Lydia is in a state to travel, we will depart; I would guess the earliest will be on the morrow," Richard told his friend.

Not long after, the Colonel accompanied the cousins to their waiting coach.

~~~~~~~/~~~~~~~

The laudanum knocked Lydia out until about three in the morning on Wednesday, when she woke up screaming. She had slept fitfully for more than four and twenty hours. Jane and Lizzy held her and rocked her when she started to cry again as she came to terms with the fact the world as she knew it had been shattered.

"He never loved me, did he? Everything I denied about him was all true, was it not?" Lydia asked between sobs.

"No Lyddie," Elizabeth replied gently as she wiped her sisters tears away. "That man loves none but himself."

"Mama's lessons about how to catch a man are all wrong, are they not?" Lydia asked as she at last attempted to control her tears.

"Yes dearest. Mama is not correct in her instructions," Jane agreed. "Are you able to eat a little Lyddie?"

"I will try if it makes you happy Jane," Lydia replied.

"Let me see if Aunt Cat is up," Elizabeth informed her sisters. "The sooner we depart for Kent the better." Jane nodded as she continued to comfort their sister.

After seeing light under Lady Catherine's bedchamber door, she knocked and was given leave to enter.

"How is Lydia?" Lady Catherine asked.

"She is upset, understandably so, but I think she finally understands how bad her behaviour has been," Elizabeth opined.

"Would it be forward of me to send an express to your

father *inviting* him and your mother to Rosings Park? It is, after all, their failings which have led to your sister being in this situation," Lady Catherine stated. Elizabeth had long known this confrontation was coming.

"I believe I can speak for Jane in saying we would not object. It is high time my parents were faced with the results of their decisions," Elizabeth stated bitterly.

"They have both disappointed you and your sisters, but they are still your parents. I will take them to task; that way you need not worry about an irrevocable break in the family," Lady Catherine declared, and Elizabeth could not but be grateful.

They decided to depart for Rosings Park by seven. Not many minutes later, an express rider was on his way to Hertfordshire.

~~~~~~~/~~~~~~~

Mr. Bennet felt most vexed on Thursday morning. He had received an express from the great Lady Catherine de Bourgh, and the rider was waiting in his kitchen for an answer. As much as he would have preferred to continue reading his book, he broke the seal and read his letter.

*10 April 1811*
*Rosings Park, Westerham, Kent*
*Mr. Bennet,*
*You need to rouse yourself from your study and join us at Rosings Park, with your wife, as soon as possible.*
*Your daughter Lydia has just been saved from ruin, and along with her, all of her sisters. I am writing this from an inn in Brighton. We depart for Kent within the hour.*
*I cannot impress upon you the seriousness of this situation enough,*
*Lady Catherine de Bourgh*

Bennet's first reaction was to consign the missive to the fire, but then he remembered Lizzy begging him not to allow Lydia to go to Brighton in the letter she had written from Kent.

Could it be Lizzy's warning had presaged events that had come to pass? Fear gripped Bennet, fear he had not felt for many years, that he had failed in a father's primary responsibility—to protect his children.

He wrote a quick note informing her Ladyship he and his wife would arrive at Rosings Park on the morrow. He issued instructions to Hill to pack his trunk and have the carriage made ready for immediate departure, then went to find his wife.

As was her wont, she was late in rising and was only now breaking her fast, thinking she would be off to visit and gossip, as she had since they had been without daughters at home.

"Mrs. Bennet," Bennet called her attention to himself sharply. "Mrs. Hill is packing your trunk. We will depart for Kent via London within the hour."

"Oh, Mr. Bennet, what has happened?" Mrs. Bennet asked as she fanned herself furiously with her lace handkerchief. "Is it that Lizzy? What had she done now?"

"It is most certainly *not* Lizzy! It is your favourite, Lydia," Bennet stated without any further information.

Mentioning Lydia was all Bennet had to say to motivate his wife into making haste to be ready for departure.

~~~~~~~/~~~~~~~

The two carriages came to a halt under Rosings' portico, where they were met by the residents of the manor house. When Lydia saw Kitty, she fell into her arms, crying. "Thank you for telling our sisters about my folly," Lydia told her surprised older sister.

Within minutes, the Collinses were seen walking briskly through the gardens toward the group returning from Brighton. Collins had been working in his study when he spied the two carriages and had informed his wife of their sisters' return, so they had set out for Rosings immediately.

"It is good to see everyone, but can we go inside the house please," Lady Catherine suggested. Soon all were ensconced in the largest drawing room.

Lydia was seated between Kitty and Jane, with Gigi next

to Kitty and Elizabeth next to Jane, and introductions were made between those who had previously not met. Lydia looked around the room and then she leaned over to Jane.

"Does everyone here know what almost happened to me?" Lydia asked bashfully.

"Yes, but only those of us who were in Brighton know what that terrible man planned for you," Jane replied softly.

"It is my opinion that Lydia should stay at the manor house with Kitty and Gigi," Lady Catherine stated.

Seeing that Lydia did not recognise the second name, Gigi touched Lydia's arm softly. "Gigi is the name my friends and family call me, you are welcome to do so as well," Georgiana told the youngest Bennet.

"Lydia dear, although you showed an inordinate amount of bad judgement, none here will judge you. You are not the only one here who has almost been ruined by that wastrel. You will, however, be the last one as he will never be free to ply his seductions and manipulations ever again," Lady Catherine told Lydia gently.

"Thank you for rescuing me," Lydia said to all of them. She looked to Richard and Darcy, forcing herself to ask the question she had been afraid to hear the answer to. "I did not kill him, did I? Even if he deserves it, I do not want to take another's life."

"No Lydia, he is very much alive—worse for wear, but alive," Richard shared. She did not ask how badly he had been injured, so no one told her.

"Hopefully, you will soon be able to move on from this experience. Do not forget it, but start down another path, for it is critical we learn from our mistakes or we are doomed to repeat them," Lady Catherine declared. "I suggest we all rest and reconvene here for dinner. Mary and Collins, you have no prior commitments, do you?"

"No Aunt Cat, we made sure our evening was open as we were sure our sisters would be returning. We would be happy to join you for dinner," Mary accepted.

Lydia hugged her three departing sisters tightly, and for the first time she hugged her brother Collins. Before they could start their walk, Richard called Jane aside. "Jane, when you are here this evening, will you grant me a private interview?"

"Yes Richard, it would be my pleasure to hear anything you may have to say," Jane replied as she blushed deeply. With her heart racing, and feeling like she was floating on a cloud, Jane walked back to the parsonage with her brother and two of her sisters.

# CHAPTER 19

The Hunsford party arrived within a few minutes of the designated time. Once everyone was served sherry, orgeat, or port, Lady Catherine cleared her throat. "It is good to have *all* of the Bennet sisters with us at Rosings Park. Jane," Lady Catherine turned to the oldest Bennet present, "it is my understanding that you have granted my nephew Richard an interview." Jane blushed scarlet as she nodded, not expecting it would be so openly discussed beforehand.

"Your help is always appreciated Aunt Cat," Richard grinned at his aunt, then stood and approached Jane. "Shall we?"

"It is unavoidable now," Jane teased.

"About time brother, rather slow in my opinion," Andrew ribbed. The Earl and Countess beamed as their younger son left to ask for the hand of a woman worthy of him in every way.

"Mrs. Annesley is seated outside the parlour opposite," Lady Catherine stated matter-of-factly.

Elizabeth bent toward Darcy, "You know William, without your help in highlighting Mr. Bingley's character, Jane may not have been open to another. Now I believe she will be the happiest woman in the world."

"The more I see her and Richard together, the more convinced I become that they are a perfect match. Besides, my days of matchmaking, or whatever the opposite office is, are done," Darcy told Elizabeth. She laughed, again impressed how the man was able to make fun of his own past foibles. Darcy loved to hear the lilting, tinkling sound of Elizabeth's laugh.

"I heard a reply from Mr. Bingley was waiting for you when we returned," Elizabeth noted.

"Indeed there was, and to no one's surprise, he accepted. If I were a wagering man, I would bet Pemberley that Miss Bingley tried to convince him to arrive at Rosings earlier than the date of the invitation," Darcy informed Elizabeth. "I am so ashamed of how blind I was to the behaviour of that woman for so long."

"We promised to move forward, remember? As Aunt Cat says, learn from the past, but do not live there," Elizabeth prompted.

Ladies Catherine and Elaine were sitting together on a settee. "I see that our William is truly interested in Elizabeth, does she return his regard?" Lady Elaine asked her sister.

"I believe he loves her, although he has a long road to travel to earn her affection. It was not long ago she thought him insufferable," Lady Catherine replied, her amusement evident.

"These girls are not impressed by wealth, connections, or rank from what I have noted," Lady Elaine said.

"As far as I can tell, unless they esteem and respect their partner, and receive the same in return, they will not be tempted into marriage regardless of the pecuniary advantages," Lady Catherine relayed.

"If William can win Elizabeth's heart, then the dream that Richard and William hold of being brothers will become a reality," Lady Elaine opined as she watched the two peripherally so they would not be aware of her scrutiny enough to cease talking.

~~~~~~~/~~~~~~~

"Bennet, Fanny, what caused you to leave Longbourn and travel to London?" Edward Gardiner asked. "You are welcome, of course, but this is unexpected."

Madeline Gardiner looked at both Bennets and, like her husband, was curious about what had happened to separate their brother from his books and port. She suspected it had to do with Lydia. Her three oldest Bennet nieces had written to her and informed her, and by extension her husband, of their

SHANA GRANDERSON A LADY

fears regarding their parents allowing Lydia to be close to so many officers without substantial supervision.

"We are only asking that you host us overnight," Bennet said. "We will leave for Kent and Rosings Park after we break our fasts in the morning."

"What has happened? Does this relate to Lydia?" Gardiner asked the question both he and his wife most wanted answered.

"How do you know?" A flabbergasted Bennet responded.

"We were not sure until you just confirmed it," Gardiner stated.

"What has happened? What do you know?" Madeline asked, gravely concerned.

"Not as much as we would like to." Bennet handed the express he had received to his brother Gardiner.

Neither of the Gardiners missed the almost catatonic state that Fanny Bennet was in. Given the situation concerned her favourite and baby, they could understand her reaction. Her reaction was alarming, but better than one of her contrived attacks of her so-called nerves.

Madeline guided Fanny out of the room so she could change and rest a little before dinner. As soon as the door was closed, Gardiner turned to his brother. "What were you thinking, allowing a girl—who you yourself call the silliest in England—to go to a place teeming with officers, under the care of one no older or wiser than she?"

"It...I...I was not thinking clearly. In my quest for peace, I ignored the pleas of both Jane and Lizzy. When Lizzy wrote to me, rather than listen to what she was saying, I scolded her. Now my family may be ruined," Bennet confessed shakily.

"Let us pray it has not come to that. The fact you have been asked to journey into Kent may not bode well, but you will not be certain until you arrive on the morrow," Gardiner opined.

"Would you and Maddie join us?" Bennet asked hopefully.

"My business is running smoothly, so I would be able to

take some days. Let me speak to Maddie as I am not sure she will want to leave the children, but mayhap for a few days only, she will agree," Gardiner replied.

Before dinner, Gardiner requested his wife join him in his study. He relayed Bennet's plea that they travel into Kent with them on the morrow. His wife stated as long as it was no longer than four or five days, she was amenable.

~~~~~~~/~~~~~~~

Leaving the door slightly ajar, Richard joined Jane in the centre of the parlour. Taking her hands in his own, he sank to one knee. "Jane Eloise Bennet, when I requested a courtship, I told you I was not in love with you *yet*. Though only a short time has passed since then, I find I have fallen irrevocably in love with you.

"You are the one I want to fall asleep next to each and every night for the rest of my life. I want to have the pleasure and honour of waking up next to you each and every morning. I lost part of myself on the battlefields of the Peninsula, but with you Jane, I am again whole. I do not want to experience the joys of life with anyone but you at my side." Richard looked at Jane, relieved to see her love for him in her eyes, her expression, in her very essence.

"I am not looking for someone to decorate my arm so we can live separate lives and come together to impress the *Ton*. What I want, what I need, is you. A woman I love, respect, and esteem—one who will be my partner in all things. You are compassionate, charitable, and one of the kindest people I know; however, I know you will defend the ones you love with all that you are. Yes, you are the most beautiful woman I have ever beheld, and for that I cannot but add it to the list of blessings that are part of you.

"Jane, will you make me the happiest of men and agree to marry me?" Richard remained on his knee, looking up hopefully at the woman he loved.

"Until I met you, I did not know what true love was. It was not many days after our courtship began that I knew I loved you. I am convinced you are the ideal man for me, so yes Richard. Yes, I will marry you—the man I love and respect above all others," Jane replied happily.

Despite his racing heart, Richard's hand remained steady as he withdrew a ring from his pocket. It was a gold band with a grouping of sapphires around a diamond. Jane proffered her left hand as Richard stood and slid the ring onto her finger.

They moved toward one another in mutual, but silent, agreement. Jane closed her eyes and lifted her chin as Richard closed the distance until their lips met. Both felt a tingling sensation, and Jane let out a soft moan as she experienced her first kiss.

The first kiss was chaste, but then Richard captured her lips and deepened the next one. Without any hesitation, Jane's arms snaked around Richard's neck while his arms wound around her slender waist. Jane felt her heart race as Richard's tongue explored her mouth.

If it were not for Mrs. Annesley clearing her throat outside the door, their interlude would have continued, but they each took a step back, feeling bereft at the loss of the other in their arms. "My brother Collins will be here shortly," a flushed Jane informed her betrothed.

Jane waited a moment for the heat she was feeling in her face to subside, then she gave Richard a kiss on the cheek and exited hastily before she was tempted to kiss him more intimately. She had been surprised, pleasantly, at how soft and welcoming his lips had been when they were against her own.

When she entered the drawing room alone, all conversation stopped and all eyes looked at her expectantly. It was the Countess who noted her maternal grandmother's ring on Jane's finger.

"William, Richard is awaiting you in the parlour opposite," Jane managed as she smiled with the warmth of a rising sun.

Collins made his way to the parlour while Jane was surrounded by her family, both current and soon-to-be. The Earl reached her first, showing how spry he was even though he was the oldest person in the room, enfolding his daughter-to-be in a hug.

"It pleases me more than I can say to welcome you to the family. I hope you will call me Father Reggie as Marie does." Lord Matlock beamed with pleasure, as did his wife.

Privately, he and his wife had begun to doubt Richard would find a woman worthy of him, one who would love him for himself rather than his estate. Now, having met this perfectly sweet young woman, they were sure he had found his true match in Jane.

After the Earl moved to the side, Jane was surrounded in a group hug consisting of three sisters and Gigi. "Jane, the only time I was happier than I am for you now was when my William proposed to me," Mary gushed.

Elizabeth turned and saw Lydia watching the joy unfold before her. "Lyddie, are you not one of our sisters?" Elizabeth invited warmly.

"You are not angry with me?" Lydia asked tentatively; for her sisters it was odd to see the normally brash and outgoing Lydia so unsure of herself.

"We still have much to discuss, but this is a time for all of us to be happy for Jane, and you are one of us Lyddie. You will always be our sister," Elizabeth clarified.

Lydia stood, relieved at the welcoming looks as she joined the circle of hugs. When the five young ladies stepped back, they were replaced by Ladies Catherine and Elaine.

"You will call me Mother Elaine, will you not?" Lady Elaine invited, her smile growing even wider when Jane nodded, and received a kiss on the cheek from her future mother-in-law before Lady Elaine stepped back.

Lady Catherine drew Jane into a fulsome hug. "Oh, I knew how it would be. You and Richard will do very well together. When you marry, I will move to the dower house so you may establish yourself as mistress."

"You will do nothing of the sort Aunt Cat! You will *always* be welcome, nay expected, to stay in this house. How will I bedevil you with questions all day long until I learn my duties?" Jane teased her lovingly. Jane had come to love her Aunt Catherine as another mother, and it was obvious the love was returned. She was certain Richard would not hear of her moving to the dower house.

"I love you and your sisters too Jane," Lady Catherine emoted. No one would ever replace Anne in her heart, but as she kept adopting surrogate sons and daughters, her heart swelled to make room for her new *children*.

Darcy was about to step forward and wish his soon-to-be cousin happy—one he hoped he would be able to call sister one day—when Collins and Richard returned to the drawing room. Collins went directly to Jane, took his sister's hand and placed it in Richard's. The ex-officer was sporting a stupid grin of absolute joy.

"Even though it seems redundant, it is my pleasure to inform you of the official betrothal of Jane and Richard. I join everyone in wishing them happy for decades to come," Collins announced.

Darcy slapped Richard on the back in congratulation and wished Jane happy. "Welcome to the family," he stated sincerely.

"Thank you William. I assume you will be able to join Andrew in telling me stories of how my betrothed got into trouble as a young boy," Jane suggested with a teasing smile.

"We were always well-behaved lads," Richard prevaricated.

"Are you telling me Aunt Catherine was inaccurate about the three of you and the mud?" Jane challenged.

"Well, besides the day we involved Anne in the mud bath with us, we were perfectly well behaved," Darcy claimed.

"Yes, I am sure that was the *only* instance," Jane replied playfully.

"Kitty," Lydia spoke softly as she sat next to her sister to watch their eldest sister's welcome by her new family. "Thank you for helping to save me from my terrible decisions."

"Let us just rejoice you are safe and he will never be able to harm another," Kitty offered as she squeezed Lydia's hand in return.

Once all the congratulations and wishes for felicity were bestowed, Lady Catherine rang for the butler to request celebratory champagne. To her surprise, Mr. Toppin arrived with the silver salver in hand. "An express, your Ladyship."

Lady Catherine thanked the butler and asked him to return with the sparkling wine. As soon as the butler withdrew, Lady Catherine broke the seal. It was a short note. "Mr. and Mrs. Bennet will arrive on the morrow," she announced. "It seems they will overnight with your aunt and uncle in Town, then depart early in the morning."

"If I know my father, he will request that my aunt and uncle accompany him to help with whatever he imagines he will have to exert himself over," Elizabeth stated pointedly, and none of her sisters said a word to contradict her.

"Then Mr. and Mrs. Gardiner will be most welcome," Richard insisted. "Not too far in the future, they will be my aunt and uncle too."

Toppin returned with two footmen and handed out champagne. Once everyone held a glass, Lord Matlock raised his. "To Jane and Richard. May their happiness and companionship only grow." There was a universal response of "hear, hear," and then, after much clinking of glasses, they enjoyed the French libation.

~~~~~~~~/~~~~~~~~

In Brighton, the surgeon had just completed his work. He had tried to save the man's arm, but the break was too severe, and the bone was shattered. The Dragoon's battle surgeon, Mr. McLamb, explained that he had no choice.

He informed his Colonel and the commander of the Derbyshire Militia it was amputation, or the man would surely die from infection. Also, many stitches had been required on the man's face, where his left eye had once been.

"How soon will I be able to transfer Wickham to the Clink?" Colonel Forster asked.

"It could be as soon as a sennight or as long as a fortnight," Mr. McLamb explained.

Before Wickham had succumbed to the laudanum, he wished he had never heard the name Bennet in his life. He wondered again how everything had gone so very wrong. He had not only lost an eye and his looks but was about to lose an arm. If that was not bad enough, he would live out the rest of his life in the Clink, for he was being sent to the most notorious of all of the debtors' prisons in the Kingdom.

As the laudanum had taken hold before the amputation, he had been asking himself why he had not let things be. As his eyes closed, he finally realised who his worst enemy was—himself!

# CHAPTER 20

Friday morning, by prior agreement, Mr. Collins and the three sisters residing at the parsonage arrived at the manor house to break their fast. After the morning meal, the Bennet sisters and Gigi met with Lady Catherine in her private sitting room.

"Lydia dear, you understand the necessity of this talk before your parents arrive, do you not?" Lady Catherine asked gently, for she did not want the youngest Bennet to feel as if she were being attacked.

"Yes Lady Catherine, I understand," Lydia replied, her voice quiet and subdued.

"Tell us what you think you did wrong," Lady Catherine prodded.

"In my determination not to heed anyone but myself, and my absolute belief that good looks meant good character, I wilfully believed *that* man, despite so many telling me the truth about him. I allowed my romantic notion of marrying young to override my ability to think about the impropriety of what I was about to do. I never gave a thought to the consequences for my sisters or myself. I should not have offered the seducer my virtue before being married." In a more self-aware fashion than her sisters had ever seen, Lydia enumerated her follies dispassionately.

"It seems that the moniker of silliest girl in England is undeserved." Lady Catherine raised her hand to stop any protests. "I am not saying that your *behaviour* was not silly, stupid, and immoral; do I need to go on?" Lydia shook her head. "The fact you are able to look back so soon after the event and highlight the chief issues shows you are an intelligent young lady, but you *chose* not to show it. Kitty, what did she miss?" Lady Catherine turned to the second youngest Bennet.

"Chasing after officers, or any other men," Kitty offered.

"And?" Lady Catherine prodded.

"Flirting with any man who looked in her direction, like I used to do; never listening to anyone else; allowing them to kiss her and possibly more and thinking that at fifteen she was ready to marry and it would be a good joke; thinking she should be the first to marry," Kitty added.

"Yes, and all of these things are related. Thank you Kitty." Lady Catherine turned back to Lydia. "Why do you think your three oldest sisters know how to behave, both in private and public? And tell me why Kitty is so very different than she used to be?"

"Jane and Lizzy have spent much time with the Gardiners..." Lydia trailed off. "Mama and Papa did not teach us how to behave. Jane and Lizzy learnt from Aunt Maddie, and they passed what they knew onto Mary to help her change a few years back. Then, more recently, Kitty opened herself to learning from them which has occasioned the changes in her."

"You made terrible choices and decisions, and your behaviour was atrocious." As Lady Catherine spoke Lydia's head dropped until her chin was pressed against her chest. "Lydia, look at me dear. As I have said more times than I care to remember, there is no need to live in the past, but if we are to move on we *must learn* from our past mistakes. I have no doubt you have begun to do so and I believe you will continue on this new path."

"Why did Mama encourage me to chase after men to *catch a husband*? Should Mama not have been the one to teach us what Jane and Lizzy learnt from Aunt Maddie?" Lydia struck at the crux of the matter.

"Remember Lyddie, Mama was not born a gentlewoman as we were. She did not know better, and Papa, rather than correcting and educating her, made sport of her—he still does," Elizabeth stated coldly. "Papa—if he had so desired—could have started saving for the future as soon as he married Mama, but he left it to his future son rather than trouble himself. By the time he realised there would be no son, he decided it was too late to bother with the effort it would require."

"What Elizabeth just mentioned is the central problem. Much blame lies with your parents, but that does not change the horrific decisions *you* made," Lady Catherine added truthfully. "Did you not revel in the fact your mother spoilt you to the detriment of your other sisters—except Jane, who was praised to the skies for only her physical beauty? Did your mother not praise your liveliness and womanly looks? My dear, you may have a woman's body, but you are still very much a child. Your mother should never have pushed any of you out at fifteen; no girl is ready for society at that age."

"Yes, I very much enjoyed being spoilt by Mama," Lydia owned.

"You could not control how your mother treated you or your sisters, nor could any of you force your father to take his responsibilities seriously or not to find amusement where he should have corrected. However, all of this had a profoundly bad effect on your behaviour. It will sound harsh, but all of it combined with a rather selfish and brazen streak led to the near disaster we put a stop to in Brighton." Lady Catherine sat back and allowed her words to sink in.

"How can I go back to Longbourn if my mother and father will be the same?" Lydia asked.

"Lyddie," Jane called her youngest sister's attention to herself. "Elizabeth and I are going to extend our stays until I marry Richard, at the very least." You are welcome to stay at the parsonage with us, and Kitty? We think it would be best if you remain as well."

"You will all move to the manor house. We need to give the Collinses a modicum of privacy," Lady Catherine stated. Mary blushed but did not dispute her words.

"Will Papa, and especially Mama, allow us younger girls to stay?" Lydia worried.

"You leave that up to me. You may call me Aunt Catherine, or Aunt Cat, as a certain impertinent sister of yours does," Lady Catherine granted as she smiled warmly at Elizabeth.

After her aunt nodded, Gigi cleared her throat. "Lydia, you are not the only girl to be manipulated by that libertine."

"I am now aware there were some in Meryton and other towns across England," Lydia owned.

"And there is one in this very room..." Georgiana told Lydia about Ramsgate and her own narrow escape.

"Was there anything he ever said that was true?" Lydia asked rhetorically. "Nothing he said about your brother was true either, was it?"

"Do not forget I too was taken in by him on that score," Elizabeth reminded her sister. "As much as I pride myself on being able to sketch characters, I failed abysmally with both William—Mr. Darcy—and the profligate liar."

"What I think I need is to go to a school, a strict one," Lydia stated.

"That may be best. Let us see how the meeting with your parents goes this afternoon," Lady Catherine declared.

"Aunt Cat, are you sure all of us staying at Rosings Park is not an imposition, and what about Jane, as she is betrothed to Richard?" Elizabeth enquired.

"Propriety will be observed. The master suite is on a different floor and at the opposite end of the house from the guest chambers. In addition to myself, Richard's parents, his brother, sister, and William are in residence. If that were not enough, with Gigi there will be four young ladies and Mrs. Annesley. I will assign double the footmen on duty in the halls at night. I will suggest to William that Mrs. Annesley become Jane's companion temporarily, and she will sleep in the second bedchamber in the suite with Jane. Each of you will be assigned a maid; Jane's will sleep on a cot in her room." Lady Catherine paused as she saw Elizabeth's eyebrows elevate as high as possible as each additional layer of protection was listed. "None of this is because I—or any of us—suspect that either Jane or Richard would do anything inappropriate or dishonourable—quite the contrary. It is to make sure there can be no question of propriety being fully observed."

"It seems my wise aunt has thought of everything," Elizabeth conceded.

"It is what I do," Lady Catherine winked at Elizabeth. The two chortled as they linked arms and followed the rest out of the sitting room.

Lady Catherine did not mention to Elizabeth that the same precautions would suit when her nephew Darcy worked up the courage to request a courtship.

~~~~~~~/~~~~~~~

As the Bennet carriage approached Rosings Park, Bennet was grateful his wife was awed into silence. The biggest house she had ever seen was at Netherfield Park, and that dwelling was dwarfed by this manor house.

Bennet felt a great deal of trepidation, as if massive consequences from his poor choices and disinterest as a father were about to be revealed. It made him feel no easier to see his two oldest waiting with the Collinses and two other people he did not recognise under the manor's portico. Bennet forgot he had been introduced to Lady Catherine and Richard Fitzwilliam at Mary's wedding.

No one could miss the warm welcome the Gardiners received from both Jane and Elizabeth, or the tepid one afforded their parents. When one of the regal-looking ladies requested introductions, Jane performed the office calmly.

"Mr. and Mrs. Gardiner, welcome. I do not know if you remember, but we met a few times at your warehouse off Gracechurch Street in London." Lady Catherine put the aforementioned couple at ease, as they had been worried they would be imposing on the master of Rosings with their unexpected presence.

"Lady Catherine, Mr. Fitzwilliam, I do remember," Madeline Gardiner averred. "One of the times was when Jane and Lizzy were visiting us."

"They are now counted as part of our family," the master of Rosings stated ambiguously.

The two Bennet parents looked on in silence, but given Mrs. Bennet's disposition, it could not last too long. "What have you to say for yourself Miss Lizzy?" Fanny Bennet demanded. "What trouble have you got my dear Lydia into. She is too good a girl to..." Whatever additional nonsense Mrs. Bennet was about to spew was cut off by an annoyed Lady Catherine.

"This is neither the time nor the place for that discussion. Suffice it to say, Elizabeth was part of the solution, *not* part of the problem!" Lady Catherine stated in a tone which brooked no opposition. "Our housekeeper, Mrs. Toppin, will show you to your suite, and we will meet in the main drawing room in an hour.

Bennet half-guided, half-pulled his wife into the house where the housekeeper was awaiting the two couples to show them to their suites. As soon as the door to their shared sitting room closed, Bennet rounded on his wife.

"Are you out of your senses to attack our second daughter so? Did I not tell you that Lizzy warned me not to send Lydia to Brighton? If I had listened, none of this, whatever it is, would have happened," Bennet shot at his wife.

"Lizzy was only jealous..." Mrs. Bennet was cut off for the second time in a short while.

"Not another word Fanny Bennet. When we go to that meeting you will sit in silence and will not make any more ridiculous pronouncements until I give you leave to talk. Defy me, and you will lose your allowance for a year. Do I make myself clear?" Fanny Bennet stood slack-jawed at her husband's ultimatum.

Of mean understanding she was, but she was not willing to lose a year's worth of pin money, so her teeth came together and her mouth shut with a clack.

~~~~~~~~/~~~~~~~~

The Gardiners had just changed when there was a soft

knock on their sitting room door. Gardiner opened it to reveal their three oldest nieces. As soon as they entered and the door was closed, Aunt Maddie noticed the ring that Jane's mother had not when they arrived.

"Jane, you have been very sneaky, you did not tell us you were being courted, never mind that you are betrothed," Madeline stated with pride.

"I did not want you in the position of having to hide information from Mama," Jane admitted. She then told her aunt and uncle everything in abbreviated form, as they were expected in the drawing room in less than a half hour.

"You are betrothed to Mr. Fitzwilliam, the master of this estate?" Gardiner verified.

"The very same," Jane confirmed. Both uncle and aunt hugged Jane and wished her happy.

"Do not be angry with me, but we will marry from this house, the seventeenth day of May, a little more than a month from now," Jane revealed. "I love my mother, I know she is your sister Uncle Edward, and I understand if you call me selfish, but I want my wedding day to be about me, not her."

"Jane, my dear niece, I do not blame you. I know my sister and love her, but I am not blind to her deficiencies." Gardiner looked at his wife, who nodded as they communicated silently. "We will support you fully. I know we will hear everything soon, but please tell us, is Lydia well? Was she ruined?"

"It was close, but we retrieved her before that happened," Elizabeth informed her aunt and uncle.

"Lizzy, I am so sorry you had to hear your mother's spiteful words. I will never understand how she places the blame on your shoulders for anything that goes wrong," Madeline told her niece as she hugged her.

"Mama never forgave me for being born a girl. I was supposed to be her son, and somehow that was my fault. As if I could magically control my gender while in her belly," Elizabeth stated stoically. "It used to hurt me. It no longer does, as I have learnt there is very little truth or rectitude in any of

Mama's utterances."

"Mary, you are glowing," Madeline observed. "You must be extremely fortunate in your marriage."

"That I am Aunt Maddie. I will forever be grateful for what you told me when we met the last time before my wedding. If I had only had the wrongheaded *information* my mother imparted, I would have been a truly panicked bride," Mary thanked her aunt.

A few minutes later, the group made for the drawing room. The five of them had just descended the stairs when the Bennet parents walked out of their suite.

~~~~~~~/~~~~~~~

"Caroline, what are these massive bills from your modiste and nearly every shop on Bond Street?" Bingley demanded.

"Charles, are you addlepated? Do you not remember I told you I was to go shopping to prepare to meet my future family at Rosings Park?" Miss Bingley replied condescendingly.

"We are to be there for two days. You purchased an entire new wardrobe," Bingley replied, aghast.

"Come now Charles, you know as well as I do when they see what people of quality I—we—are, we will be invited to stay longer so my wedding to Mr. Darcy can be planned as it should be for one of my status," Miss Bingley preened.

Bingley knew he should tell his sister the truth of his friend's opinion on the matter, but he could not take that chance. Questioning her about the obscene amount of money she was spending on clothing was the extent of his gumption.

"Did my intended amend the invitation for us to arrive earlier as I said he would?" Miss Bingley asked hopefully.

"No, he did not. He reiterated that our hosts will *not* receive us under any circumstances before the date we are expected," Bingley relayed.

As was her wont, Miss Bingley only heard that which she wanted to hear, so what she heard was how Mr. Darcy could not wait to see her again but their separation was being forced on them.

# CHAPTER 21

When the Bennet parents were shown into the drawing room, all five of their daughters, Mr. Collins, the Gardiners, and Lady Catherine were present. "Lydia, my darling girl," Mrs. Bennet gushed, "who led you into trouble?" Fanny Bennet threw an accusatory look at her second daughter as she asked the question.

"Please be seated and stop spouting nonsense," Lady Catherine ordered.

Bennet sat, as did his wife, though not graciously, as she took exception to the lady's tone. However, she decided that the best way to learn how Elizabeth had allowed something to happen to Lydia would be to hold her peace—for now. "What has occurred?" Bennet asked what he most needed to know, though he did not want information revealed that would highlight the deficiency in his parenting, or more correctly, his failure to do anything whatsoever.

"Lydia, the floor is yours," Lady Catherine indicated.

"I agreed to elope with Mr. Wickham," Lydia owned, not looking at her parents directly as she informed them of her folly.

"Oh, how wonderful! You are to be married, and at only fifteen too! How is this a problem? Where is dear Wickham?" Fanny Bennet prattled on.

"Mrs. Bennet, are you completely witless?" Lady Catherine asked pointedly.

"I have never been insulted thusly in my life," Mrs. Bennet responded with asperity.

"Somehow, I find that difficult to believe," Lady Catherine shot back. "You are pleased that your daughter of fifteen, who should not have been out of the schoolroom let alone out in society, was about to elope with a seducer of woman, a libertine of the first order, and a blackguard such as you have never met before?" Fanny was about to interject when Lady Catherine proceeded before she was able. "Do you not care the scandal would have touched your three remaining daughters —not to mention your family name—which would ensure no man would have them as wives?"

Whatever retort was on her lips, it was lost as the vision of her other daughters becoming unmarriageable struck the matron. "I, that is to say, ahem." Mrs. Bennet was, for possibly the first time, at a loss for words.

"Mrs. Bennet, I hope you understand you have lost your allowance for a year," Bennet reminded his wife. He held up his hand as she was about to protest vehemently. "Would you like it to be for two years?" Fanny Bennet shook her head as tears of anger and frustration rolled down her cheeks.

"Lydia, would you inform your parents of the rest of the story please?" Lady Catherine prompted.

"In my stubbornness and zeal to marry before the rest of my sisters, I dismissed all that I had been told about Mr. Wickham's actions in Meryton. Once he was free from his confinement, the man heard me boast I had twenty pounds with me," Lydia began to relate.

Hearing the amount she had, and well knowing he had only given her five pounds, Bennet turned an accusatory gaze on his wife, who had the decency to look away in shame. "How much of that money is left Lydia?" Bennet asked.

"Most of it Papa. I stupidly turned my funds over to the ex-officer because he claimed he would ensure no one relieved me of so large an amount. Now I know that he needed the money for himself. He instructed me to tell no one in Brighton of our planned *elopement*. I did not, but I did write to Kitty to boast of my *good fortune*. I did not know it at the time, but that letter saved my life," Lydia related.

Bennet felt as though he had been punched in the gut at

his daughter's words, while his wife almost swooned but held her tongue. "When you could not be reasoned with to hold Lydia back at Longbourn, Lizzy and I urged Kitty to pretend she was once again Lydia's minion." Jane informed him; her mild tone held layers of rebuke aimed at him. Bennet felt his shame increase as his eldest daughter held his gaze, hers distant as if nothing he could say or do could make up for his failures. "As we expected she would, Lydia was only too happy to boast of her upcoming *romantic* elopement."

"As you may remember, I covered all of the worthless man's debts in Meryton and purchased his vowels held by my nephew Darcy. The amount is well over three thousand pounds combined. When Kitty reported the contents of Lydia's letter, we planned to hie to Brighton as soon as may be, for Wickham had contravened my conditions for his continued freedom from debtors' prison," Lady Catherine added.

"Rather than waiting for Monday as we originally planned, Aunt Cat—Lady Catherine—had the feeling we needed to arrive sooner. We arrived in the area this past Sunday night," Elizabeth took up the story. "Thanks to Richard's— Mr. Fitzwilliam's—contacts within the military, both Lydia and *that* man were watched, and we soon ascertained Wickham had advanced his plans to leave after midnight Monday night." Bennet looked to his eldest daughter, his most forgiving one, but found no forgiveness there. He did not miss the look of pleasure suffusing Jane's face when the estate's master's name was mentioned.

"And so, I went out to meet the man I thought I loved, and who I believed loved me. We entered a carriage, and a few minutes later the conveyance stopped at Colonel Forster's house, which was close to where I boarded the carriage, at Humboldt Square," Lydia took up the tale again. "I was angry when I saw Jane and Lizzy, and immediately accused them of being jealous and not wanting me to have fun. I was, after all, the only one following my mother's teachings about catching a man."

Fanny Bennet preened then looked at her two eldest daughters, disgusted that they had stopped her Lydia from marrying. All of this talk about Mr. Wickham's wickedness could not be true, and surely it was not so very bad to elope. Once they married, there would be no scandal, so the high and mighty Lady Catherine did not know of what she spoke. She was determined to have words with her daughters, condemning their interference, especially Miss Lizzy, who was sure to have been the ringleader.

"My sisters, Richard, Mr. Darcy, and Aunt Catherine tried to tell me, again and again, that he had no good intentions toward myself, but I refused to believe them, declaring they were wrong as my dear *Wicky* loved me. So, Aunt Catherine offered me an option: I could accept their words and all that would come, or I could accompany her, Richard, and Mr. Darcy to Colonel Forster's office in the morning where I would be able to hear Wickham's interrogation. I was sure I would be able to crow about how wrong all of them were so I agreed to the latter. I was told if I made a sound while we listened, I would be bound and gagged." Lydia related the last with a half-smile directed at Lady Catherine.

Fanny Bennet was sure Lydia was about to relate how she had been vindicated by what she heard. She would have to admonish her daughters' so-called 'aunt' for threatening her dearest girl before this interview was over. And what was this *aunt* nonsense anyway? From the rest she expected treachery, but from Lydia it was inexcusable.

"What I heard was the opposite of what I expected." As Lydia finished this statement, all colour drained from her mother's face. "He was told if he was honest, *completely* honest, he would escape the hangman's noose for desertion during wartime, which was the penalty he would face when coupled with dereliction of duty." Lydia took a deep breath, glancing at Lady Catherine who nodded encouragingly that she should continue.

"It *is* hard to relate, but you are doing well Lyddie," Kitty said in support of her younger sister.

"Thank you." Lydia offered a small smile, reaching for and finding Kitty's hand extended for her to take. She was relieved to have her sister's support. What she had to say would be humiliating, even more so than when she heard it from Wickham's own mouth. She had seen nothing to indicate his intentions then, but looking back, she saw plenty now. "He admitted he never loved me; he said he did not even like me. I had offered my virtue to him in anticipation of our wedding vows, which he refused. I thought he was being a gentleman, but instead I learned he needed me to remain a maiden so he would get as much money as possible when he sold me, a gently-bred maiden, to a *brothel*!"

Fanny Bennet started to howl in pain and then collapsed. But a moment after Fanny heard the man's vile plans for her baby, she felt a pain like none she had experienced before. It was easy to see it was not one of her swoons contrived to garner attention, but a genuine fall, her world going black the same time as the tremendous shock of her baby's words penetrated her understanding. Her family assumed she had fainted.

Two footmen were summoned to assist Mrs. Bennet to her chambers, where a maid would attend her with salts if she did not recover her senses quickly. Bennet sat still and watched his wife being carried away; his pallor white as a sheet as he began to understand the complete ruin that had come close to befalling his family.

"When I heard his disgusting plans for me, something inside of me snapped. I shot into the Colonel's office and attacked the man. I drove him into the desk, which shattered his right arm; I understand it had to be amputated, as the break was too severe to fix.

"I do not remember it at all, but evidently I scratched him deeply around his left eye, which cost him that eye, as well as other deep scratches on his face." Lydia dropped her head; thankful Kitty was on one side and Mary on the other. They held her hands firmly, each applying pressure to assure her of their support.

"Mr. Bennet," Lady Catherine addressed the shaken man. "Was your peace and quiet at your estate worth what almost happened? From what I am told, Elizabeth is your favourite daughter, yet you dismissed her concerns as if she never before had a sensible thought. Did it not pierce your consciousness when she wrote to you to plead again that there might be more at play here than you thought?"

Had Bennet not been so thoroughly ashamed of his in-action, he might have resented Lady Catherine's words. How-ever, he realised he deserved it all—and more. "There is naught I can say in defence of my failure to act as I should have. I am beyond chagrined at the man I have become. I am pleased Lydia was saved from this situation; she should never have been put in it in the first place. I abrogated all of my parental responsibility and traded it for books and port." Bennet hung his head in shame.

"Lydia dear, is your virtue truly intact?" Madeline asked, and to her aunt, uncle, and father's great relief Lydia nodded in the affirmative.

"It will not change the past, but we have begged you since Jane was born to take an interest in your family. My sister is vulgar and of mean understanding. She was not born to the gentry, but you were Bennet. Why did you not teach her rather than ridicule her?" Gardiner asked his brother pointedly.

"What do you suggest going forward?" a defeated Bennet asked.

"Your girls—all of the unmarried ones—would like to re-main at Rosings Park, and I would like them to remain. Lydia wants to go to school—in her own words, to a strict institution —and so it shall be. I think you and your wife have much to think on and will need time without your daughters dividing your attentions." Lady Catherine allowed her words to sink in.

"Is this what all four of you desire?" Bennet asked, hoping they would not wish to remain away from him and his wife.

But he was sure they would, thereby forcing him to deal with his failure as the halls of Longbourn would be filled with nothing but silence. If they were to come home, they would remonstrate with him in their every look and their every word.

"Yes Papa, it is," Jane spoke for her three unmarried sisters who all nodded in agreement. "Papa, you may tell Mama later, but I also wanted to inform you I am betrothed to Richard Fitzwilliam, the master of this estate. We will marry in mid-May—here."

"As you are of age, you do not need my consent. I am sure your Brother Collins granted his. I gave him my authority so I would not be bothered by anything that would distract me from my books." Bennet felt his shame burn hotter than before as he admitted the last. "Although you do not need it, I hope you will accept my blessing for your match."

"I am happy to accept it. I hope you will attend and walk me up the aisle," Jane requested. Bennet nodded with all the relief a man on the verge of losing his family feels when he learns he will not. "I hope you understand why I will not allow Mama to parade me around the neighbourhood or take over my wedding?"

"No more need be said on that subject." Bennet turned to Lady Catherine. "As to my daughters remaining here, they have my leave to do so for as long as all of you desire the arrangement. I can only hope I will be worthy of their respect in the future." Bennet looked toward his daughters. "You know Longbourn is still your home, and you are welcome whenever you feel ready to return."

"Thank you Papa," Elizabeth responded as she wrapped him in a hug which he returned in full measure.

"Based on the outcome, you showed some greatness of mind. I am sorry for dismissing your concerns Lizzy. I beg all of your pardons for my faults as a man and a father," Bennet addressed all of his daughters.

"As someone very wise told us, as long as you learn from your past errors, there is no reason to dwell in the past," Jane stated as she accepted a hug from her father.

Mary and Kitty also received a warm hug from Bennet. Lydia was the last daughter to approach him, tentatively. "Please do not hate me for what I almost did Papa," Lydia requested in a tremulous voice.

"No Lydia, I could never hate you, I love you. It is I who needs to beg your pardon. I failed you because I never curbed either your mother or you. It is my fault, and I should feel the pain of my failings. Now I will do what I am able to correct my past mistakes." Bennet hugged his youngest tightly as she cried tears of relief in her father's arms.

Once he released his youngest child, Bennet turned to address Lady Catherine. "You have my deepest gratitude for the care you have given my daughters. I take no umbrage at the fact they found the support outside of their family circle they should have received from me."

"We will be related soon enough," Lady Catherine averred. "And more, it has indeed been my pleasure. Your daughters have joined my nephews and nieces to claim a part of my heart reserved for my surrogate children."

"Nothing has changed for us," Gardiner spoke up. "*Any* of you will be welcome anytime with us at Gracechurch Street."

"Including me?" Lydia wondered aloud.

"Most certainly, yes, including you," her uncle responded without hesitation.

"You have met Richard before Papa, but not as my betrothed. Will you wait while I request him to join us?" Jane asked hopefully.

"I would love to become acquainted with my future son," Bennet agreed.

Jane departed to find Richard, accompanied by Elizabeth. Kitty and Lydia went to locate Gigi. By the melodious sound from the direction of the music room, they had a good idea where she was.

"Lady Catherine, my only concern..." Bennet started to say.

"Is the propriety of Jane living in the same house as Richard." Lady Catherine completed his sentence, and Bennet nodded. Lady Catherine explained the extraordinary steps which had been undertaken to ameliorate the issue.

"It seems my worry was without merit," Bennet acknowledged. "I am thankful and appreciate the lengths you have gone to avoid any speculation about something untoward occurring. You are protecting my daughters far better than I ever did."

Just then, Jane and Elizabeth returned with not only Richard, but his parents, brother, sister, and cousin Darcy. Introductions were made to the Earl and Countess, as well as the Viscount and Viscountess. When Mr. Darcy greeted Bennet civilly, the man arched his eyebrows, for it seemed the surprises would never end.

To his further astonishment, Gardiner was acquainted with Lords Matlock and Hilldale, as they had transacted business, and Madeline Gardiner was familiar with their wives, seeing that they served together on some of the same charitable committees.

Darcy watched as he saw another of his assumptions dissolve before his eyes. Mr. Gardiner might be in trade, but he was as gentlemanly as any man Darcy knew. He ruefully smiled to himself as he remembered the way Miss Bingley had denigrated the Bennets' connections when they spoke one evening at Netherfield Park, after Jane and Elizabeth had returned to Longbourn following the former's illness.

The Bennet connections he had believed his family would decry were accepted warmly by all of them. What a fool he had been! If he had proposed as he planned, he would have told her what a degradation her family and connections were. He decided to talk to Aunt Cat before he made a bigger fool of himself. He did not doubt her advice would be invaluable yet again. As Darcy gazed at the woman he loved, he was grateful he had not proposed to her yet, as he was sure she would have rejected him out of hand.

Bennet welcomed his future son to the family, then informed his host he and his wife would depart in the morning. To save them from his wife's vulgar effusions that were sure to ensue, Bennet decided he would inform his wife of their daughter's betrothal an hour into the journey back to London.

To reinforce the saying 'men plan and God laughs,' the butler entered the drawing room and summoned Bennet to his wife's chambers. Mrs. Bennet was very ill and the local physician had been sent for.

# CHAPTER 22

When Bennet walked into his wife's chambers, he suspected she had feigned illness to garner attention for herself. The sight that met his eyes almost caused him to cast up his accounts.

The left side of his wife's face was drooping—noticeably. When she tried to call out to him, the sound was unintelligible. When Gardiner and Madeline joined him, they noticed that Fanny's right arm and leg were thrashing, but her left side was not moving at all.

"This is an apoplexy, I believe," Madeline Gardiner opined. "I have seen something like this at one of the homes where I am on the committee."

"Is there anything that can be done?" Bennet asked, very much concerned. Yes, he made sport of his wife, but he could not imagine his life without her.

"The doctor has been sent for," Gardiner stated. "Rather than making uneducated suppositions, let us wait for the professional to examine Fanny. We will know how to proceed after that." Bennet calmed down to a certain extent as there was irrefutable logic in his brother's statement.

'Why are they talking about me as if I am not here and talking to them?' Fanny Bennet asked herself. As far as she could tell, she was speaking as she always had and was unable to grasp why her husband, brother, and sister-in-law would not answer any of her questions. 'They said I cannot move my left arm and leg, of course I can...' But no matter how much Fanny tried to move those limbs, they refused to cooperate. She also noticed that when she closed her right eye, she could see nothing.

The sounds emanating from the stricken Mrs. Bennet increased, as did her obvious concern. The sounds became louder, but not clearer, than they had been before. Her right arm and leg began to move alarmingly, so wildly that Bennet asked a footman to help immobilize his wife.

"Belay that," came a voice from behind them. An unknown man entered the bedchamber carrying a physician's bag; it was the doctor.

"Mr. Bennet, Mr. and Mrs. Gardiner, may I introduce Dr. David Burnett to you?" Richard, who had accompanied the man upstairs, asked. Bennet nodded and the introductions were made.

"Mrs. Gardiner, may I request your presence while I examine your sister-in-law?" Dr. Burnett asked after the relationships had been explained to him. Maddie Gardiner nodded her acquiescence. "Gentlemen, if you will wait in the adjoining sitting room, I will be with you as soon as I have completed my examination of Mrs. Bennet.

*'No, Thomas, do not leave!'* Fanny thought she had said out loud, but no one could understand what she was trying to say. *'I am so scared Thomas!'*

~~~~~~~/~~~~~~~

Not long after Bennet and Gardiner were consigned to the sitting room, they were joined by the Collinses, Richard, Jane, and Elizabeth. Kitty and Lydia remained with Gigi and the rest of the party in the drawing room.

"Papa, will Mama be well?" Mary asked the question all of Fanny's daughters wanted answered.

"Mr. Burnett is with her now," Bennet informed his daughters. "He promised to let us know as soon as he finishes his assessment. Aunt Maddie is with him and suspects it is an apoplexy. She has seen the same in another before." Bennet went on to explain the symptoms he and the others had observed.

"Our poor mother," Jane lamented. "We will pray that she recovers."

"Just tell us what we can do to help Papa, and it will be done," Elizabeth stated as she took her father's hand. He gave her a wan smile in return.

"Bennet, you know you are welcome to remain at Rosings for as long as you need," Richard invited.

"Thank you Son," Bennet responded almost absently.

About half an hour later, Mr. Burnett entered the sitting room. Richard quickly introduced his betrothed, her sisters, and their brother. "Mr. Bennet, do you wish me to disclose my findings to everyone here?" the doctor asked.

"Please do, we are all family," Bennet allowed.

"It is my sad duty to inform you your sister's estimation was correct. Your wife has suffered a massive apoplexy that has paralysed the left side of her body." Burnett paused when the patient's three daughters began to sob. "The drooping you saw on the left side of her face is due to the loss of control of the muscles that normally hold things in place. It is the same reason she can no longer talk."

"What a trial for Mama not to be able to express herself," Elizabeth empathised. All of her mother's mistreatment was forgot, and all she now wished for was some miracle recovery for her mother.

As if reading Elizabeth's thoughts, Mr. Burnett proceeded, "There is, I am sorry to say, no cure. As far as I know, there has never been any sort of recovery from an apoplexy of the severity that Mrs. Bennet has suffered." The three sisters' sobbing increased after his pronouncement. Tears ran down both Bennet's and Gardiner's cheeks. Even given the distance between him and his sister, seeing her thus and remembering the girl she used to be affected Gardiner greatly.

"Lydia will blame herself," Jane managed between sobs.

"What do you mean Miss Bennet?" the doctor enquired.

"My wife had just received some terribly distressing news..." Bennet gave the doctor a short, sanitised version of what happened before his wife was stricken.

"From everything we understand in medicine regarding

apoplexies—granted it is not as much as we would like—we believe they are the result of a fault in a blood vessel in the area of the head. Such a fault could not have been caused by anything any of you did or did not do. The best analogy I can give you is to think of the vessel as a truss on a bridge that has an unknown weakness in it. It may support the bridge for years, but each cart or carriage that crosses will weaken the fault a bit more until it gives out. It may be a fully laden cart that triggers it, or a man walking.

"The salient point is, it was inevitable, and no one person or factor is the cause. I fully believe it is the same cause in Mrs. Bennet's case. It was going to happen, and now was the time. That is a long-winded way of telling you that Miss Lydia had as much to do with the event as she does the rising and setting of the sun each day."

Burnett's explanation made everyone feel a little easier, as they were sure Lydia would blame herself. With the explanation the doctor gave, it would be simple to convince her she was not the cause of her mother's illness.

"How will my wife communicate her needs?" Bennet asked.

"Does your wife write with her left or right hand?" Burnett verified.

"She uses her right hand," Bennet confirmed.

"In that case, I suggest you give her a slate and some chalk. I do not believe she is in pain, but it is more than likely she is frustrated because no one seems to understand her. In her own mind, I am sure she thinks she is speaking perfectly clearly. Being able to make her wishes known will reduce her frustration level." The doctor paused as he cogitated. "There is something else of which you must all be aware. Once a patient has suffered an event as severe as Mrs. Bennet has, it greatly increases the chance of subsequent attacks. I must caution you the chance of her surviving another apoplexy is minimal."

The sisters who had almost ceased crying sobbed anew, and Bennet looked as if he had been punched in the gut over and over again. "We need to summon Phillips and Hattie," Gardiner pointed out, and he turned to Richard and explained, "They are my older sister and her husband."

"Anyone who needs to be here is more than welcome," Richard assured them, "for as long as needs be."

"Did you explain all of this to my wife?" Bennet asked.

"No, your sister is doing so now, but only with respect to her physical limitations," Mr. Burnett clarified. "I leave it to you if you want to make her aware of the possibility of a relapse and the probable outcome."

"The knowledge will not enhance her life, regardless of how long she has left with us," Bennet stated resignedly.

"It is more likely it would make it more difficult. If you require me to stay and attend Mrs. Bennet for a few days, I am at your disposal; however, there is naught I can do," Mr. Burnett explained. "If she is unable to sleep, or in discomfort, then administer laudanum. Even fitful rest is better than none."

"No Doctor, there is no cause for you to remain. If there is a change, we will call on you if we may," Bennet extended his hand to the physician.

"I am at your disposal Sir," Burnett stated, as he first bowed and then shook the proffered hand.

Before Bennet was able to return to his wife's room, his son Collins pulled him aside, and they had a short but animated discussion. Bennet seemed to stare with disbelief but Collins nodded vigorously.

Elizabeth could not fathom what the conversation had been about. She was sure—based on her readings on the subject—it was too early to know if Mary was with child, so she was at a loss.

~~~~~~~/~~~~~~~

Jane and Richard entered the bedchamber with Bennet, and there was no mistaking Mrs. Bennet's agitation. Although Jane tried not to, she gasped when she saw the sagging on the left side of her mother's face.

"Mama, Richard and I have some news for you." Jane saw

her mother relax slightly. "While I was here, Richard courted me. The day before you arrived, he proposed to me, and I accepted him. It is as you always said, I could not be so pretty for no reason, and now I will become the mistress of this great estate." Jane cared not a whit for any of the things she told her mother, but she knew her mother did, and she would do *anything* to comfort the stricken woman. Using her mother's oft proclaimed words was the way she attempted to provide her some small measure of pleasure.

A single tear rolled from Fanny's right eye, and the right half of her mother's face smiled. She reached for Jane with her right hand. Jane took it and squeezed gently, then Richard leaned down and kissed his mother-in-law-to-be on the right cheek, and as Jane had done, squeezed her right hand.

"We will marry from Rosings on the seventeenth day of May Mother Bennet," Richard shared. "You *will* be at our wedding."

"Fanny my dear, did Maddie explain everything to you?" Bennet asked solicitously. Fanny moved her head in what was assumed to be a nodding motion. "We will provide you with a slate and chalk so you may make your wishes known." With her good hand, Fanny made like she was clapping.

"Mama do you remember what we were discussing before you became ill?" Mary asked, and again, Fanny nodded as well as she could.

"Lyddie was never touched Mama; we arrived in time to save her," Elizabeth informed her mother as she took her mother's good hand, and no one missed how Fanny relaxed at the knowledge that her baby was well.

"The girls are being circumspect Fanny," Bennet stated with a grin. "They did not tell you that the libertine lost an arm and an eye for his trouble, thanks to angering our Lyddie."

Her daughters were not sure, but it seemed their mother approved of the outcome. "As soon as he is fit to be moved, he will be taken to the Clink Prison in London, and he will not be a free man for the rest of his wasted life," Elizabeth informed her mother.

"Fanny, I have some more news for you. I spoke to our son just before I re-joined you in your bedchamber. There will continue to be a Bennet at Longbourn, even after I leave the mortal world." Everyone looked at Bennet with question and his wife squeezed his hand urging him to carry on. "William and Mary have had discussions, and William has decided that he will change his family name back to Bennet.

"I do not know if you know this, but his grandfather changed their family name from Bennet to Collins after the dispute that arose when he compromised my aunt. He has decided he will be known as William Bennet from this day forth. Our Mary is once again a Bennet!" Bennet announced.

Obviously approving of the decision their son had made, Mrs. Bennet cried tears of joy. She was finally looking at what she had, rather than what she wanted.

~~~~~~~/~~~~~~~

"Richard has the right of it; the Bennet parents will remain as long as they need," Lady Catherine agreed. "What of Longbourn? If you are to be here, who will manage your estate? Do you have a steward?"

"My suggestion would have been that my son and daughter take over the estate, but I know Mary wants to remain close to her mother, so I am not sure how to manage the estate from here, as I will not leave my wife's side." Bennet replied honestly.

"May I make a suggestion Mr. Bennet?" Darcy asked.

"Please do so Mr. Darcy," Bennet averred.

"As we are soon to be family, will you not call me Darcy?"

"I will as long as you call me Bennet. You were saying Darcy?"

"At Pemberley I have three under-stewards. I have known for some time now that Mark Brandson, who is not yet thirty, has been ready to take the helm of an estate on his own. I was waiting for one of the stewards at a satellite estate to retire, but none have yet done so. As he is unmarried, it would be no hardship for him to run Longbourn in your absence. If you would like, I will send him a letter asking if he would accept the position at your estate," Darcy offered.

"If Mr. Brandson is willing, I would be most appreciative. Thank you," Bennet responded gratefully.

"That man is known to me," Lord Matlock added. "If my nephew had been willing to part with him before now, I would have hired the man away some time ago."

"It is good to know he has your endorsement, your Lordship," Bennet inclined his head to the Earl.

"Matlock will do just fine," Lord Matlock offered. Before Bennet returned to his wife, he was on familiar terms with all of the Fitzwilliams.

Elizabeth was amazed. She started to change her opinion of Mr. Darcy—William—significantly after they decided to begin again, but this level of solicitude to her family was wholly unexpected. Unexpected, but most welcome. Even though her father was an indifferent estate manager at best, he would not leave Longbourn indefinitely. If William's under-steward agreed to take up the post of steward at his estate, then her father would be able to remain at their mother's side without worry.

Elizabeth had not missed the long intent looks William gave her, or how his eyes sought her out as soon as they neared one another or how they followed her whenever she moved around. It was the first time Elizabeth admitted to herself that Jane and Charlotte might have been correct; William was not indifferent to her and the looks he gave her were of admiration, not aversion. Now was not the time to consider it, but she admitted to herself that, if true, she would not be unhappy about it.

"When may we see Mama?" Lydia asked.

As predicted, when her older sisters broke the news of what had befallen their mother to her and Kitty, Lydia tried to take the blame on her shoulders and became inconsolable for a short while until Jane, Elizabeth, and Mary explained to her what Mr. Burnett had told them about the causes of an apoplexy.

Once Lydia quieted, it did not take her long to understand she was not the catalyst for the apoplexy, and that there mother did not need maudlin daughters visiting her.

"After dinner, you and Kitty will have some time with her," Jane informed her youngest sisters. "Are you prepared for the altered looks of our mother?" Both younger Bennets nodded.

"As difficult as it will be, try not to stare at Mama; it will make her self-conscious," Elizabeth added. "Papa sent an express to Aunt and Uncle Phillips, so we can expect them to arrive in a few days."

"Aunt Phillips needs to be well prepared before she sees Mama, or she will start to wail," Kitty pointed out.

"I will make sure my sister is informed what to expect before she sees your mother," Aunt Maddie told her nieces.

"And I will assist my wife," Gardiner stated. "We will do what we can to help."

"When do you need to be back in London Uncle Edward?" Mary asked.

"We will wait until my sister and Phillips arrive. Once Hattie is settled, Maddie and I will depart." Gardiner turned to Lady Catherine. "As long as it is not an imposition, we will try to visit at least every fortnight."

"Edward and Maddie, you are welcome any time for as long as you need to be here," Lady Catherine assured them. "You came in the Bennet carriage, did you not?" Gardiner nodded. "Richard, you would not object sending your soon-to-be aunt and uncle home in one of your coaches, would you?"

"You know I would not; I would place any of my coaches at the Gardiner's disposal with the greatest of pleasure," Richard offered.

"As I need to be in Town on Tuesday after Easter," Lord Matlock stated, "the Gardiners may travel with your mother and me. We have more than enough room."

"Thank you Matlock; that would cause the least upheaval

and ensure the driver would not need to make a roundtrip to get us home," Gardiner accepted.

"Should I write to Bingley and rescind the invitation for next week?" Darcy asked.

"No William, that harpy needs to be taught a lesson. You do not want her damaging Gigi's reputation with her outlandish lies, do you?" Lady Catherine asked pointedly.

"You have the right of it," Darcy acknowledged.

"I have instructed Toppin to retrieve the bath chair from the attics and have it cleaned and painted if needs be," Lady Catherine informed the group. "That way, when Mrs. Bennet feels up to it she will be able to have some society outside of her bedchamber."

The five sisters were most appreciative, though unsurprised, that their Aunt Catherine was thinking of their mother's wellbeing and comfort. She was an example of a woman they could all hope to emulate.

# CHAPTER 23

The first time all of her daughters visited her together, Fanny Bennet cried. Her husband had explained what she had missed after she was stricken—no thanks to them as parents, Lydia was safe because of the care their daughters took to insure there would be no scandal attached to the Bennet name.

With her slate and chalk, Fanny was able to communicate in a rudimentary fashion. When Elizabeth took her turn to sit with her mother, Fanny wrote but one word on her slate: 'SORRY'. "All is forgiven Mama," Elizabeth told her mother between her tears. She hugged her mother tightly, something she had not done for many a year. "Do not worry about the past, your only job now is to get as well as you are able to."

Bennet sat in a corner of the room. Other than to care for his personal needs, he had not moved from his wife's bedchamber. When Mr. Burnett came to check on his patient, Bennet asked if they could return to Longbourn, as he knew his wife would prefer to be in her own home.

Jane assured him if they were able to move her mother, she would marry from Longbourn so her mother would see her and her new son on the day they married.

The doctor had recommended against it, most strenuously. He explained that any sudden movement from a bump or rut in the road could prove fatal for Mrs. Bennet. His judgement saddened them but was accepted.

Bennet did not wish to impose, but he was informed that he and his wife were welcome for as long as they needed to be at Rosings Park. Knowing his wife would feel better with someone familiar caring for her more intimate needs, Bennet requested and was given an affirmative answer to having the Hills travel to Kent.

Darcy had informed him a letter had been sent to Brandson by courier, and that he expected an answer before the end of the week. Knowing a solution to look after Longbourn was in process, Bennet was given one less thing to worry about.

The previous day was Easter, but all of his unmarried daughters wanted to remain with their mother and miss church services. Bennet had shooed them all out, telling them he was quite capable of sitting with his wife.

His future son had sent a carriage the day before Easter to collect the Hills. The driver carried a letter of explanation from the master and instructions to make Sarah, the upstairs maid who served all Longbourn's ladies, the interim housekeeper until such time as Mrs. Hill returned to Longbourn. Unless there was a problem on the roads, the Hills would arrive on the morrow.

When he told his wife he had sent for Mrs. Hill to help her, Fanny tried to smile and wrote a large '*Thank You*' on her slate.

For his part, Bennet could not thank Lady Catherine enough. She would look in on Mr. and Mrs. Bennet a few times each day. On his way to Rosings Park, Bennet had been sure there would be, justifiably, a pointing out of their deficiencies as parents. There had been some little remonstration before his Fanny was struck down, but since then nothing. The focus was on making his wife as comfortable as possible.

Bennet felt the weight of his lackadaisical, almost non-existent, parenting style bear down on his shoulders. He had never felt contrition—until now. There was no overlooking the warmth of feeling between his daughters and Lady Catherine and all of her family, even the proud and disagreeable Mr. Darcy, who seemed neither proud nor disagreeable any longer. Unless his eyes deceived him, the very man who had called her only tolerable was interested in his second daughter.

Bennet snapped out of his reverie as he watched his

youngest curled up on the bed next to his wife. The change in her was almost too great to believe. It was unnerving to observe just how much of a sea-change Lydia's character had undergone in so short a time.

If it were not for the left side of his wife's face, it would have been hard to tell there was anything wrong with her, for an air of peace had settled over his wife. Bennet was unsure if it was acceptance, or a result of the apoplexy. Whatever it was, she was almost as serene as Jane used to be.

He had been informed about the Bingleys' upcoming visit in but two days, on Wednesday. In a way, he was sorry he would not be present to see Miss Bingley put in her place, but his place was with his wife, and there he would remain.

There was no missing the light in his wife's right eye whenever Jane and Richard visited her together. Mr. Burnett opined the attack had robbed her of sight in her left eye as it no longer reacted to light, and it seemed one had to stand on his wife's right for her to see them.

As helpful, gentle, and caring as the maids who were assigned to his wife were, he would be anxious until the Hills arrived. It was not just that his wife would feel more comfortable with Mrs. Hill, but Bennet would have Hill to attend him, the man who had been attending him for over thirty years.

~~~~~~~/~~~~~~~

The coach conveying the Hills to Rosings Park arrived a little after three on Tuesday afternoon. All five sisters waited for the carriage to come to a halt. There was much hugging and not a few tears shed as each of the sisters welcomed the woman who had been more aunt than servant since the day each was born. Mr. Hill was not spared the same warmth that was accorded his wife.

"Is my mistress very sick?" Mrs. Hill asked after the excitement of the welcome subsided.

"It *is* bad Mrs. Hill," Jane informed Longbourn's housekeeper.

"Papa will be very happy to see you Mr. Hill," Elizabeth

informed their long-time retainer. "It is not that he does not have help here, but it is not the same as having you with him."

Just then, Lady Catherine exited the house. "Jane, will you make the introductions please," she requested. It took but a moment for Jane to perform the office. "Mrs. Hill, we have converted the dressing room in your mistress's chambers into a bedchamber for you. It is not much smaller than Mrs. Bennet's bedchamber, and a comfortable bed has been moved there."

"You have my deepest appreciation, your Ladyship. I prefer to be close to my mistress," Mrs. Hill responded gratefully.

"Mr. Hill, you have a room reserved for senior visiting male staff. If either of you need anything, please communicate your needs to Mr. or Mrs. Toppin, our butler and housekeeper." Both Hills were pleasantly surprised at the way the mistress of the house treated them, rather than eschewing contact as they were but servants.

The sisters then showed the Hills to their parents' suite. As expected, though they had been forewarned, seeing the mistress for the first time was a shock for both of Longbourn's senior servants, but they schooled their features as they had done thousands of times before.

The right side of Mrs. Bennet's face lit up when she saw Mrs. Hill, and her good hand reached for the woman. After spending some time with the master and mistress, the Hills were taken to the Toppins so they could familiarize themselves with anything they needed to know to perform their duties.

~~~~~~~~/~~~~~~~~

Normally, one could not bestir Caroline Bingley from her bed before midday—at the earliest. On Wednesday, the seventeenth day of April in the year of our Lord 1811, Miss Bingley was up before dawn.

As the sun's rays broke above the horizon one minute after five that morning, Miss Bingley banged on her brother's bedchamber door to roust him from his bed so they could begin the journey to her destiny as early as possible.

"Caroline, what are you doing up? I planned to depart at eight or nine. It is just past five!" Bingley whined from inside his chambers.

"The sun is up; let us leave. The sooner I—we—arrive, the sooner my dream will come true," Miss Bingley declared in her high-pitched, grating voice.

"It will be at least an hour before I am ready; go break your fast," Bingley stated. Mayhap Caroline was correct and Darcy intended to offer for her, regardless of what he had said in the past. There was no other reason he could fathom for the invitation. Perhaps once Darcy was settled, he would permit him to pursue his angel, Miss Bennet, once again.

Bingley was seated in the breakfast parlour forty minutes later as his sister stood with crossed arms and her foot beating a staccato on the floor as she tapped it impatiently. He was tempted to remind her that every other time they needed to be somewhere, she kept him waiting. In the end, he did what he always did, avoided confrontation.

By half past six, the Bingley carriage left Curzon Street on its journey to Kent.

~~~~~~~/~~~~~~~

"Once they have alighted from their coach, the Bingleys will be shown into this drawing room," Lady Catherine directed. Jane, Lizzy, and Gigi will be in the adjoining parlour and will know when to join us. I am sure the shrew will take every opportunity to denigrate you and your family. We will see if she even recognises Mary and Collins."

"Under normal circumstances, I would feel badly for someone about to be excised from society, but I find I have no sympathy for Miss Bingley," Jane said evenly. "Everything that happens to her will be by her own hand. It took me a little longer than Lizzy to see her for who she is, but my eyes are wide open now."

"Their coach has passed the gatehouse," Richard informed those in the drawing room after he read a note from the gatekeeper, just handed to him by a groom.

While the three young ladies made their way into the adjoining parlour, Kitty and Lydia went to sit with their parents. They had asked Gigi if she wanted them to wait in the parlour with her—she thanked them but told them to spend the time with their mother.

~~~~~~~/~~~~~~~

Miss Bingley expected the whole family to be waiting to greet her, but the butler was the only one there to welcome her to her soon-to-be family's estate. "Show us to my—the—family," Miss Bingley sneered at Toppin.

The man's mien did not change at all. "As you wish Madam." Toppin walked at a sedate pace, and Miss Bingley's avarice peaked as she followed the man. All this obvious wealth! If only the place had been left to her Fitzwilliam, then they would have had *two* of the grandest estates in the land.

The butler led the Bingleys into a large drawing room. The Viscount and Viscountess of Hilldale, Lady Catherine, Mr. Fitzwilliam, Mr. and Mrs. Collins, and Mr. Darcy were present. The Earl and Countess of Matlock had returned to London the day before, conveying the Gardiners home. Lady Matlock was busy sealing Miss Bingley's fate in society.

"Charles Bingley and Miss Caroline Bingley of the Bingley family that owns Bingley Carriage Works in Scarborough." Toppin made the introduction as he had been instructed to by the mistress.

Everyone in the drawing room was amused, watching the woman attired in her signature burnt orange gown, looking as though she had dressed to attend the queen—not to travel—show signs of building fury at having her roots in trade be the first thing the people she wanted to impress heard. She did not know who these Collinses were, so she ignored them. Other than Richard, the rest of the Fitzwilliams had never deigned to be introduced to Miss Bingley.

"Miss Bingley, you seem upset," Lady Catherine noted in a saccharine-sweet voice. She turned to Mr. Bingley. "Did my nephew misinform me that you are still a partner in the carriage works your father and uncle founded?" Lady Catherine asked innocently. "If he did, I would be surprised, as William does not speak anything but the *truth*."

"Ahem, I mean yes, your Ladyship, your nephew's report was accurate." Bingley almost squeaked as he watched his sister's thunderous visage build.

"I had no knowledge my brother still sullied his hands with trade; you cannot hold that against me," Miss Bingley simpered and moved slightly away from him, as if that would distance her from the truth.

"Unlike you Miss Bingley, we judge people on character, not how they earn their money," Lady Catherine stated. Miss Bingley spluttered, not knowing how to react to such a statement.

"Hello Darcy; how are you," Bingley tried to change the subject.

"I understand congratulations are in order Mr. Bingley," Lady Catherine baited her trap.

"For what your Ladyship?" Bingley responded in confusion. Miss Bingley seemed to be looking anywhere but at Lady Catherine.

'*The old bat could not possibly know what I wrote to that bumpkin Jane Bennet!*' Miss Bingley assured herself, relieved at the distance between Kent and Hertfordshire.

"It seems someone has claimed you have an understanding with my niece, *Miss* Georgiana Darcy," Lady Catherine revealed.

"It is not true. I know not who would claim something so clearly a falsehood," Bingley stated. He turned to Darcy for support, but the man was annoyingly inscrutable.

Miss Bingley began to feel the meeting might not be about the subject she had long dreamed of and shifted uncomfortably from foot to foot as she tried to determine how best to change the subject. As they had not been invited to sit, there was nothing she and her brother could do but stand where they were.

229

"I could not have said that better myself Mr. Bingley," Darcy spoke for the first time. "Who do you think would have been classless, grasping, and delusional enough to claim such a thing?" Darcy looked at Miss Bingley with a look of true disdain.

"Caroline, how could you?" Bingley turned to his sister. Even without Darcy's pointed look, he knew she was the only one who might make such an outlandish claim.

Miss Bingley thought quickly and came up with an idea to move suspicion away from her. "It seems that fortune-hunting Miss Jane Bennet has spread lies about me. I broke off our friendship, as we are not from the same circles, and she must have suspected I stopped her from sinking her claws into my brother."

"So, you are saying on your *honour* that you never made that claim about my niece and your brother in any form to anyone?" Lady Catherine sprung her trap.

"As a member of our circles, I would never do such your Ladyship. Anyone who says so is a liar and should be excised from society. I would never do anything to harm dear Georgiana's reputation..." A chill ran down Miss Bingley's spine as she heard a voice behind her.

"When, may I ask, did either my brother or I give you leave to address me by my familiar name? Do you think I ever believed your friendship was genuine? All you wanted was to recommend yourself to my brother," Georgiana stated pointedly. "Then you had the temerity to attempt to blame something you did on people who have no motive to use my name thusly?"

"It was either the 'I act all innocent' Miss Jane Bennet or her loose sister Miss Eliza who spread the lie. Do you not know how they spread their favours around to the regiment quartered in Meryton, not only to the officers, but the enlisted men as well?" Miss Bingley spewed her vitriol as she continued to dig her hole deeper.

"What proof do you have to back up such vile accusations

Miss Bingley?" Jane asked. The woman went white; both ladies she had just slandered were standing in Rosings Park's drawing room.

She felt her only option was to attack. "I did not realise you and your brown-skinned sister Eliza had taken positions as maids here," Miss Bingley sneered with false bravado.

"Us? We are guests here, and one of us will soon be the mistress of this estate," Elizabeth informed the woman sweetly. "What estate did you live on as a child Miss Bingley?" Elizabeth paused as the woman's face turned purple, a shade that clashed with her orange outfit. "I forgot, you are a tradesman's daughter, and the only time you lived at an estate was your brief sojourn at Netherfield Park, your brother's leased estate."

Bingley looked from one Bennet to the other. Miss Elizabeth said one of them would soon be the mistress of Rosings Park; surely she could not mean his angel! Just then, his worst fears were confirmed when Richard Fitzwilliam stepped forward.

"Mr. and Miss Bingley, please meet my betrothed, Miss Jane Bennet of Longbourn in Hertfordshire," Richard said, proudly.

"How did this social-climbing fortune hunter sink her claws into you?" Miss Bingley asked, derisively.

"I see only one social-climbing fortune hunter here, Miss Bingley," Lady Catherine said firmly. It was time to bring this to a close. "It is you, and you alone. You are a liar, have no fashion sense, and lack intelligence, rounding out the list nicely."

"Charles, how can you allow that old woman to talk to me so?" Miss Bingley screeched.

While Miss Bingley was fuming, Jane handed Mr. Bingley the letters his sister had written. Miss Bingley realised what her brother held in his hand and tried to snatch them, but at a nod from Lady Catherine, a footman restrained the woman.

"Caroline, how could you stand here and lie, while making vile and unfounded accusations at the same time?" Bingley demanded.

"They are not at our level of society and that one," she pointed a bony finger at Elizabeth, took *my* Mr. Darcy's attention from me!"

"Are you insensible or merely delusional, in addition to all of the rest of your myriad faults," Darcy stated angrily. He turned to Bingley in an accusatory fashion. "Do you mean to tell me in the more than a year since I told you I would *never* offer for *her*," he pointed at a scandalised Miss Bingley, "even if she compromised me, you never told her?" Bingley hung his head in shame and shook it.

"Why *not* me? I am the ideal woman to be Mistress of Pemberley and Darcy House," Miss Bingley shrieked.

"I would *never* marry one who I dislike like the plague, one who my sister cannot tolerate having in the same room? One who is so vulgar she talks about my wealth and her dowry at every opportunity? No Madam! If you were the last woman in the world, I still would not be with you, even if it meant the end of the human race!" Darcy spat out.

"You boast about your education at Miss Hathaway's Seminary for Proper Young Ladies, yet you clearly learnt nothing there," Lady Catherine drew the shrew's attention. "If you had actually studied and not attended merely to claim you were educated at a prestigious institution, you would know it is *birth* that sets the social order, *not wealth*!

"As amusing as this has been," Lady Catherine stated sarcastically, "it is time for you to go. I would suggest Scarborough or further. My sister, the Countess of Matlock, is in London making sure you will be *persona non grata* Miss Bingley. Your so-called friends, who kept you around for the entertainment you provided, will not receive you again; no one will. Let me warn you—if you attempt to use my nephew's name, or that of anyone in this family again—this will be nothing compared to what I will bring down on your head. The same warning applies should I hear of any spite directed at my *nieces*, the Bennet sisters." Lady Catherine nodded to the footman, who escorted the shell-shocked woman to her brother's coach to wait for him.

"Mr. Bingley, you looked shocked to hear I was betrothed. Did you think I would pine for the man who did not have enough backbone to follow his own inclinations?" Jane asked pointedly.

"B-but my sisters and Darcy told me you did not care for me," Bingley spluttered.

"So what? Did they lock you away so you could not try to discover the truth for yourself? Do not answer that, as it is immaterial," Jane directed. "When you abandoned me without a word, and never came to see me after I called on your sisters in London. At the time, I thought my heart was breaking. It was not. I learnt with time I never loved you; I was infatuated. I am now in love with a *man*, one who will do anything for me, as I would for him. One who does not require permission from anyone else to do what he believes is right for him—for us. Before you tell yourself it is because he is the master of Rosings Park, understand this; I would have married Richard no matter his prospects."

"Bingley, I was wrong to advise you on matters of the heart, but I was also wrong to allow our relationship to become that of father-son instead of equal friends. I can no longer be your *de facto* parent. If and when you grow up and take control of your life—including your sister—I would be happy to have you as a friend in an equal relationship. Until then, we must go our separate ways. This time, make sure your sister understands that not only will there be nothing between us, but she will not be admitted to any of my homes or those of my family. If she dares approach any of us in society, she will receive the cut direct." Darcy looked at Bingley with a measure of pity. "I wish you good luck, Mr. Bingley."

Bingley turned without a further word. Once he joined his sister in their coach, he knocked on the ceiling with his cane. There was not a word spoken between brother and sister. She was in a state of shock, as all of her dreams and pretentions had turned to dust before her eyes; he was thinking, finally, about what he needed to do to take charge of his own life.

# CHAPTER 24

By the time they reached London, Miss Bingley decided she would soon prove that which she had been told would befall her in society was so much hot air. Brother and sister arrived at Curzon Street in time for dinner. Even though the servants were surprised to see them return on the same day they left, none of them showed it.

Miss Bingley dined without her brother, as he declared he wanted to be alone; he took his tray in his study. Charles Bingley knew he had much to consider. If he wanted to keep Darcy's friendship, he was aware he would have to make significant changes in his life.

Miss Bingley rose earlier than was her wont, intent on visiting some of *her* friends to prove she was correct that the old bat had spoken so much nonsense. She was told at every house she visited that no one was at home to her—despite seeing others of their acquaintance enter.

She dismissed it as immaterial, because those she attempted to visit were not the *best* of her friends. She took herself to Gunter's, where she was sure some of her other acquaintances would be found. Breathing a sigh of relief, she noticed Miss Jackson-Hamstead seated with two other ladies. Miss Bingley could not recall their names readily, as she had always considered them below her.

"My dear Wilamena, how I have longed to spend some time with you, it has been far too long!" Miss Bingley was struck speechless and said nothing further when Miss Jackson-Hamstead stood and glared at her, disdain written on her face.

"Come, ladies, suddenly there is a foul odour in this establishment," the lady said, picking up her reticule. All three turned their backs on a slack-jawed Caroline Bingley, giving her the cut direct in public.

What Caroline had not accepted, and had ignored, was the fact that the Countess of Matlock was in London—as Lady Catherine had warned her—and she had spread word about Miss Bingley's atrocious behaviour and lies. Lady Matlock had made it clear that Mr. Darcy had broken with Miss Bingley and would not recognise her ever again. Just as Lady Catherine had informed her, Miss Bingley had become a *persona non grata* before she even returned to London.

Less sure of herself, she walked along Bond Street with her maid following behind her, passing but a few shops. Within twenty paces she was cut three more times; now she had no doubt of what had occurred. She was ruined in the eyes of the society of which she so desperately wanted to be a member. Miss Caroline Bingley turned tail and ran back to the waiting carriage, demanding to be returned to Curzon Street with all speed.

On arriving back at her brother's townhouse, Miss Bingley burst into his study without knocking. "Those despicable Bennet chits have ruined me!" she spat out, neither noticing nor caring her brother was meeting with his solicitor.

"Caroline, I am in a meeting, and I will not have you enter my study without knocking and being bade enter. That is the right only of my wife alone, to whom I would have been joined with happily but for you," Bingley stated flatly with an edge to his voice his sister had never heard before. He returned his attention to the solicitor. "Please excuse my sister's behaviour, Mr. Jakobe. If you will agree to wait in the parlour, I will have my housekeeper bring you some refreshments while I speak with my sister." Bingley pulled the bell cord and gave his housekeeper instructions, and the solicitor followed her out of the study.

"How dare you humiliate me so in front of..." Not for the first time that day, Miss Bingley was cut off.

"Shut up Caroline! I have allowed you free rein to manipulate me for far too long, but no more." Miss Bingley was about to interject; however, she closed her mouth when she saw the malevolent look her brother directed at her. "I assume you did not have a good day in society today. Let me guess—no one was at home to you, so you attempted to approach some of your so-called friends in public and were cut?"

Miss Bingley gave a sullen nod. "It is all the Bennets'..." she tried again to repeat her nonsensical claim, and she was once again cut off.

"Did the Miss Bennets force you to lie about Miss Darcy? Did they cause your delusions about Darcy and your position in society? Did they make you behave in a reprehensible way that makes no one want to be around you?" Bingley asked pointedly.

Miss Bingley was seething, but also confused. This was not the brother she could manipulate as she previously had, even as she had yesterday morning. There was steel in his look and his back was ramrod straight.

Unfortunately for Miss Bingley, her brother had taken the time since their return from Kent to look at himself, and he did not like what he saw. He decided to take his life into his own hands, to accept responsibility for his own actions, and to stop relying on others_namely Darcy—to make decisions for him. Given Darcy's final words of warning, he knew he had to start by taking his sister in hand.

"Caroline, you walk around with your nose in the air like royalty, yet you are the daughter of a tradesman," Bingley pointed out. "Socially, we are below *all* landed gentlefolk, *including* the Bennets. Your dowry, education, and your pretentions change none of that. The *only* reason we were accepted into some higher society was due to Darcy's patronage_and that is ours no more."

"What are we to do?" the dejected woman asked.

"Mr. Jakobe will find someone to lease this house, and we will move back to Scarborough. Be forewarned, I will no longer cover any of your overspending. You will live within your allowance. I am of a good mind to make you pay for most, if not all, of your extravagant spending before we travelled to Kent; to my chagrin, I did not put my foot down before this." Bingley paused to look his sister in the eye so she could not mistake his resolve. "As long as you live with me you *will* obey the rules of my house, which includes treating *all* others with kindness and respect—including our servants!"

Miss Bingley's face had a pinched look; she wanted to object, but for once controlled her sharp tongue. She simply nodded.

"If you flout my rules, I will have Jakobe release your dowry to you, after which you will live in your own establishment and I will not assist you financially at all. I suggest you find a husband at our level of society, or if anyone will have you, to a member of the third circles like Hurst. Your time of living in a delusion is over. Do you understand me Caroline?" Bingley waited for his sister to react.

"Yes Brother, I do. What time do you require me to be ready to depart in the morning?" Miss Bingley was keen to escape from London. She never again wanted to suffer the humiliation she had that day.

"We will break our fast at eight and be on the road no later than nine. As you demonstrated the day we travelled into Kent, you are able to rise early when you choose to," Bingley informed his sister. She nodded, then left his study without further response to supervise her packing.

The following morning, Miss Bingley was in the dining parlour at the specified time. Brother and sister departed Curzon Street ten minutes before the time Bingley had set for departure.

~~~~~~~/~~~~~~~

"How is your mother?" Lady Catherine asked.

"She is as comfortable as can be expected, given her situation," Elizabeth reported. "It is understandable that there are times when she gets frustrated by her limitations. Papa has been very good with her; he still spends most of his time in her chambers."

"Your father is learning the lesson I learned much too late," Lady Catherine said wistfully as she looked to the heavens. "You do not appreciate what you have until it is no longer there. I loved my Anne, but I treated her more as a possession than a beloved daughter. My Lewis was always good to me, which I saw only after he was gone."

"At least Papa has some time left with Mama," Jane opined. "Yes, she is infirm, but there is no mistaking the love and caring Papa has demonstrated since Mama was stricken."

"You have the right of it Jane," Lady Catherine agreed. "I would have given anything for more time with Lewis and Anne. Enough maudlin thoughts! Where are my nephews and other nieces?"

"Richard and William are visiting tenants this morning. Mary is at the parsonage enjoying some richly deserved time alone with our brother. The three youngest girls are having lessons with Mrs. Annesley.

"It is less than a month until you marry, Jane. What are your plans to shop for your wedding gown and trousseau?" Lady Catherine enquired.

"How can I go to Town and shop when Mama is lying in bed?" Jane lamented. "Mr. Burnett ruled out the bath chair for the same reason she should not be in a carriage. I just do not know if this is the appropriate time to travel to London."

"Jane, your feelings do you credit, but they are fallacious," Lady Catherine told the eldest Bennet.

"How so Aunt Cat?" Jane asked. Like all of her sisters Jane had finally begun to use the shortened version of Lady Catherine's name.

"If your mother were able to speak as she used to before her apoplexy, is there anything that would convince her to tell you not to shop for your wedding gown and trousseau, other than the death of a close family member?" Lady Catherine challenged.

Jane cogitated for a little while. "No, I dare say she would not. I will ask her. She is getting better at communicating her needs," Jane decided. She turned to Elizabeth, "You will accompany me to Town, will you not Lizzy?"

"For you, Jane dearest, of course I will. Where will we stay?" I am sure Uncle and Aunt Gardiner would be happy to have us stay with them," Elizabeth opined.

"Richard's mother was hoping you would stay at Matlock House so she can spend some more time getting to know you Jane," Lady Catherine informed them.

"Lizzy, you will not be intimidated being hosted in the house of an earl and countess would you?" Jane teased her sister, well knowing how false her joke was.

"You know me Janie, my courage always rises at every attempt to intimidate me," Elizabeth returned her sisters jest. "If Aunt Elaine has invited us, I would be happy to reside there while we are in London. Aunt Maddie will understand, I am sure."

"You will be able to see your Aunt and Uncle Gardiner," Lady Catherine relayed. "Elaine will invite them to dinner at least once while you are there; in fact, they have dined at one another's houses since returning to London. Unless there are pressing needs at home, I would wager that your Aunt Maddie will join your shopping party. I would recommend you go to your Uncle's warehouse before your appointment at the modiste. That way you can select bolts of fabric that have not been seen by anyone in Town yet."

"You took the words out of my mouth," Elizabeth informed her aunt. "Should we go talk to Mama?" Jane nodded.

The two sisters each kissed lady Catherine on the cheek and then proceeded to their mother's chambers.

~~~~~~~/~~~~~~~

Hattie Phillips was a fixture at her sister's side. Other than to sleep and for her personal hygiene, Fanny's eldest sibling had refused to move from her position next to her sister's bed. She read to her sister, fed her, and did anything else Fanny needed.

The decision of the Gardiners to wait for the Phillipses to arrive before they departed had been an excellent one. With the support of her husband, the Gardiners, her nieces, and Lady Catherine, Hattie had been prepared to see her sister.

As anticipated, her initial reaction when informed what had befallen Fanny was extreme. There had been wailing and an almost-swoon, but after a half hour with Lady Catherine, Hattie Phillips pulled herself together, straightened her back, and decided she was here for her sister. It was not about her sadness but helping her stricken sister.

Her reaction on seeing Fanny was muted compared to what it would have been without being as prepared as she was. That first visit, she had been accompanied by her sister Maddie, Jane, Elizabeth, and Mary.

Since then, Hattie had been a balm to her sister, and there was nothing that was to be done for Fanny that she did not do herself. If her husband had not put his foot down, she would have tried to remain with her sister four and twenty hours per day.

Frank, Hattie's husband, sat with Bennet for an hour or two each day to discuss the legal issues that needed to be dealt with during Bennet's absence from Longbourn. An express had arrived from Pemberley indicating Mr. Brandson's acceptance of the post of steward of Longbourn.

Phillips took copious notes each day, so when he met with his brother's new steward he would be able to pass on information in the absence of the master. The brothers had discussed how difficult it would be for his wife when the Phillipses had to return to Meryton in a few days.

"Jane and Lizzy, it is good to see you again so soon," Bennet welcomed his two eldest back to their mother's chambers after his brother's departure. "You just missed the youngest three. Gigi played the upright while Kitty showed your mother some new sketches she is making, and Lydia lay next to my Fanny talking to her."

Lady Catherine had some footmen move an upright

pianoforte into Fanny's chambers. It had been gathering dust in Mrs. Jenkinson's old room, just off of the late Anne de Bourgh's suite. It had been cleaned until it shone like new, moved, and then tuned.

When Fanny desired it, either Elizabeth, Mary, or Gigi would play soft music for her. Lydia started learning from Gigi, but so far she had only mastered her scales. She looked forward to the day she could surprise her mother by playing a basic tune.

Lydia's misadventure had not been mentioned in company since the Phillipses arrival. Even though she was sure her Aunt Hattie would not spread word abroad of her near ruin in Brighton, Lydia was pleased the tale had not been told to her mother's sister.

"We need to ask Mama about Jane travelling to London to shop for her clothing needs," Elizabeth informed their father. "Do you think it will upset her if we go?"

"Not nearly as much as if you did not go. When we spoke last night, she made it clear to me that she wanted life to carry on—she would agree Jane needs to shop for her trousseau and wedding gown. I dislike discussing lace, but I know what will be needed before Jane marries Richard," Bennet assured his daughters.

Lydia had an ingenious suggestion. She wrote all of the letters on a large slate as well as a goodly number of commonly used words and phrases on another. Fanny Bennet was given a shortened stick such as gardeners would use to support a plant, and she would point at a word or letters. If all else failed, she had her own slate on which to write. Due to Lydia's brilliant idea, Bennet announced to one and all he no longer had *any* silly daughters.

The system had proven most effective and had eradicated much of the frustration Fanny had due to being unable to communicate normally.

With her eldest nieces attending their mother, Hattie Phillips made for her chambers to take a short rest. Jane and

Elizabeth sat on the bed near their mother, each holding one of Lydia's slates. "Mama, would you object if Lizzy and I travelled to London for less than a sennight to find a wedding gown and to order my trousseau?" Jane asked.

Fanny pointed first to '*No*', then to '*of course not*'. "Are you sure Mama? If you want I will remain here to be with you," Elizabeth offered.

'*No, you go too*', Fanny pointed to with her stick. Then she pointed to the one Jane was holding with the letters. '*A-s-k M-a-d-d-i-e b-e-s-t f-a-b-r-i-c*'.

"Yes, Mama, I will go to Uncle Edward's warehouse before I go to the modiste. Aunt Cat reminded me we will be able to find fabric no other has seen before," Jane told her mother. Fanny's head moved vigorously which by now they knew was her way of nodding agreement. Jane wanted to tell her mother how much she wished she was well enough to join the expedition to London, but she refrained, not wanting to occasion her mother more pain, having to think about one more thing she was unable to do.

'*Where you stay*'? Fanny pointed to words on the slate her second daughter held.

"We have been invited to stay at Matlock House Mama," Elizabeth informed her mother. "Richard's parents' house."

'*Good tired now*', Fanny indicated. Both of her older daughters kissed her cheek, then their father's, and made their way back to the drawing room to plan for their journey to London. Per their father's instruction, they did not inform Aunt Hattie they were no longer with their mother, allowing her some well-earned rest.

~~~~~~~~/~~~~~~~~

When the two sisters entered the drawing room, both Richard and Darcy had returned and were talking to Lady Catherine. Based on the melodic tones emanating from the music room, the three younger girls were there.

As soon as Jane spied her betrothed she lit up with pleasure, as did he on seeing her. Elizabeth blushed lightly at the intense approving stare she received from William. Jane sat next to Richard after greeting him, while Elizabeth sat next to her sister, opposite William.

The sisters informed Lady Catherine of their mother's agreement with their plan to go to London. "I will send a note to my sister. When will you depart?" Lady Catherine asked.

"Lizzy, as today is Friday, what say you to Monday?" Jane asked.

"I am at your disposal Sister; I have no prior engagements," Elizbeth agreed.

"As much as I wish to accompany you both, I am in the middle of the spring planting," a disappointed Richard informed his ladylove.

"Richard," Darcy called his cousin's attention to himself. "We are at the end of the process. If you choose to, you could make the trip without any negative consequences." Both Jane and Richard were happy at Darcy's statement.

Marie entered the drawing room after spending some time with little Reggie. "Andrew and I need to return to London for a few days; we would be more than happy to convey you two to London. I will be available to assist my soon-to-be sister with her shopping," Marie offered.

"They will be going to the same house as you," Lady Catherine informed her niece.

"You will be staying at Matlock House? How much fun— the more the merrier," Marie gushed.

As the Bennet ladies stood to leave the drawing room, Darcy called Elizabeth aside. "Elizabeth, do you intend to walk your favourite route tomorrow?" he asked.

"Yes, William I do," Elizabeth averred. "Why do you ask?"

"Would you object if I walk with you?" he asked, hopefully.

"You will hear no objection from me," Elizabeth replied. She then turned to Lady Catherine. "Who will escort me on the morrow?"

"Jeffers will be ready for you when you depart," Lady

Catherine informed them. The pleasant footman was Elizabeth's escort when he did not have other duties to perform.

As far as Darcy was concerned, her verifying her escort so as to avoid any possible impropriety elevated her in his mind. Before this, he could not imagine Elizabeth could rise any higher in his estimation, but now she had reached the pinnacle of his approbation.

Jane and Elizabeth collected the three younger girls, then the five walked toward the parsonage to have tea with Mary and William Bennet.

# CHAPTER 25

A few minutes after sunrise, Elizabeth, accompanied by the footman, waited for her walking partner to arrive. She did not have to wait for long. "I apologise for being tardy," Darcy gave a half bow.

"Seeing as I did not have to wait for you for more than a minute, I find there is nothing to forgive; I do not consider you tardy," Elizabeth granted.

"In my mind, I should have been waiting for you, not the other way around," Darcy insisted.

"If there is reason to do so, you are forgiven. Shall we?" Elizabeth led off and Darcy offered her his arm. She placed her delicate hand lightly on his forearm causing a fission of pleasure to shoot up his arm and into his chest.

Darcy was certain his walking partner was the only woman he would ever want to marry. There was no doubt he loved her, and he was sure, given his marked attentions to her since his arriving in Kent, she would be expecting him to pay his addresses.

He was confident there would be an opportunity on their walk to propose. He knew from the times he had met her walking in the morning that the glade was a favourite spot of hers. Yes, that would be the perfect spot to declare his love and become betrothed to *his* Elizabeth.

As she walked, Elizabeth surreptitiously stole glances at the man who had offered her his arm. Yes, he was no longer insufferable, and yes, she did enjoy his company. She appreciated that he treated her as an equal when they debated and was not in any way condescending.

She was just starting to know the real William, and could

imagine tender feelings developing for him, but she needed to know him better first. She had accepted that he admired her, and now she was beginning to admire him.

He was loyal; he treated Gigi as well as, if not better than, any brother could. She was aware his pride had allowed him to overlook the faults in Gigi's former companion and he still berated himself for that lapse to this day. It had impressed her when the Gardiners were in residence how respectfully he interacted with them.

Elizabeth had not missed his surprise at the gentility of her aunt and uncle. She was sure he had expected Uncle Edward to be a male version of his sisters.

Since her arrival, Aunt Hattie had been subdued, given her sister's health. To Elizabeth's relief, her aunt had not indulged in gossip, there had been no vulgar effusions, and she had been calmer than was her wont in Meryton.

Upon further consideration, she realised not even Lydia's near ruin had caused William to revert to the haughty, disdainful, and insufferable man he had been in Meryton. He had tried to take the blame for Lydia's actions onto himself. It was one of his faults; he tried to assume responsibility for that which was not his.

There was much to admire about the man, but she did not have tender feelings for him quite yet. There were perhaps the beginnings of them, so she hoped she would have the time to sketch his character correctly.

Elizabeth realised in that moment if he were to offer a courtship she would accept gladly. She was reasonably confident that, given more time in his company, her feelings would develop until she came to love him. That thought brought her pleasure.

~~~~~~~/~~~~~~~

"Richard, did I hear Frank Phillips saying he must return to Meryton to take care of his law practice?" Lady Catherine asked as the two sat in the master's study, going over the schedule for the coming week.

"You did. You miss nothing. Although he knows his wife would like to stay with her sister, he feels their return cannot be delayed any longer. He has taken on a clerk, but the man is not yet ready to do the more complex work needing to be completed," Richard informed his aunt.

"I will issue an invitation for Hattie to remain as long as she wishes; hopefully she will, unless her husband requires his wife to travel home with him," Lady Catherine decided. "Her comfort is a balm to Fanny, so there is no question of her departing unless she desires it."

"William hopes to be the recipient of our best wishes for the future when he and Lizzy return from their walk," Richard observed.

"Is that boy finally going to request a courtship?" Lady Catherine asked.

"Courtship, no; he intends to propose." Richard's confusion was plain to read when he saw the look of dismay on his aunt's face.

"Elizabeth is not ready to hear a proposal from him! Based on what she has told me she wants to get to know him better," Lady Catherine related. "I am sure *he* is in love with *her*, but she is only getting to know him and will not accept a proposal if she feels she is not ready. I am afraid William will assume her feelings equal his. We will see what his demeanour is when he returns from their walk."

"William, I hope you control your anger if she refuses you," Richard beseeched, eyes towards the heavens.

~~~~~~~/~~~~~~~

"Would you like to sit on the bench in the glade?" Darcy asked hopefully.

"Yes, I think I would enjoy that," Elizabeth responded as they branched off the main pathway onto the one that led to the glade.

It was already a warm day with nary a cloud in sight, but the glade was cooler from the shelter the trees ringing it provided. The pond in the centre of the glade was not large, and the sounds of frogs and toads could be heard along with the hum of insects. A little breeze caused the leaves on the highest branches to sway gently, but at ground level very little air movement could be felt.

The wildflowers were plentiful and in full bloom, making a carpet of riotous colour. There were two benches in the glade, one near where the path entered the peaceful, verdant area, and the other on the opposite side of the pond.

Darcy led Elizabeth to the farthest bench to create some distance from the footman, who remained at the end of the path. The servant would be able to see them at all times but would not be able to hear unless one of them raised his or her voice.

"Jeffers," Elizabeth addressed the footman. "There is no need for you to stand the whole time; there is a perfectly good bench near you."

"Thanks ya, Miss," the footman returned as he made for the bench and took a seat.

"It is so beautiful here," Elizabeth sighed as her arm swept from left to right in front of her, indicating the area. "Nature has been given free rein, and no one has imposed the awkward tastes of man on this wonderful place."

"Anne used to love this glade," Darcy remembered. "She would drive her phaeton to the beginning of the path that leads here, walk the short distance, and then she would sit and drink in the beauty of the place. She was usually accompanied by Mrs. Jenkinson—her former companion—or her father, or sometimes both. One time she told me she was never more at peace than she was when she sat and ruminated here."

"It has been more than six years since your cousin and uncle were taken, has it not?" Elizabeth verified.

"It will be seven years in July," Darcy confirmed. "As much as I miss my cousin and uncle, it is the future I would like to discuss, not the past."

"What is it you would like to discuss?" Elizabeth asked, her head cocked to one side as a beam of early-morning sunlight shone behind her head creating the effect of a halo of light.

Darcy paced back and forth for a minute or so. Elizabeth had learnt that rather than a sign of disdain, as she had thought it to be in Hertfordshire, she knew it was what he did when he was considering a weighty issue.

"It will not do, in vain I have struggled, my feelings will not be repressed. I must tell you how ardently I love and admire you," Darcy began, forgetting to get down on one knee as he intended. "When I thought you below me, your connections non-existent and the behaviour of your family, except for you, Jane, and Mary of course, was unacceptable, I fought against my inclination, thinking an alliance with you would be a degradation to the Darcy name and my family."

Darcy was so intent on making his speech that he did not notice the look of dismay on Elizabeth's face. She was wondering how he expected to request a courtship after telling her how unsuitable he had thought her to be.

"After my family humbled me at Christmastide, I came to realise many of my former scruples were fallacious. When I look back on my former behaviour, I cannot but view it with abhorrence." Darcy paused as he walked back and forth some more.

He stopped in front of the object of his desire. "Having found all of my former arguments to be specious, I came to acknowledge there was nothing about you or your family which is objectionable. After meeting the Gardiners here at Rosings, I could not but own they are among the most genteel persons I know."

"William, I am still not sure where all of this is going," a confused Elizabeth told Darcy. "You are saying a lot and not asking anything, if that was indeed your intent to do so."

"It is so much easier for me to order my thoughts when I write. When I speak—unless I have rehearsed at length what I mean to say—what I am attempting to say will often times come out all wrong as I become disconcerted. An example was my reaction to Bingley at the assembly when I was attempting to stop him from trying to coerce me into dancing. Instead, I insulted you," Darcy explained.

"Just speak plainly," Elizabeth prompted.

"What I have been attempting to do was ask for your hand in marriage. Elizabeth will you honour me and be my wife?" Darcy asked, relieved and pleased he had finally managed to ask the question uppermost in his mind.

Elizabeth gasped. Marriage! She was not ready to make that commitment! Darcy, hearing her gasp thought it was in response to the pleasure and honour of his proposing to her.

"You have bestowed a great honour on me, but I am sorry, I am not ready to become betrothed to you," Elizabeth said gently. "It was a different question I was hoping for."

All Darcy heard was that she was refusing him, the second half of her statement was lost to him. "Is this all the answer I can expect as you reject me out of hand?" Darcy asked, as he allowed his anger to rule. Before he said something he would truly regret, Darcy turned on his heel and stormed off without so much as a by-your-leave.

Elizabeth was stunned. She was willing to enter into a courtship with William, but how could she when he was not willing to listen to her words? Would he ignore her opinions and show her no respect? One thing Elizabeth knew is she did not want a marriage such as the one her parents used to have; she wanted a partnership.

She stood, in a daze, and with the footman trailing behind her, Elizabeth began the walk back to the manor house. She noticed that the sky had begun to darken as heavy clouds were scudding across the sky.

The change in weather represented the change she felt in her mood.

~~~~~~~/~~~~~~~

Darcy walked like a man possessed; he neither knew nor cared in what direction. He did not see that the weather had changed, the wind increasing and dark grey clouds invading the formerly blue sky. Before he knew where he was, he was at the folly on a hill overlooking Rosings Park, a replica of a small Greek temple his late uncle had built for Anne.

By the time he arrived at the folly, his anger had abated to a degree; it was replaced by shame. Elizabeth had been trying to say something to him, and what had he done? He had turned and run away like a petulant child who had been told he was not allowed to play with his favourite toy.

What must she think of him? Had he just destroyed any chance he had of winning her hand? He made circuits of the folly trying to regulate himself. After ten minutes he was no less confused as to what his next step—if any—should be, so he sat down with his back against the wall of the structure, his head in his hands as despair fell on him.

Without warning, the sky opened and rain poured down with such force it seemed to fall horizontally. Earlier, he noticed there were few clouds in the sky, but in his distraction, he had not noticed the changing weather. Darcy barely reacted; the weather was merely a reflection of his mood. Given the angle at which the rain was falling, he was not well protected and was becoming soaked, but he did not care; it was no less than he deserved, after all.

All he hoped was that Elizabeth had been able to return to the house before the heavens opened.

~~~~~~~~/~~~~~~~~

Lady Catherine visited Fanny before she went to break her fast. She found Hattie feeding her sister with Mrs. Hill's assistance, and Bennet was with Mr. Hill preparing for the day. As agreed, Frank Phillips met his wife in Fanny's bedchamber.

"Hattie, I need to return to Meryton. I am sorry, but there is much I need to take care of, so I pray you will understand," Phillips relayed to his wife.

"I do understand, but I am loathe to leave Fanny's side," Hattie stated as she held onto her sister's right hand.

"That is why I am here. In my capacity of mistress of this estate—as temporary as the title now is—it is my pleasure to invite you to remain at Rosings for as long as you choose," Lady Catherine explained.

"Frank, you do not object if I remain with Fanny, do you?" Hattie asked hopefully.

"Not at all," Phillips assured his wife. "I need to get Longbourn's new steward situated, and there are a few matters Gregson does not have the experience to deal with. As soon as I have completed all I need to do, I will return. Fitzwilliam and Lady Catherine have assured me that, like you, I am welcome any time. Remember, the Gardiners will return with their children in a sennight."

"Thank you Catherine, for inviting me, and Frank for agreeing to spare me," Hattie said appreciatively. She felt Fanny squeeze her hand and give her half smile, indicating her pleasure at not being deprived of her sister's company.

~~~~~~~/~~~~~~~

Elizabeth looked at the change in the weather as she walked briskly back to the manor house. She hoped she and Jeffers would gain the house before the skies opened up. *'Insufferable man! I was right about him; he has not changed,'* Elizabeth told herself, then she checked her emotions.

*'No, that is a prevarication. He has changed and is not the same man I disliked so intensely in Hertfordshire. Did he not tell me how he can become flustered when he tries to speak if he had not practised or made notes to assist him? Assumptions were the problem when we first met; I cannot make that same error again. When he returns, we must speak. I hope he is sheltered from the hard rain!'*

When Elizabeth entered the breakfast parlour, Lady Catherine saw that her equanimity had been disturbed. "Elizabeth, be a dear and accompany me to my study. I would like to show you something."

Richard and Jane were intent on talking to each other between bites of their fast-cooling meal, so they hardly noticed. Kitty, Gigi, and Lydia looked up from their plates, but soon lost interest in whatever Lady Catherine and Elizabeth were up to, while Mrs. Annesley sat across from them eating quietly.

"What happened Elizabeth, if you do not mind my asking?" Lady Catherine asked after she closed her study door. "Did William do something to upset you?"

"Yes—no—yes!" Elizabeth stammered.

"Are you willing to share what happened with me?" Lady Catherine requested.

"It was such a pleasant walk, and we ended up sitting on one of the benches in Anne's glade, and then he *proposed*! I refused him as I do not know him—the true him—well enough as yet. I tried to tell him it was not the question I had expected, but he stormed off before I had a chance to explain," Elizabeth related.

"It is as I feared. William has had, for some time now, the deepest feelings for you," Lady Catherine stated. "He assumed your feelings equalled his. Will you allow me to talk to him about this? Not on your behalf—you and he need to have that conversation—but to try to help him understand he needs to talk to you and truly *listen* rather than be ruled by his desires alone."

"I almost slipped into my old way of thinking about him, but thank goodness I caught myself," Elizabeth answered. "Yes, you may talk to him on the subject. I do care for him, but I am not in love with him yet, and I will not marry without *mutual* love and respect."

"Well I know that. Let us return to the breakfast parlour. You have yet to break your fast, am I correct?" Lady Catherine surmised. Elizabeth nodded.

The two were about to re-enter the breakfast parlour when Darcy, soaked from head to toe, arrived in the hall. The butler was trying to dry what he was able as the man came to an abrupt halt, suddenly facing both his aunt and the woman who owned his heart as he stood in a pool of water.

# CHAPTER 26

Elizabeth and Darcy stared at one another, neither knowing what to say. Before the silence became uncomfortable, Lady Catherine took charge. "William, you look a sight," she stated, breaking the tension. "Go have a warm bath, change, and then seek me out."

"Yes Aunt Cat," Darcy responded, relieved that he was not the one who had to break the silence first. "Did you make it back before the rain Elizabeth?"

"I did. Thank you for asking." Both knew their conversation was stilted, and both hoped they would soon be able to move past the awkwardness.

"William, why are you soaked?" Georgiana asked as she, Kitty, and Lydia were departing the breakfast parlour.

"It is what happens when one is caught in a sudden downpour Gigi," Darcy replied drolly. "You should try it sometime," he jested.

"Very droll William," Georgiana remarked as she joined the two youngest Bennets on their way up to see their mother.

"Off you go," Lady Catherine shooed her nephew. "At this rate, you will leave more water in the entrance hall than will be in your bath."

"*Yes* Aunt Cat. I will see you both later," Darcy stated, leaving a trail of water on the marble floor and up the grand staircase. He was thankful Richard had not finished his meal yet, as the teasing from that quarter would have been merciless.

"Please notify Mrs. Toppin there is some water to dry up before someone slips in it," Lady Catherine addressed the nearest footman, who gave a bow and left to deliver the mistress's message to the housekeeper.

Lady Catherine and Elizabeth proceeded into the breakfast parlour.

~~~~~~~/~~~~~~~

"Sit," Lady Catherine instructed as her nephew entered her study freshly bathed, shaved, and wearing dry clothes.

"You wanted to see me?" Darcy asked, even though he knew the answer, and why his aunt wanted to talk to him.

"Do you think that we all think and feel the same way?" Lady Catherine began.

"Of course not," Darcy returned with a quizzical look.

"Then why did you assume Elizabeth would be at the same point you are?" Lady Catherine asked pointedly. "It was not many months ago she thought you insufferable, haughty, proud, and disdainful of anyone you deemed lower than yourself. Need I go on?"

"No Aunt, I think I understand what you are saying," Darcy said as he hung his head.

"It would take a blind man not to be able to see that Elizabeth has changed her thinking about you, but this is all new for her; that is not so for you," Lady Catherine explained.

"I was so hurt when she refused me, I did not listen," Darcy related with shame.

"Did she just reject you, or did she also try and tell you something else?"

"The latter, but all I heard was she would not accept me. And what did I do? I stormed off without listening to her. Will I never learn?"

"You are eight and twenty, by no means an old man; however, the formation of your character was the work of many years while your desire to change has been of much shorter duration. It will take time," Lady Catherine soothed her nephew.

"If she will hear me, I would like to talk to Elizabeth," Darcy stated with a little hope.

"It is my belief she would like nothing more than to remove this latest misunderstanding between you. But, William," Darcy looked up and met his aunt's eyes, "listen to her. Truly *hear* what she tells you, rather than filter her words through your interpretation of what you expect her to say."

"And stop thinking because I feel one way others do as well?" Darcy offered.

"You see William, you are not too old to learn," Lady Catherine teased her surrogate son.

"I obviously have your blessing to proceed," Darcy observed.

"Even were Jane not betrothed to Richard, I could not imagine anyone of good sense objecting to Lizzy. You do not need my blessing William; you are a big, tall fellow and your own man," Lady Catherine stated lovingly. "You have seen how I esteem the Bennet sisters, so you must know how I feel."

"I would like your blessing, all the same," Darcy stated warmly. His conversation with his aunt had him feeling much better as he now believed there was still hope for him and Elizabeth.

"Then you have it. Go to it," Lady Catherine said with motherly affection.

~~~~~~~~/~~~~~~~~

Darcy waited in the drawing room until Elizabeth returned from visiting her parents and Aunt in her mother's bedchamber. When she and Jane entered, the three younger ladies quit the room for the music room.

"Elizabeth, may I talk with you?" Darcy asked, tentatively. His aunt had told him Elizabeth was amenable to speak with him, but until he heard it from her, he would feel some trepidation.

"Yes, I would like that," Elizabeth returned in a friendly tone, which put Darcy at ease.

"Mrs. Annesley, please accompany my niece and nephew to the parlour opposite. I will remain here with Jane and Richard until you three return," Lady Catherine instructed.

"And here I thought you would leave us alone," Richard jested saucily, earning him a light slap on the arm from his betrothed and his aunt's gimlet eye.

Mrs. Annesley found a chair as far from the couple as possible so she could not hear what they said. The two principals sat on opposite ends of a settee on the other side of the room.

"I need to apologise for childishly walking away without listening to what you were trying to say to me," Darcy opened. "Try as I may, I still revert back to my old way of expecting everyone to grant what I wish, without taking their desires into account."

"You are not the only one who needs to apologise for falling back into old attitudes," Elizabeth acknowledged. "I think rather than each of us trying to argue over who was more at fault, let us move forward rather than living in the past. For my part you are forgiven in full measure."

"Not being sure you have anything for which to beg my pardon, I give it none the less," Darcy allowed. "Aunt Cat pointed out that I have always had a tendency to assume if I feel strongly about something, or someone, as in this case, the other person's feelings must match my own."

"William, let me speak plainly." Darcy nodded. "I am attracted to you. In fact, I may be starting to develop warm feelings for you, but that does not mean I am ready to accept a proposal of marriage from you quite yet," Elizabeth explained. "Like Jane, I swore I would only marry for the deepest of love, regardless of rank, connections, or wealth. We grew up in a house where we were subjected to daily examples of the evils in a match of unequal affections, one devoid of respect. It is sad that only now, after my mother has been stricken with an apoplexy, we finally see there is affection between them." After a moment Elizabeth added, "If only they had treated each other this way when Mama was healthy!" It was a wistful wish, as Elizabeth knew there was no way to correct the errors of the past.

"On the other hand, I grew up seeing the depth of love and respect my parents had one for the other, and I still ended up being the man you despised in Meryton," Darcy stated contritely.

"Did we not agree to move forward?" Elizabeth asked archly.

"Yes, we most certainly did," Darcy acknowledged.

"In that case, let us concentrate on today and on the future. Do you want to hear what I tried to say after I told you I could not accept a betrothal *yet*?" Elizabeth asked one eyebrow arched.

"Please," was Darcy's succinct reply.

"What you did not hear was the following: I would have gone on to say although I was not ready to accept a proposal *today*, there was another question I was expecting you to ask," Elizabeth informed Darcy. "In fact, I was *hoping* you would ask *that* question."

"Are you telling me that you are willing to enter into a courtship with me?" Darcy asked. His heart sped up. He felt the staccato in his chest and the sound of his rapidly beating heart in his ears.

"As the man, you must ask the question before I may answer it," Elizabeth teased. How he enjoyed being teased by this impertinent woman he loved beyond all reason.

"Elizabeth Rose Bennet, will you do me the honour of entering into an official courtship with me?" Darcy asked. How she enjoyed the sonorous sound of his deep baritone voice. It did not hurt that he was the most handsome man Elizabeth knew.

"Most certainly yes. That is *exactly* what I would like so I can get to know you better," Elizabeth replied happily.

Darcy took each of her dainty hands in his large ones, turned them over, and bestowed a kiss on the underside of each wrist, his lips lingering over each one for longer than strict propriety would allow. Even better, Elizabeth did not seem to object to his taking such a liberty. Now it was Elizabeth's turn to experience a racing heart, as the pleasurable sensation of his kisses caused her to draw in a deep breath.

"As your father is in residence, I will go see him to ask

his consent for our courtship," Darcy stated, almost giddily. *'If I had not rushed things this morning, I would have known this joy for some hours already,'* Darcy admonished himself. *'I never thought I would attain this level of happiness again; she is my world.'*

"Let me accompany you, as my father may have questions for me. That way we will be able to give my mother joy at the same time," Elizabeth stated.

~~~~~~~/~~~~~~~

When Elizabeth and Darcy entered her mother's bed-chamber, they were not surprised to see Lady Catherine, Andrew and Marie, Jane and Richard, and the younger girls had decided it was time to visit Mrs. Bennet as well.

"Bennet, may we have a word in *private*?" Darcy requested.

"Yes, you may court my second daughter," Bennet granted. There was no mistaking the look of joy which suffused both of their faces when they heard his words. Lady Catherine had apprised Bennet of the morning's happenings, and it was obvious Darcy finally had asked the question his Lizzy was expecting.

"Thank you, Papa," Elizabeth threw her arms around her father's neck and kissed his cheek. Darcy approached after Elizabeth went to her mother's bedside after receiving the well wishes of those assembled.

"If you kiss me, I will call you out," Bennet admonished Darcy in jest—mostly in jest.

With a wide grin on his face, Darcy extended his hand to the man he hoped would become his father-in-law. Darcy took Bennet's hand and lifted it towards his lips. The action, combined with the look of horror on Bennet's face, led to a round of raucous laughter.

Bennet was usually the one making sport of others, so becoming the butt of a joke was new to him, but he found he could not repine it. It seemed his Lizzy had met her true match. Who would have thought so after the ignominious beginning between the two in Hertfordshire?

Darcy joined Elizabeth at her mother's side, after being waylaid by his hopefully soon-to-be Aunt Phillips. After wishing their brother and sister joy, Gigi and Lydia held up the big slate with all the words on it. There was a sentence prepared which Fanny pointed to: '*I am very happy for you both.*'

"Thank you Mama," Elizabeth said, squeezing her mother's right hand.

"I look forward to being allowed to call you Mother Bennet, as my undeserving cousin Richard does," Darcy ribbed.

Fanny pointed to two words on the slate being held by the girls. '*Can*' and '*Now*'. Now, they all understood why Fanny seemed so happy at that moment.

"It seems you asked the correct question this time William," Jane teased after she congratulated him. "If you ever hurt my sister, you will have me to contend with."

"Is no one here unaware of my humiliating behaviour this morning?" Darcy asked.

There was a chorus of "no," and Fanny jabbed at the word '*no*' on the slate as she made a sound everyone recognised as laughter. Darcy just shook his head.

"Buck up William," Lady Catherine said softly near her nephew's ear so only he could hear her, "it could have been worse—she could have refused you again."

Darcy did not even want to imagine the depths of his despair if she had done so. He thanked God he did not need to know such pain. "I have a suggestion," Darcy announced.

"What is it?" Lady Catherine asked.

"Jane and Elizabeth are to London on Monday, are they not?" he asked. That was quickly verified as fact. "Might I join the trip with Kitty, Gigi, and Lydia? That is, if Aunt Cat will be my hostess," Darcy stated. "If you come, Aunt Cat, then Richard may as well. Before you object, Richard, the planting is all but over so you could choose to do so."

"In that case, I will consult with my steward, and if all is well," Richard responded looking into Jane's eyes as he spoke, "I will be happy to join the party travelling to London."

Lady Catherine and the youngest three girls looked uncertain about leaving some of the guests plus the patient alone in the house. "Catherine, you and the girls should go. You have all been waiting on us hand and foot, and it is high time you took some time for yourselves. Hattie will be here with Fanny and me, not to mention the Hills and a house full of servants," Bennet insisted.

"You will hear no disagreement from me," Hattie stated emphatically. "Thomas is correct, you all deserve some time without worry."

"That being the case, we will accompany you," Lady Catherine pronounced.

A little later, Mary and William Bennet came for tea, and were both delighted with the news of the courtship. William Bennet did not feel it was a good time to be away from his flock, and Mary declined an invitation to join the trip to Town, stating she had too much to do in the upcoming weeks. Even if she had nothing planned, she would not have considered going without her beloved husband.

She did not inform anyone that she had recently started to be sick most mornings, and that some foods she used to love, she could not stomach any longer. Mary also did not mention she needed to rest in the afternoons, something she had not done since she was a little girl in the nursery.

~~~~~~~/~~~~~~~

Sunday was a quiet day. Come Monday morning, four carriages, one of which was for the servants, stood ready to depart for London as soon as everyone boarded.

# CHAPTER 27

As if being ruined in society were not punishment enough, her traitorous sister Louisa agreed with her brother Charles that it was no one's fault but her own.

Miss Bingley's sister and brother-in-law had come for a short visit to Scarborough. She was living in the home of an uncle and her traitor of a brother, both publicly active in trade, but the Hursts refused to invite her to live with them.

Louisa had reminded her of the number of times she had been warned Mr. Darcy was not interested in her and had tolerated her only because of his friendship with Charles. She also pointed out the occasions she had warned Caroline her behaviour would only end in her ruin because they were not members of the first circles—no matter her pretentions. Members of the first circles would not excuse her bad behaviour as eccentric, as they would for one of their own.

Louisa and that lout Hurst told her—as they had previously—she would *never* be welcome at Winsdale. Louisa also told her younger sister how much happier she was with her husband since Caroline was no longer around to cause trouble between them.

When Louisa and Hurst departed for the Hurst estate, Caroline Bingley finally understood she had managed to alienate everyone in her life. She wrote to some of her so-called friends, and without exception, every letter was returned unopened.

To her vexation, her brother was no longer malleable. He had warned her he would not cover her overspending, and she had ignored him—as she had in the past. To feel better about herself, she went to the local mantua-maker and ordered a completely new wardrobe—she would be the one to show the locals true class, after all.

When the proprietor, who had never received such a large order before, asked how the bill would be paid, Miss Bingley presented her brother's card. She had not counted on the owner being a sharp-witted steward of her business. The owner dispatched a note to Mr. Bingley, asking for his acquiescence to cover the bill. He had returned a short note of refusal.

It was soon made known throughout the town that unless Miss Bingley had funds on her person to pay for her purchases, those extending her credit not authorised by him beforehand, in writing, would not be able to collect from her brother; he would refuse to cover any of her bills not approved ahead of time by himself.

Returning from an embarrassing trip to the mantua-maker—where she was informed her order had been cancelled—Caroline discovered none of her stratagems worked on her brother any longer. All her effort produced was the loss of a quarter's allowance.

Even though Miss Bingley had lived in the lies she told herself for some time, she was not devoid of intelligence. It took some time, but she finally accepted she had been the author of her own expulsion from society, and it was not something that would be forgotten.

Watching her brother ignore her made it clear he did not appreciate her company, she had an epiphany—unless she wanted to be alone for the rest if her life, she needed to make real changes, including addressing her inappropriate airs, graces, and pretentions.

~~~~~~~/~~~~~~~

"Welcome to Matlock House, Jane and Lizzy," Lady Elaine received her guests enthusiastically. "It is good to see you again, Andrew and Marie. Marie, please let me hold little Reggie; I have missed him so since we left Kent."

Lady Marie, who had been holding her son when they

entered the house, handed the babe over to his grandmother. "I understand my parents are in Town," Lady Marie observed. "I will take little Reggie to visit them tomorrow morning. Would you like to come with me Mother Elaine?"

"That will depend on Jane and Lizzy, and what they have planned," Lady Elaine replied.

"In the morning, Aunt Elaine, we are to visit with our sisters, Aunt Cat, Richard, and the Darcys at Darcy House, and then we will go to Uncle Edward's warehouse to look at fabric in the afternoon," Jane responded.

"Jane dear, did you forget I gave you leave to call me Mother Elaine?" Lady Elaine reminded.

"I beg your pardon. Yes, you did," Jane said in apology.

"Think nothing of it." Lady Elaine turned to her daughter, "I will accompany you to Jersey House in the morning, but I will return in time to join the party travelling to the Gardiner warehouse," Lady Elaine stated. She would not miss seeing the new fabrics.

"We will return in time, as I too am looking forward to seeing what new bolts the warehouse has," Lady Marie stated.

"My Reggie will be home from the Lords after four, so I think it will be good to have a family dinner tonight. I suspected we might have a few more to dine, so I warned cook ahead of time," Lady Elaine relayed. "I will send a footman with a note to Darcy House and invite them to join us. Jane and Lizzy, how is your mother?"

"She is as well as can be expected under the circumstances. Thank you for enquiring after her," Elizabeth responded. "She is very pleased her older sister remains with her, and I know she is looking forward to the Gardiners returning with all of us to Kent. Aunt Elaine, I have news."

"Did William finally speak?" Lady Elaine asked perceptively. "It was not a state secret Lizzy dear; there was no difficulty noticing that William is besotted with you."

"He did, and we have commenced an official courtship," Elizabeth confirmed with a light blush.

"You are on the family floor," Lady Elaine informed the sisters. "My housekeeper," she indicated the grandmotherly looking lady standing off to the side, "will show you to your chambers. When you have changed and rested, if you so desire, just request any servant you see to direct you to the family sitting room on the same floor."

Lady Elaine accompanied her daughter-in-law to hand little Reggie to the nursemaid in the nursery while Jane and Elizabeth were shown to the suite they would share.

~~~~~~~~/~~~~~~~~

Elizabeth was up at sunrise the next morning, as was her wont. She had been informed of the proximity of Hyde Park the previous evening during the family dinner, which everyone enjoyed.

Darcy, who knew her love of walking, had told her of Hyde Park's wonders for one who enjoyed the exercise. She had mentioned her intention to take a ramble at sunrise, and he had informed her that he might very well feel like an early morning walk himself.

It was not surprising that Darcy was waiting outside Matlock House when Elizabeth emerged with a maid and footman. "Good morning William," Elizabeth greeted Darcy cheerily. "Did you sleep on the doorstep last night?" Elizabeth teased.

"There was no need," Darcy returned with a dimpled smile. "Like you, I do not sleep past the rising of the sun."

Elizabeth had to force herself not to give into the weakness she felt in her knees when she noted how devastatingly handsome William was when he smiled. He offered his arm, and she gratefully curled her arm around it, steadying herself.

"So, this is the infamous Rotten Row," Elizabeth observed after the two had entered Hyde Park.

"The only time I enjoy it is when it is empty, as it is now," Darcy revealed. "I do not do well in large crowds of people with whom I am unfamiliar, as you know. I find the so-called fashionable hour a trial. I avoid this place at that time as if it were where the plague could be found."

"In that we agree," Elizabeth acknowledged. "When I walk, it is for the enjoyment of nature and the exercise. I care not one whit to see or be seen."

"That is one of your many attributes I enjoy and love," Darcy informed Elizabeth.

"You talk of love, not for the first time." She noted quietly and Darcy nodded. "How is it you fell in love with me when I was so combative and revelled in arguing with you? When did it begin?"

"As to when, it was when I truly looked at you the first time. No, that is not true. I was attracted to you, but not yet in love," Darcy divulged. "You began to invade my dreams first, then my waking hours. The night I first heard you play the pianoforte at Lucas Lodge, when your friend Mrs. Jamison urged you to play, I could not take my eyes off you. When you refused to dance with me, it only raised you in my estimation. You should know your refusal of my inept proposal showed your strength of character—showing me beyond all doubt that you would not accept a man for anything but the right reasons.

"I fell in love with you during your sojourn at Netherfield Park, while you were nursing Jane. Unlike Miss Bingley, who would agree with me if I said the sky was red, you always re-butted my assertions. You never fawned and did not attempt to flatter me, instead you constantly challenged, disagreed, and debated with me; it was exciting to have such conversa-tions."

"You had the right of it when you said I sometimes ex-press opinions not my own. I despised you so much I thought I was hurting you by arguing—what you call debating. There were times I honestly disagreed with you, but when I did agree, I would take the other side of the argument so we would have a reason to fight," Elizabeth owned.

"I did not know you did it every time, but I suspected you did espouse that which you did not believe on occasion. It was at Netherfield I decided you had no interest in my fortune, or any of the things society deems important. I could not help but fall in love with you.

"Imagine the blow to my ego during Christmastide at Snowhaven, when I was informed that you disliked me intensely. I thought myself so superior and then was forced to realise I was not. Worse, I was made to see I did not behave as a gentleman should." Darcy ceased talking and placed his other hand over Elizabeth's gloved one.

They reached the Serpentine and continued to follow the path next to it as it snaked through Hyde Park. "When you left after the ball with the Bingleys, you knew you loved me?" Elizabeth asked.

"Yes, I did," Darcy admitted. "Although I erroneously believed Jane indifferent to Bingley, I knew I needed to be away from you before I offered for you, which at the time, was anathema to me. Even though I knew I loved you, I fought my inclination for the reasons I blurted out at the glade. I allowed that need to drive me to be much more forceful in convincing Bingley."

"Jane and Richard thank you. We all thank you for exposing Mr. Bingley's weak-willed character," Elizabeth stated.

"After I arrived at Rosings Park and proffered my apologies, it was easy to see you were no longer indifferent to me," Darcy said. "Then I made unwarranted assumptions—as I have explained—which led to my ill-fated, and horribly worded proposal. When I am nervous, I spew nonsense, which accounts for all of the words that escaped my mouth when I attempted my proposal."

"Here is my promise to you—when I feel I am ready to hear your proposals, I will give you a sign," Elizabeth offered. "I will tell you we are closer to that point now than we were in the glade."

Her admission caused another face-splitting dimpled smile from her walking partner. For the rest of the walk, they discussed their favourite books.

~~~~~~~/~~~~~~~

"All of the bolts not yet consigned to shops are in the back room," Gardiner informed the group of intrepid shoppers.

Kitty, Gigi, and Lydia were joined by Lilly Gardiner. At almost thirteen, she was the eldest of the four Gardiner children and the most excited to have girls close to her in age present. The four decided to explore the main area of the warehouse as a group under the watchful eyes of Mrs. Annesley, the head clerk, and two Darcy footmen.

Ladies Catherine, Elaine, Marie, and Sarah—Marie's mother, Lady Jersey, who had been invited—joined Madeline Gardiner, Jane, and Elizabeth as they all made for the back room. There they discovered a cornucopia of bolts of Indian muslin, silk, satin, and many more fabrics. The shades, textures, and colours were unique, which made the ladies keen indeed as they touched the bolts reverently.

"This is the one for a wedding gown," Jane told her sister. It was a shimmering ivory Indian muslin with interwoven gold thread.

The rest of the ladies stopped examining their bolts and joined the sisters. "Oh Jane, that suits you perfectly," Lady Catherine opined. There was unanimous agreement from all of the ladies.

An hour later, Jane had selected more than enough bolts of fabric to be taken to Madame Chambourg's, some of the new fabrics and some from the main warehouse. The ladies had an appointment at Madame Chambourg's shop on Bond Street on the morrow.

Each lady selected fabric for herself, except for Lady Catherine. "As I intend to continue to wear half mourning and am blessed with more than enough gowns and dresses, I see no need to purchase more," Lady Catherine explained when asked why she had not chosen anything for herself.

Besides fabric, the three youngest ladies selected other items of interest. Lydia chose things that would be of use to her when she went to school. It had been decided, with Jane's wedding in mid-May and the school year ending weeks after, Lydia would commence school in August. Although none said so to Elizabeth, they suspected Lydia would attend another wedding before she started the school chosen for her in Bedfordshire.

~~~~~~~/~~~~~~~

Darcy and Elizabeth had managed to meet and walk in Hyde Park three mornings in a row, thanks to the good weather. The previous night, their party, except the three young ladies not yet out in society, went to see *A Midsummer Night's Dream*—one of Elizabeth's favourites—at a theatre in Covent Gardens.

Once the absolute approval of the Matlocks, Hilldales, Mr. Darcy, and the Jerseys was known, no one dared denigrate the unknown country lady who had 'stolen' the master of Rosings Park from under the noses of the daughters of the *Ton*.

In clear view of the gawkers, at the start of the first intermission the Duke and Duchess of Bedford, accompanied by the Marquess and Marchioness of Birchington, visited the Matlock Box. It became obvious that Mr. Fitzwilliam's fiancée and her sister both had the approbation of Queen Charlotte's cousins, since they paid the compliment of visiting them in their box and not vice versa.

Seeing leading doyens of the *Ton* offer their unreserved approval dampened any plans of the few spiteful ladies who thought to snub the upstarts. Knowledge of the way Miss Bingley, a lady who had crossed these very ladies, had been ostracised was enough to cause all who came in contact with the Bennet sisters to treat them with every arrear of civility.

Each successive day the two walked together, Elizabeth discovered more about William. The more she learned, the more she liked. She admitted to herself he had wormed his way into her heart and she had developed tender feelings for him.

Elizabeth had no doubt William respected her. She was certain off his love for her and realised she was close to being in the same state. She had yet to admit to herself she had fallen over that particular precipice.

She remembered how impressed she had been when

visiting Darcy House the first time. She was not given a tour but had paid attention to how the master of the house interacted with his servants. What Elizabeth saw warmed her heart. William treated his servants with respect, not like nobodies.

It was easy to see the servants had genuine affection for their master. Seeing him thus convinced Elizabeth that Gigi's opinion that William was the best master and landlord was not hyperbole; it was nothing more than the truth.

Dinner had been held at Darcy house after the play, and Elizabeth had seen William in candid moments talking to one or two of his servants, discovering he was the same even when he did not know he was being observed. William's belief that everyone deserved respect regardless of their station, was a major plus in Elizabeth's eyes.

On the fourth day, Friday, the day they would all return to Rosings Park, Darcy and Elizabeth met as they had on the previous three days. They walked together in companionable silence for a while, enjoying one another's company. They needed no words, as they felt entirely comfortable with one another.

While they were walking, Elizabeth's head admitted what her heart already knew; she loved the man whose arm she held. He was her perfect match in every way. She had needed time to know him better, but not as much time as she had thought.

Any doubts she thought she had, had been erased. All that was left was the surety she wanted to be his wife. That realisation made her lightheaded, almost giddy with happiness. Once she was able to regulate her breathing she stopped, causing Darcy to stop. He looked at her with concern, for when they walked Elizabeth never wanted to stop.

"Elizabeth, are you well?" Darcy asked.

"Why yes William. Never better. I just realised something, and the realisation stopped me in my tracks," Elizabeth stated cryptically.

"Should we continue?" Darcy asked, still confused.

"I would like to walk to the glade tomorrow morning. Will you join me?" Elizabeth asked saucily.

"It would be my pleasure to do so," Darcy averred.

"This time try to ask your question without getting tongue-tied," Elizabeth stated innocently as she strode forward, leaving behind a man with a silly grin on his face. It took a moment before he could command his feet to move to chase after the woman he loved who was walking ahead of him.

'I need to retrieve something from my safe before we depart for Kent,' Darcy thought to himself as wave after wave of pleasure washed over his body.

# CHAPTER 28

The line of carriages approaching Rosings Park was considerably longer than the one that made the journey to Town on Monday—by three additional vehicles. The entire Fitzwilliam family joined those returning to Kent from London, as did the Gardiners.

Lady Catherine rode in the Darcy coach with Darcy, Georgiana, and Kitty Bennet. The three ladies looked at each other questioningly during the journey, wondering why William, whose face sported a huge grin, seemed so distracted.

Lady Catherine was sure there was no betrothal between him and Elizabeth; she surmised, correctly, that neither of them would have been able to keep such news secret. William was somewhere in his own world and seemed perfectly happy to remain there. No one knew what had occurred to affect him so. Lady Catherine was sure his mood was connected to Elizabeth somehow—perhaps the courtship was proceeding in a way which gave him hope for the future.

When the convoy stopped so everyone could refresh themselves and stretch their legs at Bromley, Elizabeth and William met in full view of all to maintain propriety, walking together deep in private conversation.

Jane and Richard were applied to for an explanation, but they were not sure what had affected the two so. After Bromley, Jane left the Matlock carriage and rode with Lizzy in one of the Gardiner conveyances.

Jane quizzed Lizzy and she was given the same answer as the Gardiners had received: "All will be revealed on the morrow." As soon as her sister made that statement, Jane had a very good idea of what would happen.

As the carriages turned into the estate, Mary and William Bennet waved to their returning family and friends from their garden. As soon as the equipages were brought to a halt, they were swarmed by footmen placing steps and removing trunks.

Jane's purchases, including her wedding gown, would be delivered in the middle of the coming week, along with the gowns and dresses the other ladies had ordered. Two of Madam Chambourg's seamstresses would accompany the delivery to make final adjustments. Jane could not wait to preview her gown for her mother, knowing it would bring her great pleasure.

~~~~~~~/~~~~~~~

After a quick wash, Darcy sought out his Aunt Catherine. Because she was the closest person he had to a mother, he felt the urge to tell her what had happened to give him so much joy. He thought she might think something was afoot, but that did not lessen his desire to share his happiness with her. He did not know why he said nothing to her in the carriage; mayhap he did not want to temp the fates.

"I am sure what you want to talk about is Elizabeth," Lady Catherine stated as her nephew seated himself in her private sitting room.

"It is," Darcy owned. "Before our departure this morning, we walked in Hyde Park, as we did each morning in London. She told me to ask her the question I tried to ask so poorly last time on the morrow. I am beyond happy, but I am worried I will again become tongue-tied and say the wrong thing."

"William, my dear boy, just keep it simple," Lady Catherine advised. "Sometimes an idea can be conveyed more effectively in few words rather than many. With the former, there will be less opportunity to ramble or have your meaning misunderstood."

"That is sound advice," Darcy accepted, "I will eliminate any four-syllable words I was considering using."

"My other suggestion is you inform Thomas first; request his permission to propose to his favourite daughter. It will show respect for his position as Elizabeth's father," Lady Catherine recommended to Darcy.

The suggestion was a good one, and after kissing the proffered cheek, Darcy set off with determination towards Mrs. Bennet's chambers.

~~~~~~~/~~~~~~~

Darcy found Bennet sitting with his wife and sister Hattie. The four just-returned Bennet sisters, Gigi, and Lilly Gardiner followed him into the room. "Bennet, can you spare me a few moments?" Darcy asked.

"Thank you for rescuing me. I needed an excuse to escape the talk of lace and fripperies." The two decided to use Darcy's sitting room, as it would be quieter. "How may I assist you?" Bennet asked as soon as they each had seated themselves with a glass of good port.

"I am seeking your consent to propose to Elizabeth," Darcy informed the man he intended to call "father" soon.

"Your courtship has been of a short duration. I am aware you were precipitous once before; what makes you think Lizzy will be amenable now?" Bennet asked pointedly.

"Because she instructed me to ask the question again, only without placing my hessian in my mouth this time," Darcy revealed. In the past, he had been loath to lay his private dealings before anyone—that had changed.

"That certainly sounds like my Lizzy," Bennet shook his head. "What do you think made her change her mind so soon?"

"We spent many hours walking and talking…" Darcy informed Bennet about their morning walks, and the goodly number of other times they had found chances to talk while in Town. "She asked me many probing questions and in turn told me much of herself and all of your family. I suppose she has decided she knows enough about me now. More importantly, I know she would not marry unless she could love and respect her partner," Darcy stated. "If she were not secure in her feelings for me, she would not have prompted me to ask my question again."

"Has she declared her love for you?" Bennet enquired.

"Not yet, but the looks she has given me with her fine, excuse me, expressive eyes have spoken volumes," Darcy stated.

"Since I know Lizzy would never say what she did without wanting you to propose, you have my consent to address my daughter. I know your honour is impeccable, so I have no qualms about your accompanying her on her rambles." Bennet sat back and drained his port.

After he left his meeting with Bennet, which could not have gone better, Darcy counted the minutes until he could see Elizabeth again. He was too excited to sleep that night. It would be a long night as the minutes ticked away until he could offer for the woman he loved beyond all reason.

~~~~~~~~/~~~~~~~~

After all of the young ladies exited Fanny's bedchamber, Elizabeth returned to her mother's side and sat on the bed facing her, taking her good hand in her own. "Mama, I have signalled William I am ready to hear his proposals to me in the morning. If he renews his addresses, I will accept him," Elizabeth shared with her mother, whose face radiated joy at the news.

'*Very Happy for you*'. Fanny told her second daughter as she pointed to words on the large slate her sister held for her.

"Thank you Mama. I love him so very much," Elizabeth said out loud for the very first time.

"We are so happy for you Lizzy," Aunt Hattie said quietly. Fanny nodded in agreement—as well as she was able to.

"You remember that the Jamisons—Stuart and Charlotte—will arrive today for a week, so they will have some time with us before the wedding," Elizabeth stated.

Her mother pointed to '*Yes.*' Then Fanny thought to herself, '*I made both of Jane's early suitors run away. My behaviour was so embarrassing! The way I used to denigrate my poor Lizzy, as if she had the power to determine her gender before she was born. In a way, like William and that spineless Bingley, I did Jane a favour. There is no mistaking how well-suited Jane and Richard are.*'

Fanny realised.

She wished she was able to speak, if only for a few minutes, so she could beg her daughters' pardon. *'How did I ever think Mary plain? I was blind! She is anything but, and she is happy in her marriage. The fact that her husband is to inherit Longbourn played no part in her decision to marry him; she fell in love with the man.'*

No matter what happened to her, Fanny could rest easy now, knowing her family members were all happy and closer to one another than any other time she could remember.

~~~~~~~/~~~~~~~

Darcy stood ready outside the manor house's entrance a few moments after dawn on Saturday. The early morning light revealed an almost cloudless day. He hoped the day would be like his mood: bright.

Darcy patted his inside pocket and felt the ring box securely where he had placed it. It was the fifth time he had made sure it was there, perhaps the sixth if he were to count when he checked it on the stairs on his way down. He heard a sound behind him, turned, and saw the most welcome sight in the world, Elizabeth. She was wearing a pale-yellow walking dress with short sleeves that revealed her arms. She had beige kid leather gloves on her hands, and a light bonnet covered most of her mahogany locks, although some had escaped her coiffure.

"I see you were determined I would not be the one to wait for you this time, unlike our last walk to the glade," Elizabeth teased with arched eyebrow. How he enjoyed her teasing!

"There is much about *that* walk which I am resolved to correct," Darcy returned.

"In that case, should we proceed?" Elizabeth prompted. Darcy offered her his arm, which she accepted gladly, and they walked towards the woodlands. This time she did not rest her hand lightly on his proffered arm—she wound her arm around his.

When they arrived at the glade, Jeffers stopped a little before it to allow the couple privacy for the interview Darcy had been granted, instead of sitting on the bench opposite. Thankfully, there was a tree stump for the man to sit on so he would not have to remain standing. Bennet had instructed him to allow the couple ten minutes of privacy.

Just as they had the previous time, William led Elizabeth to the bench on the far side of the pond. In contrast to his earlier, rather inept attempt, Darcy remembered to drop to one knee as soon as Elizabeth was seated.

"Elizabeth Rose Bennet, I must tell you that you have bewitched me body and soul, and I love you most ardently. I never wish to be parted from you from this day forward. I need you to bring the joy to my life that has been absent for many years. I have been living a half-life, going through the motions. Materially, I have much, but I have not had the love between a man and a woman. Not just any woman, only you. I have not experienced life as I should; I merely existed and tried to do the best I could for Gigi. Please end my suffering and loneliness and agree to become my wife," Darcy proposed.

"Fitzwilliam Robert Darcy, it is only recently I admitted to myself that I love you with all that I am. You are the *only* man I could ever agree to marry. So yes, William, yes, yes, yes, YES! There is nothing I desire more than to become your wife," Elizabeth answered, speaking the words he dreamed of hearing from her for so long. Yes, she had hinted it was time to ask her, but he thirsted to hear the words from her lips and he only allowed himself to believe fully after she accepted him.

Darcy reached into his pocket and withdrew a velvet-covered box. He opened it and removed the most beautiful ring Elizabeth had ever seen. It was gold with one large emerald surrounded by a ring of alternating, very small diamonds and emeralds.

As she watched, he gently removed her gloves, then slid the ring slowly down her finger until it was in place. "I have never seen a more beautiful ring," Elizabeth gushed.

"It belonged to my paternal grandmother. She told me to

place it only on the finger of the lady I loved. That, my dearest, loveliest Elizabeth, is you." Without further words, Darcy stood and gently drew Elizabeth to him. She knew—hoped—she was about to experience her first kiss.

Their heads moved closer together and, closing her eyes, Elizabeth felt the gentle pressure of his moist lips on hers. She grasped the lapels of his coat and felt his hands rise to the sides of her head, then slowly slide down to her shoulders, finally stopping at the small of her back. He pressed her body a little closer to his before breaking their kiss gradually; then he rested his forehead against hers. Her body tingled all over and her heart raced like never before.

Had they not been holding onto each other, she felt as if she might float to the heavens, for she was drunk with love. His kiss had sent her normally sharp mind reeling. She smiled even as she blushed; he was staring intently at her, seeing into the depths of her soul. Their eyes locked as she silently granted permission for more, and then his lips once again captured hers. There was a certain fervour to their movements, an urgent need to become closer. He sat on the bench and drew her onto his lap, and she twined her arms about his neck.

In his wildest dreams, Darcy had not thought her kisses would be so sweet, like the nectar of the gods. As a sudden shock gripped Darcy's body, he thought '*The poets were right, it is like being struck by lightning.*' Elizabeth was soft and welcoming, and it felt as though his entire being was concentrated on where their bodies touched.

She was as passionate as he had dreamed she would be, and he realised with a soaring heart that although unpractised in the art of kissing, she learned quickly, holding nothing back. She was calm until the moment his tongue slipped between her parted lips.

He opened his eyes and noted her initial look of surprise as he explored her mouth. He paused in case she did not want him to proceed. Gratified by her little mewl of frustration, he proceeded with renewed urgency. The taste of her was overwhelming, and he growled from the depths of his throat as he pulled her tightly to himself with the hand he had on the small of her back. Heat poured off him in waves and into her as she answered his daring attempt by sliding her tongue over and about his.

He pulled back, intending to end the interlude, knowing they would be out of time soon, but she pressed closer and he was lost again. His kiss was hot and wet, and her arms wound more tightly around his neck when he tried to separate from her. Then she removed a hand from his neck and raked her fingers through his curls. Ever since the first blush of an attraction, she had longed to do just that, to feel if they were as soft as they looked. They were.

In response, Darcy pushed her bonnet off and ran his fingers through her mahogany tresses, sending pins flying every which way, but he cared not. For months he had been nearly desperate to thread his fingers through her hair. How he could not wait to see her with her tresses free from all restraints.

Her legs trembled as she seized his lapels to draw him as close to her as possible. Luckily, they were seated, as she did not believe her legs could have supported her at that moment. Her heart was hammering in her chest, and she was conscious of the press of her breasts through the thin layer of muslin against his waistcoat; the contact only increased her arousal.

Neither wanted to separate, but they knew they did not have much time before Jeffers made an appearance. By mutual agreement, the newly betrothed couple drew apart. As gently as he could, Darcy slid Elizabeth off his lap onto the bench just as the footman made his presence known.

Both felt bereft of the warmth of the other's body. Now they had committed one to the other, they were desperate to explore the depths of their shared passion. They suspected, privately, that they would never be able to get enough of each other.

"Unless you object, I suggest a short betrothal period," Elizabeth stated saucily.

"Either that or we can make for Gretna," Darcy jested. That statement earned him one of her tinkling laughs he loved to hear.

Darcy tried to gather up her hairpins, which had flown everywhere, but Elizabeth laid her hand on his arm. "Do not bother; I have many more," she told him as she gathered her tresses into a makeshift bun, which she secured by tying her bonnet in place.

Just then, Jeffers cleared his throat tentatively. Elizabeth was about to stand when Darcy placed a restraining hand on her arm. She turned to him in concern, but when he met her eyes and remained silent, she looked downward and she noticed a distinct bulge in his breeches and understood his need to remain seated a while longer.

Not too many minutes later, Darcy gave his fiancée an imperceptible nod and they both stood. With her arms wrapped around his forearm, and his other hand covering hers, the couple started their return to the great house.

"William, may we go by way of the parsonage first?" Elizabeth asked as they reached the main path.

"You must know I would never refuse you anything it is within my power to grant," Darcy averred.

"I want to inform Mary and William first," Elizabeth stated. "When the two of you are in the same room, we will have to find some way so you both do not answer whenever 'William' is spoken."

With Jeffers following, the newly betrothed couple turned in the direction of the parsonage.

# CHAPTER 29

"Lizzy, I am so very happy for you!" Mary exclaimed. "What a fine brother you are gifting us with."

Mary and her husband conveyed profuse wishes for the future felicity of the newly betrothed couple, then Mary had a thought. "Have you told Mama yet? Do you have Papa's consent?"

"You are the first we informed," Elizabeth replied. "I did tell Mama there was a high probability of William proposing to me today."

"Your father gave me permission to pay my addresses to Elizabeth, so it will be no surprise to him when I make my request," Darcy reported.

"You requested Papa's permission to address me before you proposed to me?" Elizabeth asked, and he nodded. The fact William showed her father the respect and deference to make such a request spoke well of him. "Thank you; that pleases me."

"In the spirit of honesty, Aunt Cat suggested I do so." Darcy revealed, "You know disguise is abhorrent to me, so I will not take the credit for the initial inspiration."

"Regardless of who made the suggestion, you still decided to follow their advice and talk to my father," Elizabeth pointed out. "Please do not sell my betrothed short," she teased.

"What are we to do with my William and yours in the family? We cannot call mine Bennet when Papa is near, and with two Williams it will be confusing." Mary asked after Elizabeth's reply

"There is a simple solution," Darcy offered as he shook his

soon-to-be brother's hand again. "When we are together, your husband will be William and I can be called Darcy. As I am the only one, it will reduce any confusion. I would have suggested Fitzwilliam, which is my Christian name, but with Richard in the family, that would be just as problematic."

"Then Darcy it will be," Mary decided.

"It will take me a while to get used to calling you Darcy when we are all together. I apologise in advance for the times I might forget," Elizabeth stated contritely.

"Do not trouble yourself Sister, I will know which William you mean," William Bennet stated with a grin.

"As will I," Darcy added with a grin of his own.

"William, do any of your parishioners need you this morning?" Mary asked.

"No my love, they do not," William Bennet replied.

"In that case, we will join you on your walk to the manor house," Mary stated. "Lizzy and Darcy, you must know how much I—we—appreciate that you told us first."

~~~~~~~/~~~~~~~

"Bennet, may I please have a word in private," a beaming Darcy requested.

Bennet watched his second daughter as she practically floated to her mother's bedside. "We can do so in private Son but given the look of unadulterated joy I see on both your faces, I assume she accepted you," Bennet said.

"Yes Sir. Elizabeth accepted me as her betrothed," Darcy confirmed.

"Then you have my consent and unreserved blessing. Just make sure I never repine bestowing my permission and strive to make her happy all the days of her life." Bennet looked his future son in the eye.

"Her felicity will be my priority for the rest of the time I am granted on this earth," Darcy assured Bennet.

"Mama," Elizabeth took her mother's hand. "We are officially betrothed with Papa's blessing; I am to be married. He did indeed ask and I did not refuse him—this time."

Fanny pointed to the slate with the words on it and Elizabeth held it up for her and handed her mother the stick. '*Happy for you*' Fanny indicated. Elizabeth bent down and kissed her mother as a tear of happiness rolled down her mother's cheek, leaving a salty taste in Elizabeth's mouth.

Elizabeth extended her left hand so her mother could admire the elegant ring she had been gifted by her betrothed. Fanny's good right eye grew wide, then she pointed to '*Very nice*'.

"God has been good to us," Elizabeth told her mother. "With me, there will be three of your daughters well married, all to men we love."

Just then, Mrs. Phillips returned to her sister's bedchamber. When she saw the joy reflected on the right side of her sister's face and the ring her niece was displaying, she knew what had occurred. "Lizzy, you could not have been so intelligent for nothing. You caught such a wealthy man! He is as good as a lord. He has an estate in Derbyshire, a house in Town, and ten thousand a year—likely more. What pin money, jewels, and carriages, you will have; you will have even more wealth than Jane!" Hattie effused.

Elizabeth simply hugged her aunt, sure the words she had just verbalised would have been spoken by her mother before her illness struck. The only thing she worried about was whether her fiancé would take exception to the rather vulgar outburst.

A concerned Elizabeth looked over to where her betrothed and father sat next to one another and was relieved to see rather than take offence, William seemed amused. Her father was shaking his head and sporting a large grin.

"William," Elizabeth reached out her hand. Darcy stood and joined his beloved next to her mother.

Darcy kissed the hand of his mother-in-law-to-be. She pointed at the slate with the letters and Elizabeth held it for her.

'*A-l-w-a-y-s t-r-e-a-t m-y g-i-r-l w-e-l-l*' Fanny spelled out.

"You have my most solemn promise Mother Bennet. I will make it my life's mission to respect and love your daughter," Darcy promised.

Fanny turned her head as much as she could to expose her cheek, and Darcy bestowed a kiss on it. "Now that your betrothal is official, are there not some people you would like to tell?" Bennet asked. "You will need to see Mary and my son at the parsonage."

"Mary and William already know," Elizabeth informed her father. "We stopped there on the way back to the manor house."

"They are with the rest of the family waiting for us in the drawing room," Darcy explained. Before the happy couple made their way downstairs, they explained the method they would use so there would be no confusion about the same names being in use when they were in company with Mary and her husband.

~~~~~~~/~~~~~~~

When the beaming couple entered the room, Lady Catherine saw William's grandmother's ring on Elizabeth's finger. She remained quiet to see if anyone noticed the ring before the newly betrothed couple made their announcement. The parsonage Bennets had not said a word, not wanting to steal the newly betrothed couple's thunder.

"Elizabeth!" Georgiana squealed as she noticed the ring, "You accepted William!"

"No, Gigi, I did not accept William as he is happily married to my sister." Elizabeth teased. At first Gigi was flummoxed. "However, *Darcy* proposed to me and I did accept him." She clarified as Gigi's face lit up with absolute joy. There was a brief explanation of the use of the names "William" and "Darcy" to avoid confusion.

Within seconds there was a cacophony of well wishes, many hugs, and not a few kisses.

"It is about time," Lady Elaine stated as she hugged her nephew.

"Your parents would have been very happy for you," Lord Matlock said as he clapped his nephew on the back. "My sister and brother would have loved your Lizzy."

Gigi did not say a word, she simply hugged her brother with all of her might, as did Kitty and Lydia, while Elizabeth was wrapped in Jane's arms.

"I am so happy for you Lizzy. I saw that you loved Darcy when I looked into your eyes in London, even before you admitted it to yourself," Jane shared. Then in a soft voice Jane added, "We need to talk as soon as possible."

Her Aunt and Uncle Gardiner pulled Elizabeth into a joint hug, and each kissed her on a cheek. "You will be a very happy woman," her Aunt Maddie told her.

"Yes, I believe I will," Elizabeth agreed.

Richard pulled both members of the newly betrothed couple into a bear hug. "You two are almost as perfect for one another as my Jane is for me," Richard exclaimed.

Lady Catherine held back, knowing she would have her turn. Andrew and Marie were the last two to wish the betrothed couple happy before Lady Catherine. As she stood up, the two approached her and opened their arms, enfolding their aunt in the cocoon of their love.

"This is a glorious day," Lady Catherine stated after she kissed each of them on the cheek. "Even though I knew how it would be, there were times I thought one or both of you would not be able to get out of your own way and come together. But all of that is in the past now. You do not understand how much joy I will find in your union. You are so well suited one to the other.

"I have considered you another surrogate daughter for some time now Elizabeth, so nothing has changed for me." The lady turned to her nephew, "She is the only one for you William. Cherish her for the rest of your days, and make sure there is always respect between you. If you ever disagree, let it be in private and not in front of any other," Lady Catherine advised.

"We will always keep your advice in mind," Elizabeth

promised. "You have long been a surrogate mother to me, and I love you." Elizabeth leant forward and kissed Lady Catherine's cheeks once again.

Elizabeth's declaration caused more than a few tears to run unchecked down Lady Catherine's cheeks. "I second that Aunt Cat," Darcy added. "You have been a mother to Gigi and me since father died."

"Away with you two now, before you turn this old lady into a watering pot," Lady Catherine admonished playfully.

"Lizzy do not forget I need to speak to you," Jane reminded her. Elizabeth nodded. "Please join Richard and me in the parlour opposite, with your betrothed, of course."

~~~~~~~~/~~~~~~~~

"You requested we join you?" Elizabeth asked, after both couples chose settees across from one another with a low table between them.

"Yes I did. I have not yet mentioned to Richard what I am about to suggest," Jane opened.

"Now you have piqued my curiosity," Richard stated.

"You all remember that Mr. Burnett said that Mama may —no, probably will—have another apoplexy and the chances of her surviving a second attack are close to naught," Jane stated.

"Yes, I was in the meeting with him. Are you about to suggest that William and I marry with you and Richard in a double ceremony?" Elizabeth deduced.

"That is exactly what I am suggesting," Jane confirmed. "I know it may be much quicker than either of you planned, if you have even yet discussed wedding dates."

"We have not yet," Darcy informed the other couple. "Although we agree we do not wish for a long betrothal." Elizabeth nodded her concurrence.

"If by the Grace of God Mama survives like this for a long time, then you will have married sooner than you might have otherwise. However, if the worst happens after our wedding, marrying earlier will be a good thing, will it not?" Jane enquired.

Seeing the consternation in his betrothed, Darcy made a request of Jane and Richard. "Will you give us a few minutes to talk? Please, wait for us in the hall and leave the door partially open."

Jane and Richard stood and exited, pulling the door three quarters closed on their way out. "What is your opinion?" Darcy asked gently.

"My hesitation is not because I object to marrying you in just over a fortnight; it is the spectre of my mother's mortality that grips me. I found the mother I had always hoped she would be since she was stricken. All life is tentative, but Jane is correct, Mama's life is threatened more than most others' are," Elizabeth explained. "You lost your mother when you were young, did you not?"

"Yes, I was but twelve, and Gigi was a few weeks old. I at least knew my mother; Gigi never did," Darcy replied.

"Enough melancholy," Elizabeth decided. "Do you object to Jane's plan?"

"Not at all. As long as you do not object to marrying with Jane and Richard, the sooner I am married to you, the better," Darcy stated.

"Jane's suggestion could not please me more, as it always has been a childhood dream of mine that Jane and I marry in the same ceremony," Elizabeth relayed. "I do think we need to request Papa join the four of us and allow him to advise us."

Darcy called the other couple back in and explained what they had decided. Richard sent a footman to request Mr. Bennet's presence.

~~~~~~~/~~~~~~~

"What trouble are you four cooking up now?" Bennet asked with a sardonic smile as he joined his betrothed daughters and their affianced.

Jane and Elizabeth explained what Jane had suggested and why. They informed him Elizabeth and William had agreed to the plan, pending his consent. "Darcy, are you sure you do not object?" Bennet asked.

"I do not, not at all," Darcy replied.

"As much as I would prefer the situation were otherwise, there is no denying the wisdom of your decision. It will give my Fanny a great deal of pleasure to see you both marry," Bennet agreed. "Do you have any thoughts on how we might ensure your mother will be able to witness the ceremony? You know she would love to see you marry, not just see you before and after the service."

"Would anyone object if I ask Aunt Cat to join us?" Richard asked, and when no one did, he went to find her.

A few minutes later, Richard returned with Lady Catherine, and she was quickly informed of what the two couples had decided, and the problem they were wrestling with. "The family sitting room," Lady Catherine stated after cogitating for a little while. "It has not been opened since Anne and Lewis were taken from me, but it is large and close to Fanny's chambers. We can move her in the bath chair with a minimum of jostling since there are no stairs to negotiate."

"Are you sure you are ready to reopen the family sitting room?" Richard queried. "We are all aware it was a special place for the three of you before the accident."

"Yes I am, it is time," Lady Catherine assured her nephew. "There can be no better affirmation of continuing life than a wedding."

"As long as you are sure," Darcy verified. "We would not want you to be pained for any reason."

"If I were not ready, I would never have suggested it," Lady Catherine confirmed. "All will be well."

"Papa, will you inform Mama?" Jane asked.

"Yes my dear daughter. I thank you both for trying to give your mother as much pleasure as possible," Bennet replied warmly.

"Thank Jane. I agreed to the plan but it was her idea," Elizabeth owned.

"I am on my way to see your mother," Bennet relayed as he stood to return to his wife's bedchamber. "Catherine, thank you for all the accommodations you are making in order to assure Fanny is comfortable."

"It is my pleasure," Lady Catherine demurred.

"What dress should I wear?" Elizabeth asked after her father had departed.

"Did you not choose some Indian muslin similar to mine?" Jane asked her sister.

"Yes! You are brilliant! Mine is cream, interwoven with light yellow silk thread. It will be perfect," Elizabeth gushed. "How lucky the seamstresses will be here in a few days."

"Do not concern yourself with your trousseau now Elizabeth," Darcy interjected. "When we return from our wedding trip, we will make a stop in London and you may order everything you require or desire. Lambton does not have a Madame Chambourg, but the dressmaker there is excellent. She makes most of Gigi's gowns and dresses."

With their decisions made, the two couples and Lady Catherine returned to the drawing room to inform the rest of the assembled party of the upcoming double wedding.

~~~~~~~~/~~~~~~~~

As was her wont, Miss Bingley read the society pages when they were delivered to Bingley House in Scarborough. The Saturday papers were delivered to Scarborough each Tuesday following.

When she read the announcement of the betrothal of Mr. Fitzwilliam Robert Darcy to Miss Elizabeth Rose Bennet, she was, for a moment, fit to be tied. When she cooled down, she reminded herself the man had never been interested in her.

If he had looked at her the way he had looked at Eliza Bennet even once, Miss Bingley admitted to herself she would have ordered her wedding clothes the very same day. With her new self-awareness, she acknowledged she had never had a chance and closed the paper. It was the last day she scanned the social announcements.

# CHAPTER 30

Charlotte and Stuart Jamison and their three children arrived, as scheduled, on the tenth day of May 1811. Two years after their son was born, Charlotte had birthed a daughter, then three years later the newest Jamison arrived. He was a little more than a year old, and his looks seemed to favour his grandfather, Sir William Lucas.

"Eliza, I was shocked to hear about your mother," Charlotte told her as the two walked arm in arm into the manor house. She then turned to Jane. "And you are to be mistress of all of this in eight days?"

"Yes, I am, but Miss '*Mr. Darcy does not admire me*' will be the mistress of a far larger estate, not to mention several satellite estates," Jane teased her younger sister.

"You two are invited to remind me how wrong I was in my estimation of William at your leisure," Elizabeth sighed.

"There is no need, Eliza dear, you know I was correct. That is more than enough for me; after all, you are the one who is *never* wrong when she sketches characters," Charlotte jested with her friend.

"It seems we must rethink our invitation," Elizabeth teased back. "Charlotte, your children are darling. How old is Stuart Junior now?"

"He will be six in July. Yvette Sarah will be four in November, and this little man, Jacob, was one in January," Charlotte shared. "After I settle them in the nursery with their nursemaid, I would love to visit with your mother."

"You know that Eddy, May, and Peter Gardiner are here do you not? Your two older children will have children of similar ages with whom to play," Jane informed their long-time friend. "I want to make sure you are prepared to see Mama. She is much altered, especially her left side, including her face." Jane went on to give their friend a detailed description so she would be prepared when she saw their mother.

"She will be pleased to see you, as will our father and Aunt Hattie," Elizabeth added. "We just want to make sure seeing Mama as she is now will not be a shock to you."

"I understand," Charlotte responded.

"Mr. Jamison, after you change, you can find the rest of the men in the billiards room. Any servant will be able to direct you. Charlotte, ask to be directed to the main drawing room where you will meet our soon-to-be relations, and then Lizzy and I will accompany you to see Mama," Jane offered.

~~~~~~~/~~~~~~~

As Elizabeth waited in the drawing room for Charlotte to join them, she was lost in her reverie as she remembered what Mary told her the day she and William had informed everyone about their betrothal.

*Mary had requested she accompany her to see their parents. "Mama, Papa, Lizzy, I have news for you," Mary had said. "I am including you Lizzy, as you told me about your betrothal first." Mary paused for a few seconds. "I am with child."*

*Mama had Papa hold her word slate. 'How long' Mama indicated.*

*"This month was the third time I have missed my courses," Mary blushed as she looked at Papa. "Sorry Papa."*

*"My dear daughter, if I were to run for the hills every time anything feminine was discussed, with a wife and five daughters in the house, I would never have been home," Papa had stated sardonically. "Do not forget I was with your mother through five confinements."*

*Mama had begun to cry and make the sound she would when happy at the same time. With her slate, she asked if Mary had seen a doctor regarding her suspicions yet.*

*"No Mama, I have not, but Mr. Burnett will pay me a call*

on the morrow and hopefully he will confirm my state," Mary explained. "No, I have not felt the quickening, and no I have not been ill—yet. I cannot abide fish any longer, and you all know how much I love it. I must rest in the afternoons or I become too tired." Mary gave as much information as she could to satisfy Mama's curiosity and pre-empt possible questions.

"Our first grandchild," Papa had exclaimed. "Between that and the weddings, our cup runneth over."

"Thank you for including me Mary. You know it will be hard to keep this from our sisters. I will have to share the news with my William, as I do not want secrets between us. When will you inform the rest of the family?" I asked.

"Of course you may tell Darcy. As to the rest, after Mr. Burnett confirms my state, I will inform everybody, so you only have to keep the secret for a day," Mary replied.

As Mary and her William had expected, the doctor confirmed her state on Monday morning. Mary had forgotten the next day was Sunday—Aunt Cat told me it happens to ladies who are with child. We had a family dinner that night, and Mary and my brother William informed every one of their wonderful news.

Elizabeth snapped out of her reverie when Charlotte entered the drawing room. "Elizabeth, will you introduce us to Rosings Park's new guest?" Lady Elaine requested as the highest-ranking lady in the room.

It was Elizabeth's distinct honour to introduce Charlotte to those whom she was unknown, the three older ladies and Gigi. After introductions were made, Charlotte, Jane, and Elizabeth made for Mrs. Bennet's bedchamber.

"Never did I imagine I would meet such pleasant members of the *Ton*," Charlotte commented as they exited the drawing room. "Mary!" Charlotte exclaimed as she saw the middle Bennet sister arriving to visit for tea. "Are you comfortable and fitting into the area as Mrs. Collins?"

"It is Mrs. *Bennet* now, and I am well. Yes, I have become comfortable in my new role," Mary returned with an eyebrow arched just as her next older sister was wont to do. Jane,

Elizabeth, and Mary explained the former William Collins had changed his name back to Bennet, as it had been before his grandfather changed it. The news had not yet been shared with their friends, so Mary took no offence at Charlotte using her previous married name.

"Mary, are you with child?" Charlotte blurted out before she could stop herself. "I am sorry; I should have asked you in private. Since I have been in that state three times, I find it easy to spot another who is *enceinte*."

"Do not make yourself uneasy; everyone in the family knows I am increasing," Mary assured Charlotte. "Are you three going to see Mama? If so, may I join you?" As would be expected, Mary was welcome to join them.

Jane led the ladies into her mother's bedchamber. "Welcome Charlotte," Bennet said as he looked up from the book he was reading.

Charlotte was pleased her friends had prepared her before seeing their mother. She had not wanted to believe it was as bad as Jane and Eliza had told her, but on seeing the Bennet matron, she felt they might have understated the truth of the matter.

Charlotte greeted Mrs. Phillips, who then took her leave, as the four ladies would keep her sister entertained. "Mrs. Bennet, I am sorry you are afflicted so," Charlotte greeted her friends' mother.

Fanny pointed to three words '*Not your fault*'.

Charlotte spoke to Mrs. Bennet as she would have had she not been afflicted. She told her about her three children and her husband. In the past, Fanny Bennet would become angry, feeling that Charlotte had *stolen* Jane's suitor.

With so many hours trapped in her own head, Fanny now knew the truth. It was she, and she alone, who had chased Stuart Jamison into Charlotte's welcoming arms. The fact that life was too short for petty recriminations had been driven home for Fanny Bennet in the starkest terms. She now intended to look at the positive for whatever time God allowed her until she was called home. She had adopted the philosophy she had heard both Lady Catherine and Lizzy espouse: Think only of the past as those thoughts give you pleasure.

Charlotte told Mrs. Bennet her mother and all of the ladies of Meryton sent their love and were praying for her. She shared how much her mother, Mrs. Long, and Mrs. Goulding were looking forward to seeing their friend, and that they would arrive on the Tuesday before the wedding.

~~~~~~~/~~~~~~~

Lady Catherine requested a family meeting the day after Charlotte arrived. Bennet and Lydia were asked to attend also; Kitty and Gigi were sent to entertain the younger children, with Lilly Gardiner's assistance.

"I requested you meet with me today, especially you, Lydia dear, because I wish to discuss George Wickham with you." Lady Catherine saw the look on Lydia's face and moved to reassure her. "He is very much in the Clink; he is not free and cannot harm you or any other." Lydia visibly relaxed.

"What about the wastrel?" Richard asked.

"We aimed to punish the man, and punished he has been," Lady Catherine stated. "Before any of you protest, I am not suggesting he be given leave to walk out of the Clink."

"I am confused," Darcy verbalized what most of them in the room were thinking.

"The man is without his right arm and his left eye; his greatest asset, his looks, are no more," Lady Catherine enumerated. "I would like to make him an offer—either leave for Australia with two hundred pounds and a one-way ticket with the understanding if he ever sets foot in England again, he will be returned to the Clink, or he can remain where he is."

"That seems to be a fair offer," Elizabeth opined. "He will be unable to work his charm on anyone ever again."

"Even though he does not deserve it, he was my father's godson. I would not oppose making him that offer," Darcy stated.

"Lydia, what do you think?" Lady Catherine asked. If

Lydia did not agree, she would leave well enough alone and the man would stay where he was.

"I care not, one way or the other," Lydia stated with no emotion. "As long as he can never hurt another again, whether it be in the Clink or on the other side of the world, it will make no difference to me."

"Does anyone object? Reggie? Thomas?" Lady Catherine asked.

"I agree with Lydia, Catherine; as long as he can harm no one, I do not object," Bennet stated.

"I am with Bennet on this," Lord Matlock added.

"In that case, the offer will be extended to him," Lady Catherine informed them.

Ten days later George Wickham boarded a ship and left the shores of England forever.

~~~~~~~~/~~~~~~~~

A betrothal ball had been discussed, but with Fanny lying stricken upstairs it was deemed an inappropriate time for it. On her husband's orders, nothing was mentioned to the Bennet matron, as he was sure she would have urged them to proceed.

Lady Matlock offered to hold a ball in both couple's honour at some time in the future. What was left unsaid was there would likely be a mourning period for the sisters to observe beforehand.

Each morning, Elizabeth and Darcy walked out, usually to the glade, with the ever-faithful Jeffers following behind. Once or twice, they walked to the folly where Darcy had gotten soaked that day and they both laughed at their former behaviour. Some days, rather than return directly to the manor house, they would stop at the parsonage to break their fasts with the Bennets.

A few days ago, Jane and Richard had joined their walk to the glade, but only that one time. With the positioning of the benches, each couple was afforded a modicum of privacy; neither could hear what the other couple was saying.

On this particular morning, Elizabeth and Darcy sat on their favourite bench. "Elizabeth, have you ever been sea bathing?" Darcy asked.

"No I have not. I have never seen the sea," Elizabeth revealed.

"Then how would you like to spend our wedding trip at a house overlooking the sea, on a bluff near Brighton?" he asked.

"Like it? I would love it. Is there enough time for you to reserve such a place?" Elizabeth wondered.

"There is no need to reserve it, I—and soon we—own it. It is called Seaview Cottage. My parents enjoyed part of their wedding trip there, and my mother liked it so well Father purchased it for her," Darcy explained. "Cottage, however, is a misnomer. The house is a little larger than Longbourn's. There is a private cove with a small beach which cannot be seen from the sea and can only be accessed from our property." Darcy waggled his eyebrows at his now-blushing fiancée.

"It sounds ideal. I would like it very well if we were to spend our wedding trip there," Elizabeth gushed, giving her betrothed a quick peck on the cheek. She was reminded they were not alone when Jeffers cleared his throat.

"My preference would have been to take you to the continent, but thanks to the little tyrant, that is not possible," Darcy stated.

"I am perfectly happy to go to Seaview Cottage. Once the French dictator is dispatched, you will be able to show me the wonders of the continent. Do you know where Jane and Richard plan to go?" Elizabeth wanted to know.

"Our aunt and uncle own a house in the Lake District, Lakeside House. I believe they will go there," William informed his betrothed. "At some other time, we can return to Seaview as a group. It is very peaceful there. I find I sleep better than normal with the sound of the sea to lull me."

"As long as you do not sleep too much," Elizabeth stated and then blushed scarlet at her wanton statement.

"Trust me, sleep will be the last thing that will interest

me when you are there with me," Darcy told her, causing her blush to deepen. One of her tinkling laughs Darcy loved to earn burst from Elizabeth to cover her embarrassment.

"We will visit the Lake District at some time will we not?" Elizabeth asked. Her betrothed nodded vigorously.

Not long after, the couple walked back to the manor house. Darcy did not want to tarry long as his and Richard's solicitors were bringing the final draft of the settlements. Luckily for Bennet, Frank Phillips had returned a few days earlier so he would be able to review the documents with both of his brothers.

As they neared the house, they noticed three carriages traveling down the drive. The friends from Meryton were arriving.

# CHAPTER 31

When Jane and Elizabeth were included in the reviewing of the settlements, they finally realised just how wealthy their soon-to-be husbands were. Richard had been left a sizable fortune in addition to Rosings Park, as well as Fitzwilliam House in London.

In spite of Jane's protests, he had settled fifty thousand pounds on her. She protested vociferously that it was far too much, but Richard was unwilling to bend on this point. It was nothing to the protest her sister made when she saw the amount Darcy had set aside for her.

"One hundred thousand pounds? William, that is far beyond the pale!" Elizabeth insisted.

"Did you note of the actual state of my—soon to be our—wealth?" Darcy asked calmly, having expected she would resist. "The income from all the estates and investments is more than thirty thousand pounds per annum. It is not known that Gigi's dowry is the same amount as I have settled on you, and it will not be revealed until she has found a man worthy of her. We can have ten daughters, and there will still be enough for each to have a large dowry. It is the same for me as Richard told Jane, it lifts a worry from my shoulders to know my wife will always be taken care of if I am called home to God early."

Just as it had halted Jane's objections when Richard applied the same logic, Elizabeth ceased her opposition—her vocal opposition. She still felt that the enormous amount was three or four times what she would need, but she remained silent on the subject.

"There is nothing I would recommend changing," Phillips informed Bennet and Gardiner concurred.

"Jane and Lizzy, you have no further objections, do you?" Bennet asked.

"None Papa," the two chorused.

Each of the grooms signed their four copies, and Bennet signed all eight. Darcy and Richard set one aside for their solicitor, gave a copy each to Bennet and his brother, who was his solicitor, and retained one for their wives to keep.

Richard poured a finger of the best cognac he possessed for the six men and a small glass of sherry for the two ladies. Everyone present toasted to the felicity of the two betrothed couples.

When the rest had vacated his study, Richard placed Jane's copy of the marriage contract in his safe. His soon-to-be brother, Darcy, sent Elizabeth's by express to his steward at Pemberley with instructions to leave the document on the master's desk.

~~~~~~~/~~~~~~~

Lady Lucas, Mrs. Long, and Mrs. Goulding had to catch themselves before they gasped when they first saw Fanny Bennet. Even though they had been warned and thought themselves prepared, the reality of seeing the woman who had been very pretty for her age—as well as vivacious and so full of life—was a shock.

Sarah Lucas always considered Fanny Bennet as much a rival as she was a friend. When Charlotte married Stuart Jamison after he had first courted Jane Bennet, Lady Lucas crowed about her daughter's success to Fanny Bennet whenever she could.

Seeing her friend as she now was; all thoughts of their petty rivalry dissipated. Instead, she thought about how tenuous life was, and how much time was wasted on inconsequential nothings.

When Kitty and Lydia came to visit their mother, accompanied by Gigi, and after the introductions were made to Miss Darcy, the three ladies shook their heads to be sure they were not imagining the well-behaved young Bennets they saw before them. Kitty had always been a bit boisterous and a follower of her younger, brash, and flirtatious sister Lydia. The Kitty they saw in front of them was a confident, mature, well-behaved young lady.

If they were shocked to see Kitty's transformation, the three ladies were completely taken aback when they noted the astounding change in Lydia. There was no brashness, no evidence of her devil-may-care attitude, and not one word about officers or any of the other inane subjects she used to speak of.

When Lydia informed her mother's friends she was to attend a school for young ladies in Bedfordshire at the start of the new school year, and it had been *her* idea to attend, the three almost fell from their chairs, so complete was their surprise.

All three regretted their decisions to leave their younger daughters, or in the Longs case their wards, at home. In the past, they had discouraged contact with Kitty and Lydia due to their behaviour. If the behaviour they saw today continued when they left Mrs. Bennet's sickroom, there would no longer be need of such discouragement.

Another change they noted was neither Fanny—with her slates—nor Hattie mentioned one word about how fabulously wealthy Jane's and Lizzy's betrotheds were. All either would discuss was how happy they were the two had found men who loved and respected them.

Mr. Bennet was present almost the whole time the ladies visited with their friend. It was another major change they noted, as in times past he would remain in his study reading when his wife had visitors; if he did enter the room, it was to mock or make sport. This was a very different Bennet family than the ladies had known before.

~~~~~~~/~~~~~~~

Lord and Lady Jersey arrived the day before the wedding. Lord Jersey joined the men on a hunt, while his wife, after greeting all of the ladies, made for the nursery to spend time with little Reggie. The De Melvilles were the only ones who were not extended family or close friends invited.

Jane and Elizabeth had met the Countess on their shopping trip to London and liked her very well. While there, they became close to Marie's mother which led to the invitation to the wedding.

After visiting her grandson, Lady Sarah joined Catherine, Elaine, and Marie in the mistress's private sitting room. "Are you moving to the dower house Catherine?" Lady Sarah asked.

"No, I am not, but not for want of trying," Lady Catherine revealed. "Jane will not hear of it, but by tonight I will move to the Rose Suite. I had been living in my Anne's old chambers, but it is time to move on."

"Your two nephews were most fortunate to be accepted by Jane and Elizabeth Bennet. I find I like them both very well," Lady Sarah stated.

"Sarah, thank you and Cyril for helping when we were in London. The vipers of the *Ton* have been defanged after the overwhelming show of support when we were at the theatre together. The Rhys-Davies bestowing their approval was the thing that drove home the futility of attacking them," Lady Catherine stated with satisfaction.

"I, for one, am most pleased to be gaining another wonderful daughter," Lady Elaine said as she squeezed her daughter-in-law's hand.

"It should come as no surprise to you that I am very partial to your current daughter-in-law," Lady Sarah teased.

"For me, in addition to the fact I like Jane and her sisters very well, I am happy I will no longer be the only daughter in the Fitzwilliam family," Marie told the ladies.

"The only change for me will be on paper," Lady Catherine stated. "They have been my family of the heart for some time already."

"Is it sure that Mrs. Bennet's prognosis is so dire?" Lady Sarah asked.

"As much as I wish it were not the case, it is," Lady Catherine replied. "I have asked Thomas, Mr. Bennet that is, if he preferred we bring in some London experts, but he is happy with Mr. Burnett and accepts there is little or nothing to be done."

"I applaud you holding the ceremony in the family sitting room so their mother will be able to witness the wedding." Lady Sarah stated.

"It was the only good solution. According to Mr. Burnett, moving her is fraught with danger, but her husband agrees it is worth the risk as she would become upset were she unable to attend," Lady Catherine related.

"Were the banns read?" Lady Sarah asked.

"For Jane and Richard, yes. However, due to the location of the ceremony, both grooms acquired special licences so they could marry outside of a church." Lady Catherine responded.

"Will the rector from Hunsford marry the couples? If I remember correctly, his name is Collins is it not?" Lady Sarah asked.

"The Parson, William Bennet, who will conduct the ceremony is married to the middle Bennet sister, Mary." Lady Catherine explained how his name had been changed.

"Is what I heard true Sarah? Is your daughter-in-law increasing with her fourth child?" Lady Elaine asked.

Lady Sarah confirmed it was a fact, and the ladies discussed the wonders of childbirth. Lady Catherine looked forward to a time when her *girls and boys* became mothers and fathers, and she, too, would be surrounded by surrogate grandchildren.

~~~~~~~/~~~~~~~

That night there was a family dinner, a loud and carefree event. Given the weddings in the morning, Bennet and Hattie Phillips gave in to Fanny's urging them to join the festivities. Mr. and Mrs. Hill would stay with their mistress, and before leaving his wife's bedchamber Bennet extracted a promise from Hill to send for him if there was the slightest reason to do so. His man swore he would—but only if needed.

As it was the night before the wedding, Mary, who would stand up with Jane and Elizabeth, would remain at the manor house, while the two grooms would stay at the parsonage for the night, as would Viscount Hilldale, who would stand up for both his brother and cousin.

Lady Catherine did not repine the fact it was the last time she would preside over a dinner at Rosings Park as the mistress. While Jane and Richard were on their wedding trip she would be the acting mistress, but as soon as Jane and Richard signed the register she intended to take her lead from Jane. Lady Catherine was determined to see Jane become the best mistress the estate ever had and would do anything she could to assist.

She knew how important it was for her to step back so Jane would not hesitate to assert herself as the new lady of the manor. It would not be a difficult transition, as the servants already loved her. Lady Catherine smiled to herself, thinking no one should mistake Jane's serene countenance for weakness. If anyone tried to take advantage of that perceived weakness, they would find out just how much steel there was in Jane's spine.

She turned her head, hearing Elizabeth's tinkling laugh fill the dining parlour. It warmed Lady Catherine's heart to see the way William stared at his betrothed, the love he felt for her obvious to any who cared to look. He seemed to light up whenever he earned one of her laughs.

Yes, Elizabeth would be the making of her nephew. She had the intelligence and quickness to learn what was needed in order to take charge as mistress of Pemberley, Darcy House, and their satellite estates. Lady Catherine was sure she would charm the housekeepers in each location, especially Mrs. Reynolds at Pemberley. Once the long-time housekeeper—who had been at her post since William was four—saw how happy the master was with his wife and how much Gigi loved her, any reservations she might have would be lost.

Lady Catherine shook her head as she remembered the nonsense she used to spout about the distinction of rank being maintained. Before her were two peers of the realm sitting with men active in trade, and they were all one big happy family.

She looked to the heavens, hoping her husband and Anne were looking down on her with pride. She missed them, but she had been gifted a second chance with such a wonderful family as this. As she looked at the joy on all sides, Lady Catherine decided after almost six years it was time to put aside her half mourning clothes.

Before the sexes separated, William Bennet stood and claimed everyone's attention, announcing that Mary had felt the quickening that day, informing those from Meryton who did not yet know of their happy news that his Mary was with child.

~~~~~~~/~~~~~~~

As it would have been too hard for Fanny Bennet to use her slates for the talk before the wedding, Jane and Elizabeth were joined by Mary and by their Aunt Maddie, who would provide the truth sensibly. Had the three sisters not been so close, it might have been awkward that their younger sister was present.

"Your mother wrote a short note to you," Aunt Maddie said as she handed the note to Jane. Jane opened it as Elizabeth read over her shoulder.

*16 May 1811*

*My dearest daughters, Jane and Lizzy,*

*I am well aware of my faults, and I am sorry for anything I ever did to hurt either of you, especially the way I used to treat Lizzy. A mother could not be prouder of her daughters than I am of all of you.*

*It is obvious when I see you with your young men how much each of you love and respect each other. Love and respect are the most important things in a true marriage. Do not give into stratagems as I did with my nerves and flutterings; all that earns you is distance from your husband.*

*Listen to what Maddie and Mary have to tell you as they are both in loving, felicitous, and respectful unions. They are far more qualified to talk to you on this the eve of your weddings, than I, even were I able.*

*Please tell Mary when I think back to what I told her before her wedding, I cannot but think on that drivel with abhorrence.*

*Do not make the error your father and I did by allowing yourselves to go to bed angry. I am sure you will succeed where I failed, as you both will understand your husbands so much more than I ever understood my Thomas.*

*Keep love alive, my darling daughters.*

*With all my love and wishes for long and felicitous marriages for both of you,*

*Mama.*

Jane and Elizabeth had tears in their eyes as they completed their mother's missive. Her handwriting used to be flowing and steady, nothing like the shaky, uneven script on the parchment. The change in her handwriting was but another reminder of their mother's precarious health.

Aunt Maddie and Mary allowed the two brides to dry their eyes. "You both have a good idea of the physical act of joining after having grown up on a working farm, do you not?" Aunt Maddie began. Both nodded with blooming blushes. "There is far more to it…"

Between their aunt and married sister, Jane and Elizabeth learnt much useful information_the most important being that the taking and giving of pleasure between a married couple in private was never wrong or wanton. Their formerly quiet, pious sister imparted some enlightening tips, including laying to rest the fallacy one should lock their door to their husband when with child.

After their aunt and sister departed the bedchamber, Charlotte Jamison knocked on the door and asked if her friends had any questions, but as they did not, and after sharing her own advice that occasionally being the one to initiate intimacy was never remiss, the three friends talked for an hour.

Eventually, after Charlotte returned to her husband, the sisters fell asleep, unintentionally, in the same bed as they had often done at Longbourn.

~~~~~~~/~~~~~~~

"No thank you, Andy and William, *I* certainly do not need any tips and pointers from either of you," Richard exclaimed. The four were sitting in the parlour at the parsonage with snifters of brandy, and it was inevitable the two grooms would be subjected to some good-natured ribbing from the married men.

"Although I did not experience as many ladies as Richard did, I do not need any of your so-called help, thank you," Darcy stated.

"I did not experience that many—well I suppose there were several more than you. And, unlike you, I never had them running in the opposite direction," Richard returned the jest from whence it came as he waggled his eyebrows. The truth was although Richard had some experience, he had been just as careful as his more serious cousin, the difference being he had loved to flirt—now he would only flirt with his Jane.

"In all seriousness, here is to brothers, as it is what we will all be after I conduct the rituals on the morrow," William Bennet stated as he raised his snifter.

"To brothers," the other three chorused and then all four drained their glasses.

"No more for me," Darcy insisted when their host offered. "I want to be bright eyed and aware when I marry Elizabeth."

"Same for me," agreed Richard. "I cannot wait to start my married life with Jane."

"Then we should retire for the night," Andrew suggested.

The four made their way to their bedchambers. For the two married men, it was a foreign experience sleeping in a bed without their wives, and as for the two grooms—bachelors no more after this night—both were looking forward to never sleeping alone again.

# CHAPTER 32

The maid assigned to Elizabeth almost panicked when she discovered her charge's bed had not been slept in. Remembering the sisters sometimes slept in the other's bed, she had the presence of mind to check with her counterpart, who was serving the soon-to-be new mistress.

That is where the maid found Miss Elizabeth, curled up asleep in Miss Bennet's bed. Each maid woke her lady as gently as she was able. "Good morning Jenny," Elizabeth greeted as her sleep laden eyes flickered open.

"Good morning Lizzy," Jane offered as she forced her eyes open. "What do you think we should do today?"

"My intention is to meet the man I love and marry him. What you plan, I know not," Elizabeth teased her sister in return.

"Come now, you two, it is time to get ready," Mary commanded as she breezed into Jane's bedchamber. "Lizzy, you caused poor Jenny here worry when she went to your bedchamber to wake you." Mary turned to the maids, "Are their baths ready?"

"They are Mrs. Bennet," the two girls chorused.

"I will assist Jane to dress, and Charlotte will help you Lizzy," Mary informed her sisters who had risen from their shared bed.

"What is that divine smell?" Elizabeth asked as her nose detected an aroma she loved.

"It is hot chocolate and pastries which await both of you in the sitting room. I suggest you have something to eat and drink now, as it will be a while before the wedding breakfast,"

Mary informed her sisters. Both donned a robe and made for the sitting room.

"Clotted cream on top of the hot chocolate, just as we like it," Jane exclaimed happily as she munched on a strawberry pastry.

Elizabeth took a big sip of her drink as it was her absolute favourite decadent treat, resulting in a moustache of cream as she lowered the mug to seek out a raspberry pastry. "Lizzy dear, you need to shave," Mary pointed out. Without embarrassment, Elizabeth used her tongue to remove the cream from her upper lip.

With the cups drained and two pastries each consumed, the brides made for their bathing rooms to luxuriate in warm baths.

~~~~~~~/~~~~~~~

Lady Catherine reviewed the family sitting room one more time to make sure all was as it should be. It had not been as difficult as she thought it would be to enter the room, though it was the first time she had after suggesting it be the location of the wedding.

Rather than being overwhelmed with sadness, she found it was a relief to be back in this sitting room. Instead of grief, the good memories she had of her late husband and daughter flowed through her.

The room was perfect and would accommodate the number of attendees for the ceremony without issue. There were five rows of chairs separated by an aisle, and the maids had decorated the walls with flowers from the gardens. Her footmen had placed a raised platform in the front of the room where the couples and their attendants would stand in front of the rector. To one side of the platform was a bookstand where the register sat open to the relevant page for the two couples to sign at the appropriate time.

On the wall that faced the gardens, fabric was draped to make sure the windows were covered and the morning sun would not shine directly into the eyes of those seated, which would have made it hard for the guests to view the ceremony. There was a space for Fanny's bath chair in the front row, allowing her a clear view of her daughters binding their lives to the men they loved.

Pleased everything was as she wished, Lady Catherine left the makeshift wedding chapel to seek out Mrs. Toppin and to thank and compliment her for a job well done.

~~~~~~~/~~~~~~~

At the parsonage, Darcy was awake before the sun peeked over the eastern horizon. He had slept for only a few hours. In his dreams, Elizabeth had been in his arms. He was still marvelling at the fact that after all of his missteps, he was being rewarded with Elizabeth as his wife, partner, and helpmeet in a few short hours. From tonight onward, his dream would become reality.

It was less than four hours to Seaview Cottage, unlike Richard and Jane, who would travel for more than three days. As soon as Elizabeth agreed to his proposed wedding trip venue, Darcy had dashed off a missive to Mrs. Agatha Spencer and Mr. Riddell Burrows, the housekeeper and butler at the cottage, so the house would be opened, aired, and ready to receive its new mistress.

In the next bedchamber, Richard was just waking. Due to his days as an officer, with his combat experience, he could sleep anywhere. He woke imagining the vision of beauty he would wake up next to on the morrow.

They would spend the night at Fitzwilliam House in London which would be ready to receive his wife when they arrived. There would be three days of travel from London to the house above Lake Windermere. The largest suite had been reserved at the three inns where he and his wife would spend their nights during their journey north.

Richard hoped he was right in thinking his Jane would be happy to travel with the shades lowered in their coach so they could enjoy one another's company without being seen. He knew from their stolen moments together that Jane's serenity hid a deep well of passion.

He still marvelled at the fact that such a woman had accepted him, and he would do anything within his power to make her happy for the rest of their mortal lives together. Richard was snapped out of his reverie by William Bennet knocking on his door to inform him a repast would be served in the dining parlour shortly.

The grooms met in the hallway outside their bedchambers, and when they arrived at the dining parlour they found their host and Andrew seated at the table. "That is not what you are wearing to get married in, is it?" Andrew ribbed his brother and cousin.

"No *Andy*, it is not. I am sure Darcy plans to change after we have broken our fasts. My bath will soon be ready, and Darcy has already availed himself of one," Richard responded with mock indignation.

The four men made short work of the meal, then Richard made his way up for his bath while Darcy returned to his bedchamber where Carstens assisted him into the suit he had chosen for the day. He chose a light-coloured waistcoat to match his beloved's dress.

Less than a half hour later, the four men made the short walk to the manor house.

~~~~~~~/~~~~~~~

Once the two brides had bathed, each was assisted by her designated helper. "Eliza, for someone who had such a short betrothal, your dress is perfect," Charlotte proclaimed once Elizabeth's gown settled over her.

"Thank you Charlotte..." Elizabeth explained how she had selected the fabric when they were in London and added it was merely good luck the dress had been ready in time for her wedding. Thankfully, the seamstresses who had accompanied Jane's gown and trousseau had not needed to make any adjustments to the garment.

Jane and Elizabeth eschewed wearing a bonnet and instead each wore a gossamer veil. Once they were dressed, the two brides met in the sitting room they had shared since moving into the manor house.

"Jane, how beautiful you look!" Elizabeth exclaimed when she spied her sister. "How well the gown looks on you!"

"The same is true of you, in both cases," Jane returned serenely.

"You both look wonderful," Mary stated as Charlotte nodded her agreement.

"It is time to see Mama," Jane reminded them. Charlotte left to join her husband in the makeshift wedding chapel as the three older Bennet sisters made their way to their parents' suite.

"You two look like princesses," Lydia exclaimed as she, Kitty, and Gigi were exiting the Bennet parent's suite.

"Thank you Lyddie," Jane answered for both brides. "Is Mama in the bath chair?"

"Yes she is. The footmen and Mr. Hill were so very careful when they placed her in it," Kitty reported.

As much as they wanted to, the younger girls knew it was not the time to hug their sisters. As far as Gigi was concerned, she was already sister to all the Bennets and the wedding would merely formalise that fact.

When Jane, Elizabeth, and Mary entered their mother's bedchamber, their father and Aunts Cat, Elaine, Maddie, and Hattie were there already. "How well you look," Aunt Hattie exclaimed when she saw them. She arrested herself knowing it was not the time to hug her nieces.

"My sister has the right of it," Aunt Maddie agreed.

"My boys are very lucky men," Lady Catherine informed the group.

"Richard has found the perfect lady in you, Jane," Lady Elaine added.

"Thank you Mother Elaine," Jane averred.

Bennet stood next to his wife, holding her right hand. Both had tears at seeing the magnificence of their daughters in their wedding dresses. Without relinquishing his wife's hand,

Bennet used his handkerchief to dry her eye. "It is time," he stated as he unwillingly released his wife's hand. The footman, Jeffers, was standing by to push the chair. Before he did, Bennet gently lowered the darkened veil his wife had chosen to wear.

Everyone other than their father and three daughters followed the bath chair out of the room. "I could not be prouder of you girls if I tried—indeed, I am proud of all five of you," Bennet informed his daughters. "I believe Jane and Elizabeth you will be as happy as Mary, or more so." He lifted each veil as he gave each bride a kiss on her offered cheek and then bestowed a kiss to Mary's as he hugged her.

~~~~~~~/~~~~~~~

When Fanny was wheeled into the makeshift wedding chapel, everyone spontaneously stood. Once she was in position, the congregants sat. The back of the room was lined with some of the servants of the estate, including the steward, housekeeper, and butler.

Richard and Darcy, who had been talking quietly to Reverend Bennet and Andrew, approached their mother-in-law-to-be. First Richard, then Darcy, lifted her veil and bestowed a kiss on her cheek, and a look of pleasure suffused the right side of her face. After Darcy lowered her veil, he took his place on the platform opposite Richard with the pastor between them.

With a huge smile directed at her husband, Mary made her way to the raised platform to take her place opposite Andrew. When Mrs. Toppin nodded to Reverend Bennet; he gave the signal for the witnesses to stand.

Bennet, with Jane on his right and Elizabeth on his left, made his entry. Although their gowns were similar, each bride looked like the only woman in the world to her groom. No one missed the way each bride's eyes locked with her groom's as they seemed to glide down the aisle on their father's arms.

Bennet stopped just before the dais. He lifted Jane's veil, kissed her cheek, and then placed her hand on Richard's arm as he stepped forward to meet her. He then repeated the same sequence for Elizabeth and Darcy.

Once Darcy led her to their place, Bennet stood to the right of his wife and took her hand. His son-in-law then gave the signal to sit.

As had been discussed two days before, when the betrothed couples had gone over the order of service with William Bennet, he conducted one ceremony, addressing both couples rather than first one and then the other.

When it came to the vows, Jane and Richard recited their vows first, followed by Elizabeth and Darcy; they did the same for the giving and receiving of rings. Defying convention, each bride presented her groom with a ring after she had received hers from him.

"Those whom God hath joined together let no man put asunder," William Bennet intoned.

"Forasmuch as Richard and Jane, and Fitzwilliam and Elizabeth have consented together in holy wedlock and have witnessed the same before God and this company, and thereto have given and pledged their troth either to the other and have declared the same by giving and receiving of rings, and by joining of hands; I pronounce that each couple be man and wife together, In the Name of the Father, and of the Son, and of the Holy Ghost. Amen."

"God the Father, God the Son, God the Holy Ghost, bless, preserve, and keep you; the Lord mercifully with his favour look upon you; and so fill you with all spiritual benediction and grace, that ye may so live together in this life, that in the world to come ye may have life everlasting. *Amen*"

"You may kiss your brides," was the final statement from the clergyman.

Darcy saw the mischievous glint in his new brother's eye. "Do not even think about it, Richard. We are not swapping wives; you kiss Jane and I will kiss my Elizabeth."

Each groom did just that, albeit with a quick, chaste kiss —but with the anticipation of far more when they were in private. Before signing the register, and amidst cheering from the other witnesses, each newlywed couple stopped to hug and kiss Fanny Bennet again.

After they signed the register where Jane and Elizabeth signed the last name Bennet for the final time, the next hugs and kisses were for Lady Catherine, who had played such a positive role in their arriving at this point.

"Aunt Cat," Elizabeth said softly to her as she grasped her hand. "Please promise you will spend part of each year with us at Pemberley. I am told that the winters are much harsher, but I understand we have milder summers. I want to make sure when we are blessed with children, they will know their Grandmother Cat well indeed.

With tears of gratitude in her eyes, Lady Catherine simply hugged her niece and nodded with both promise and joy. "Thank you Lizzy. I love you too."

"Jane cannot be selfish, she is not the only one who needs to learn from you," Elizabeth teased.

Darcy and his new brothers were standing back watching their wives and sisters hugging. All of them were amused and warmed as they heard Gigi exclaim how she had always wished to be part of a large family.

All the witnesses to the ceremony spent a moment with Mrs. Bennet to congratulate her on having three daughters so well married before they made their way to the ballroom, where the wedding breakfast was being held.

Once only the two newly wed couples and Mr. and Mrs. Bennet remained, Bennet pushed his wife back to her chambers himself. As the Hills, in addition to both maids and footmen, would be in attendance with his wife, Bennet felt easier about joining the celebrations in the ballroom.

~~~~~~~/~~~~~~~

Rosings Park's butler announced the Honourable Mr. and Mrs. Richard Fitzwilliam and Mr. and Mrs. Fitzwilliam Darcy to the assembled guests, which resulted in another round of cheering. It was not a large crowd, but those present were vocal in their joy for the two couples.

Just before Jane and Richard completed their circuit of

the room, they came to where the rest of the Fitzwilliams and the De Melvilles were seated. "Welcome to the family Jane," her father-in-law said, hugging her yet again.

"Thank you Father Reggie, I could not be happier about becoming part of your family," Jane returned.

"When you all return from your wedding trips, we will plan your wedding ball," Lady Elaine insisted.

"Please call on me to assist you as needed," Lady Sarah offered.

"Although my *little* brother does not deserve a wife such as you, welcome to the family Sister," Andrew offered as he ribbed his brother.

After greeting everyone, the new Mr. and Mrs. Darcy found a seat near Mary, her husband, and Charlotte and Stuart Jamison. They were soon joined by the newly minted Mr. and Mrs. Fitzwilliam. Although the four newlyweds were excited beyond what words could express, they did manage to eat and drink.

"What if Mama has another attack while we are on our wedding trips?" Elizabeth asked.

"If it is serious, we know how to contact you. Let us pray it is not necessary to summon you. Just enjoy yourselves," Mary advised.

"At least you will be less than four hours from here," Jane stated. "Richard and I will be days away."

"There is little your worrying can accomplish except to spoil your honeymoons," Charlotte opined. "If you were here, sitting with your mother every day instead of on your wedding trips, would it change anything? Would your mother want you not to go?"

Jane and Elizabeth looked at one another and shook their heads. Good, practical Charlotte—she took charge when needed. "You are correct Charlotte," Jane responded quietly.

"In fact, if Mama knew we were worrying about her now, I believe she would not be happy," Elizabeth added.

"Then, my love," Darcy said as he took his wife's hand and

kissed it, "we will honour her and have the best time we can."

"And so shall we. Jane, are you ready to say your good-byes?" Richard enquired.

"Allow me to change," Jane told her husband. "Are you coming Lizzy?"

Elizabeth rose to follow Jane, as did Mary and Charlotte to assist the same bride they had before the ceremony.

~~~~~~~/~~~~~~~

Two coaches stood ready under the portico while the brides were hugging their father. "Your mother and I want you to enjoy yourselves and not spend your time worrying what might happen here. It is in God's hands and He will call your mother home in His own time. It is her fervent wish you two have as good a time as possible," Bennet conveyed to his newly married daughters.

"Charlotte advised us the same, as did Aunt Cat when we spoke to her after changing," Elizabeth revealed.

"Wise women, those," Bennet quipped.

Lady Catherine stood with her two nephews as they watched their wives talk to their father. "Each of you have married the best woman for yourself. Do not make me come and paddle either of you if you ever think of mistreating them," Lady Catherine jested.

She had no doubt her nieces would be treated like the queens they were. There was so much love and respect between them, it was not something she would ever have to concern herself with.

"I second my wife's invitation to you. You know you have been far more than an aunt to me and Gigi." Darcy hugged his aunt tightly.

"We will consider giving Aunt Cat up for a few *weeks* at a time," Richard jested.

Once all the aunts, uncles, sisters, and brothers made their farewells, the two couples boarded their coaches. The Fitzwilliam conveyance led off and turned north out of the drive, while the Darcy carriage turned south.

The group of farewellers returned to the house after the Darcy coach was no longer visible.

# CHAPTER 33

On their second day at Seaview Cottage, Darcy introduced his wife to the wonders of the private cove. There was only about fifty yards of beach, but as her husband had described, it was completely private. The clifftop protruded some yards out from the cliff face, so if someone were willing to risk life and limb to attempt to see the beach below, they could only see the water.

As it was private property, well-guarded by footmen—one of them the ever-faithful Jeffers who Richard had agreed to release if he wanted to work for the Darcys, which he did—and outriders, no one would wander onto their land, either in error or by design.

On this day about a sennight after they arrived, Elizabeth reclined on an enormous blanket her William had spread on the shaley beach. Like her husband who was cooling off in the water, she was as naked as the day she had been born.

From the first night when she had become his wife in every way, there was no shyness between them. Aunt Maddie's and Mary's words had been proven over and over again during the days Mr. and Mrs. Darcy had been in residence.

The first time they had joined, there had been some little pain, but William had been so solicitous of her. She had not required it of him, but he had waited until all traces of the pain were gone, and not long after he continued he had attained his release.

It had taken several more times, but as they learnt from one another, both being fast learners, her husband routinely brought her to release before they joined, and at least once, she had achieved a second wave of bliss as her husband reached his own climax.

Between love making, when they had a little time, Elizabeth wondered at the beauty of the house. The ground-level drawing room had large windows facing the sea, while at the same time giving an unimpeded view up the coast towards Brighton. The master suite was above the drawing room and had similar windows. At night, they could see the lights of Brighton along the shore.

So far, on this day, they had joined in the sea once and on the blanket a second time, which had led to Elizabeth's husband's need to cool off in the green water of the cove. Elizabeth allowed her eyes to rake over her husband's statuesque form as he returned to her.

"William, I thought the cold water would inhibit that," she stated as she looked at the growing evidence of her husband's arousal.

"It is all your fault, minx. How can I look at a naked nymph lying on a blanket and not be in this state?" No more words were needed as the two again enjoyed the physical manifestation of their love.

~~~~~~~/~~~~~~~

On the fourth day after their wedding, Jane and Richard Fitzwilliam arrived at Lakeside House. During their days of travel, the shades had been lowered many times as both found it nearly impossible to keep their hands off one another.

Much to his delight, the night of their wedding Richard discovered his supposition about the depths of Jane's passion, had been underestimated. When she had cried out softly as her maidenly barrier was breached, Richard tried to stop to give her time to recover, but Jane had urged him on instead.

They had slept mayhap an hour the first night, and not much more each of the following three nights at inns along the way. And as for their activities in the conveyance, one need never count the hours of a drive when so pleasurably occupied. Luckily the driver, his assistant, and the two footmen on the rear step never let on they heard any noises from within the coach.

As the coach came to a stop, Richard, who needed to stretch his legs, had the door open before the footman could move, turning to assist his wife to alight. "Richard, what a view," Jane exclaimed as she looked down on Lake Windemere.

"We will explore the area, my Jane—in a few days," Richard added as he waggled his eyebrows at his wife.

"If you expect me to complain that we will be *confined* to the house for a few days," Jane replied saucily, "you will be waiting until the Second Coming."

"You are a woman after my own heart," her husband replied contentedly.

The house was on a hill near the summit, allowing a magnificent view of Lake Windermere and some of the smaller lakes as well. Husband and wife stood with fingers intertwined, drinking in the beauty of the view laid out before them before making their way into the house where the housekeeper and butler awaited them.

~~~~~~~/~~~~~~~

Almost ten days after the wedding, the only ones left in residence at Rosings Park were Thomas and Fanny Bennet, Hattie Phillips, the two unmarried Bennet sisters, Gigi, and Lady Catherine.

As Lady Catherine approached Fanny Bennet's bedchamber, she heard the wailing of Fanny's sister. Lady Catherine knew immediately that Fanny Bennet had been called home to God and no longer inhabited the mortal coil.

Even before she entered the bedchamber, Lady Catherine instructed a footman to make haste to summon Mr. Burnett. Her supposition was confirmed when she entered the bedchamber. Thomas Bennet was holding his wife's hand and crying silently, while his sister Phillips lamented.

"Please accept my condolences, Thomas and Hattie," Lady Catherine offered softly as she approached the new widower.

"She is no longer suffering," Bennet managed. "She was

able to witness her daughters marry, and I believe—notwith-standing her physical limitations—she lived some of the hap-piest days of her life. We fell in love all over again. She passed away knowing her family's future is secure and all of her daughters will do well for themselves. How much time I…"

"This is not a time for self-indulgence," Lady Catherine admonished gently. "As you said, Fanny is at peace and there is nothing *any* of us can do to change the past. Do you think your wife would want you to berate yourself when you had just proven these last weeks you did indeed love her, or would she want you to take care of yourself and the two daughters still under your protection?"

"Thank you Catherine, I needed a kick to the…head to wake me up. You are absolutely correct; there is much to do. I must inform my daughters who are here," Bennet stated as he started to stand. "Would you mind sending for my daughter and son at the parsonage?"

"Of course I will," Lady Catherine waved off his even hav-ing to ask.

"We must send for Jane and Lizzy," Hattie Phillips inter-jected between her sobs.

"No!" Both Bennet and Lady Catherine replied simultan-eously.

"Hattie, Fanny and I discussed this eventuality while you were resting one day, and she wrote—I have the letter for you to see if you desire—under no circumstances are we to call the newlyweds back from their wedding trips." Bennet raised his hand before his loquacious sister could reply. "And, under no circumstances will I go against Fanny's wishes in this, as I know she would be very upset if we did."

"I suppose if you put it like that, it must be so," Hattie thankfully capitulated quickly.

"Telling them now will change nothing. Allow them some peace, and when they return, they will begin their mourning for their beloved mother," Lady Catherine soothed.

Bennet gave Lady Catherine a look of appreciation for her

intervention and for calming his sister on the subject. "May I use Richard's study after I talk to my family? I have many letters to write," Bennet requested.

"Of course you may. Let me know if I can be of assistance with anything," Lady Catherine replied.

~~~~~~~/~~~~~~~

As soon as Mary and William arrived at the manor house, they were shown into a parlour where Bennet awaited them. Just after the two sat, Kitty and Lydia were shown into the room.

"Mama is gone," Lydia stated as her tears begun to fall, for there was no mistaking their father's sadness.

"As much as I would love to refute your supposition Lydia, I cannot," Bennet responded. "Mr. Burnett arrived a few minutes before I joined you and he surmises your mother passed away while she slept. She is at peace now, with no pain or further suffering.

"Aunt Hattie discovered your mother this morning. She was already gone," Bennet explained. "We will all miss her, me more than anyone, but she is with God now."

By now all three girls were crying quietly. Bennet sat between Kitty and Lydia and hugged them to himself, giving each a shoulder to cry on. Mary was in her husband's arms as he whispered soothing words to her.

"What about Jane and Lizzy?" Mary asked. Bennet explained what their mother wanted and how he agreed, and none of them could find it in themselves to disagree with Mrs. Bennet's preference.

After informing his daughters, Bennet sat down and wrote a number of expresses. One to his brother Phillips, one to the Gardiners, one to Mr. Dudley—Longbourn's parson—and the final one to Sir William Lucas to ask him to make the news known in and around Meryton.

By the next day, Rosings had been closed, and the whole party left accompanying Fanny Bennet on her final journey back to Longbourn.

~~~~~~~/~~~~~~~

Fanny Bennet was in her final resting place alongside generations of Bennets who had come before her. The funeral was well attended, men from each of the four and twenty families in the neighbourhood were at both the service and the graveside. The service itself had been led jointly by Mr. Dudley and William Bennet.

Mr. Bennet asked Lady Catherine to be acting mistress, thus allowing Mary to be free to mourn with her sisters rather than worry about the running of the house. Additionally, she made sure to involve the three ladies who had attended the double wedding. They were grateful they had been able to see Fanny in person one more time.

Any questions about Jane and Elizabeth ceased once word circulated that it was one of Mrs. Bennet's final wishes that her daughters were not to be informed of her death or be recalled from their wedding trips if she succumbed in their absence.

Gigi, having lost her father six years previously, was able to empathise with Kitty and Lydia and comfort them in their grief. In addition, the two subdued and mourning girls were surrounded by all of their peers in the neighbourhood.

Once the three families who had attended the wedding returned and reported how calm and well behaved the two youngest Bennet daughters were, especially Lydia, the parents who had warned their daughters away from the two lifted any embargo they had formerly put in place on associating with the youngest Bennets.

After a few days, the number of callers returned to a normal level. The Gardiners chose to stay with Frank and Hattie Phillips so they would not crowd Longbourn. Later in the week, the Phillipses and Gardiners joined their family for dinner at Longbourn to discuss how best to notify the Darcys and the Fitzwilliams once they returned. They expected the couples would be angry and hurt, but it was necessary to discuss this now, because the Darcys were to return in three days, and the Fitzwilliams a few days afterwards.

"If it were me, as much as you do dislike travel, I would meet my daughters in Town and tell them. It would be best coming from you," Lady Catherine suggested to Bennet.

"I know you are correct Catherine. Gardiner, you and Maddie return to London on Saturday, do you not?" Bennet asked. Gardiner allowed it was so. "In that case, as you came with only Lilly, would I be able to ride with you?"

"Of course you would be welcome," Gardiner spoke for his wife and himself.

~~~~~~~/~~~~~~~

The second Monday in June, on the tenth day of that month, Elizabeth and William Darcy returned to Darcy House after a most enjoyable sojourn at Seaview Cottage. They had promised themselves they would return there for at least a month each summer, with any family members who wanted to join them.

"If only Mama could travel to the cottage! She always wanted to bathe in the sea," Elizabeth told her husband as they walked up the steps.

After greeting the lined-up servants warmly, the master and mistress were about to go to their suite when Killion handed his master a note addressed to both of them. "William, it is in Aunt Maddie's hand," Elizabeth exclaimed. "What does it say?"

"It asks us to visit the Gardiners as soon as we are able, nothing more," Darcy told his wife as he handed the short note to her.

"Can we leave right away?" Elizabeth asked, a feeling of foreboding growing in the pit of her stomach.

Within minutes, the two Darcys were back in their coach and on their way to Gracechurch Street. When they arrived, Elizabeth saw the black wreath on the door and went weak at the knees.

"Surely, it is not your uncle," Darcy surmised.

"No, I am sure it is Mama," Elizabeth stated as her tears began to flow.

When the door opened and the first person she saw was her father standing there with a black armband, she was certain. As she had done so many times when she was a young girl, Elizabeth ran into her father's outstretched arms.

Once they were all seated, Bennet told them Fanny had passed almost a fortnight previously. Not unexpectedly, Elizabeth turned to her father while she held her husband's hand tightly. "Why were we not notified when Mama passed?" she asked accusingly.

"I prefer to let your mother answer that," Bennet said as he handed his second daughter a letter in her mother's shaky script.

*18 May 1811*

*Jane and Elizabeth,*

*Yesterday was one of the best days of my life. I saw two of my beautiful daughters marry men worthy of them.*

*If you are reading this on your return from your honeymoons, then I am now with God and at peace. Please understand I made your father and Cathy promise neither of you would be notified of my passing before you returned.*

*For me it is too late, but you, my darling daughters, will only have one wedding trip. It was my decision, and mine alone you were not summoned, so please, if you want to be angry with anyone, let it be with me.*

*I love you, my girls,*

*If I may make a last demand of you, go live the best lives you are able.*

*Your mother.*

Elizabeth fell against her husband as great, wracking sobs emanated from her chest. What her mother said resonated with her, and any anger she felt at not being notified drained from her body. Her mother had wanted her and William to have as good a time on their trip as possible, and they had honoured that wish.

The next day, Elizabeth had two of her dresses died black

and ordered additional mourning dresses and gowns. By early afternoon, the two Darcys were on their way to Longbourn to be with their sisters.

~~~~~~~/~~~~~~~

Two days later, when Jane and Richard arrived at Fitzwilliam House, they were met with a note identical to the one handed to the Darcys. They also turned around and made for Gracechurch Street immediately.

The scene that played out was similar to the one two days previously. Jane felt a great deal of guilt, which was assuaged when she read her mother's wishes penned in her own hand.

Just over four and twenty hours later, the Fitzwilliam coach, with Bennet as one of the passengers, was on its way to Hertfordshire.

~~~~~~~/~~~~~~~

As it can be imagined, the reunion of all five Bennet sisters and their newest sister, Gigi, was bittersweet. So they could all be together for their three months of deep mourning, Richard and Darcy signed a short-term lease for Netherfield Park. After a few weeks in residence, the two decided to make a joint purchase of that estate, so they would always have a place close to London and next to Longbourn to stay at when needed.

Mary and William Bennet accepted Bennet's offer for them to move to Longbourn so William could learn the running of the estate; the new steward had already made improvements which would lead to higher yields and profits.

The acceptance was made after a discussion with his patron, who happened to be his brother. Richard accepted his brother's recommendation that his curate would be an excellent candidate for the Hunsford living. Mary and William sent a note to their housekeeper, asking the parsonage servants to pack their belongings as they would not return during their deep mourning period and send everything to Longbourn.

One afternoon, Bennet was sitting next to Lady Catherine in the park, watching the *youngsters*—as they called everyone younger than they—spending time in the park. "How did you move on after your husband and daughter were taken from you?" Bennet asked.

"I do not believe I ever did, not fully. It is only around the time of the weddings I finally put aside my half mourning and dared enter the family sitting room. You would not have liked to know the person I was before I re-evaluated my life," Lady Catherine shared.

"I understand that, and I know I am not the same man I was before Fanny was stricken. I have a feeling you were about to berate me before the tragedy struck, and it would have been well deserved," Bennet observed.

"We both have pasts we are not proud of," Lady Catherine pointed out.

"How did you do it? How did you point your nephews and my daughters in the direction they needed to travel without seeming to do so?" Bennet wondered.

"Once I thought all it took was an imperious command and my will would be done. I learnt to ask questions, questions which would make the person think, to make their own decisions, to allow them to choose their path," Lady Catherine explained.

"Catherine, you were in charge the whole time, even though they did not know it," Bennet realised.

"I was not in charge, just nudging those who needed to find their correct paths," Lady Catherine clarified. As she looked around, she saw part of her much-enlarged family. She would miss her late husband and daughter until her dying day, but she had much to live for.

# EPILOGUE

March 1823

"Thomas, it is time to depart for Rosings Park. I do not want to miss any time with our grandchildren," Lady Catherine Bennet insisted.

"You know I hate to disappoint you, my dear we will leave on time," Bennet assured his wife. "I know how important punctuality is to you."

Bennet had mourned his Fanny for more than a year. It was three more years before he convinced himself there was a chance for happiness with another woman. If that lady had offered him one or two hints along the way, he had not objected.

They married a little after four years from the date Fanny passed away. The wedding took place at Snowhaven, as Lady Catherine, who had not married the first time from her childhood home, requested of her brother and sister to have the ceremony at Matlock Church and the wedding breakfast at the estate.

This time Lady Catherine married for love. For the first two years after his late wife passed, Thomas Bennet spent most of his time between Pemberley and Rosings Park, allowing Mary and William to establish themselves at Longbourn.

The two saw each other only briefly during that time, though they maintained the friendship they formed during Fanny's convalescence at Rosings Park. Much of the time Bennet was at Rosings, Lady Catherine had been with one of the Derbyshire or Staffordshire families. Bennet had not believed he would marry again, and he certainly had not expected to fall in love.

They had seen each other occasionally at Rosings Park, such as when the family met in Kent for Easter each year. Lydia split her holidays from school between Longbourn, Rosings Park, and Pemberley.

Kitty and Gigi became even closer, and for most of the year Kitty lived wherever Gigi was. Even though Kitty would be twenty and Gigi nineteen, the two decided to wait until Lydia was eighteen so the three of them could come out together.

Mary safely delivered Thomas Collin Bennet—Tommy— the heir to Longbourn, in October of 1811. Elizabeth and Darcy were gifted with Francene Anne Darcy—Franny—in November of 1812. Johnathan Fitzwilliam—Johnny—was born in June of 1813.

By the second Easter visit after the double wedding, Jane was heavy with their first child, a son an heir. When the family assembled for the birth of Jane's first child, Bennet started to allow the attraction he had felt for Lady Catherine for some years to progress beyond friendship.

After the birth of Jane's and Richard's babe, Lady Catherine and Bennet began to gravitate toward one another whenever they were in company. In July of 1815, while the two walked around the lake at Pemberley, Bennet proposed and Lady Catherine accepted his hand.

The wedding was held at the end of August. Tommy Bennet, almost four, was the page, and the nearly three-year-old Franny Darcy was the flower girl. By the time the two married, Mary and William had added two more children to their family, twins_ a boy and a girl_born a year and a half before the wedding. When Thomas and Catherine lived in Hertfordshire, they resided at Netherfield Park to avoid intruding on their son and daughter at Longbourn.

Elizabeth gave birth to Bennet Robert Darcy—Ben—six months before the wedding. Jane was with child again, about five months along. Richard was not shy about telling one and all he wanted a daughter just like her mother.

Lydia completed two years at her school. She loved the education she received and became an extremely accomplished young lady. If one had never known Lydia as she used to be, one would have thought they were being teased if told about the old Miss Lydia.

Kitty worked with a drawing master for just over a year. He had honed and developed her innate abilities. She had a prodigious talent and found pleasure in sketching her growing brood of nieces and nephews.

The three girls made their curtsies before the Queen and came out during the season of 1814. All three had suitors in their first season, but none captured their interest. During the little season of 1815, Gigi met Lord Mark Creighton, Marquess Hamworthing and heir to his Grace, the Duke of Devonshire. After a month-long courtship, followed by a three-month betrothal, the two were married in March of 1816.

When the Duke of Devonshire was felled by a heart attack less than a year after she married, Lady Georgiana Creighton became a duchess when her husband ascended to the dukedom. It was at her sister Georgiana's wedding that Lydia Bennet met Lord James Carrington, Viscount Amberleigh. He was heir to the Earl of Holder, whose seat was Holder Heights in Staffordshire.

When the Viscount requested a courtship, Lydia first told him all about her youthful indiscretion and allowed him to withdraw the offer without his honour being engaged. He only cared who Lydia was currently, not who she had been when she was a gullible girl of fifteen. Lydia married her viscount from Longbourn in November of 1816.

Although she had given up her childish desire to marry before her older sisters long ago, Kitty could not help pointing out Lydia had married before at least one of her older sisters. In December of 1816, when the family met at Pemberley for Christmastide, Kitty renewed her acquaintance with Mr. Patrick Elliot, the clergyman holding the livings of Pemberley,

Lambton, and Kympton.

One day, Kitty was sketching when the rector was walking the grounds of Pemberley, his not yet two-year-old daughter Grace in his arms. She had known, along with the rest of the family, that his wife had died after birthing the pretty little girl.

Grace had demanded her father allow her to see what the pretty lady was doing, and not able to deny his little angel anything, he had requested permission, which Kitty had granted.

Kitty had fallen in love with Grace first, and not long after with the darling girl's father, who returned the sentiment in full measure. By February of 1817, the two were married, and for the first time in her almost three years, Grace had a Mama.

After her son, Elizabeth became with child four more times. A son was followed by a daughter, and then by a miscarriage before she felt the quickening. Both Pemberley's doctor and a well-noted accoucheur opined she would not be able to become with child again. Both were proven wrong when identical twin Darcy girls—to their father's delight, as they grew they became exact replicas of his beloved wife, in looks and character—arrived in February of 1821, just before the couple's tenth wedding anniversary.

Jane and Richard's second child had been another son. After him the couple were gifted with two daughters, the first of whom was the splitting image of her mother—to her father's pleasure. The couple had no more children but did not repine the fact given how happy they were with their four offspring who were each an enjoyable mix of their father's affability and their mother's serenity, strength, and sweetness.

Andrew and Marie Fitzwilliam had five children after little Reggie, four daughters and then a second son. The two were happy at Hilldale and hoped Lord Matlock would remain as spry as he was for many years to come, as Andrew was in no hurry to inherit his father's title.

The Earl and Countess of Matlock spent much of their

time visiting grandchildren, grandnieces, and grandnephews. By 1822, Lord Reggie had turned over the running of the Matlock holdings to his son Andrew and effectively retired.

Three years after their twins, the Bennets of Longbourn were gifted with another daughter; two years after that, yet another girl arrived. William Bennet became a conscientious landlord and master, who worked hard with his steward and was never uninvolved in the running of his estate. He was never indolent like as father-in-law used to be before his first wife's illness.

As parcels of land abutting Longbourn became available, he purchased them, thereby expanding Longbourn's land and the number of tenants. His holdings doubled when he purchased all the land his brothers owned at Netherfield other than the home farm and park. He suspected the land was sold for a fraction of its real worth. Nothing he said moved his brothers to raise the price, and they threatened they would lower it further if he did not accept graciously.

The expanded estate earned around eight thousand pounds per annum. In consultation with his wife, William Bennet decided to rebuild the manor house, more than doubling its size. The family lived at Netherfield until the new manor house was ready for occupation in August of 1818.

Gigi and her duke had two children; a son followed by a daughter when she fell with child again. Her brother, who had always dreaded the day he would have to give over protection of his sister to another, could not have been more pleased his sister lived less than three hours from Pemberley.

Lydia and Jamey had a daughter, born two years after they married, and a son three years later. The Earl and Countess of Holder had been good friends of Lord Reggie and Lady Elaine, which helped them integrate seamlessly into the large extended family.

In April of 1818, Kitty Elliot bore her husband a son. As happy as Grace had been to have a Mama, she was even happier when she became a big sister. Grace loved that she suddenly had a plethora of family members, because her birth mother was the last living member of a very small family. Patrick Elliot did have family in Shropshire, but they were estranged as his family had felt he should not have chosen the church as a career.

By the time the families converged on Rosings Park for the Easter holiday of 1823, Kitty and Patrick had two sons and three daughters. Grace felt herself the luckiest of girls to have four younger siblings to help look after.

Even before her wedding to Thomas Bennet, Lady Catherine had been a grandmother to the children born to their family. The greatest change was that rather than Aunt Cat, she was now called Mother Cat by all of her former nieces and nephews, save for Andrew and Marie.

~~~~~~~/~~~~~~~

As for the Bingleys, Charles Bingley ran and expanded his carriage works. Two years after Darcy and Elizabeth were married, Darcy bumped into Bingley, who was in London on business.

After a few meetings at their club and a number of conversations, Darcy was happy to see Bingley had matured and grown a spine of his own. They would occasionally see one another over the years, but their relationship was never as close as it had been. In 1815, Bingley married the daughter of one of his business partners.

The Hursts were happy together. After five childless years, Louisa Hurst was granted a son, followed by a daughter two years later. They lived at the estate in Yorkshire, and when the elder Mr. Hurst went to his final reward in 1820, Hurst became the master of Winsdale.

After her epiphany, Miss Bingley never reverted to her former self. When she was five and twenty, she met a man with a small estate in Scotland while he was visiting her brother's business. The two courted briefly, were betrothed, and married within a month.

The irony was the new Mrs. McTavet lived with her husband and three children on their small estate, only twenty miles from the Darcys' Scotland holding. The former Miss Bingley saw the Darcys in the town near the estate on one occasion, but wisely never approached them.

Of George Wickham, nothing was known except he arrived in Australia. He was never heard of or from again.

~~~~~~~/~~~~~~~

"Look, Mama and Papa," a ten-year-old Johnny Fitzwilliam exclaimed excitedly. "I see Grandmama's and Grandpapa's carriage."

"Good eyes Son," Richard stated proudly. Jane, Richard, and their four children, the youngest now three, waited under the portico to welcome the arriving family members.

The Darcys, Elliots, Creightons, and Carringtons had all arrived earlier that day from London. The Longbourn Bennets and the rest of the Fitzwilliams were expected the following morning.

"Mother Cat and Papa, you are very welcome," Jane hugged and kissed the cheek of each in turn.

"I second that," Richard stated. He was soon drowned out by the excited voices of their four children, each wanting their grandparents' attention for themselves.

"We are very flattered at the welcome," Lady Catherine stated warmly. "We saw your other grandparents recently and they will arrive on the morrow."

"We know Grandmama, but we have missed you and Grandpapa," Johnny, the eldest, explained. "We missed Grandmother and Grandfather just as much and will be happy when they arrive."

"Where are all of your cousins?" Bennet asked as he ruffled the boy's hair.

"Our sisters, brothers, and their children are washing and changing," Jane reported. "As much as the children all wanted to play, their parents insisted they get settled first."

"Thomas, will you take a turn with me in the gardens before we see the horde?" Lady Catherine requested with a smile.

"Of course Cathy; it will be my pleasure," Bennet offered his wife his arm, and she wound hers around it.

They walked in silence for a little while, and then Lady Catherine indicated a bench under an extremely old oak. "All those years ago, after Lewis and Anne were taken from me, if you had told me I would be part of the family I have today, married to a man who I love with all that I am, I would have had you consigned to Bedlam."

"Just as I never imagined I would find love again after Fanny died," Bennet stated. "At least from the time she was stricken until she passed, Fanny and I rekindled the love we had when we married." Bennet paused. "This is the place where we both lost parts of our family, but it is also the location you and I found love for one another."

"True. Just look at the magnificent family we have," Lady Catherine said softly. "I do not wish the pain either of us suffered on anyone, but without events happening just as they did, we would not be here now, and it is likely some of our children would not have found each other."

"Except it did happen, and as I told you some years ago, you, my darling Cathy, had a hand in all of it," Bennet challenged.

"Be that as it may, it is time to make for the house," Lady Catherine informed her husband. "Are you prepared to face the mob of children waiting for us there?"

"Yes Wife, I am more than ready to be with our beloved grandchildren and children," Bennet owned.

"In that case," Lady Catherine teased with a sparkle in her eyes, "into the breach once more we go."

Catherine and Thomas Bennet stood. They kissed languidly, and then made for the house and their waiting family, arm in arm.

## *The End*

# COMING SOON

## Banished (Dec 2021/Jane 2022)

If you do not like a bad Jane Bennet, this one will not be for you.

The story takes the point of view that Bennet supports Fanny, who is being egged on by Jane, in demanding that Elizabeth marry Collins. As she dislikes Mr. Collins even more than Mr. Darcy, Elizabeth refuses point blank.

Bennet points out that no clergyman will marry the couple of Lizzy, as he knows she will does not consent to the marriage. Fanny demands he banish Elizabeth, which Bennet does. Bennet is weak and never stands up to his wife.

Elizabeth is taken in by the Gardiners who are disgusted at the actions of her parents.

## Book 3 of the Take Charge Series: Georgiana Darcy Takes Charge ( Jan/Feb 2022)

As in the preceding Take Charge books, We see the effects of Miss Darcy asserting herself in this tale.

# BOOKS IN THIS SERIES

*The Take Charge Series*

The Take Charge series are all stand-alone books. There will be at least four books in the series and as they are not sequels or not connected one to the other, you may read them in any order you choose.

The series tells a Pride & Prejudice Variation/Vagary tale in which one of the characters we know and love from canon takes charge and assert themselves. We see how the actions of that particular character affects the others and the trajectory of each individual tale, both known from canon and some non-canon characters.

We know Elizabeth Bennet and Fitzwilliam (William) Darcy well and how they are depicted in the original, they will not have a book in their names, but will, as it should be, feature very heavily in each of the stories where someone else takes charge.

## Charlotte Lucas Takes Charge

None of the books in this series are just about the title character, but how their taking charge affects those around them.

Fanny Bennet dies of an apoplexy two years prior to the start of this story.

As in canon, the Bingleys, Hursts, and Darcy arrive in the area residing in the leased Netherfield Park. Up until the Reverend William Collins arrival, things are not far from canon. Collins is the sycophant we all love to hate and sets his sights on Jane. Bennet tells him in no uncertain terms he will not consent to such a man marrying ANY of his daughters.

Charlotte Lucas overhears Collins ranting to himself about how he will evict the Bennets from Longbourn the day Bennet passes. He then tried to woo Charlotte hours later and she too rejects him. He is derisive when she rejects him out of hand, he tells her that no man would ever offer for one on the shelf, without fortune, and as homely as her.

Collins then proposes to Matilda Dudley, Lizzy's friend and Longbourn's widowered parson's daughter. Matilda accepts him much to Elizabeth and Charlotte's surprise.

Collins's words to her spur Charlotte to take charge, the story tells the tale of what she does and how it affects the lives of not a few people. The book examines how Charlotte actions change the trajectories of some of our favourite (to love and hate) characters.

# BOOKS BY THIS AUTHOR

## A Change Of Fortunes

What if, unlike canon, the Bennets had sons? Could it be, if both father and mother prayed to God and begged for a son that their prayers would be answered? If the prayers were granted how would the parents be different and what kind of life would the family have? What will the consequences of their decisions be?

In many Pride and Prejudice variations the Bennet parents are portrayed as borderline neglectful with Mr. Bennet caring only about making fun of others, reading and drinking his port while shutting himself away in his study. Mrs. Bennet is often shown as flighty, unintelligent and a character to make sport of. The Bennet parent's marriage is often shown as a mistake where there is no love; could there be love there that has been stifled due to circumstances?

In this book, some of those traits are present, but we see what a different set of circumstances and decisions do to the parents and the family as a whole. Most of the characters from canon are here along with some new characters to help broaden the story. The normal villains are present with one added who is not normally a villain per se and I trust that you, my dear reader, will like the way that they are all 'rewarded' in my story.

We find a much stronger and more resolute Bingley. Jane Bennet is serene, but not without a steely resolve. I feel that both need to be portrayed with more strength of character for the purposes of this book. Sit back, relax and enjoy and my hope is that you will be suitably entertained.

## The Hypocrite

The Hypocrite is a low angst, sweet and clean tale about the relationship dynamics between Fitzwilliam Darcy and Elizabeth Bennet after his disastrous and insult laden proposal at Hunsford. How does our heroine react to his proposal and the behaviour that she has witnessed from Darcy up to that point in the story?

The traditional villains from Pride and Prejudice that we all love to hate make an appearance in my story BUT they are not the focus. Other than Miss Bingley, whose character provides the small amount of angst in this tale, they play a small role and are dealt with quickly. If dear reader you are looking for an angst filled tale rife with dastardly attempts to disrupt ODC then I am sorry to say, you will not find that in my book.

This story is about the consequences of the decisions made by the characters portrayed within. Along with Darcy and Elizabeth, we examine the trajectory of the supporting character's lives around them. How are they affected by decisions taken by ODC coupled with the decisions that they make themselves? How do the decisions taken by members of the Bingley/Hurst family affect them and their lives?

The Bennets are assumed to be extremely wealthy for the purposes of my tale, the source of that wealth is explained during the telling of this story. The wealth, like so much in this story is a consequence of decisions made Thomas Bennet and Edward Gardiner.

If you like a sweet and clean, low angst story, then dear reader, sit back, pour yourself a glass of your favourite drink and read, because this book is for you.

## The Duke's Daughter: Omnibus Edition

All three parts of the series are available individually.

Part 1: Lady Elizbeth Bennet is the Daughter of Lord Thomas and Lady Sarah Bennet, the Duke and Duchess of Hertfordshire. She is quick to judge and anger and very slow to forgive. Fitzwilliam Darcy has learnt to rely on his own judgement above all others. Once he believes that something is a certain way, he does not allow anyone to change his mind. He ignored his mother and the result was the Ramsgate debacle, but he had not learnt his lesson yet.
He mistakes information that her heard from his Aunt about her parson's relatives and with assumptions and his failure to listen to his friends the Bingleys, he makes a huge mistake and faces a very angry Lady Elizabeth Bennet.

Part 2: At the end of Part 1, William Darcy saved Lady Elizabeth Bennet's life, but at what cost? After a short look into the future, part 2 picks up from the point that Part 1 ended. We find out very soon what William's fate is. We also follow the villains as they plot their revenge and try to find new ways to get money that they do not deserve.
Elizabeth finally admitted that she loved William the morning that he was shot, is it too late or will love find a way? As there always are in life, there are highs and lows and this second part of three gives us a window into the ups and downs that affect our couple and their extended family.

Part 3: In part 2, the Duke's Daughter became a Duchess. We follow ODC as they continue their married life as they deal with the vagaries of life. We left the villains preparing to sail from Bundoran to execute their dastardly plan. We find out if they are successful or if they fail.

In this final part of the Duke's Daughter series, we get a good idea what the future holds for the characters that we have followed through the first two books in the series.

## The Discarded Daughter - Omnibus Edition

All 4 books in the Discarded Daughter series are combined into a single book. They are available individually, in both Kindle and paperback format.

The story is about the life of Elizabeth Bennet who is kidnapped and discarded at an exceedingly early age. It tells the tale of her life with the family that takes her in and loved her as a true daughter.

We follow not only Elizbeth's life, her trials and tribulations, but that of the family that lost her and all of those around her, immediate and extended family, and the effect that she has on their lives. There is love, villains, hurt, and happiness as we watch Elizabeth grow into an exceptional young woman.

If you are looking for a story that only concentrates on our heroine, then this is not for you.

## Surviving Thomas Bennet

**Warning: This book contains violence, although not graphically portrayed.**

There are Bennet twins born to James Bennet, his heir, James Junior and second born Thomas. They boys start out as the best of friends until Thomas starts to get resentful of his older brother's status as heir.

The younger Bennet turns to gambling, drink, and carousing. In order to protect Longbourn, unbeknownst to Thomas, James Bennet senior places and entail on the estate so none of his son's creditors are able to make demands against the family estate.

Thomas Bennet was given his legacy of thirty thousand pounds when he reached his majority. He marries Fanny the daughter of a local solicitor in Oxford where Thomas is teaching. He is fired for being drunk at work. He manages to gamble away all of his legacy while going into serious debt to a dangerous man in not too many years.

When James Senior dies, Thomas and Fanny Bennet arrive at Longbourn demanding an imagined inheritance. They find out there is no more for them and leave after abusing one an all roundly swearing revenge.

James Junior, the master of Longbourn, and his wife Priscilla have a son, Jamie, and daughters Jane, Elizabeth, and Mary. Thinking he can sell Longbourn if his brother and son are out of the way, Thomas Bennet murders them and James' wife by causing a carriage accident.

The story reveals how the three surviving daughters are protected by their friends and how they survive the man who murdered their beloved parents and brother. Netherfield belongs to the Darcy's second son, William. There are many of the characters that are both loved and hated from the canon in this story, some similar to canon, a good number of them hugely different, there are also some new characters not from canon.

## Unknown Family Connections

**This is a book of two volumes, but all in one book. It is a one off, standalone story.**

Over 150 years in the past an Evil Duke plotted to separate his first and second sons. He was a man who had two interests: money and status. Lord Sedgewick Rhys-Davies, the 3rd Duke of Bedford sets off a chain of events that ultimately ends up doing the exact opposite of what his original evil intent was in the far future.

Mr. Thomas Bennet lives with his second wife and family on his estate Longbourn in Hertfordshire. As far as he knows, he is an indirect descendant of the last Earl of Meryton whose line died out with him over 150 years ago. The family has owned Longbourn and Netherfield Park for as long as anyone remembers. There is an entail on Longbourn, but not the one we are used to. As in the canon, this Bennet dislikes London, and the Ton and he and his family keep away from London society. His second wife is the daughter of an Earl but just goes as Mrs. Bennet.

The Bennet's new tenants at Netherfield Park are the Bingleys. One of the major deviations from canon in this tale, Jane Bennet has more than a little backbone while Bingley has little or none. How will Darcy behave, will he make assumptions and act on them? Will Elizabeth allow her prejudices to rule? When Wickham slithers onto the scene will he cause havoc?

The 7th Duke of Bedford is ill, and he will be the end of the line as there are no living relatives to inherit the dukedom and vast Bedford holdings. He removes an old letter from a safe in his study written by the 4th Duke. Witten on the outside of the letter is: 'Open ONLY if there are no more Rhys-Davies heirs.'

The Duke opens the letter and learns of the 3rd Duke's evil and there is in fact an heir, although a direct descendant, he is not a Rhys-Davies.

This is the story of different families and what happens when their lives intersect and are changed for ever. There is quite a bit about Lizzy & Darcy, but there are not always the main focus of the story as the title infers.

## Cinder-Liza

**No fairy godmother or magic in the story although there is some imagery we would expect to see in a Cinderella story – my apologies to those who thought there would be magic based on the title.**

Mr. Thomas Bennet married the love of his life: Miss Fanny Gardiner. She gave him three children, Jane, Elizabeth and Tommy. 2 years after Tommy, Fanny was taken from her loving family birthing a second son, who was stillborn.

Another branch of the Bennet family, cousins to the Longbourn Bennets, are titled, the Earl and Countess of Holder, who live in Staffordshire with their 5 children. The two families are extremely close and after Fanny dies Bennet's cousins, at his request, keep and raise Tommy. In his grief Thomas Bennet doesn't think he can raise a 2-year-old at the same time as his two daughters. He also feels Tommy needs a mother figure in his life.

Martha Bingley is the widow of an honourable tradesman, Mr. Arthur Bingley, who had died of a heart attack. Bingley senior was a minor partner of Edward Gardiner in Gardiner and Associates. They had three children, Charles, Louisa, and Caroline. Unlike canon, the Bingleys are not very wealthy, and the girls have small dowries of £2,000 each.

Bennet is introduced to Martha at his brother-in-law's house. The Bingleys live in a leased house a few houses down from the Gardiners on Gracechurch street. Martha has always dreamed of climbing up the social ladder, raising her family above their roots in trade, so she compromises Bennet as he is a landed gentleman with an estate. Being an honourable man, and against advice of friends and family, he marries her.

Our 'prince' in the story is of course none other than His Grace Fitzwilliam Darcy, Duke of Derbyshire, Earl of Lambton. Like canon his parents have already passed away. Dear old Lady Catherine de Bourgh will do anything to make her sickly daughter with a nasty disposition a Duchess. At some point the Duke purchases Netherfield to be closer to London so his sister, Lady Georgiana, will have her preferred music master close by.

Bennet never reveals the existence of his son or his relations, who are peers of the realm, to his new wife, who he dislikes intensely. The neighbours, none of whom like the new Mrs. Bennet or her children, keep the Bennet's secrets without question. Bennet allows his new wife to believe the entail on Longbourn is away from female line giving her the impression that on his death, she and her three spawn will be evicted from the estate by a distant unnamed cousin.

Sometime after sending Jane to live with his cousins, for reasons that will be revealed in the story, with Lizzy refusing to leave her father's side, Bennet has an accident which kills him. When no heir presents himself to throw her and her children, still at Longbourn, into the hedgerows, the stepmother feels more secure at the estate.

Several the usual suspects are present as well as some other characters. This is a story of hope and survival and the eventual triumph of good over evil.

## A Bennet Of Royal Blood

**This is an 'Elizabeth is not a Bennet' Story**

This story starts with one of King George III's sons marrying the love of his life secretly. The woman is a daughter of an Earl. After more than a year of marriage, all of the time with his beloved wife spent at her estate of Netherfield Park in Hertfordshire, the Prince reveals his marriage to his father hoping the elapsed time will protect them. The King orders his son to leave the lady and plans to have the marriage annulled. The King was at least convinced by his son not to annul the marriage, so instead he orders a speedy divorce.

The reason was NOT that the lady was unsuitable, the opposite was true, but for political reasons, the King has promised his son's hand to a European princess to strengthen alliances for England. It saddens the King to do so, especially as this son is one he is very close to, knowing he is breaking his son's heart the King forces the divorce as the other country in question is one England sorely needs as an ally.

In the meanwhile, the lady had become best of friends with Mrs. Francine Bennet of Longbourn. They met not many months after Jane was born, shortly after the lady moved into Netherfield Park. When her devastated husband informs her of the forced divorce, his wife does not inform him she is with child to try not hurt him more. It so happens Fanny Bennet is also pregnant with her second child.

Due to the ignominy of divorce and worried about the social ramifications coupled with making assumptions about what the royals would expect of them, the lady's family cut ties with her when she needs her parents more than ever. The only one she feels she has left is Fanny Bennet. A few other friends write but the broken-hearted lady is not ready to accept their overtures and respond yet. As both ladies near their confinements Thomas Bennet is called away—for what he tells his wife—is to assist his good friend from Cambridge the Earl of Holder in

Staffordshire. He is actually investigating ways to break the entail on Longbourn.

Fanny moves into Netherfield to be with her best friend during their confinements along with 2-year-old Jane. Before the final confinement, her brothers, Phillips, the solicitor, and Gardiner, the man of business are summoned. Phillips draws up a will for the lady and Gardiner is given management of her fortune.

Just in case the worst happens, the lady writes a number of letters, among them one to her child, one to the Prince, one to Bennet, and one to her parents as she has a plan in the event of her death.

The best friends go into labour within hours of each other. Fanny delivers a still born son and some hours later, her friend delivers a healthy baby girl, who is the legitimate daughter of a Prince, making her a Princess of the United Kingdom of Great Britain and Ireland. The friend has complications of birth and will not survive long. She implores her best friend—her sister of the heart—to take her daughter and raise her as her own and she will claim the dead baby son. Fanny cannot deny her friend her dying wish.

The Lady names her baby Elizabeth after her maternal grandmother. She charges Fanny with waiting until Fanny feels Elizabeth is ready, to reveal her birth right to her explaining her reasons for waiting. Other than a few small bequests to some, the lady's will bequeaths her child all of her worldly possessions, including an enormous fortune and Netherfield Park on reaching her majority of 21. When Bennet returns he is introduced to, and falls in love with, his second daughter. Jane and Lizzy are the loved equally by their parents.

The story looks at how the Bennets' lives are different with a much different—completely opposite—Fanny than canon.

How will Elizabeth and the world around her react to the news when she finds out her true heritage. The Bennets meet the Darcys and Fitzwilliams much earlier than in Miss Austen's masterpiece.